MARTHA GRIMES

FADEAWAY GIRL

NEW YORK TIMES
BESTSELLING AUTHOR OF
BELLE RUIN

"COLORFUL AND
BEAUTIFULLY REALIZED
CHARACTERS...
GRIMES IS, AS USUAL,
IN SUREFOOTED
AND INVENTIVE FORM."
—*THE SEATTLE TIMES*

A NOVEL

PRAISE FOR THE NOVELS
OF MARTHA GRIMES

Fadeaway Girl

"The colorful characters . . . all quicken to life under Grimes's Dickensian touch, but none more so than Emma. She may keep losing herself in the past, but she's far too vital to fade away."   —*The New York Times*

"Colorful and beautifully realized characters. . . . Grimes is, as usual, in sure-footed and inventive form."   —*The Seattle Times*

"Thoughtful and touching. . . . Grimes has lost neither her storytelling touch nor her desire to concoct a winning tale."   —*Richmond Times-Dispatch*

"The writing is often lovely in *Fadeaway Girl*, with an occasional setting evoked so beautifully that it takes the reader's breath away."   —*The Boston Globe*

"Emma is as enchanting as the eccentric cast of her hometown."   —*Kirkus Reviews*

"Grimes's strength is in her appealing characters, from the inquisitive Emma and her dipsomaniac great-aunt, Aurora, to the pretentious sixteen-year-old Ree-Jane Davidow and philosophical auto mechanic Dwayne."   —*Publishers Weekly*

"An agreeable thriller from a seasoned hand."   —*Booklist*

Belle Ruin

"Rings with laughter . . . an entertaining tale of old crimes and faded glory. . . . *Belle Ruin*'s strength is as a showcase for Grimes's wry and wacky humor. Hilarious subplots and secondary characters are her signature."   —*USA Today*

"Laced with Grimes's trademark imagination and humor . . . *Belle Ruin* is an entrancing read."   —*Richmond Times-Dispatch*

continued . . .

"Grimes saves her loveliest writing for the gloomy images of empty train stations and tumbledown houses in which Emma takes such melancholy pleasure. But there's also an explosive comic exuberance to the scenes of Emma's high jinks around town and at her mother's hotel, a rich source for the oddball characters who give these novels their charm . . . [a] beguiling young sleuth."

—*The New York Times Book Review*

"Her novels centered around Emma—*Hotel Paradise*, *Cold Flat Junction*, and now *Belle Ruin*—show how compelling and complicated a mystery it is growing up."

—*South Florida Sun-Sentinel*

"A superior literary mystery continuing a story the formidable Martha Grimes began in *Hotel Paradise* and *Cold Flat Junction*. . . . Grimes's strong suit is her knack for vividly eccentric characters, especially the narrator. . . . [Emma is] irresistible."

—*The Seattle Times*

"Grimes . . . has struck gold. . . . [Her] pungent prose and catchy dialog breathe life into her charming young narrator and the novel's idiosyncratic cast of characters."

—*Publishers Weekly*

"Readers willing to sink softly into a nostalgic atmosphere of small-town timelessness will be content . . . amusing and eccentric."   —January Magazine

Cold Flat Junction

"A marvelous gallery of idiosyncratic characters . . . a thoroughly delightful reading experience."

—*The San Diego Union-Tribune*

"A master of nuance, Grimes brings every corner of *Cold Flat Junction* to vivid life . . . melds classic mystery with a coming-of-age story in which the young protagonist must face the hard and often shocking realities of adulthood. . . . Grimes gets that—and everything else—just right."

—*The Baltimore Sun*

"Beguiling. . . . Eccentric characters keep [Grimes's] enchanted, time-forgotten towns alive."

—*The New York Times Book Review*

"Character-driven psychological fiction . . . smartly written . . . surprisingly satisfying."

—*Publishers Weekly*

"A tour de force."

—*Kirkus Reviews*

Hotel Paradise

"Utterly engaging . . . Emma's voice [is] sharp, funny, perceptive."

—*The Washington Post*

"Rich with metaphors and imaginative characters . . . provocative . . . *Hotel Paradise* takes on the mood of a lazy Sunday afternoon with its slow unveiling of events. Meandering and atmospheric, the novel reads with the ease of a daydream. . . . [Grimes] proves herself a writer of delicate sensibility whose work is notable for its delightfully quirky details, insightful perceptions into human relationships, and graceful prose." —*Los Angeles Times*

PRAISE FOR MARTHA GRIMES'S RICHARD JURY NOVELS

"Grimes is a gorgeous writer whose lyrical evocation of the lost innocence of the past invests her strange stories with the aura of grown-up fairy tales."

—*The New York Times Book Review*

"Her wit sparkles, her plots intrigue, and her characters are absolutely unforgettable." —*The Denver Post*

"Martha Grimes . . . writes the British mystery better than most Brits."

—*The San Diego Union-Tribune*

"Sure to please. . . . Grimes's writing has rarely been more lovely." —*Chicago Tribune*

"[Grimes] excels at creating a haunting atmosphere and characters both poignant and preposterous." —*USA Today*

"Grimes is not the next Dorothy Sayers, not the next Agatha Christie. She is better than both." —*The Atlanta Journal-Constitution*

"[Grimes's] gift for evoking mood and emotion is as keen as her talent for inventing a demanding puzzle and solving it." —*The Wall Street Journal*

MARTHA GRIMES

FADE AWAY GIRL

GIRL

A Novel

NEW AMERICAN LIBRARY

New American Library
Published by New American Library, a division of
Penguin Gro up (USA) Inc., 375 Hudson Street,
New York, New York 10014, USA
Penguin Group (Canada), 90 Eglinton Avenue East, Suite 700, Toronto,
Ontario M4P 2Y3, Canada (a division of Pearson Penguin Canada Inc.)
Penguin Books Ltd., 80 Strand, London WC2R 0RL, England
Penguin Ireland, 25 St. Stephen's Green, Dublin 2,
Ireland (a division of Penguin Books Ltd.)
Penguin Group (Australia), 250 Camberwell Road, Camberwell, Victoria 3124,
Australia (a division of Pearson Australia Group Pty. Ltd.)
Penguin Books India Pvt. Ltd., 11 Community Centre, Panchsheel Park,
New Delhi - 110 017, India
Penguin Group (NZ), 67 Apollo Drive, Rosedale, North Shore 0632,
New Zealand (a division of Pearson New Zealand Ltd.)
Penguin Books (South Africa) (Pty.) Ltd., 24 Sturdee Avenue,
Rosebank, Johannesburg 2196, South Africa

Penguin Books Ltd., Registered Offices:
80 Strand, London WC2R 0RL, England

Published by New American Library, a division of Penguin Group (USA) Inc. Previously published
in a Viking edition.

First New American Library Printing, February 2012
10 9 8 7 6 5 4 3 2 1

Copyright © Martha Grimes, 2011
For author permissions and copyrights see page 326
All rights reserved

 REGISTERED TRADEMARK—MARCA REGISTRADA

New American Library Trade Paperback ISBN: 978-0-451-23564-0

The Library of Congress has catalogued the hardcover edition of this title as follows:

Grimes, Martha.
Fadeaway Girl: a novel/Martha Grimes.
p. cm.
ISBN 978-0-670-02244-1
1. Graham, Emma (Fictitious character)—Fiction. 2. Missing children—Fiction.
3. Cold cases (Criminal investigation)—Fiction. 4. Summer resorts—Fiction.
5. Hotels—Fiction. I. Title.
PS3557.R48998F34 2011
813'.54—dc22   2010035332

Printed in the United States of America

Designed by Daniel Lagin

To the memory of two of my favorite writers,
Gary Devon
and
Stuart M. Kaminsky

So long, Lew.

This saying good-by on the edge of the dark
And cold to an orchard so young in the bark
Reminds me of all that can happen to harm
An orchard away at the end of the farm.
. . . .

I wish I could promise to lie in the night
And think of an orchard's arboreal plight
When slowly (and nobody comes with a light)
Its heart sinks lower under the sod.
But something has to be left to God.

—ROBERT FROST,
"GOOD-BY AND KEEP COLD"

RED, RED ROBIN

1

We were talking about the kidnapped baby.

Me, Emma Graham, age twelve, standing in my great-aunt's room with a tray under my arm; her, Aurora Paradise, who never left the fourth floor, probably wouldn't even if someone shouted "FIRE!"

The fourth floor of the Hotel Paradise is made up of only four rooms. These are her domain. One is her bedroom, but I've never actually seen her in it. Maybe she never goes to bed; maybe she sleeps in her chair; or maybe she doesn't sleep. She's so stubborn.

Aurora Paradise stirred the straw around in what remained of her Rumba, a drink I had fashioned from rum and banana. It was five o'clock, the cocktail hour, a time that was held in as high esteem as Sunday communion with wine and wafers, only here it was rum, gin, and whiskey. I was the chief drink maker.

"What baby?" She clicked her fingernail against her nearly empty glass. That was to let me know she was due another drink before she'd talk, but I wasn't having it.

"You know what baby. The Slade baby, Baby Fay. The one kidnapped from the Belle Ruin twenty years ago." Then I added, cleverly, "When you were around fifty." My great-aunt Aurora was ninety if she was a day. Back then, she would have been seventy.

Aurora shut her eyes as if she were pondering the kidnapped baby, which she wasn't. She was probably remembering herself at the Belle Ruin balls.

I moved my small round tray from under one arm to the other. She never invited me to sit down, even though I was the chief rum supplier. Her drink was one-third Myers's rum.

"I'm not making another Rumba till you tell me why you said Miss Isabel Barnett was lying about seeing the baby."

For a moment she pouted and adjusted her black crocheted mittens with the pearl buttons. Aurora was dressed for a ball a lot of the time, a ball of fifty years ago. Behind her was her steamer trunk spilling out gorgeous gowns. It was a stand-up trunk with drawers and everything, the sort people used to take on ocean voyages.

When she saw I wasn't budging, she sighed and said, "Isabel Barnett is about as dependable as a firecracker in the snow. She'd say anything to get herself noticed. You seem to forget she's a klep-to-maniac." Aurora smirked as if this disorder pleased her.

It was true Miss Isabel took little items from McCrory's Five-and-Dime, but she always paid them back. Since Miss Isabel was very well-off, no one could figure out why she stole twenty-five-cent Tangee lipsticks. "That's got nothing to do with the baby."

"I'm saying Isabel Barnett is barmy. You can't depend on anything she says or does. She's lived all by herself for so long she probably talks to the walls. I know she's got a parrot and they probably sit up half the night jawin'." She stiff-armed her glass at me. "It happened over twenty years ago; why would she remember what this infant looked like even if it had solid gold teeth? Now get me another Rumba, if you please!"

I knew I couldn't make her say more, and maybe she'd said all that she could, anyway. "It'll have to be something else. The rum's down to a ghost of itself."

"Just something sweet. Make up one of your Count of Monte Cristo at Miami Beach drinks."

I set the glass on my tray, deciding there was nothing more to be gained by further drink blackmail. So I left, still wondering about Miss Isabel Barnett. The trouble was that one of my theories about this baby that disappeared from the Belle Ruin years ago was that there never had been a baby at the hotel, for no one had actually seen one, not even the babysitter, Gloria Spiker. I figured maybe the baby had sickened and died and for some reason Imogen and Morris Slade, the mother and father, didn't want anyone to know. It probably had to do with a big inheritance or something. I also had a theory that the Slades had arranged the kidnapping so they could collect the ransom. But no ransom demand had been made.

Then Miss Isabel Barnett claimed to have looked into the carriage when the Slades were in La Porte, getting medicine for the baby. She had seen the baby, she said.

Now Aurora Paradise was claiming Miss Isabel had always been a liar.

I walked heavily down the stairs with my serving tray and Aurora's glass, thinking truth was hard bought.

2

Behind the hotel are several buildings: a cottage where we used to live when we were little, now set aside for guests who preferred the privacy of separate rooms; and two garages, one big and one small, the small one now filled with cast-off furniture, empty paint cans, and spare timber. The Big Garage was once used for guests' cars and it could hold at least twenty of them. Now it was used as a theater, housing Will and Mill's productions.

Mill is Brownmiller Conroy. His first name passed down through his family. No parent could be so mean as to make up such a name. We shortened it to Mill.

As usual, there was a lot of commotion inside the Big Garage. And, as usual, at my knock, silence fell like a blanket dropped over the clamor. I don't know how they did this—I mean, silenced everything like flipping a switch. Will and Mill demanded total secrecy. They did not want anyone to know anything in advance of the production. I wondered why and decided that they wanted to burst onto the scene with all of it so new it looked like the opening of the world. As if none of us had really lived until the moment the curtain went up; as if the sun and moon had sailed around with blinkers on.

It was no good trying to bang on the door. I just sighed and waited. Finally, the side door opened reluctantly, and Will appeared— that is, half of his face appeared through the opening.

"What?"

"Paul's mother's looking for him." That was a lie and Will probably knew it, as Paul's mother was hardly ever looking for him except when it was time to go home. "What've you got him doing?"

"Nothing."

"Listen, let me in."

"No."

I smiled. "Okay, then I'll tell everybody about your airplane set." They'd been working on this set ever since *Medea, the Musical* had closed a week ago to thunderous applause. Will and Mill had made scads of money on that production; they had even extended its "run" (one of the many Broadway show terms Will liked to use). But they seemed to spend all their money on Orange Crush and Moon Pies and the pinball machines over across the highway at Greg's Restaurant.

My seeing the new set had been by chance, when they'd had Paul strapped into the plane's cockpit.

Will was disgusted. "My God! You're nothing but a blackmailer." At the same time he opened the door and then walked away from me. He had traded his pilot's cap for a top hat, I noticed.

The plane was even more refined by now. It was the inside of an airliner, one side shaved away so that you were looking into the interior. They had moved this craft up to the stage.

Mill, sitting at the piano, said, "Hi." He was never as hostile as Will. But then, he wasn't my brother. He started trilling away at "When the Red, Red Robin," singing in his nasal voice.

"Why are you wearing a top hat?" I asked Will, over the "bob, bob bobbin'" of Mill and the piano.

"For my number." He began to tap-dance, which was an irresistible cue to join Mill:

There'll be no more sobbin'
When he starts throbbin'
His ooold sweet SONG!

The piano pinged, the shoes tapped, and I yelled:

"What's all this got to do with *Murder in the Sky*?" That was the title of the new production.

Will stopped dancing and said, as if this were an answer, "I'm the pilot." But, incapable of stilling himself, he raised and dropped his top hat to the rhythm of Mill's piano, and went to tapping again.

"The pilot's a tap dancer?"

"Why not? Hey, Paul!" He shouted up to the rafters. "Come on down; your ma wants you."

This order was barked to the dishwasher's son, Paul, a boy of eight, more or less. No one knew his age. Paul clambered down one of the posts like a monkey and came over to where we were standing. "Hello, missus," he said to me. It was all he ever said.

"Did you finish the clouds?" said Will.

Paul shook his head.

"Well, finish 'em before you go to the kitchen." To me, Will said, "It won't take long. You can tell his mom."

I was going to ask what he was doing with clouds, but I knew the question would be asked in vain.

Paul, in the meantime, had sat down on one of the big stones left over from *Medea, the Musical,* and was dozing off. This didn't surprise me; Will and Mill were afraid to let him sleep up in the rafters in case he fell off.

Mill rippled the keys and sang,

Wake up! Wake up! You sleepy head!

Will joined him with

Get up! Get up! Get outta bed!
Cheer up! Cheer up! The sun is red!

Piano keys tinkling, feet tapping, as if the world were just waiting for a duet.

I wasn't, so I went bob bob bobbin' along.

Feeling put upon, I walked the gravel drive and then the path to the back door of the kitchen. I saw a robin along the way, maybe a refugee from the Big Garage. Grumpily, I stood and watched it pulling a worm from the wet grass. Its breast was nowhere near red; it was a dusty shade of orange. And it certainly didn't "bob."

In other words, it was nothing like the song, but then, I guess things seldom are.

3

Rather than take the chance of running into Ree-Jane Davidow, whom I'd last seen in the hotel lobby, I went down the back stairs and down the hall to the front office, where I could call Axel's Taxis.

There was a poet named Emily Dickinson, who I was told was called the Belle of Amherst. Ree-Jane Davidow thought she was the Belle of Everywhere—Spirit Lake, and La Porte, and Lake Noir. Anyplace roughly in a twenty-five-mile radius, Ree-Jane was the Belle of.

She was sixteen, going on seventeen. Her name was really Regina Jane, but one day she decided she wanted it pronounced in the manner of a famous French actress, Réjane. She kept after me to pronounce it throatily, but I couldn't or wouldn't. What I came out with was "Ree-Jane," which of course made her furious. I have called her that ever since, and so do a lot of people now, thinking that's her real name. I don't correct them.

No one was in the hotel's back office (although I could hear Ree-Jane declaiming out in the lobby), so I phoned Axel's and asked the dispatcher to send a cab to the Hotel Paradise. "And make sure it's Axel that comes, please, Wilma." It was never Axel who came.

"Sure, hon. He'll be back soon from taking a fare over to Lake Noir."

I told her I wanted to be picked up at the bottom of the first driveway—the hotel had three drives—and *not* in front of the hotel.

As I said all of this I was studying the shelf that held Mrs. Davidow's liquor bottles. The shelf was right by the big rolltop desk where she usually had her drinks around five o'clock. I took note of the empty Myers's rum bottle and wondered if Lola would take note too. There was another bottle of a brand called Pyrat, about which Mrs. Davidow had said she better not catch anyone touching it because it was really good and really expensive. I had considered pouring a little of the Pyrat into the Myers's bottle (which I had used up in the Rumbas), but decided that would be chancy; for all I knew she might have the Pyrat bottle measured off.

After I put down the telephone, I stood chewing my lip, wondering what tasted most like rum. I thought of pouring some of the Jim Beam into the Myers's bottle, but Mrs. Davidow would know the taste was funny. I decided it would be better just to take the bottle away.

I left the hotel by the back door and walked the stone path to the cocktail garden, intending to leave the bottle on the table there. But then I decided, no, it would only call attention to its empty self.

Will said Mrs. Davidow was definitely an alcoholic. One way you can tell you're an alcoholic is if you do crazy things with bottles. Like in *The Lost Weekend*, a movie I was told I was not allowed to go to, which only meant I went as soon as it came to the Orion. (The owner, Mr. McComas, liked old movies.) Ray Milland was hiding bottles all over his apartment, even one in the chandelier.

So here I was carrying an empty Myers's rum bottle around, hoping I wouldn't run into anybody unless it was a movie producer who might see possibilities in this situation. I needed to stop fooling around, so I walked down to the end of the drive, where there were a lot of thick rhododendron bushes by the badminton court. I went up the bank and stuffed the bottle in the rhododendron. I felt like Ray Milland.

I stood at the end of the gravel drive, waiting for Axel and staring at the spot on the highway where our dog Rufus was hit and killed by a car. I'd been standing here just like this when it happened. Rufus had run out into the road, so it probably wasn't the driver's fault, but that didn't matter. I didn't remember the car or the driver. As I looked at that spot, it grew farther away and smaller—the way on a movie screen, at a fade-out, there's a circle of light in blackness, the circle getting smaller and smaller. What was in it was Rufus dying, getting tinier and tinier until he was gone altogether and there was only the black screen.

I blinked.

I could call him back anytime by some awful magic of blinking. Blink, he was there; blink again, he wasn't.

The trouble was that I thought I could still get Rufus back only if I blinked in the right way. It happened when I was little; I was only five, so it didn't surprise me I might have felt this way. A little kid might believe her dog was still around somewhere. When you get older you know death is only death and that's all there was to it.

But I still blinked.

Axel's taxi pulled up at just that moment. It wasn't Axel driving, either; it was Delbert. I knew it would be Delbert because it always was, no matter how much the dispatcher said it would be Axel. I would have thought there was no such person except I'd often seen Axel in his taxi, driving somewhere. Only he never had a fare with him.

"You gonna just stand there all day?" Delbert stuck his head out of the driver's-side window. "Meter's runnin'." He thought this was funny and slapped the steering wheel.

"You haven't got a meter," I said, sliding in and down in the backseat so he couldn't see me in his rearview mirror.

The cab lurched forward. "No, we ain't got meters, but if we did, it woulda been runnin'." His laugh was more of a pig snort. "So where're you goin'? As if I didn't know." He laughed again.

That made me really mad. "Oh really? Where?"

"Well, it's either the Rainbow or the courthouse. Though bein' they're across from each other it don't make much difference when it comes to stopping."

We were passing Britten's store, where the Wood boys and Mr. Root were sitting on the wooden bench. Or rather, two of them were, Ubub and Mr. Root. Ulub was standing with a book in his hand. I rolled down the window and called and they all turned and waved.

Then I told Delbert to drop me at the bank.

"The bank? You never go there."

"I guess you don't know everything. Do you?"

Ten minutes later we pulled up in front of the First National and I got out and handed him the fare. I considered not tipping him, but then I gave him fifteen cents.

It was annoying to have to walk from the bank on Second Street all the way back to the Rainbow Café, five blocks up and over, though the walk did take me by stores I liked. I found all of them mysterious in some way, like Sincell's Haberdashery. The word itself seemed to belong to a past full of red-jacketed men and women, horses and foxes.

Sincell's was appropriately dark and cool inside, with tall, narrow rooms. The room in the rear sold shoes and (I liked to think) rich brown hunting boots. The front room was stocked with dark silk dresses and men's three-piece suits. Among hats nested behind tall glass cases were, I was sure, dark velvet hunting caps. And over among the canes were riding crops. I liked to think all of this.

Just past the haberdashery was McCrory's Five-and-Dime, where Miss Isabel Barnett practiced her kleptomania. Around the corner was Souder's Pharmacy, with its unchanging window display of Evening in Paris toilet water and pale face powder spilling delicately from a silver compact by whoever had been wearing the long blue satin evening gloves. There was a story! I could make up half a dozen scenes on the spot to fit that perfume, those blue gloves. It made me feel warm and comfortable somehow, the notion that I could think up all of these stories and write them down. It was like always having another me around, a friend to help out.

Along the next street and closer to the Rainbow was the tiny Oak Tree Gift Shoppe, owned by Miss Flagler. Across the narrow alley from that stood the candle store run by Miss Flyte, who was no stranger to mystery. Her shop was the one that was most mysterious, for lighted candles flickered in the windows themselves and trailed in and all the way to the back of the store.

All of these stores had a backstory, and it occurred to me that our newspaper could do a piece on each of them. If I couldn't actually dig out a story on each one, I could still write down my impressions of them.

I was the youngest reporter the *Conservative* had ever had. Of course, I had got the job as a result of almost getting murdered at Spirit Lake, and what I was doing now was writing up the whole experience. But "Impressions of Souder's," "Impressions of the Haberdashery," and so forth, that could keep me on the staff and keep me famous for many months to come.

Ree-Jane liked to point out at least once a day that I was only a "cub reporter, not a real one," but given Ree-Jane's notion of reality, I was justified in not paying much attention to her opinion.

I walked on to the Rainbow.

Donny Mooma, the Sheriff's deputy, was in the Rainbow, standing in front of the bakery case with a doughnut in his hand, talking to Wanda Wayans, the new waitress. We didn't like each other, Donny and I. He was too dumb to be doing police work, and I never understood why the Sheriff kept him. Maybe Donny was what's called a "political appointment." The Moomas had been involved in police work in the county for several generations. There was a Mooma who'd been sheriff when the Slade baby had been kidnapped, but I guessed he must be dead now, or maybe the Moomas never died, just walked the earth forever. Donny walked around kind of dead.

I should say *alleged* kidnapping and for that matter even alleged baby, for, as I said, I wasn't even sure there'd *been* a baby. One of the reasons I wanted to go to the Rainbow Café was to see if Miss Isabel Barnett was there. I wanted to ask her again if she'd really seen Baby Fay in that carriage. I would put it, of course, in a more polite way, not meaning to suggest that Miss Isabel's word was unreliable. Just because she was a kleptomaniac didn't mean you couldn't count on her to know the difference between an empty carriage and one with a baby in it.

I said hello to Wanda and she said hi back. Donny grunted. He was still smarting over the time I got him out of the office (so that I could inspect police files) by telling him he'd won the doughnut competition across the street—that is, in the Rainbow Café. Of course, there wasn't any competition, but he fell for it and left without locking the office, telling me I wasn't to go in it. Well.

Donny was waving his doughnut with chocolate sprinkles around and talking six to the dozen about some "crazy guy" walking around town yelling at people.

"I says to Sam we should take him in for disturbing the peace is what he's doing—"

"Who's doing?" I asked.

Donny treated me as if I were invisible. "I said, 'Sam, the man's a menace, a m-e-n-a-s-e—' "

"C-e," I said, looking at the doughnut display.

He glared at me and ate some of his doughnut while he thought up an insult. "You think you know it all, don't you?"

"No. I just know how to spell 'menace.' " I decided on a doughnut with different-colored sprinkles. I would've preferred chocolate, but I wasn't going to eat the same kind Donny was eating.

But Donny couldn't think of any retort so he went on about the crazy person. As he munched the rest of his doughnut, he said, " 'The guy's out there scarin' little kids,' I says to Sam—"

"Not me," I said, going to the unusual extreme of allowing myself to be lumped with little kids.

"Oh, *you-u-u-u,*" he said, snarling and picking up his mug of coffee from the counter, which was next to the glass cases. There were stools lining the soda fountain counter, but the idea was that Donny was just too busy, too much in demand, to take the time to sit at the counter.

"I don't think he's crazy," I said, wondering who it was I was defending.

"You? What do you know about it? You don't even know what that sign he's carrying means. Ha!"

I could have just asked what he was talking about, but why do that when I could squeeze it out of him without his knowing. I'd already found out the "crazy" was carrying a sign. I asked Wanda for the doughnut I wanted. As she got it out of the case, I said to Donny, "It's pretty obvious what it means, isn't it?" I thanked Wanda and took my doughnut and looked at Donny as I munched on it.

"Obvious? *Obvious?*" He was standing over me with a mean look in his lizard eyes and one thumb hooked in his belt while the other hand waved his coffee cup around. "Well, supposing you just tell us what the expression 'end of days' means, then?"

I licked a few sprinkles from my doughnut and looked thoughtful. "One thing is, it's not an 'expression.'" That was good, I thought. That made it sound more like I knew what was going on than if I'd just waded in explaining "end of days," which I didn't know what it meant either. And it was always safer to say what something wasn't, rather than say what it was. Since I had no idea what "end of days" meant. If I knew the context, now . . . Was Rudy's or the haberdashery having a sale? Was the county trying to get liquor legal again and now some old prune who didn't believe in drinking was going around shouting "It's the end of days" about it? Having a liquor store right here in La Porte would save Lola Davidow the trouble of having to go into the next state to get hers. For her, it would be the beginning of days.

"What d'ya mean not an expression?"

Donny should watch more *Perry Mason.* Perry was always telling greenhorn lawyers you should never ask a question of a witness if you don't already know the answer. "I mean 'end of days' means what it says, It's literal." Before he could ask me again what it meant, I said, "I don't see why you think this person is scary."

"Oh, you don't? Well, a course, what with all your exploits lately, I guess the end of the world coming wouldn't bother you at all!"

"Not especially." So there I was: end of the world. I wanted a Coke and climbed up on a stool, my end of days set aside for the moment. I hoped Will and Mill never got wind of "end of days." *Murder in the Sky* was putting us at enough peril.

4

I needed to see Mr. Gumbrel at the *Conservative* office, so I went back the way I'd come. The newspaper was beside Sincell's, in another narrow building.

The window of Souder's Pharmacy stopped me again, as I looked at the Evening in Paris toilet water and the pale gloves and a photo I hadn't noticed before, down in the corner of the window, that showed a sad-looking dog with HAVE YOU SEEN ME? beneath his face. He seemed so woeful, I wondered if, when the picture was taken, he'd known he'd go missing.

I picked up my pace and walked around the corner on Second Street, but nearly stopped as I was going past McCrory's Five-and-Dime. When I glanced through the glass door, I saw Miss Isabel Barnett at the makeup counter. I debated going in and striking up a conversation, but I didn't want to interrupt a kleptomaniacal fit, and anyway, it would have been too hard for her to keep her mind on the Slade baby if she was considering the Tangee lipstick colors.

When I got to the *Conservative*'s building I took the old oak stairs two at a time.

"Emma!" Mr. Gumbrel was standing beside Suzie Whitelaw's desk, reading some pages.

"Hello, Mr. Gumbrel."

He slid his glasses up on his forehead and said, "Hope you've brought me that last installment."

He was, of course, referring to "The Spirit Lake Tragedy," the story that had been selling a lot of newspapers lately, the last installment of which featured me.

I put on my woebegone look and sadly said, "I'm really sorry. I've nearly finished"—I hadn't even nearly begun—"but I just can't get that final bit about the shooting and then I thought, 'This isn't exactly right.'" I frowned earnestly.

"What's not right?"

I hitched myself up on the copy editor's desk, trying to think up an answer to what might not be right. "Well. Well . . ."

And then it came to me, and it wasn't just an excuse for not doing my job. "Maybe what happened that night, maybe that's only part of the story; maybe that's not the end of it."

Mr. Gumbrel put down the pages he'd been reading. "Enlighten me."

You can imagine how many times anyone ever asked me to enlighten them. "Look: What happened to me is just part of something bigger." It was unheard of for me to suggest, when given the opportunity for myself to be big, that there was anything bigger, but I managed to do it. "There's Ben Queen, don't forget."

"I haven't. He's in your story. He saved your life."

I nodded. "But Ben Queen's story amounts to more than that. His story is also Rose Queen's story, and that old murder. Now, that was twenty or more years ago, and that was around the time of the Belle Rouen—" I tried to pronounce it the French way but then thought of the way Ree-Jane sounded and gave that up. "Belle Ruin. Remember the disappearance of the Morris Slades' baby?"

"Of course I do, Emma. I had my theory about that. You recall?"

I did, but I was more interested in my own theory. "I bet it's all connected." There were jumping jacks in my mind.

Mr. Gumbrel frowned, thinking. "So what you mean is, all this is something else than the Spirit Lake tragedy—"

I was shaking my head hard. "No. I mean it's still the Spirit Lake tragedy. It's just more of it. It goes on and on. Like the Greeks did. You know, like Medea."

Mr. Gumbrel laughed. "*Medea, the Musical*! That was some production! Your brother is some kind of genius—"

"Yes, but he's not part of the tragedy." I certainly didn't want the conversation to get sidetracked onto my brother's "genius." "I mean, Medea and her revenge. With the Greeks it's all about revenge; all they ever think of is revenge." With my mind lighting momentarily on Ree-Jane, I could understand why. "The police are finally convinced that Ben Queen didn't murder Rose." (I didn't add, though I could have, "Thanks to me.") "I'm almost sure it was their daughter Fern—"

"You got any evidence for this?"

I sighed. "I'm a reporter, not a policeman. No. But it just seems logical. Anyway, my point is, somebody murders Fern out of revenge for her murdering her mother, Rose."

My mind was frantic with possibilities. It felt like one of the pinball machines up at Greg's that Will and Mill played. Each little steel ball aimed and rolling into a hole. I pulled back the plunger and *whicssssh* went one thought after another, *clack, click, clack* into its hole.

"We wrote that up about Fern Queen. But we don't know who did it."

I wished he'd stop interrupting the sinking of the pinballs. "Then, don't forget, there's the murder of Mary-Evelyn Devereau before all of this, and I just know she was drowned because they thought she was their sister Iris's child. 'Bastard child' is what Isabel called her."

Mr. Gumbrel sat down in front of Suzie's old Royal typewriter and tapped a few keys as if words should come out the tips of his fingers. "You're saying the Devereau sisters killed that poor child?"

"Yes, I am." I shouldn't have had to remind him that one of those sisters almost killed this poor child, me. "You remember she tried to kill me? She was crazy, of course. She thought I was Mary-Evelyn. So I guess she had to finish killing me."

He slapped his hand against the carriage return. "Now, maybe we should get the dates of all these things right."

Oh, how boring. It was the atmosphere I wanted to get right, the feelings, the looks of things. . . .

"Because you just might have something here, Emma."

I knew I did. My mind was loaded down with pinballs, so that I could hardly move. "What I came to do today was search around in the archives"—I liked this word; it was weighty, like my mind at the moment—"for more details. You said before you thought Morris and Imogen themselves might have taken the baby somehow."

"I wouldn't've put it past Morris Slade." He narrowed his eyes against the smoke from his cigarette and looked grim. "That boy was a gambler. He was forever at that poker club, 'club' being what they called it. He'd bet anything just to stay in the game, anything. Had a lot of debts, I'd guess."

"But no ransom was ever asked for."

"None we know of." He shook his head. "I should've spent more time on this, but we were short on reporters then."

I tried to think of what could have been more important back then than a disappeared baby from a grand hotel. You could have written books about it. My mind sparked at the mere idea. I slid off the desk. "I want to search around the archives and see if I can figure out the connection."

"You got a head full of ideas, Emma."

Since I didn't have a face full of prettiness, I thought it just as well.

The back room was as musty as ever, perhaps even mustier in my eyes because it contained the past, and nothing could compare with the past. The comforting words of William Faulkner came back to me, that the past wasn't dead; it wasn't even past. I had typed out his exact words and put the slip of paper on my mirror. It was Dwayne, over at Slaw's Garage, who was the big William Faulkner reader. He called him "Billy." A mechanic, even a master mechanic, reading William Faulkner was something to note.

Not that I'd actually read Faulkner, except for a few story beginnings (so I could impress Dwayne), or words rooted out here and there. I wasn't actually going down the mines myself as much as I was panning his words for gold.

Faulkner's words were delaying the last episode of the "tragedy." I was trying to look at things the way he did, trying to find words like "bugswirled" and "stumppocked." Trying to think up words like that was holding up the writing, but I couldn't help myself.

From one of the shelves stacked high with old papers, I dragged out the edition with the story of the Slade baby's kidnapping. The paper was so old I thought it might crumble in my hands. No, I didn't think that; I just wanted to make up a word like "crumbcracked." I would have to stop doing this, making up things to fit words.

I doubted I would find anything new in the newspaper accounts, as I had seen them before. And anyway, I'd seen the police report. I lined up the papers: the account of the "tragic accident" that wasn't an accident, but a murder—the drowning of Mary-Evelyn Devereau in Spirit Lake; the murder of Rose Devereau Queen in Cold Flat Junction; the shooting of Fern Queen over near White's Bridge; the attempt to murder me in Spirit Lake (this written by yours truly); the kidnapping of the Slades' baby; the burning down of the Belle Rouen Hotel. That's an awful lot of violence for a couple of small towns.

Connecting all of this, I thought, might be the Girl, the mysterious Girl who came and went. I had seen her six times now, twice at the old Devereau house—once at the edge of the wood and later on the other side of the lake. It was the odd way she'd looked, unmoving, statue still. I remembered her from a distance, a lake away, and up close at the railway station, on the platform in Cold Flat Junction, where she boarded the train that stopped there on its way to Hebrides and points north. What struck me about her—I mean, after the way she looked—was that she carried nothing except for a tiny purse. No suitcase, no coat, nothing, so it was as if, like me, she lived not too far from the train station.

It surprised me that my friends in the Windy Run Diner hadn't noticed her, for she was the spitting image of Rose Devereau Queen, who was held to be the most beautiful girl Billy and Don Joe and Mervin, all of them in the diner, had ever seen.

Thinking about this resemblance, and Rose's daughter, Fern, I decided, well, the Girl must be Fern's daughter. But Fern was not at all pretty. Rose's looks had skipped Fern, I decided, and carried on to the Girl.

I imagined a line of light around her, the way she looked carved out of her background. She looked misplaced. Yet at the same time the background seemed to absorb her and she became a necessary part of it.

I got up from the table and the newspapers and went to the table by the door that held the past copies of magazines like *Life* and the *Saturday Evening Post*. I had seen the cover before and wanted to see it again. It was right on top, where I'd left it. The cover showed a woman in red against a red background, a black wrought-iron fence in the foreground, and a black mailbox. She was mailing a letter, or probably a Christmas card, for it was clearly a Christmas issue. Light snow was falling, the flakes just a few white dots, coming down here and there.

Mr. Gumbrel once told me the artist had done a lot of these il- lustrations for magazines. His name was Coles Phillips and he was famous for them. I went through the stack but didn't find another of them. Red against red, the outline of her coat was invisible. She blended into the background.

It was a trick of the eye, I guess. I could pick out the whole figure if I wanted to, if I looked at it in a certain way. Only there was some- thing restful about seeing it as the artist intended, letting the red coat fade into its background.

He called them Fadeaway Girls.

5

was too tired out from all of that thinking to put up with Delbert, but I had no choice, as Axel had "just left" to pick up a fare on Red Bird Road.

I sat in sullen silence in the backseat, hoping that would discourage Delbert from talking, but of course it didn't. I considered lying down in the well of the floor between front and rear seats to make him think I'd fallen out of the cab when he went over that last bump in the road.

He was going on about the First National and my business there. "You come into money, ha-ha?" and "Maybe you was robbin' it. Well, I could've been drivin' the getaway car, ha-ha." And on and on, saying dumb things that made me feel like they were eating up the air that I needed for breathing, chomping all the oxygen out of it.

"I had to get something out of my safe-deposit box."

"Huh?"

In the rearview mirror I could see Delbert's beady eyes narrow with suspicion. "Safe-deposit? You got valuables? I don't believe you got valuables." He gave a scornful snort.

I was down in the seat now, playing out strands of hair to see the sun through; the sun turned their color, which according to Ree-Jane was mousy brown, to a kind of burnt umber. I had no idea what color that was; I just liked the sound of "umber." And the sound made by "burnt" along with it. I didn't care what it meant, really. I guess that was why writers like William Faulkner went around making up words.

"Well?" said Delbert. "What valuables?"

"Delbert, if I needed a safe-deposit box, I'd hardly be going around telling people what was in it." By now, we were in Spirit Lake, coming up on Britten's Market. "Stop!" I yelled.

Delbert braked so hard it threw us forward.

"Gawd sakes alive!" he said, white in the face.

I smiled. "I'd prefer to get out here." I went into my change purse and brought out three quarters and handed them to him.

"You coulda just said you wanted me to stop." Grudgingly, he thanked me for the quarter tip.

Mr. Root was still on the bench, Ulub still on his feet, his book raised high. I knew he was reading poetry.

Mr. Root had set Ulub upon a course of reading aloud, thinking it would help his speech predicament. Ubub, Ulub's brother, had been excused from this practice, as Mr. Root did not find Ubub's speech problem nearly as bad. It was a little easier to understand Ubub, but not so easy that he couldn't have stood a few lessons in elocution. As far as I was concerned, it didn't make sense to put either one of them through this, but Mr. Root was determined. Of course, I will admit Mr. Root's ear was more finely tuned than mine. He was the only person who could understand either of them without much thinking about it. It was rather amazing.

Their real names were Alonzo and, I think, Robert. They had been christened "Ulub" and "Ubub" by Dodge Haines and Bubby Dubois and the other uncharitable sorts who held up the counter at the Rainbow Café. They'd taken the nicknames from the license plates of "the boys'" old pickup trucks: UBB and ULB. But "the boys" were too good-natured to mind this bit of meanness.

I crossed the highway, waving to them, and on the other side, had to watch Delbert coming back and honking, "shave-and-a-haircut, honk honk!" That was Delbert being funny.

I didn't wave. As I went up the grassy embankment where the bench was, I heard Ulub recite:

Ah unthuse memunse eh ah ah on.

I liked the way he did this with gestures, arm flung above his head, hand against heart. I didn't understand a word except for "I" at the beginning and "an" toward the end.

"Pretty good, Ulub," said Mr. Root.

Actually, Ulub sounded much as he'd always sounded. We'd all spent some time deciding what poet would be the best for this job. One of the first had been a poet I'd never heard of, Vachel something. Ulub came across a poem of his in some old book lying around their house. The poem was "The Congo." Mr. Root liked it because it had a real beat to it; he could tap his foot to it.

I recalled that Will had made drums by stretching thin canvas (or was it dead human skin?) over empty beer kegs. I don't know what they'd used the drums for, but they were still in the Big Garage. So I said we should all troop up there and borrow them. (I knew I wouldn't get anywhere with this request on my own.) When they saw it was all of us, and heard the request, Will actually smiled and let us in. This, I knew, was so they themselves could do the drum beating while Ulub read "The Congo." Which they did. They were loud and insistent to the point where Ulub forgot the poem and went into a kind of Indian-on-the-warpath dance.

So we decided "The Congo" was not the best choice for Ulub's reading. I suggested Shakespeare.

Mr. Root shook his head. "Too old-timey."

Robert Frost?

Another shake. "Too easy."

My storeroom of poets was about as full as my safe-deposit box, but I knew Robert Frost wasn't "easy." My mind hunted around for one of his poems. "He can't be easy, not if he's considered our greatest living poet."

Mr. Root was already thumbing through his battered book and came upon a poem. He read the first lines of "Stopping by Woods on a Snowy Evening." Then he snapped the book shut, as if he'd proven his point.

"Mr. Root, that's one of the most famous poems in the language; that's the one about the woods—"

"Famous and woods don't necessarily cut it."

Mr. Root was as old as forever but he had a modern way of speaking sometimes.

He went on: "I'll bet any one of us could write a poem this good. Couldn't we, boys?"

Considering who "anyone" was, he'd better not bet too much on it.

"Yes, sir, we could walk over to the lake and the woods where that Devereau house is and write us a poem right there." He pounded one small fist into the other hand.

I said, "Mr. Root, let's just choose another poet." Though I couldn't see what easiness had to do with Ulub's reading one or another.

"Well . . ." He was miffed but he turned some pages. "Here's this Wordsworth fellow going on about the daffodils. Try this, Ulub: a host of golden daffodils."

Ulub tried it: "Ah ghost uh oldna duvudus."

Mr. Root said, "See? Now that's too easy. It don't give Ulub enough range."

The back of a Rice Krispies box would give Ulub enough range. If I hadn't first heard the line, I don't think I'd have known "knee" meant "sea."

Then it was that Mr. Root decided to go back to Emily Dickinson, a poet he had earlier discarded as too crazy. *"How does 'space toll'? What's 'an amethyst remembrance'?"* But now he was back with her. He read off:

I know a place where summer strives
With such a practiced Frost . . .

We all stood or sat there while Mr. Root debated in his own mind about this poem. He drummed his fingers on the book, stared at the sky, murmuring *hmm-hmm* and repeating words from it. "'Practiced Frost.' Now that's got some zing to it. Ulub, you try that right there." He turned the book for Ulub to see.

Ulub saw and Ulub said: "Mon uh ah macused mros."

"Good," said Mr. Root. "That's got just the right amount of hardness to it."

So Emily Dickinson had the honor of just enough hardness and if she'd been alive and around, I would have liked to invite her to a reading.

Today, Ubub had gone into Britten's and brought back bottles of Nehi grape and handed them around. Mr. Root asked Ulub to repeat the Emily Dickinson lines he'd been reciting when I came along to the bench.

Ulub cleared his throat and solemnly raised the book.

Nee ee ear nees er aisee ack,
Eoden eefly ost.

"Hot spit!" exclaimed Mr. Root. "See? That little lady knows about poetry, don't she?" He turned to Ubub, who was drinking his Nehi grape. "What d'you think? Pretty good, wasn't it?"

"Mritty wood." Ubub nodded with enthusiasm.

Mr. Root said, "You hear how much better he sounds."

I didn't, but I said I did, then said I had to get back to the hotel to wait tables.

6

My mother was making soufflés, a bad sign, for it usually meant a dinner party. Vera, our head waitress, was also there, so there was definitely an increase in dinner guests. She was in her black uniform, long sleeved and white cuffed. All I ever wore was a short-sleeved blue uniform, or a white one that would have made anyone with more compassion look like a nurse.

I said hello to Walter, who was behind his big sink, the huge dishwasher making the kitchen sound like a building site. It clattered away beside him. But if not for the dishwasher, I'd be beside Walter, dishrag in my hands. Even Ree-Jane had been forced to wash dishes once or twice before we got the dishwasher. She complained all the while and picked on Walter. But Walter wouldn't rise to the bait; he just went on saying, "I reckon so."

I wondered if Walter was the exact opposite of Aurora Paradise. Maybe of all of us. I stopped poking at a lettuce to ponder this. The lettuces were, to quote Mrs. Davidow, who seemed to set lots of store by them, "personal Bibb lettuces"—baby Bibbs—for we were serving each guest a whole small lettuce. To hear Mrs. Davidow talk, you'd think they walked all the way from our vegetable garden, shaking off soil as they came.

Ree-Jane called Walter a retard, but he wasn't; he was just slow.

He might have been anywhere from thirty to forty-five. He wore black-rimmed glasses and lived alone in a big house that sat at the curve of the highway where Spirit Lake starts to fold into the far outskirts of La Porte.

Lola Davidow was in the kitchen with her martini, which reminded me that this was Aurora's cocktail hour too, and now would be a good time to get her drink going, while Mrs. Davidow was not in the office. Mrs. Davidow had dressed up in pink linen and powdered her face. She had one of those wonderful fair complexions that powder lies across like a fine veil.

She came to oversee the baby Bibbs, telling me to be careful. Careful? It was a lettuce. All I could picture was throwing one like a tennis ball across the kitchen to Walter and have him bat it back. We played tennis in my mind for a minute until Vera walked in with a reminder I hadn't done the butter patties.

I said how could I while I was doing the salads and she just squawked and walked away like a rooster. Never had I known anyone so this-and-that as Vera. My mother was a perfectionist, true, but she didn't have her ten fingers into everything around: the butter patties, the Pyrex coffeemakers, the ruby goblets, the place settings, the plates, glasses, coffee cups, and so on.

I finished the twelve "personal" lettuce salads, which were no fun because I wasn't allowed to stick things on them like hard-cooked-egg faces. I tried dressing them up with a slice of black olive on top of each until Vera saw them and told me to remove them, which I did; when her back was turned I hid the olives inside the tight little lettuce leaves.

What would be wonderful would be Miss Bertha finding hers and thinking it was a bug. I studied an olive slice, then searched the jar for an end slice, which would not have the hole in the middle. I found one, more buglike. I exchanged it for the one with the hole, tucking it into the salad I would serve Miss Bertha.

In life, just as in my mother's Angel Pies and Ham Pinwheels, it's the little things that count. Father Freeman once said to me, "God's in the details." The Sheriff said, on the other hand, "The devil's in the details." So it made no difference which one of them was planning something, God or the devil, it was the details that mattered.

I patted Miss Bertha's Bibb lettuce and took the ice-hard butter patties into the dining room.

Again, I remembered Aurora's drink. Mrs. Davidow was on her second martini, so that meant she planned on staying in the kitchen. I grabbed up a ruby goblet, rooted some ice from the butter patty dish, and tossed it in. I hightailed it through the long hall to the lobby and the back office.

Ree-Jane was standing by the fireplace again, posed with her arm draped across the mantel, talking to herself. She had changed into one of her expensive Heather Gay Struther dresses, this one a pearly blue with a crowd of knife-sharp pleats in the skirt.

In the back office, I looked over the bottles that sat double deep on the shelf. There was a bottle of Southern Comfort that I checked for fullness: half full, which made it safe to use.

I hadn't made a Cold Comfort in some time and wasn't sure of the recipe. Recipe? Who was I kidding? Who cared, least of all Aurora? I poured an inch of the Southern Comfort into the glass and added a little crème de menthe, then a little brandy. It really needed some juice or something light, such as club soda, but I couldn't go back to the kitchen. Then I remembered that Will liked to keep a bottle or two of Orange Crush in the bottom drawer of the typewriter table in the outer office.

I moved to the outer office, staying out of Ree-Jane's line of vision, and looked in the drawer. I uncapped a bottle and poured until the glass was full. I recapped it, put the bottle back in the drawer, returned to the inner office, and finished the drink with a maraschino cherry on a plastic swizzle stick.

I had no tray, so I had to hand-carry the glass, a practice strictly forbidden in the dining room. Any item of food or drink had to be transported to the diner on a tray. That was probably why I had become so adept at carrying trays. Vera wasn't the only one who could hoist a tray on five fingers.

Ree-Jane had her back to the staircase and was so engrossed in what she was saying to herself that she didn't hear me. It was another opportunity. You'd think she'd have learned by now.

I stood on the wide stairs for half a minute, watching her. She could have been talking to herself, talking to an invisible companion, rehearsing a part for a play—though not *Murder in the Sky,* for I knew Will and Mill wouldn't let her within a country mile of that. But there were other possibilities: she could have been rehearsing a speech to be given to the United Nations; rehearsing her acceptance of the Duke of Oxford when he proposed; making her screen test for Cecil B. DeMille; or throwing kisses to the people on both sides of the runway as she pivoted down it at the Paris fashion show.

Aurora's drink was warming in my hand, but I just had to say something. "There's only one female in the play and she's dead and she's me."

Ree-Jane twirled like a drum majorette (which she also could be rehearsing) and the pleats in her skirt made a pretty fan. "What are you doing here?"

"I live here."

"You're spying on me!"

I shrugged.

With a toss of her head she had learned from Veronica Lake (her future costar), she said, "Oh, *that* play? I found out about the female lead and turned it down."

I was stunned. Ree-Jane was actually thinking on her feet! I almost applauded. Of course, so did she. I marveled at this shred of thought coming from Ree-Jane (as if I'd been rooting for her all along), and continued my trek up the stairs.

"About time, miss! The yardarm's way over the bow."

That didn't sound exactly right but I knew what Aurora meant. "I do have other things to do," I said. "There's a dinner party tonight. Ten people."

She was agitating her Cold Comfort, prior to drinking. "Whose?"

Aurora was as interested in gossip as a normal person. "The Baums."

She made some lip-smacking sound of disapproval. "They're just throwing themselves around, trying to buy their way up the social ladder." She held her red goblet up to the window, and the setting sun made it look like blood splashed on her silver crocheted mitten.

"Into what?" I was truly curious.

"High society, of course." She took a long swig of the drink.

"In La Porte? There's no society in La Porte, much less a high one."

Aurora put down her drink long enough to waggle her finger at me. "That's where you're wrong, miss: There certainly is and I was once its leader!"

If she had been talking about a pack of sled dogs, I could have believed her. But high society? "There isn't one now, is there?"

"Oh, one or another of them thinks she's got the toehold and then *Wham!*" Down came her glass on the chair arm. "She's on the ground, flat on her ass—pardon my French. What's wrong? I could plant beans in the lines on your forehead." She emptied her glass in a couple of long swigs.

I guess I had on my stupefied frown. "This is a little town on the tag end of Maryland, nearly in West Virginia—"

"Where they got liquor stores, as I recall—" She jiggled her glass in a meaningful way.

I did not attend to it. "Maybe we've got the poor and the well-off, but we have not got high society."

She looked as if she could spit bullets. "My lord, girl, that's how much you know? After all your talk about the Devereaus and Woodruffs and the Belle Ruin?"

"The Devereaus? They were society people?" And here I thought they were just killers.

"Well, of course. Look at Iris. Look at Elizabeth."

"I can't look. They're dead." I was suddenly overcome with a sense of dread that there were too many people I couldn't look at. I had to depend on the likes of Aurora Paradise and Isabel Barnett, which brought me out of my mood, remembering the reason I'd come up here: to check on the snapshots. Aurora held out her glass.

"In a minute. First, I want to see those pictures again, the ones of the Slades and the Woodruffs."

"Lost them. So get downstairs and make me another Cold Comfort."

"You didn't lose them. They're in a blue satin box that you keep in your steamer trunk." I pointed to the trunk, draped with beautiful dresses.

Heavily, she sighed and set down her glass. And wearing her put-upon face, wheeled her swivel chair over to the trunk and opened one of its drawers and pulled out the blue box. Sighing again, she wheeled back. Then she rooted in the box and drew out the snapshots. But then she said, "There's one of Morris Slade that's gone missing. Last time I had it was when you were looking at these." She fanned several of them out. "So where is he?"

"I have no idea." Yes, I had. The snapshot was lying in my drawer under my socks.

"I bet you don't. Here, what about them?" She held several snap-shots out.

I took the picture of Imogen Slade holding her baby, tightly wrapped in a blanket. You couldn't see its face. "This one with the baby in it. You said they were at the Belle Ruin. Now if they were, that means Miss Isabel isn't lying about seeing the baby."

Aurora gave a fake sigh. "She's a liar, all right. But I guess the poor soul can't help herself."

Aurora calling her a "poor soul" really said Aurora didn't care. There was no care in her. I kept to it: "I'm talking about this baby being taken from the hotel. Kidnapped, snatched, whatever. The only person who actually saw the baby and who's around now is Miss Isabel—"

"Well, there's whoever took that picture."

"Yes, but all you see here is the blanket, not the baby."

Aurora looked absolutely pained. "Girl, you got more ways to explain away what you don't want to believe than a politician. Why can't you just go for the simplest thing? A mother holding a blanket like it had a baby in it *does* have a baby in it."

I said, "Just listen: It's natural that anyone might have taken for granted that if there was a carriage, there was a baby in it, or in its mother's arms. But remember, not even the babysitter actually *saw* the baby."

Aurora waved that away. "Oh, that Spiker girl. You can't depend on what she——"

I stepped on her words. "Imogen Slade told her not to bother the baby. Now, if this snapshot was taken that weekend when they were at the Belle Ruin——" Then I recalled that before, Aurora had said the Slade baby was only a few weeks old. Not months. "You said the baby was weeks old. But it was four months old according to the police report."

Aurora squeezed her eyes shut and motioned with her fidgety fingers. "God's sakes, girl, don't you ever stop thinking? What in the tarnation difference does it make? Could've been weeks, could've been months. No wonder people drink." She thrust her glass toward me.

I ignored it. "Because if the parents went to so much trouble to make out the baby was there, then maybe something happened that they wanted kept secret. So look again: Was that snapshot done on the occasion of the Belle Ruin ball?" To get her closer to saying, I took the glass from her fingers.

She perked up a little. "Hell's bells, give me my specs. They're in that little top drawer." She motioned to the steamer trunk.

I opened the drawer. Small as it was, I had to rummage through it. My fingers lit on something steely and cold and I pulled it out. "What are you doing with a *gun*?" I held it away from me as if it were a dead rat. It was small, with a short barrel.

"That? I've always had that. Woman alone has to protect herself. Well, for goodness' sakes, it ain't loaded. It's just a twenty-two, little revolver is all."

"Where'd you get it?"

"One of my men friends gave it to me. A gift." She looked off, dreamily.

When I saw her eyes were lighting up with the past, I shoved the gun back in the drawer and handed her her glasses. "The snapshot."

"Now, hand over my spyglass."

By this, I supposed she meant the magnifying glass atop one of the trunks. I gave that to her also. Stems of her glasses hooked around her small ears, she studied the snapshots with the magnifying glass, which I bet she didn't need. After a moment she said, "No. Couldn't have been that weekend." She tapped one of the pictures with her fingernail.

I looked. It was the one of old Mr. Woodruff.

"See there, he's got that mustache. Well, he never had it that weekend, not at that ball. I should know, as he danced with me all night."

I should have felt relieved to know that Miss Isabel could have been wrong, but it was then I realized the snapshot would settle nothing, whether it was taken that weekend, or the one before, or the one before that; the picture would be nothing more than a little chink of possibility—a possibility that Miss Isabel had seen the baby, a possibility that the baby had been there. Or, on the other hand, the possibility that she hadn't seen the baby. But that proved nothing.

At that point, I was so keen to get away I grabbed the glass and nearly ran out of the room. Behind me Aurora called, "Just why are you so all-fired interested in this?"

I turned back. "It's because the baby disappeared. I'm interested in disappearances."

Fadeaways, I could have said.

7

I t was to Mrs. Louderback's I went whenever things got complicated or when whatever I saw in my mind's eye looked like another
one of the devil's details.

This part of Spirit Lake sat across the highway from the hotel. It
was quite pretty, for the streets were tree-lined and the houses almost
all white clapboard with green trim and wide porches. It was as if
everyone had banded together and decided to make the houses look
alike, which was probably true.

We were in the very bottom of Maryland, where we could fall on
our faces into West Virginia. But West Virginia's okay. My mother
always said you could build a fence around West Virginia and you'd
have everything you needed. It would certainly have everything Lola
Davidow needed: a state liquor store was right over the line. It's about
twenty miles from La Porte, an easy drive (especially if you stay in
the ruts worn by Mrs. Davidow's station wagon).

My mother was from there and so was my grandfather, not a
Paradise but a Dunn. My mother's father. My grandfather had owned
a hotel there too, so maybe the hotel business was in my mother's
blood.

Yet, close as it was, my mother never wanted to visit it. If it were
me, and my old home was practically next door, I'd be over there all

the time, nosing around. But maybe their left-behind homes are too painful for some people.

I would knock on the door of my old house, and when the person who lived there now came to the door (an elderly woman in a flowered apron) I would say, "I'm sorry to bother you but I used to live here. I mean, my family did, but they were all killed in a train wreck and my mother, as she was dying, pleaded with me to go back home— Emma, go back and find those photographs!" By now, of course, I'd be inside and saying something about a photo album buried upstairs, perhaps in a window seat . . . and so forth. I would certainly want to see my old room.

I had sat myself down on the curb outside of the Moomas' house (although I didn't know which Moomas, as there were so many of them). Baskets of petunias and pansies hung along the porch roof, looking thirsty. Then I got up and walked on, kicking pebbles.

Mrs. Louderback's house was called "Traveler's Rest," which I thought especially appropriate for a fortune-teller. As if finally you could stop trying to fix your own messed-up life and let something else take control. Of course, it didn't actually work that way for me, but then I thought (being philosophical), just look at my life; how could it?

The woman who opened the door to me lived here with Mrs. Louderback and was always silent and grim. I thought she was bad-natured and wondered why Mrs. Louderback let her be the door greeter. Maybe she thought that if one of her clients could be discouraged from coming because of this woman's peevishness, well, maybe that person's fortune was already set in stone and no turning over of cards would change things.

Inside, the house was very cool and shadowy. I was led through the living room full of dark lion-footed furniture to a small room off the kitchen. It was in the kitchen that fortunes got told, and this small room was a parlor, a waiting room.

There were two other people there who looked to be mother and daughter. The young one might have been my age, and was dumb-looking. Say what you will about me. I am not dumb-looking. This girl sat with her head against her mother's shoulder and stared at me. I was never a person to hide from a stare; I stared back. She did not move an inch, and her eyelids did not flutter. She stared and stared.

The mother just flipped the pages of a *Ladies' Home Journal,* flipping, not reading, as if she were mad at the magazine for its uselessness. She was unaware of her staring girl, certainly. I was about to get up and go over and ask the mother if she knew her daughter was dead, when the door opened and a middle-aged woman walked out and crossed the room woodenly and left without looking at anybody or anything. I wondered if Mrs. Louderback hypnotized people and left them to find their own way home.

"Emma, hello."

Seeing I was next, I got up from my chair. But I felt some reluctance to go on. I didn't know what it was I wanted.

The kitchen smelled of recently baked bread. It was a very neat and clean kitchen. There wasn't a mark on the white counters, and the white enamel stove looked as if it had just come from the new Sears outlet.

Mrs. Louderback started placing cards in a row and the first was (yes, there he was) the Hanged Man.

"This does not mean bad news," said Mrs. Louderback.

It would to me if I were hanging upside down. I nodded and waited for the next card.

Orphans in a Storm. "Here they are again. Don't tell me *they're* okay."

She laughed, briefly. "It depends on what you think is 'okay.'"

"For one thing, not having to tramp through snow and rain in ragged clothes."

Mrs. Louderback grew thoughtful. "But they may be moving toward something brilliant."

I hoped this was not a cue for God to walk onstage. I changed the subject. "Last time we were talking about the Slades' baby being kidnapped. You know, from the Belle Ruin."

"Yes."

"Do you know what I think? I think maybe the baby wasn't even there. At the Belle Ruin, I mean. They just wanted people to believe it was."

Mrs. Louderback looked astonished. "But why would parents do such a thing?"

"I don't know. To make sure people thought baby Fay was alive at that time. And remember, the baby's nurse wasn't with them. They said she was sick. They said their baby was sick too, maybe to keep people from insisting on seeing her. What if the parents had to account for the baby's absence for some reason? Now if Fay was *allegedly kidnapped*, well, that would sure account for it."

Mrs. Louderback was looking at the cards but I don't think she was seeing them. Then she said, "This Spiker girl, the babysitter. She said she left the room and was gone for twenty minutes talking on the phone. When she returned, the baby was gone and Morris Slade was in the room."

I nodded. I thought Mrs. Louderback was doing awfully well in remembering details for a person her age.

She continued: "There's a problem there, isn't there? How would the kidnappers know she'd leave? And be gone long enough to get up that ladder and out again? You'd almost have to say it was arranged beforehand."

I slumped in my chair, hardly knowing what to say. I'd never thought the phone call was planned. "But how could it have been arranged beforehand unless Gloria Spiker was in on it? And not just Gloria, but her friend. For she did talk to a friend for twenty minutes. The operator confirmed it." A conspiracy? That was even more exciting.

"Could the kidnappers have been watching the room? Perhaps with binoculars? And see her leave?"

"Maybe. But she might have just turned around and come back." It looked as if I should go to Cold Flat Junction and talk to Gloria Spiker Calhoun again to try to see if she was telling the truth.

"Now, Emma, we really should get back to you."

I frankly thought we *were* back to me.

"This Orphan card keeps coming up. This is the third time."

Actually, it was the fourth, but I wasn't going to dwell on that. "Well, there are ten orphans that Miss Landis—that's Miss Louise Landis—do you know her? She's from Cold Flat Junction."

Mrs. Louderback pursed her lips, thinking. She was never one to toss out answers without thinking about them. "No, I don't believe I do."

"Anyway, as a treat for them, she brought ten orphans to the Hotel Paradise for lunch."

"How thoughtful."

I frowned. It had been my idea, actually. But not out of thoughtfulness. It was more like a bribe, the lunch, and I also threw in a performance of *Medea, the Musical.* "Those orphans weren't much like these, though." I had my chin cupped in my hands on the table, getting a different view of the cards for no reason. "They had terrible table manners."

"That's too bad. I expect your mother went to a lot of trouble for them."

My *mother* went to trouble? I was the one who nearly had to horsewhip Will and Mill into doing the performance. I said, poking the card, "Of course these Orphans aren't real; they just stand for something."

"What might they?"

I shrugged and shook my head. I was sitting back now and looking at the ceiling. I wondered if I was avoiding something. I thought of the Devereau house across the lake that in the fog seemed to float like a tall gray ship. I thought of the misty pond near the Belle Ruin, where the deer came almost like phantom deer to drink. I thought of the Girl. Then I said, "Sometimes I wonder: How can you tell the difference between what's real and what's not?"

I didn't expect Mrs. Louderback to come up with *the* answer— you know, the one that solves all problems, past, present, and future. But I certainly didn't expect her to say,

"Maybe you can't."

8

I forgot my two-dollar contribution on the way out, which was probably why Mrs. Louderback's housekeeper or whoever she was gave me an extra-stern look, although on her face it was hard to tell the difference from her other looks.

Maybe my hand that was now feeling the dollar bills hadn't wanted to let go because Mrs. Louderback hadn't told me anything that made me feel better, and was there any other reason to pay a person?

I kicked an empty Nehi can for a while down the road and then over to the curb when I saw a car coming. It was a buttercup yellow Chevy convertible, much bigger and fancier than Ree-Jane's white one, and it was driven by Scarlett Bittinger. I liked her because she was so much competition for Ree-Jane, who, of course, hated her.

Scarlett honked the horn and waved to me as she sped by. It was nice having someone her age treat me as if I was visible. Around her neck was a vivid green chiffon scarf that was raked by the wind, and as it sank from sight, I imagined Scarlett, in a night of wind and rain, on a dark road, and the scarf just whipping over her face, blinding her, and the car going over an incline, busting through the white safety guard, and away.

I hoped that wouldn't happen to her. But it did give me an idea for Ree-Jane's Christmas present: a chiffon scarf. I would describe how pretty Scarlett had looked in her scarf, driving her yellow convertible.

After crossing the highway, I walked up the hotel drive, the one in the rear, wondering what was going on in the Big Garage, and if they still had Paul in there. Paul's mother, who was our second dishwasher, was kind of slow. She forgot Paul a lot of the time. I could understand why.

I cut around the cocktail garden, which looked as if the Baum party had been there. Half-empty glasses were scattered about and napkins balled up and tossed anywhere. There was a wreck of an hors d'oeuvre plate sitting on the table.

I could see light through chinks in the Big Garage and walked over that way. Mill's piano was going full speed ahead, and I heard loud laughter and talk and a high-pitched squeal that probably came from Paul. At my knock, all of this noise stopped so suddenly you'd have thought the night had swallowed it. It made me feel like not waiting around for Will to come to the door and do his who-are-you? act.

I walked back toward the hotel and along the stone path to the rear door that led up to my room on the third floor. I met up with the hotel cat going from somewhere to somewhere and held the screen door for him in case he'd like to come with me. But he was far too busy. He did pause, though, to look up at me before he went on. I wished I had some business to take care of that made me that determined to do it.

I heard voices drifting back from the front porch and the hyena-like laugh of Helene Baum, so I figured that the dinner was over and now they had gathered for more drinks on the porch. Mrs. Davidow always counted her own self into any dinner party if she knew the people at all. So if places were set for ten, it could end up eleven, with Lola squeezed in between the others.

There was music too. Maybe Ree-Jane's phonograph had been carted downstairs. I sat on the bottom step, my skirt pulled over my knees like a tent and my chin resting on my knees. "Tangerine" was playing.

I remembered how I had sung this at the club along the Tamiami Trail and at the Roney Plaza. Rather, how I had pretended to sing it, since I hadn't been invited along on the trip to Miami Beach. And it all seemed so long ago. I couldn't understand why, as they'd come back from Florida hardly more than a week ago.

I trudged up the steps like a person going to her doom. I told myself to stop being so dramatic, but it still had a kind of doomish feel to it.

In my room was a toy chest that I didn't open often, as I thought I was getting too old to play with stuffed animals and certainly dolls.

There had been a big argument going on over my toy chest—still was, I supposed, for Ree-Jane hadn't got it yet. Lola Davidow wanted me to give it to Ree-Jane to keep her things in it.

"What things? I'm keeping *my* things in it." It seemed to me that was a reasonable question although I admit I said it in a lofty way.

Mrs. Davidow's mouth worked in that way she had when she wanted to deliver a squelching comeback: lips bunching, relaxing, bunching again; mouth opening and shutting, saying nothing. It was like the characters in the cartoons we saw at the movies before the feature came on.

I said to her that this chest had been mine since I was a baby. Her mouth finally worked and she told me I was just being selfish.

Then Ree-Jane limped in (I like to picture her with a gimpy leg or even a clubfoot) and called me selfish too.

"What do you want it for?" I said. "Do you have a dead body you want to stuff in it?"

"Don't be stupid."

"I'm using this chest."

"It's just junk you've got in there."

"How do you know? Have you been in here looking around?"

"All you've got in that chest is kid stuff."

"I know. I'm a kid." That was the second time lately I'd allowed myself to be categorized that way. I hoped it wouldn't become a habit. "Anyway, I haven't got anyplace else for my mice to live." I scratched my head as if I were really thinking.

"Your what?"

"Mice. There's a mother and father and she has babies. You want to see?" I lifted the lid.

Ree-Jane dragged her foot off, muttering.

What was all this? If she really needed a chest like mine with its chipped and faded pink paint, well, her mother had plenty of money to buy one. She'd bought into the Hotel Paradise a few years ago and owned half of it. Maybe that was why she thought I should let go of my toy chest—because she owned half of it.

And why would Ree-Jane want to be associated with a toy chest, especially mine?

I knew my mother would probably be along soon, for both of them would complain to her about my selfishness. All my mother wanted to do was keep the peace.

I opened the chest and looked inside, feeling now that all this stuff was of a value no one could guess. It might as well have been full of diamonds and rubies. There was a ragged doll—not a Raggedy Ann, but just plain ragged. Her hair was patched and one ear was missing. I felt sorry for her, mostly because I couldn't remember when I'd last played with her. I couldn't imagine playing with her now, although I wasn't above getting a gauze square for her ear, as ears bleed a lot.

As I took out one item after another, it struck me how much this chest was like Mary-Evelyn Devereau's toy chest in that old house across the lake.

Mary-Evelyn. She was my age when she drowned, *was* drowned, her head shoved underwater until she couldn't hold her breath any longer. I breathed deeply and wondered, How long could I hold my breath?

Mary-Evelyn. If Rose Devereau had not run off with Ben Queen, Mary-Evelyn might not have died as she did. But it's not fair putting it off on them, as they meant to come back for her. But then it was too late.

Mary-Evelyn had owned a Mr. Ree game, the same as I did. For each player there was a character, a small hollow tube with a tiny doll-like head, removable for hiding the tiny weapons a player might pick up if the cards told him to do so. The thing is, two of these tubes had turned up, Artist George at Crystal Spring and the other, Niece Rhoda, at Brokedown House, and I thought the Girl had left them as some kind of clue—to what, I didn't know. Perhaps simply that she'd been there.

For all I know, I had left them myself.

That wasn't something I wanted to dwell on.

9

But dwell I did.

It's hard on a person to think she's going crazy, especially when she's only twelve. I haven't come across many crazy people.

Over in Weeks's Nursing Home, where I sometimes went with my mother to take cakes and pies, I remembered a lot of old people sitting around with their mouths open. That looked kind of crazy, but that might instead just be what happens when you're old.

Sitting now by my toy chest, which might not be mine much longer, I inspected one of the tubes from the old Mr. Ree game: the Aunt Cora tube. I removed her head and stuck my finger inside. It would be a perfect place to leave a little rolled paper. But the two tubes I'd found, one at the spring and the other at Brokedown House, had been empty. I was almost glad for that now, for if I'd been writing messages to myself, I might soon be on the doorstep of Weeks's with a suitcase instead of a pie. Since there were never any kids there, I figured there were probably places like that for kids too.

And then I thought of Mary-Evelyn's Mr. Ree box. *Had* two tubes been missing from hers? I thought back, hard. I remembered taking the game out of her toy chest and looking at all the pieces, but I might not have noticed a missing character tube.

What if the same two pieces were missing there?

Maybe I should go back. That idea didn't appeal to me, not after what happened, not after I had almost gotten murdered.

But the house itself, I had to think, was harmless. Places didn't absorb the evil waves that vibrated off some people. The fourth floor of our hotel, the four small rooms up there, the floors and furniture and doors and walls: they hadn't gone crazy just because Aurora Paradise lived in them.

The Devereau house was just a house. It just happened to have been lived in by at least one totally crazy person and a couple of others that the house would have been better off without.

Take Ree-Jane's room, for instance. The bed and dresser didn't think they were better than other beds and dressers just because Ree-Jane lived there.

Ree-Jane.

Ree-Jane had been in my room; otherwise, she wouldn't have known what was in the toy chest. She could easily have taken Niece Rhoda and Artist George away. My mind moved swiftly to that ghastly-turned-wonderful ten minutes in the Rainbow Café when I'd come upon Ree-Jane sitting in *my* booth (mine and Maud's and the Sheriff's) with the Sheriff, when he showed me what she'd given him: an Artist George tube that she claimed she'd found at Crystal Spring, saying maybe that's how I contacted Ben Queen. The Sheriff had told her off in five seconds flat (the wonderful part) and later given me the Artist George tube.

Now this was not proof she'd taken Artist George from my game, because I had also found him in that stone alcove in Crystal Spring before she'd been there. But that piece might have been the one from Mary-Evelyn's Mr. Ree, and Ree-Jane could still have taken mine.

The Niece Rhoda tube Dwayne found in the woods around Brokedown House, which was near Lake Noir. I don't think Ree-Jane had ever been there; it just wasn't her kind of place. It was deserted, owlish, thickly wooded, and without anyone there to admire her beautiful self. Also, Fern Queen had been murdered very near there, at Mirror Pond, and I couldn't imagine Ree-Jane going to a murder site unless under full police escort.

10

The next morning after my breakfast of lingonberry pancakes with powdered sugar sifted across them and syrup-swarmed (Faulkner, again), I was down at Slaw's Garage.

If there was one person to talk to about insanity, it was Dwayne, who worked at Abel Slaw's. Dwayne was the William Faulkner expert, which I thought unusual for a mechanic, but the mere fact of reading him would make a person an expert around here, since nobody else did.

Slaw's Garage was down the highway maybe a mile or so, and across the highway from the railroad station. An old boardwalk could be taken from near the hotel past some tennis courts. It ran parallel to the highway. People had long used the boardwalk for strolling to the post office or the general store, or to Jessie's Restaurant, which was something like the Windy Run Diner.

Abel Slaw employed Dwayne, master mechanic, and a couple other ordinary mechanics, but they were never all there at once. One was You-Boy, whose strange name he'd had from when he was little, and his mother always calling to him: "You, boy! Get in here!" Things like that.

I looked to see if Mr. Slaw was in his office, and he wasn't, which was a relief. He didn't like me going into the garage.

You-Boy was under one of the car lifts and saw me and tilted his wrench toward me by way of greeting. I heard a clanging coming from under another car, not up on a lift, and figured it was Dwayne. The car was one of those fancy foreign models, and I recognized it as belonging to Bubby Dubois, the Chevrolet dealer in La Porte. I'd rather be called You-Boy than Bubby. Imagine, a grown man still letting himself be called Bubby.

Harsh metallic sounds came from beneath Bubby's car. I don't know why Dwayne didn't just raise the car on the other lift, but then he was the master mechanic, so I guess he had his reasons.

I hoisted myself up on the stack of new tires to wait for Dwayne to roll himself out. I sat there thinking how I liked the clanging sound of metal against metal and the smell of the new rubber. Then I stopped watching myself, posing as if the photographers were all gathered at Slaw's today, taking my picture, and slid down onto the floor, then down on my knees. I had to squat even more until I could see under Bubby's car where Dwayne lay on his rolling board. He was tightening up something under the car. A caged light hung from the car's undersurface.

"Dwayne?"

He turned his head. He shook it slowly and in a wondering way, lying there on the pallet. "Of all the gin joints in all the towns in all the world, she walks into mine."

My cheek was now down on the cement. Dwayne had picked up his wrench and started tightening something. The underside of a car held no fascination for me, but as he wasn't rolling himself out, I just lay down on the oil-stained floor and propped my head on my hand.

"Dwayne," I said. "Do you think a little kid"—that was the fourth time for the kid category, and this time with "little" in front of it—"could go crazy, even insane?"

The noises stopped. He turned his head to look at me again. Even in the half dark of the car, he was handsome. Ree-Jane had a terrific crush on him; he did not have a crush on her, I am happy to say. I thought I would mention to her that there were a lot of handsome men in my life and how many could she say were in hers?

He surprised me then by pushing himself out from under the car. He said, "Are you talking about that little kid that's the dishwasher's son?" Dwayne was getting up now and wiping his hands on the oily rag that he kept in his back pocket. All mechanics had one.

"Him? Paul? No." Paul was already insane, not going.

"Okay, so who?"

"Well, me, maybe."

"*You?* Christ almighty, you're too ornery to go insane. Come on." He nodded for me to follow him.

"Ornery? What's that got to do with it?" I walked after him.

"With you, everything." On the way out he said to You-Boy, "Tell Abel I'm over at Jessie's when he gets back."

"Sure, Dwayne." You-Boy smiled and gave him a wrench salute, hitting himself in the forehead coming back.

Poor You-Boy. It was like something I'd do. "Wait up!" I called to Dwayne, who was now almost at the highway's edge.

We crossed the highway, then crossed the railroad tracks. I loved the old station. It was nearly as wonderful as the one in Cold Flat Junction.

We got to Jessie's Restaurant and Dwayne actually stepped back and held the screen door for me and I thanked him. I was still amazed that he'd be leaving work and going over here with me.

The restaurant was bigger than the Windy Run Diner, but it always struck me as having diner intentions. There was a horseshoe counter, and the people now sitting there could have been the same ones who sat there every day. It was clear some at least knew some others. The ones sitting at the counter nodded to Dwayne, and he nodded back and then said hello to Jessie.

I sat wondering if she had a crush on Dwayne too, the way she kind of came up to the other side of the counter as if in a moment she might be over it. Jessie was a pretty brunette, only she looked kind of worn.

"Hello, lover," she said.

I might retch. And Dwayne took it without even a tenth of the smackdown he'd have given me if I'd tried saying something so silly.

Of course, I was twelve and Jessie was probably a hundred and twelve. Ha-ha.

She got him his coffee and me my Cherry Coke, and after we'd taken our first sips, he said, "So what's all this insanity stuff?"

"Remember at Brokedown House you found that little game piece on the path that you didn't know what it was?"

"Yeah. Hollow tube thing."

I pulled the Mr. Perrin tube from my pocket and put it in front of him.

Dwayne held it up, inspecting it. He had really nice hands with long fingers, a pianist's hands, or, I guess, a master mechanic's. "The one I found had a woman's head."

"Niece Rhoda."

"And this one's—?"

"Mr. Perrin."

"Go on."

Then I took Artist Geroge from my other pocket. "This one's the tube I found over at Crystal Spring. It was behind the tin cup in a kind of stone alcove. It was missing from Mary-Evelyn Devereau's Mr. Ree game." I leaned in closer to him so no one else would hear. "It was missing from mine too. My Mr. Ree game. And so's my Niece Rhoda tube. Like the one you found. What I'm wondering is: *Was* that the one you found?"

"And somebody stole it and tossed it on the path? Is this the insane part of the story?"

Nervously, I nodded. "Was it me? Could I have done that and not remembered?"

"No." Dwayne was turning Mr. Perrin in his fingers. "You never forget *anything*. Better if you did."

"But the point *is* if I was *insane*—" I whispered the word, not wanting to give it too much life.

"If you were insane, we wouldn't be having this conversation. You wouldn't be sane enough to wonder if you weren't." He drank his coffee.

"Huh?"

"What about that ditzy brother of yours?"

Will? Ditzy?

"He could've taken those game pieces."

"But he didn't know I was going to Brokedown House."

"He was over at Mirror Pond, you told me. Where that murder happened."

"Oh, Will's too busy with their production to be playing tricks."

Dwayne guffawed. "From all I've heard, I'd say your brother is *never* too busy to be playing tricks."

I considered that, knowing it was probably true.

He said, "Besides you, who else knew what was in the toy chest?"

"In mine?"

"Yours and what's-her-name's. The little drowned girl?"

"Mary-Evelyn Devereau. I don't know about hers. But mine, I think Ree-Jane's been into mine, from something she said."

"Well, there you go."

"You think it was her?"

"Could be. After all, she's jealous of you, so it would seem likely she'd want to mess with your mind."

"Jealous? Of *me*?"

Dwayne turned upon me a look of surprise. "You tellin' me you don't know that? For God's sakes, you're a ton smarter than she is, and she knows it; you've practically got yourself a whole career in reporting going, which must really get her goat; and you're prettier. Of course she's jealous." He was getting out some money.

I sat there, gape-mouthed.

"Come on, I gotta get back to that Mercedes." He left a tip on the counter. "Some of us have to work for a living."

I slid off my stool, complaining. "I work for a living."

"Oh yeah. Sure you do."

And we argued back and forth across the tracks and the highway about working for a living.

I really wanted to discuss my being prettier than Ree-Jane.

11

"N o'd bye nd neep nold—"

I was on the Britten's Market bench, listening to Ulub practice his elocution.

"First thing people notice is how you say your words. For instance, 'ask,' not 'ast.'"

Somehow I felt "ask" was light-years behind Ulub's problem; I didn't think he needed to worry about mispronouncing words.

I had come here after visiting Dwayne. Not to put myself in the way of Ulub's elocution lesson, I sat patiently, trying to understand his words before Mr. Root barged in and translated. It was a particular point of pride with Mr. Root that he was the only one of us who could understand Ulub.

Ubub could understand his brother, but that came from a lifetime of listening. Ubub's speech wasn't exactly like FDR's or Winston Churchill's, but it wasn't as bad as Ulub's.

Mr. Root was reciting, "'Keep cold, young orchard. Good-by and keep cold.'" He turned to me. "That still sounds like dumb advice."

Dumb advice? What was he talking about?

Back to Ulub: "Now, you say that, Ulub." Mr. Root held up his hands as if he had a symphony orchestra he was trying to conduct.

"Ong . . ."

" 'Young, *young,* orchard—' "

"no-or—"

Mr. Root shook his head. "Well, 'orchard' is a pretty hard word. Let's take it from 'Dread fifty above more than fifty below.' Okay? 'Dread,' 'Dread fifty . . .' " and down came his hand on the beat.

"Ed. Ed ifny."

I heard no improvement, though Mr. Root apparently did, or pretended he did, for he slapped Ulub on the back and told him he was getting much better. There was a small notebook on the bench; Mr. Root picked it up and made some kind of note with a pencil. "You get good marks today, Ulub."

I hoped he wasn't actually giving Ulub grades. "What's the poem, Mr. Root?" I asked.

He took the book from Ulub. It was a paperback, not very thick. I saw it was the poetry of Robert Frost. "But I thought you didn't like Robert Frost. You were all against 'Stopping by Woods on a Snowy Evening.' Remember?"

"That one, yeah. But he's wrote a couple good ones. I kind of put 'em in between Emily's, you know, to give Ulub a rest." Mr. Root cleared his throat and intoned in a singsong fashion:

This saying good-by on the edge of the dark—

It shut my eyes, that line did, as sure as a hand passing over them. "Oh," I said.

"What?"

"Nothing."

He read on, although I was still back there on the edge of the dark. Then he came to:

I wish I could promise to lie in the night
And think of an orchard's ar-bor-e-al plight
When slowly (and nobody comes with a light)
Its heart sinks lower under the sod.

My eyes snapped shut again. I had never heard anything so fearfully sad. I bit my lip to keep from crying. I could almost see it, the trees too young to be left alone, waiting for someone or something to come, and finally knowing no one ever would.

"Yep," said Mr. Root. "Some of his, well, I'd say he knows what he's talking about. Straight talk. That's what Frost was really good at, none of those namby-pamby poems about your Greek urns and stuff. Nope"—he held up the book—"just your plainspoken, to-the-point words about nature and stuff." He handed the book back to Ulub.

Ulub did not look happy to receive it.

"Mr. Root," I said, "I don't think he's plainspoken. He means a lot more than what he seems to be saying."

Mr. Root pushed his feed cap back on his head and scratched his forehead.

Ulub bobbed his head up and down, briskly. I thought he wanted to agree with me because I might be a way out for him.

"What do you mean by that?" His eyes narrowed as if I might be insulting him.

I didn't really want to talk about it; I don't know why I had to open my big mouth. "Well, I think he means something different from what he's saying. Or seems to be saying."

Ulub felt free enough now to come and sit beside me on the bench.

Ubub was coming out of Britten's with a Grape Crush. He asked me, in his way, if I wanted one, and I said no, thanks. I asked Mr. Root if I could just borrow the book for a minute, and he handed it to me.

"And could I have a piece of paper and use your pencil?"

He tore off a little sheet and handed that to me too, along with his pencil. "Whatcha doin'?"

"Just copying."

I wrote the last lines on the paper and folded it up and stuck it in my change purse.

12

My mother told me I was late (which I already knew) and that Miss Bertha and Mrs. Fulbright were already in the dining room waiting for their lunch.

I asked what they were having and when my mother said Ham Pinwheels I perked up; a lot of the sadness left me. Ham Pinwheels might be the only thing that could compete with Robert Frost.

Yes, the day was getting heady with the luxury of having me in it: me, prettier than Ree-Jane, about to eat Ham Pinwheels for lunch. And about to serve this to Miss Bertha, who hated Ham Pinwheels and the last time she'd been served them scraped off the cheese sauce and rolled the pinwheel across the floor. It had collided with a chair leg.

Mrs. Fulbright was mortified. I was gleeful, except she'd put a perfectly good pinwheel out of commission. Depending on how dirty it was, of course.

"You know she doesn't like these," I said to my mother, happily unhelpful.

"The old fool. Well, if she wants something else you can tell her we have one serving of chicken pot pie from last night's dinner. I'm sure she doesn't like leftovers, either."

Miss Bertha and Mrs. Fulbright have been coming here summers since I was born. They could be a hundred but are probably in their eighties. Mrs. Fulbright is one of those old women with a complexion as luminous as crushed pearls. Her disposition matches: never a complaint, always a compliment.

Miss Bertha just looks, well, crushed, period. She is bent over, her head getting closer and closer to the polished floor of the dining room every summer. Her hump certainly doesn't help the situation, and, of course, she needs a cane, which comes down on the floor like a drill. She never married and I wonder if she ever had a boyfriend and if she always had that hump. Was she a humpbacked baby? Just a tiny hump, no bigger than a knuckle?

The luncheon plates also held a shimmering tomato aspic cupped in a lettuce leaf with a dab of mayonnaise on the side and a couple of radish curls. The cheese sauce poured over the Ham Pinwheel was thick and golden, with a dusting of paprika across its top.

The plate looked so pretty I thought it criminal to serve it to someone bent on hating it. I raised the tray like Father Freeman raised the communion cup (which I had never tasted, as I was not a Catholic) and marched the food into the dining room.

"You know I don't eat these things!" She gave the pinwheel a little push and left a fingerprint in the cheese sauce. "Bring something else." She sat back, or as far back as her hump allowed.

Mrs. Fulbright, of course, received her plate with a pleasantly surprised look.

I said to Miss Bertha, "Well, there's one serving left of leek and eel pie."

"What? Eel pie? Don't be ridiculous. Jen Graham never cooked an eel in her life."

Said Mrs. Fulbright, "Bertha, now you don't know that."

"Of course I know it! Don't be a fool."

Mrs. Fulbright took a bite of her pinwheel and pronounced it delicious. "You do like the cheese sauce, Bertha."

You'd have to have had your taste buds burned out of your mouth to not like it.

Miss Bertha demanded something else with cheese sauce.

"You can have it over the eels." It was the most disgusting way of putting it I could think of offhand.

She made a face, although you could say Miss Bertha's face was always making one.

I looked at the paprika sprinkled across the cheese sauce and smiled. I had, for once, the perfect solution. "Welsh rarebit," I said.

Miss Bertha looked at me with suspicion, but my face was as clear as a glass bell, and my voice was carefully modulated to match it. I was all sympathy. "White or whole-wheat toast, Miss Bertha?" I fluttered my eyelashes a little.

"White. And I want an egg, a hard-boiled egg sliced up on the toast, and then the sauce over everything."

"Coming up!" I said cheerily.

"Oh, for God's sake," said my mother, slapping down her chef's knife, then marching to the refrigerator and hauling out a dish of hard-boiled eggs. "Walter, shell one of these under running water. The shell comes off more easily."

Walter loped over and took the egg and did as instructed. I took the ground red pepper from the little shelf of spices and held it behind my back and hummed, watching my mother slice up the egg. Waiting, I turned (shifting the red pepper to my front) and saw through the kitchen window over the distance to the back door on the other wing of the hotel. There was a man walking out and up toward the cocktail garden. I could not make out whether he was old or young.

"Who's that?"

"Who?"

I sighed. "I don't know or I wouldn't be asking." The toast popped about a mile high and my mother slapped it down and started trimming off the crust as she looked off more or less in the direction of the back door. "I don't see anyone."

"Not now you don't. It's a fellow in shirtsleeves who came out and walked up the back. He's light-haired."

"Oh, that's Ralph." She arranged the sliced egg on the toast and reached for the cheese sauce.

Oh, that's Ralph? As if "Ralph" had been her sous chef for years, in addition to managing the books and making martinis. "Well? Who's Ralph?" I had the small canister of pepper ready, holding it below the counter. I had the paprika in my other hand up on the counter. "I've never come across any Ralph around here."

"Ralph Diggs. He calls himself 'Rafe.' That's the way the *English* pronounce Ralph. To rhyme with 'safe.' " She poured the cheese sauce and I held up the paprika, showily. "I can't say I care for him much."

Although I was nearly drowning in impatience, I managed to give the cayenne pepper several shakes over the sauce when my mother turned her back. As she turned around I placed the innocent paprika on the counter. "Well, I probably wouldn't care for him either if I knew who he was. Who *is* he?"

"Mrs. Davidow hired him to carry bags and help out generally."

"But Will's the bag carrier, the bellhop. *Will* is." In case she'd forgotten her son and his hotel role.

"Will's just too busy with his theater work." She shook a cigarette loose from a pack of Kools and lit it and said, "Take the lunch in before it gets cold."

I ignored this. "His *theater* work? Well, what about my *newspaper* work? Why don't you hire someone to take my place in the dining room?"

"You're indispensable." She smiled through the smoke, insincerely.

I smiled back, insincerely. "Why is *anyone* needed to carry bags, anyway? We hardly get that many guests, and most of them carry their own bags."

"Will's not let off completely. He's to be hotel concierge. In case guests have questions."

Concierge? Will? "The only question he can answer is, 'Where is the Big Garage?' Where did he come from, this Ralph? We haven't hired anybody new in years."

My mother merely looked grimly at the plate still sitting on the tray. "Lunch."

Angrily, I hoisted the tray, marched it into the dining room, and placed the cayenne-peppered-up rarebit in front of Miss Bertha. I walked over to a window to stare out and brood.

I was so irritated by Will's being let off his hotel duties, especially by this brand-new Ralph-Rafe person, that I hardly noticed when Miss Bertha cried out, *"Water! Water!"*

Let her burn.

13

I was out of the dining room and out the side door, hot on the trail of Ralph Diggs.

As he was no longer in sight in the back, I could only guess he might have gone to the Big Garage to get tips on bellhopping from the Hotel Paradise concierge.

Unfortunately for Ralph or Rafe, Will's real work was "charm," charming the guests, especially if there was trouble.

Like a few weeks ago, when he'd wanted another kid to join the Hummers in the production of *Medea, the Musical*. He'd discovered this little girl wandering around the croquet court with a mallet, not knowing where she was or, possibly, who she was. So Will had hauled her up to the Big Garage, not mindful (or at least not caring) that her parents would be anxiously searching for her.

It turned out that her name was Bessie, and she'd been "missing for hours." Will and Mill were brought to the front desk with Bessie in tow. The parents were white-faced. Did Will apologize? Of course not. He sidestepped the entire issue by telling Bessie's mom and dad what a marvelous stage presence she had and how she had a real future in the theater. This was all delivered with a million smiles. Since Bessie, who was only four, had about as much stage presence as Paul, the wonder was how the parents swallowed all of this malarkey.

Charm, charm, charm, that's all.

It really irritated me. Will had it and I didn't. I was the one who *worked*; I was the one who deserved it; I was the one who almost got murdered.

As I crunched along the gravel up to the Big Garage, I noticed a black Chevy coupe parked up on the verge. I didn't think we had any guests coming today, which was not an unusual event, and wondered whose it was.

I was astounded to find the garage door open. *Open*. It was like finding the pearly gates unattended by Saint Peter so that any screwball could just walk in. Back there in the shadows were Will, Mill, and the fellow I supposed was Ralph Diggs.

Ralph was years older than Will and Mill, so no longer in his teens. Some girls I guess would find him "cute": he had curly blond hair and a straight nose and hazel eyes. He was taller than Will.

When we were introduced, he as "Rafe," me as "Emma" (my name resistant to a fancy pronunciation), I said, "Ralph, isn't it?"

His smile was lopsided and he gave me a splintered look, as if the irises had broken up into tiny shards of green, blue, and brown.

Will answered for him. Apparently Ralph Diggs was not to be put to a lot of bother answering questions. "Rafe's taking over for me as front man," said Will.

That was a good description of either of them, I thought, having the strong ring of dishonesty and deceit. "Oh? Where are you going?"

"Don't be dumb. Nowhere. I'll be the hotel concierge. You know, helping guests with problems and questions."

"They'll have to come to the Big Garage to ask them."

Will just rolled his eyes. Ralph kept up that smile that I decided was pretty cold.

"What things? Aside from carrying bags only occasionally, you don't do anything. Did Mrs. Davidow outline your job? Ralph?"

The smile was still on only one side of his mouth. And his eyes looked those shards at me. But he did answer. "Helping out generally. Bags. Kitchen. Dining room. Getting groceries, since I have a car."

He did not appear to be trying to impress us with the car. I assumed it was the old black Chevy that I'd passed. But at my age, any car would impress me; I mean owning one.

He said, "What do you do?"

"I work. Seven days a week, three meals a day. Waitressing."

"Wow." He said this without emphasis, quite sarcastically.

Ralph did not like me, probably because he was onto the fact that I did not like him and, consequently, might be trouble. But his dislike seemed more focused. "Excuse me," he said, "but I've got to get my stuff out of my car."

We said good-bye and I watched him leave and then followed. I stood outside of the garage and I looked as he walked to the Chevy and opened the trunk. He took out two cheap-looking suitcases and a hatbox.

A hatbox.

A bellhop.

Wow. With emphasis.

I watched him carry these things, shoving the smaller case up under his armpit and holding the larger one underneath by its handle, as if he'd had bellhop experience. The hatbox he held in his other hand.

He was heading toward the back door in the far wing, and I wondered if Mrs. Davidow had put him up on the third floor, where the least of us had our rooms. In other words, the third floor was empty except for me.

Keeping well behind, I followed him. He went through the door to the back staircase, which lay down a short hallway. I made sure I heard his feet ascending before I put my own foot on the stair. His feet stopped at the second-floor landing and continued along that hall.

He wasn't to sleep on the third floor, for which I was grateful. When I saw him turn the corner on the second floor and keep on down the long hall, I followed.

His room was on that hall, where Will's was, and Mill's beside it.

I peeked around the corner and saw Ralph Diggs had entered a room halfway down; number 51.

Now, all of this following was, of course, unnecessary simply to find out his room number. But I think it was in the nature of Ralph Diggs that he should be followed.

The hotel was often silent when you got above the main floor, especially as we had so few guests. So I could tell when Ralph Diggs left his room after a few minutes. I realized that if he came back this way, I'd be exposed, and was about to slip into an empty room, but then I heard his footsteps getting farther away. He would go down by way of the stairs that ended up outside of the dining room.

I waited until the silence became even more silent, as if a thick layer of fog had come down to muffle every sound. Then I crept down the hall to number 51, on the right. The door, I was surprised to see, was open, or halfway open. I put my hand to it and pushed a little. The suitcases were on the bed, also open. It was as if Ralph Diggs had nothing in the world to hide.

Except the hatbox. That I didn't see. He must have put it in the wardrobe.

I stood there, scratching my elbows and debating. I had never searched a guest's room, never tried to look at their possessions, opening drawers, looking under beds or in wardrobes. That was mostly because our guests were boring and probably wouldn't have anything I wanted to see.

But that hatbox, now, that was interesting. There was a movie called *Night Must Fall*. Robert Montgomery played a bellhop in a big hotel, who carried a hatbox around. He charmed a rich old lady in a wheelchair so much that she had him move into her little house. Her companion, played by Rosalind Russell, was really suspicious of him, and he knew it.

The house was in the woods, where it always seemed to be dark or in deep shadow, and where the branches of trees dripped rain.

There was a great mystery surrounding one of the hotel guests, a woman who had disappeared. Finally, they found her body in the woods. It didn't have a head—

"Looking for me, are you?"

The voice fell like the hand on my shoulder that I lurched to shake off.

Ralph Diggs stood there with one of the towels from his room slung over his shoulder. How stupid of me! He hadn't walked down to the stairs; he'd simply walked the few doors down to the hall bathroom. Few of our guest rooms had private baths.

"No," I said. "I mean, I just wondered if you were going to help out at dinner."

"Am I supposed to? Lola didn't say anything about it."

Lola? He was calling her by her first name?

"Maybe"—I looked upward, as if I could see all the way to the fourth floor—"you could take a drink up to my great-aunt Aurora Paradise." I smiled. "She always has a drink before dinner. It would help because there's a dinner party tonight and I'll be really busy."

He did not say yes or no, as if it were his choice. "Doesn't she come down to dinner?"

"Oh, no. No. She never comes down. She lives up on the fourth floor." I jabbed my finger toward the staircase at the end of the hall. "You could say she's a . . . recluse."

"Sounds a little crazy." He pulled the towel from his shoulder. We were both still standing in his doorway.

That, I thought, was impertinent and forward. I wondered how far forward he would get with Aurora Paradise. "I was just wondering— why are you here? In Spirit Lake?"

A shrug that hardly touched his shoulders. "Just passing through."

But he wasn't, was he?

He was stopping and staying.

14

hightailed it back up to Squirrel Hall and banged on the door. I wanted to see if I could get any information out of Will and Mill about him.

Blood out of a stone would have been easier as well as a bit less frustrating. Did they know anything about Ralph Diggs? No. Why was he here? Shrug shrug. Where had he come from?

Mill stopped trailing his fingers along the piano keys, like lifting his hand from river water. "Doylestown."

"Doylestown? Where's that?"

Mill shrugged. "Pennsylvania?" He returned the hand to his river of music.

Will said, looking at his "production notes" book, which looked to me like one of the Hotel Paradise registers, "We'll find a part for him."

"Part? Well, good grief, he's not a *kid*! He wouldn't want to be in a play with us."

Will looked at me as if I'd gone crazier than usual. "Are you joking?"

That, apparently, was all that needed to be said. He turned a page of the book.

I gave up on Ralph. I didn't know what to ask. So I just said, "Why do you need that clumsy, hard-to-hold book?"

"All producers have them."

"They also have money, Broadway, and paid actors."

He smiled, undaunted. "Well, they don't have me and Mill."

To Will, this was just stating a fact. If David O. Selznick had given him the nod, he would have nodded back and checked his schedule. I have never known anyone, not even the Sheriff, with such steely confidence as Will. I can't imagine where he got it.

As a musical backdrop for our conversation, Mill's fingers were flying all over the keyboard. He was probably making up his variation of a gospel piece they'd heard over at the Tabernacle. Putting their own words to gospel music was a favorite pastime.

"Okay," Will said. "You can be Patty Flynn." He snapped the book shut.

I frowned. "Who's Patty Flynn?"

"The murderee. The victim."

"That's my whole part?" I'd only been guessing when I told Ree-Jane I was the victim.

"As of now." He was chewing his Teaberry gum mercilessly.

"Wait. You mean you haven't finished writing it?"

"We've got most of it down. We're kind of hung up on who killed you and why."

I just looked at him. He was unfazed by the look. "In *Perry Mason*, the whole *point* is who did it and why."

"That's TV." He moved his gum to the other side of his mouth. "This is theater."

I ignored that distinction. "But it's a *mystery*. That's what they *are*. They go by certain *rules*—"

Will interrupted with a blubber of his lips.

"What's that supposed to mean?" Why was I arguing?

He didn't answer. Instead, he yelled over to Mill, who was pounding out a tune I didn't know. "You finished that number?"

Mill raised a hand with a thumb up.

"Great! I'll be over if Emma ever stops talking."

"What number?"

"Look. I haven't got time to go into all the details right now." He looked at his big-faced cheap and showy watch.

"Wait. Wait. It sounds like *Murder in the Sky* is going to be one of your musicals."

"Yeah. So?"

"A murder-mystery musical?"

"Yeah. So?"

"Those two things just don't go together." I nearly whined this out.

"We've got some neat numbers. The one we do at the beginning after you drop down dead is terrific. So. Are you playing Patty Flynn or not?"

"But all I know about her so far is she's dead."

"Well, she's alive when the curtain goes up."

"Then does she— Do I have lines?"

Will had to think, which meant he was right now inventing one. His gum was stilled and his lips moved ever so slightly. He was being Patty Flynn. "Okay. Patty is pretty old, around fifty—"

"Don't let Mrs. Davidow hear you say that."

"—and she's kind of arrogant. Rich, filthy rich. A lot of her money is tied up in jewelry. Diamonds, mostly. She's carrying it with her on the plane—"

"The jewelry?"

"Yeah."

"Is she wearing some?" I had never worn diamonds. This was not surprising, given I was twelve.

"Yea-ah, I guess she is."

He guessed. It was clear that very little, if any, thought had been given to the story or Patty Flynn. "Who else is in it?"

Will opened the production notes again and ran his finger down the page as if he had so many possible actors to choose from, he couldn't remember the ones he'd picked. Picked? He didn't have any to pick.

"Chuck. He's playing an airplane steward and maybe someone else."

They had to double up on parts, there were so few performers.

His finger stopped again. "There's Paul. He may be a stowaway besides handling the clouds."

Paul was, at the moment, up in the rafters, and I hoped he was tied there.

"You mean you're using those fake clouds again, the same ones we used in *Medea, the Musical*?"

"Sure. That creates the illusion of being up in the air."

"Listen, I don't want to be up in the air if that's where Paul is. I don't want to be anywhere near Paul."

"Well, you won't care. You're dead."

Dead was no protection against Will's and Mill's imaginations.

He went on. "Then, June. She'll be a passenger."

"June *Sikes*? You can't have her again!"

"She did a great job as Medea."

I stepped closer. "She's got a *reputation*."

"So did Medea." He snorted out a laugh. "Then we might bring back the Hummers."

That was truly outlandish. "They're just little kids you scared up because you needed a Greek chorus. And one of them you even shanghaied!"

"Who? Bessie?" He shrugged. "She's gone now."

This was the lonesome child who'd been wandering the croquet court; only four, and if she'd stuck around, she might never have gotten to five.

"When will they hum in this one? That's all they do is go *huuummm*." I drew it out to make a point. Not to Will. I never scored a point there.

He didn't bother answering that. "And we've got June's sister for the stewardess."

"Reba Sikes. Oh, swell. Well, except for her, all the cast is the same as in *Medea*."

"Yeah. It's repertory."

"It's what?"

"Repertory. Exclusive. It's when you use the same actors again and again. Look, I can't stand here jawing with you all day. I've got things to do."

"Well, but when do you hand out scripts?"

"After we're finished, of course."

"When will *that* be? I want to know what Patty Flynn is like."

Mill's piano started up, and so did Will:

> *O Patty Flynn,*
> *Where have you been?*
> *In your granma's basement bathroom*
> *Drinkin' bathtub gin again?*

It was all I could take, so I left.

15

ours later, I came downstairs to find Ralph sitting on the porch with the Duchess of Devonshire, rocking and smoking, sending streams of smoke upward as if he owned the air.

Ree-Jane was doing her appreciative laugh in answer to something he'd said, her head thrown back, ruby lips parted.

Their backs were to the front screen door, so I stood behind it and listened to hear if either said anything quotable.

"So how . . . be staying?"

". . . business . . ."

"What . . . ?"

The tall backs of the rockers muffled their voices, especially Ralph's as his was deep. Ree-Jane's was often high and screechy, so her words carried better. But from the little I could make out, Ralph Diggs was here on some kind of business. Then why had he said he was just passing through? And she was speaking to him as if he were a guest, not an employee.

I heard her high-pitched laugh again. It was mirthless.

He would of course charm her to death.

I thought of *Night Must Fall*.

* * *

"Why don't you like him?" I said to my mother as she slid a chicken breast onto Aurora's dinner plate. Just a moment ago, she had said hiring Ralph might not have been the best idea in the world.

"Like who?"

I rolled my eyes. "This Ralph-Rafe Diggs."

"I don't know; he just seems suspicious. Hand me that napkin."

"It's chicken cordon bleu, isn't it?" I knew my chicken, at least my mother's. I knew my French too, if it was attached to food.

"It is." She was wiping a narrow stream of chicken juiciness from the rim of the plate. Peas from the Emerald City of Oz were spooned onto it.

"I don't think Great-Aunt Aurora likes this kind of chicken."

"I don't think I care." Mashed potatoes, pooled with butter, crowned with a snip of parsley, made up the plate.

"But if she likes chicken at all, how could she not like this?" I said.

I took note of how quickly my mother and I could change the subject of suspicious bellhops to food.

It was another "Night of the Baby Bibbs" with Mrs. Davidow hovering over them protectively. She seemed to look on these lettuces as the communion wafers of the Hotel Paradise. I liked to imagine Father Freeman on a Sunday, as he was going down the line, placing tiny Bibb lettuces on the tongues of his flock, then coming back with a chalice of French dressing.

"Emma!"

Vera jumped me right out of my church visit.

"Don't put too much dressing on them. Don't use the ladle. Use a spoon."

I liked the big ceramic pot of French dressing. At the bottom, an onion sat, marinating for a long time like a hermit in a cave. I liked to stir the dressing and watch it bind together, the oil and vinegar, the paprika, garlic, salt, pepper, sugar.

"All right," I said. "Who's coming?"

"The Custises and their party." She sniffed.

Vera had a thin, angular nose, good for disdainful sniffing. When she sailed out into the dining room in her black uniform with starched white cuffs as sharp as knives, she could have cut the Custises' throats by passing the Parker House rolls. I dwelt on this image awhile and then started ladling out the dressing.

Now Lola Davidow was back, martini in hand, to make sure herself I didn't drown the baby Bibbs. Seeing they still breathed, she grunted and went away.

I counted the salads, subtracting two for Miss Bertha and "her party" and one more for Mr. Muggs, our traveling salesman.

That left eight salads, so that was the number of the Custis "party." I myself couldn't stand the Custises. They lived in one of the big white frame houses across the highway on nearly an acre of land. They were "summer people" and liked to take over each and every holiday and event they could. Every summer there was a tennis tournament, where they'd play mixed doubles, but were always so hungover they had a hard time seeing the net. But they made sure they were at the center of every cocktail party, every corn and weenie roast, every dance and prize award.

Ree-Jane drifted in (she didn't seem tied to earth) and came over and leaned on the salad table. She'd lean on one hand, jutting her shoulder up and hip out in what I guess she thought was a model's pose. All she wanted was to make sure I noticed her new dress.

"I don't think I'll have a salad tonight."

Eleven baby Bibbs breathed a sigh of relief.

When I didn't mention the dress, she said, "We went to Europa today."

Europa was Heather Gay Struther's dress shop. It was expensive, and that's where the Davidows got their clothes. She was wearing a caramel-colored, off-the-shoulder silky dress; she held out the skirt. "How do you like it?"

"It's okay. Excuse me." I brought a ladle of dressing dangerously close to where she leaned.

"Rafe thinks it's beautiful." Here, she gave me a big-eyed look, as if she really wondered. "Or haven't you met Rafe yet?"

"You mean Ralph? The bellboy replacement?"

"Rafe. It's the English pronunciation."

"I know. It rhymes with 'safe.'"

"He prefers to be called Rafe."

I wondered if this was true, or if she was telling me he did so she could keep saying *Rafe, Rafe*.

She watched me do the salads for a minute, then said, "I might have a lobster tail for dinner."

I was glad these were frozen because the sight of a live lobster dropping into a pot of boiling water just for Ree-Jane's dinner would have made me cry. I never got to eat lobster or filet mignon, as they were too expensive. On the other hand, Ree-Jane turned her nose up at Ham Pinwheels, calling them leftovers. So who was the loser here? I asked the Bibbs and they all cheered for pinwheels.

"Why are you staring at those stupid salads?"

She hadn't impressed me yet, not with the dress, with Ralph, or with the lobster, and it really got her down. Then she smirked. "I'm going to the Double Down after dinner, but don't tell anybody!" This was spoken in a raised voice that told everybody.

The Double Down was a club outside of Hebrides, run by a man named Perry Vines. He must have been twenty or thirty years older than Ree-Jane and had been married a zillion times. Ree-Jane said he was crazy about her.

"If he's so crazy about you, why doesn't he put himself out and come here?"

That was an unwelcome question. "Because he's too busy with the club, of course."

"You're a minor. Or didn't you know?"

Haughtily, she smiled as she flipped her Veronica Lake locks out of her eyes. "Well, Rafe isn't."

"I never knew that the person you were with changed your age."

I don't know whether she just ignored that or didn't understand it. She said, "I hope Perry isn't too jealous."

"Ralph just got here and already he's moving on the heiress. That's quick work."

It was clear she didn't know whether to take this as a compliment. Her mouth worked it over, but came up with nothing.

"I wouldn't worry about Perry. He'll never go hungry. There's always Scarlett Bittinger." I think I must have been mixing up images from *Gone with the Wind*. I hummed and picked up my tray of salads.

That brought her almost into this life. "*What?* What about Scarlett?"

"Hm? Oh, you know, in that yellow convertible of hers? I saw it whizzing down Alder Street."

Ree-Jane was so fast on my heels she nearly fell through the swinging door into the dining room. "Perry was with her? *Perry was?*"

"Did I say that?" I asked in just that tone that said I said it.

16

I had no idea how Ree-Jane's big night at the Double Down went, if it went at all. The last thing I recall is seeing her climb into Ralph Diggs's black Chevy and the two of them go fizzing off down the drive. Since she wasn't bragging the next morning about Perry's undying devotion to her—indeed she was pretty grumpy—I assumed they'd never gotten into the back room and the gambling. Probably they'd never gotten very far into the front room.

After what I referred to as my Double Down stack of silver dollar pancakes and maple syrup, I decided to walk along the highway to the Belle Ruin. I needed, I guess, some taste of faded glory.

The Belle Ruin sat on several acres of wooded land once called Soldiers Park. I had no idea where that name came from. Probably it had something to do with World War Two, or even the Civil War. I wasn't sure what side we were on, South or North. Hadn't this state taken some kind of cantankerous view of the war back then? Some for South and some for North? Wasn't anything black or white? Did I have to reside in a state that probably couldn't choose up a volleyball team?

I wondered if Soldiers Park could have been some kind of army cemetery, and I looked as I walked for signs of grave markers, but saw none. Of course, they could have been toppled or buried when the ground was torn up to build the Belle Ruin. But then I thought, probably not, because there would have been some kind of survey, something that told the lay of the land, and I doubted they'd have gone on to build over a Civil War graveyard of dead servicemen. That was called desecrating the land or the graves or something like that. I didn't like the idea I was stepping on a soldier's grave. It gets you thinking, though, if not about the Civil War (about which I knew nothing), then about dying.

I was sitting on a log from a fallen tree, most of which had rotted. I was looking at the part of the Belle Ruin that had not burned down—the huge ballroom. A lot of the walls had burned, but oddly enough, not the floor, not the bandstand. There had been a big dance on the night of the Slade baby's alleged kidnapping. The thing was, I was coming more and more to believe that she hadn't been and that it had been made to look like a kidnapping.

Why? To collect a ransom from the rich grandfather, Mr. Woodruff. At least, that would be the obvious reason. Only there had been no ransom demand, at least as far as we knew around La Porte. For after the Slades and Mr. Woodruff had gone back to New York City, nothing more appeared about the kidnapping. Its similarities to the Lindbergh baby kidnapping had been noted, like the ladder up against the wall outside the hotel and, of course, the baby's being snatched from its crib. The ladder belonged to Reuben Stuck, who'd been one of the men painting the hotel at the time. I'd interviewed him and listened to his woeful account of being under suspicion.

Here was a kidnapping very like the Lindbergh case, and then nothing further had been reported. It was as if nothing had happened at all, and I was thinking that maybe nothing had, and that Mr. Woodruff had paid off the police because he had discovered it was his daughter Imogen and Morris Slade who'd set up the whole thing.

But what—as both Dwayne and Mrs. Louderback had pointed out—about the phone call? Gloria Calhoun, who used to be a Spiker, and that friend of hers, Prunella-somebody, had been on the phone at the time. I thought it was worth talking to Gloria again. She would hardly want to admit she'd had anything to do with the kidnapping, but I might be able to get something useful out of her.

I got up and walked over to the ballroom, where my phonograph sat. I didn't want it out in bad weather, and I could always bring it back if I felt like dancing. I had brought only three records. The last one we had played a few nights ago, when the Sheriff and Maud and Dwayne had been out here. That was "Moonlight Serenade." The one that was now on the turntable was "I'll Be Seeing You."

How could that be? I looked around almost as if I expected to find a roomful of dancers. Who had put on "I'll be Seeing You"? I imagined a hundred uniformed World War Two soldiers dancing with stage-door-canteen hostesses in print dresses. The ghosts of them, the soldiers and their partners, floated across the dark hardwood floor. And I imagined one of them was the Girl, who fit in perfectly with her pale hair and mild blue dress.

I snapped the lid shut and stuck the records under my arm and left the Belle Ruin and Soldiers Park.

As I trudged along back to the Hotel Paradise, I thought of the Waitresses, for this had really been their phonograph, an old Victrola with a crank handle, left forgotten in one of the storage rooms on the second floor for six or seven years. It was hard to believe they'd been gone that long. When I see a picture of exotic birds, I think of the Waitresses. They were as bright and free as flamingos.

I asked Abel Slaw if he would mind my leaving the phonograph in the garage so that I could get the next train to Cold Flat Junction. Slaw's Garage was just across the highway from the railroad station.

"Just as long as you come back and get it, hear?" He was always crotchety when he talked to me.

No, Mr. Slaw, I wanted to say, *I will never be back. I am flying off into the long gone and the sweet hereafter.* But I didn't want to hear him complain about my backtalk.

I guess it was the Waitresses that made me think of flying away. I wondered what the sweet hereafter actually was. Was it heaven? Was it paradise? I wondered if that's where they'd gone.

17

I had money with me and decided for a change to actually buy a ticket to Cold Flat Junction. It was only twelve miles from Spirit Lake and didn't cost much, and it was easier than being a stowaway.

I smiled and handed my money up to the conductor after the train started moving. It was the same conductor who was always on this train, although he didn't seem to remember my stowaway status.

He punched the ticket and said, "Well, little lady, what are you going there for today?" He handed back my ticket.

"To see my gran." I looked up at him through squinty eyes, as if I might need glasses but was too poor to buy any. "She's awful sick."

He swayed a little with the movement of the train. "Sorry to hear that. She lives in the Junction? I know folks there."

Then she can't live there. I thought of the Simples, whom I had told the Windy Run Diner people about. The Simples didn't exist, of course, but I'd had need of them one day for some reason. I sorted through the family names, seeing if I'd mentioned a grandmother. I didn't remember anybody in the family except the son who was retarded. "Her name's Alberta Simple. They live a distance outside Cold Flat Junction, on a farm. You probably don't know them. Anyway, Granny Alberta fell down and hit her head. Bad."

"Sorry to hear that," he said again, with a sway and looking down the aisle, obviously wanting to move on.

I wouldn't let him. "Yes, it is. The Simples have got enough trouble in their lives without her getting hurt. She's the one who takes care of Miller Simple. He's retarded and kind of dangerous."

"You don't say? Well, now I got to be—"

"Once, Miller—" Was that his name? "Once, he hit his daddy over the head with a chair leg, just ripped the leg right off the chair to do it, and now he's got to be watched closely."

The conductor tipped his hat, like a wave good-bye. "Got to see to my tickets."

I turned and watched him move quickly along the aisle. "Good-bye!" I called.

Well, he'd asked me, hadn't he?

When the train pulled into Cold Flat Junction, I stepped down to the station platform and stood while it pulled back out, then looked across the track at the dark line of trees in the distance. I always looked at them for a longer while than a person would ordinarily spend on trees. They looked, from this distance, sometimes dark gray-green, and sometimes navy blue, and the line was as straight as an arrow. They almost stood at attention, like ranks of soldiers. I thought of Soldiers Park. I supposed that behind them lay only the same wasted land that ran between them and the railroad tracks, yet I couldn't be sure. I think they hid a mystery that drew me.

I had started out thinking I'd go to see Gloria Spiker Calhoun again, but then I thought, no, it's her friend, this Prunella-someone, I should talk to. It was Prunella whom Gloria had called. It was just too much of a coincidence: the telephone call and the baby being kidnapped during that twenty-minute call.

Prunella. The reason I remembered that name was because I had never liked it. I wouldn't like to be a Prunella. Ree-Jane would call me Prune-face.

So once again, I needed to stop in the Windy Run Diner to find out about Prunella and where she lived. The best thing to do was think about this over a slice of pie. So it was to the diner that the sandy path from the station led me.

It was pleasant—I might even say a comfort—to find the same old faces in the Windy Run, three at the counter, one in a booth.

"Well, look't what the cat dragged in," said Don Joe, with a snuffly laugh.

"Lo and be-*hold*," Billy added, not wanting to be shown up in the greetings department. Evren, sitting on the other side of Don Joe, just smiled.

Louise Snell was wiping down the counter. "Hello, hon. How're you today?"

"Okay." I climbed up on my usual stool, the one near the pie and cake glass shelves. There was a new one among the pies, a pale pink chiffon.

Louise Snell saw me looking and smiled and said, "We got Strawberry Chiffon today. It's real good."

"It surely does look it," I said, trying to get a little Junction twang into my speech.

Mervin, who usually sat with his wife in one of the maroon-colored leatherette booths, asked me how I was coming along with my story for the paper. Mervin was probably the only customer who didn't feel he had to make fun of other people just to prove he was alive.

He went on: "Sure is the best thing I've read in the papers in a long time."

Irritated that he hadn't thought to say that, Billy said (as if it were my fault), "Haven't them police over to La Porte found out who killed Fern Queen yet? My Lord, how long's it been since she got shot? Six weeks, like?"

"It's been three," I said.

Don Joe said, "They don't still think it was Ben, surely?"

I could hardly tell them what I knew about the murder of Fern, mostly because it wasn't official and partly because I'd be in for so much questioning, I'd be here all day. I did have a life to lead, after all.

But I did answer, as Louise Snell had set my pie before me. It had little flecks of red in it, bits of strawberry. "Well, Ben Queen is a suspect still, but there's nothing to point to him, I mean no physical evidence, nothing to say he was at White's Bridge that night." He wasn't. I knew because the same person that killed Fern had been the one to nearly murder me: Isabel Devereau. She had told me, since she didn't think I'd be telling anyone else. Ever. Yet, the Sheriff called this "hearsay evidence." Imagine. It made my blood boil.

I was glad Mervin's wife was absent, for he was much freer to speak. She was a devil, always jabbing at him and telling him to be quiet. He said, "What about that crazy woman that attacked *you*? I'd think she'd be more of a suspect than Ben Queen. Wasn't she a relation of Rose Queen?"

I looked at Mervin, amazed that he seemed to have read my mind. But it was just that Mervin gave thought to things, and sometimes seemed to be the only one in here who did. Besides Louise Snell, that is. She was pretty smart and not always talking just to hear herself talk like the others.

"Yes. Rose was a Devereau, as you know."

"Then it could've been revenge, couldn't it?" said Mervin.

Billy, who usually sat with his back to Mervin, turned around on his stool to face him. "Now, Mervin, you never knowed Rose Queen, nor Rose Queen's family. But you sure are tossin' words around as if you did."

Billy was so jealous of Mervin that it hardly bore thinking about. I furrowed my brow as if I were considering the Rose Queen business, but I was really just enjoying my pie. I could think up something when I finished.

"I been here many years, Billy. And I heard stuff. Like Fern went off with her mother for several months. That sounds likely, I'd say."

"Likely what?"

"Girl goes off for a few months. It's the usual story, I'd bet."

Billy, and now Don Joe, wanted to argue against that. You could just tell, the way they sat with their arms folded tight across their chests.

Louise Snell said, "Well, all I know is that girl was trouble growing up."

Don Joe snorted. "Trouble, yes, you could say. Stabbed her mom twenty times with that knife."

"Except that never was proved," said Louise Snell. "Ben had an alibi all along and he never used it, probably because he knew it was her that did it."

He had an alibi, and I was the one who'd uncovered it, in Smitty's Feed Store, where Ben Queen had been when the murder of his wife had been committed.

Louise was wiping down the counter. She seemed to enjoy doing this. "The pity is they couldn't have another kid."

I frowned. "You mean Rose and Ben Queen? Why not?"

There was a quick look that seemed to go up and down the counter like Saint Elmo's fire. I figured adults do that only when it's something to do with sex. I sighed. "You mean Rose had to have"—I could not remember the word—"whatever removed?"

Don Joe snorted again. "You'd think someone knew all about Alaska and Hawa-yah, she'd know 'whatever.'"

"Oh, shut up, Don Joe," said Louise. "No, hon. Trouble was with her husband. You know, sometimes when a couple can't have kids, trouble's with the wife, but sometimes with the husband."

"Oh." I didn't know, so I changed the subject to the reason I'd come in the first place. "Any of you know a woman around here named Prunella?" It had suddenly occurred to me that now I was a reporter for the *Conservative* and I didn't have to make up reasons for wanting to find or talk to people. Which was not to say I wouldn't make up reasons, only I didn't have to.

Evren, on the other side of Don Joe, said, "Yeah. There's one named Prunella Rice. Don't she live in the Holler, Billy?" Evren al-

most always deferred to Billy, even though Billy was wrong 99 percent of the time.

"Well, now, let me just think on that while Louise fills up this
coffee cup." He grinned as if he'd said something really clever. He got
his coffee and opened his mouth to say something but not soon
enough.

Mervin said, "Red Coon Rock's where she lives."

That really got Billy's goat. "Now, how is it you, that's hardly
been here ten years—"

"Fifteen," Mervin corrected him, and drank his coffee.

"Well, I been here forty-five years, Mervin. How is it you know
every goddamned thing about the Junction in only ten or fifteen?"

Evenly, Mervin said, "Don't know everything, just that Prunella
Rice lives in Red Coon Rock."

That made me grin. Mervin, if he was ever called as witness in a
murder case, would be a dream of a witness for whichever side, de-
fense or prosecution. For the other side would never be able to shake
him, or make him contradict himself or back down. Mervin was solid
as a rock. More than that, he let nothing get him off the point. No
one could shy a stone and skip it around him, not even Perry Mason.

I said, "Which house does she live in, do you know, Mr. Mervin?"

Naturally, that caused an argument.

"It's the one a little ways up from Cary Grant Calhoun's. I think
it's painted brown," said Mervin, "but I'm not sure. I do know there's
a little wishing well in the yard."

Billy's hand slapped down on the counter and made the cups
jump, as well as Don Joe and Evren. He wheeled around on his stool
again. "Now, there you are *wrong*, Mervin. That wishing-well house
belongs to Earl Midge. It's his wife had that well put in."

"That may be so, but that's another house. Don't Earl Midge live
out the end of Sweetwater Road?"

"No, he does not!" said Billy.

"Oh, for pity's sake," said Louise Snell as she pulled out the Hebrides and area phone book. She flipped through it, ran her finger

down a column, and said, "There's six Rices, mostly in Hebrides, but two in the Junction. One lives in Red Coon Rock and the name's 'P. Rice.' So Mervin's right."

I snuck a smile. I wanted to say, "Again."

"That there's an old phone book," said Billy, lighting himself another cigarette.

Louise Snell rolled her eyes. "That is so ridiculous. When does anything change in Cold Flat Junction? How many people ever move? When dinosaurs roamed here, there was still a P. Rice"—here she put the open telephone directory straight against Billy's eyes—"living on Red Coon Road." Then she slapped it shut.

Billy sat and smoked, trying to think up a reply.

Evren said, "Hell, we still got the dinosaurs. You seen them Wicker sisters lately? Must be carrying six hundred pounds between 'em!"

They all managed a laugh at that, even Mervin, and so I decided to leave before the Wicker sisters showed.

18

Dubois Road, where the Queens lived, ended up at Flyback Hollow, or "the Holler" as they called it in the Windy Run. Jude Stemple lived back there. It was Jude Stemple who'd made the comment that Fern Queen had never had any kids. If he was right, then the Girl could not have been Fern's daughter. But the people at the Windy Run Diner hinted at another view of Fern.

The last time I was here, there was a girl sitting behind a stand, selling Kool-Aid, even though her sign read LEMONADE 5¢. She wasn't there, but the table and chair and sign were, along with a pitcher of green-colored Kool-Aid. There was also a box that had once held kitchen matches, and that was where she kept her money. It was empty.

I guessed the Kool-Aid must be lime, not my favorite flavor in anything, and certainly not Kool-Aid, which I didn't much like in any flavor. I thought she wasn't being completely honest, selling Kool-Aid for lemonade, but she had said it was a lemonade stand, not that she was selling lemonade, nor did she have to.

I pulled a plastic cup from a small tower of them, poured an inch of Kool-Aid into it, and dropped a nickel into the matchbox. Then I poured the drink out and mashed the edge of the cup a little so it would look as if a customer had indeed gone and taken a drink. I thought it was important; she was making an effort and this was really a bad spot for a lemonade stand. How many people had I ever seen walking about here?

The bent plastic cup I had set back on the table made me think of the dented metal cup in the stone alcove at Spirit Lake. I looked down at the little puddle I'd made, throwing away the Kool-Aid, and felt bad. So I put another nickel in the box and pulled another cup from the tower. Then I poured in a little Kool-Aid. This time I drank it; it tasted awful, but I got it down in one gulp.

Now she had two used cups and ten cents. This was more business, I guessed, than she'd had all day. I imagined her returning and seeing all this activity and being pleased.

It was a nice thought to take with me.

As I tramped from Flyback Hollow to Red Coon Rock, I imagined myself setting up a vodka, gin, and whiskey stand at the bottom of the Hotel Paradise's driveway. I could get real fancy and list a menu of Aurora's favorite drinks: Cold Comfort, Appledew, Rumba, Bombay Breakfast, the Count of Monte Cristo at Miami Beach. Probably I'd have to have bottled beer cooling in a galvanized tub full of ice, for most people around here, like Dwayne, would want beer.

It was fun thinking of this, but as whiskey and gin weren't as cheap as Kool-Aid, I told myself I'd better rethink it.

I turned in to Red Coon Rock. The hard-surfaced road got narrower here, and didn't so much end as dwindle into dirt, hard packed, looking almost as if it had been swept down with a broom.

The Calhoun house was the blue one on my left. There was an old pickup truck pulled up to the curb, and I dawdled, scuffing up dirt with my shoe, hoping I might catch a look at Gloria's husband, Cary Grant Calhoun. The diner people said he didn't look a thing like Cary Grant, but I wanted to see for myself. I might find it necessary to talk to Gloria again. Maybe she remembered something else about Baby Fay Slade being snatched from her crib.

If she had been snatched, I had to keep reminding myself. Had she been at the Belle Ruin at all? Or somewhere else? Or maybe dead? That chilled me.

Gloria said the Slades had told her the baby was sick and asleep and not to bother her. It was hard to imagine a babysitter not even taking a peek at her charge. It was my theory that the baby hadn't been with the Slades, but then Miss Isabel Barnett claimed to have seen Baby Fay and that the poor thing had something called Down disease, which knocked my theory into a cocked hat.

Then, then (you can see how hard it is being me) Aurora Paradise said Isabel Barnett was the biggest liar in three counties besides being a kleptomaniac, and I shouldn't pay attention to anything she said.

So I was back with my theory again that the baby hadn't been at the Belle Ruin at all.

I was thinking so hard I'd walked right past the wishing well, which had fortunately registered on some part of my mind, and I stopped and retraced my steps. The house was brown (as Mervin had said), plain brown clapboard with white trim and a white fence. The gate creaked a little and the small bucket above the well swayed in the fresh wind. The sky was darkening. I took all of this as a sign that I ought to pause and think. Signs are sometimes worth ignoring.

The screen door squeaked just as the gate had. I opened it in order to knock on the door. It was less than a minute before a woman came.

"Yes? Oh, hello." She'd expected a grown person to be there and was a little surprised. Most are, seeing a twelve-year-old on their doorstep.

"Miss Rice? Prunella Rice?" I looked wide-eyed.

She nodded. Her plainness was emphasized by her clothes. She wore a brown dress, the color of the house. And it had a small collar at the neck, with white piping like the trim. Her hair was almost exactly the brown of the dress and the house. It was pulled back into an old-fashioned bun. Her face had what my mother called "good bones." But they weren't good enough for prettiness.

"Did you want something?"

Now, it was true that as a reporter—or, more precisely, "features writer," according to Mr. Gumbrel—I was permitted to ask questions. Still, some kinds of questions might get a person riled. For instance, *"Were you and Gloria Spiker telling the truth about that telephone call?"* Obviously, she wasn't going to say, "No, we weren't." So I'd have to make up something, which was okay with me.

I wished I'd brought a copy of the newspaper with my story, just to prove who I was. "My name's Emma Graham. I don't know if you've been reading the La Porte paper—the *Conservative?*—but I've been writing up what happened in Spirit Lake—"

Her frown relaxed a bit. "Yes, I did hear about that. Oh, you're that poor girl!"

My expression adjusted to poorness and I asked, "Could I come in?"

She held the door open wider. I walked into a parlor ("living room," I heard my mother correct me) neat as a pin; it looked as if nobody lived there. It wasn't very inviting, actually.

Prunella Rice held out a hand, to indicate which of the heavy, dark chairs I was welcome to, and I sat down. She sat on one opposite.

"Like I said, I've been writing about events in Spirit Lake, but now I'm interested in this other story that took place in the Belle Ruin Hotel years ago." It was discomfiting to be speaking the unvarnished truth, so I varnished it up a little. "You see"—I settled back in my uncomfortable chair—"when I was talking to Gloria Calhoun, she mentioned you and what a great friend you were—"

Far from looking pleased, Prunella Rice looked anxious.

I went on: "—and how nice it was living on the same road so close to each other."

Her nervous hand fluttered up to the bun at the nape of her neck. "Well, I don't know as I'd say that. I mean, we hardly see each other, even living so close. We went to school together in La Porte. . . ." She wound down.

"Well, part of my story involves that hotel that burned down."

Faintly, she nodded. It looked to me like she'd rather un-nod.

"And, of course, the kidnapping. Now I just want to make sure I get the details straight."

As if I were bad medicine, her lips pressed together and nothing would pry them open. Why hadn't I brought at least a notebook and a pencil so I'd look like a person writing up something for a newspaper? Which is exactly what I was. I decided making stuff up was a lot easier than telling the bald-faced truth.

"I understand Mrs. Calhoun—Gloria Spiker back then—had to leave the baby for a few minutes in order to call you." I thought I put this in a forgiving way: she "had to" instead of just wanting to make a phone call because she was bored.

The prim mouth unclamped. "That's right. We was to go to a show at the old Limerick movie house that used to be in Hebrides the next night. Veronica Lake was in it and Gloria was just then reading *Photoplay*. There was an article in it about Veronica Lake. That's what reminded her and that's why she called." She sat back in the heavy chair, looking kind of pleased with herself.

Something about what she'd said bothered me, and I found I was frowning. I immediately stopped and put my hand on my temple. "Oh, sorry. I get this headachelike pain. . . ."

"Well, you're a little young for headaches, I'd say."

"It's inherited. My great-aunt Aurora Paradise gets fierce headaches. It's so bad she really can't stand being around people *at all*." I sat forward to emphasize the seriousness of this. "So she lives up on the top floor of our hotel. I take her food on trays."

That was the trick, you see. When you make things up, there has to be enough truth in it so if the person ever decides to check up, well, there'd be Aurora on the fourth floor. It was all true, except the headaches.

Prunella looked sympathetic, but only to be polite. "That's awful. And does she get lonely?"

"Oh, no." I wanted to say she got drunk. "No, she's got a lot to keep her occupied, like solitaire and things."

Prunella smoothed down her dress and reclasped her hands and looked, as I said, self-satisfied, as if she thought she'd gotten over the rough part, that telephone call.

No, she hadn't.

"Then, she—Gloria Spiker, I mean—spoke to you a few minutes—"

"Twenty minutes. We just talked a lot of girl stuff." She simpered a bit.

"Then she went back to find the baby missing and the father in an awful state." I chewed the inside of my lip as if I were thinking hard. I wasn't; I knew what I was going to say: "Now, it was she called *you,* and not the other way around?"

Her eyes opened a little wider, the look of something dawning—or darkening. Quickly she said, "Why, yes, of course. I couldn't hardly call her, could I? She was at that hotel and had to go down the hall to phone."

I cocked my head. "Did you know she was going to call?"

That drew her up even straighter than she was before. It was a while before she answered.

There was a cobweb in the corner of the ceiling. That would annoy her; she must spend every waking minute keeping this house clean.

"Well, now, what do you mean?"

Was it hard to understand *Did you know she was going to call*? "Oh, I just wondered about the movie you were going to see." Which made no sense at all: I was just trying to tiptoe around my question so she'd bend a little. I tried to make some connection: "I mean that you both liked Veronica Lake and maybe were excited about this movie."

"Oh. Now you mention it, yes, I guess we had said something about telephoning." Her nod was uncertain. She still wasn't sure about my question.

I slid down in my chair and looked off with what I hoped was a dreamy expression. "It was just all so strange, wasn't it? You would have thought there'd be a big ransom demand, but there wasn't."

"Didn't seem to be."

"You never heard anything else about the baby?"

"No indeed." Her head shake was curt.

"The Slades lived in New York City. That's where they went." As if New York City were the place to go for vanishing. I decided I would get nothing else from Prunella Rice, and said, "It's really nice of you to give me your time, Miss Rice."

"Prunella." She almost smiled. "That's with two *l*'s."

It was that old rule: Just be sure you spell my name right in the paper, whatever else you do or say about me.

I smiled. "I'll remember."

She showed me to the door as if she were turning away trouble.

It was a little past 3:00 and I wanted to get the 3:32 train back, which would be easy to make.

I scuffed my way back down the road, once again passing the Calhoun house. The pickup truck was still there, but no sign of Cary Grant Calhoun.

As I got to Flyback Hollow and Dubois Road, I saw that the lemonade stand was still set up, but the pitcher had changed from lime to orange. And the money was gone. Maybe this was to be her new way of conducting business, the honor system, just letting people help themselves. It saved sitting around being bored.

As I walked on down to the train station, I thought about that phone call and tried to bring up what had bothered me when Prunella Rice said she'd been talking about going to the old Limerick Theater. I thought about Veronica and Ree-Jane and the "peekaboo" hairstyle. After I reached the station, I stood on the platform puzzling out what Prunella had said and thinking about Baby Fay and getting nowhere.

I paid again to a different conductor, glad it wasn't the first one in case he asked questions about the long story I'd told him about Grandmother Simple.

Maybe the library, where I was going, had old copies of *Photoplay*, and I could look up the article Gloria had been reading—

Suddenly, I sat up straight. That was it! That's what had been bothering me. While she was babysitting, Gloria had been reading a copy of *Photoplay*, and she'd said, *"I was sitting, reading it. There was an article in it about Veronica Lake."* Those were almost her exact words. Then she'd said she and Prunella were going to *"the old Limerick movie house that used to be in Hebrides."*

That's also what Prunella said. The same thing. The *exact* same thing. She hadn't said just "the Limerick Theater," but the *"old Limerick movie house that used to be in Hebrides."* Twenty years had gone by and they were saying the exact same things.

I knew what Perry Mason would make of that.

The phone call had been arranged. It had been arranged that Gloria would leave the room. She'd been paid to do it, was my guess. Prunella had been paid to bear out Gloria's story. As they'd both said, there were no phones except for the one in the hall. *"Had to."* I had thought that was just an excuse: *"Had to."* But what if—?

The conductor was collecting tickets. Absently, I handed mine up to him.

"That's quite a frown you're wearing, young lady." He punched my ticket and handed it back. "Must not be having a very good trip." He stood there, smiling and swaying, swaying just as the other conductor had.

I guessed he would just stand over me all the way home if I didn't explain my frown. "My dog died."

"Oh. Oh, I'm real sorry." He moved off.

Death had a way of moving people off.

19

"I want to see the Sheriff."

Donny Mooma was talking to Maureen Kneff, the secretary, who I seemed to recall had once been a Stuck. There were as many Stucks around as there were Moomas and Calhouns.

He looked over his shoulder at me. "Then get in line, girl. You see them people out there sitting? You ain't the only pebble on the beach."

Donny knew more clichés than anyone. "Where is he?" I tried to keep from sounding too demanding.

Donny opened his mouth, but it was Maureen Stuck who spoke. "He's gone over to Cold Flat Junction, hon."

Donny raised his head to look at the ceiling as if seeking God's guidance. "Now, what'd you go and tell her for, Maureen? He's on po-*lice* business. You don't give out the whys and wherefores of what goes on in the Sheriff's office!"

Maureen just waved the words away. "It's no 'why' nor 'wherefore'; he's just gone to Cold Flat Junction, for goodness' sakes."

I liked Maureen. I always had. She didn't try to blow up her job the way Donny blew up his, as being the most important one in the county. Except, of course, the Sheriff's.

I asked her, "Maureen, are you related to Reuben Stuck?"

Donny rolled his eyes. "Excuse me for livin'."

"Yes, I am. He's my cousin. Do you know Reuben?"

Donny threw up his arms. "Well, pardon me for wanting to do po-lice business."

Reuben Stuck was the man who had come in for lots of questions regarding the kidnapping of the Slade baby, as it was his ladder that had been leaning against the Belle Ruin beneath the Slades' window. Reuben was a housepainter and had been one of several hired to paint the hotel.

"Yes," I said. "I interviewed him about what happened at the Belle Ruin."

Maureen slowly nodded. "That old, sad business." She shut her eyes against it.

"Don't mind me, girls, you just go on socializin'." Donny plopped himself down behind his desk and parked his boots on top of it. "I bet Sam'd like to know how much work gets done around here."

"When's he coming back?"

Donny said, "Well, don't ask me. Ask your friend here." He pushed his thumb in Maureen's direction. Then he rose and hitched up his wide brown belt. "Me, I'm goin' across the street for a coffee."

Maureen said, her voice all sparkly, "Get me a vanilla iced doughnut and one with sprinkles on." She winked at me. "Emma too. She'd probably like one."

At that Donny looked so heated up I thought he'd blister. "I ain't no delivery service. She can get her own damn doughnuts."

"Okay, I'll go with you!" I could sound sparkly too.

The Rainbow Café was to be my next stop anyway. Having me tag along was the last thing he wanted. He was out the door so fast I could have played cards on his coattail. That was my mother's saying for someone who was beating a hasty retreat. I've always liked that image of someone moving so fast his coat flies up behind him flat and square as a table.

I caught up with Donny as he was stopping traffic so he could cross. He always did that: held his hand palm out and stopped an old

Ford so worn-out it looked like it would have coughed to a stop anyway. I just skipped along with him.

"You get away, you hear!" he fumed, and quick-walked to the other side and into the Rainbow Café.

I waved to the Ford driver, who smiled at me, toothlessly.

Donny was standing in front of the baked-goods case, pointing and barking out his order to Wanda Wayans.

I went to the end of the soda counter, where Maud was making a milk shake, her hand jittering on the metal container.

"Want some?" She nodded at the machine. "Miss Isabel never can drink a whole one."

Turning around, I saw Miss Isabel Barnett seated in one of the wooden booths at the rear. She was looking into a small silver compact and apparently applying lipstick. "I need to talk to her," I said to Maud. "Thanks!"

"Do you mind if I sit down for a minute, Miss Isabel?"

She seemed really happy to see me. "Why, Emma Graham, just sit right down and tell me what you've been up to."

As I slid into the booth I looked at what appeared to be a brand-new lipstick she was putting away and did not want to ask what she'd been up to. "Nothing much. But I need to ask you something: Do you remember last week we were talking about Morris and Imogen Slade's baby, Fay?"

First, she looked a little puzzled.

"The Slades were in La Porte one day, you remember; it was over twenty years ago, and you told me you saw the baby in her carriage?"

Her face grew tight with thinking, as if she were flinging her memory back twenty years. "Yes! The poor little thing. Well, it couldn't have been more than a few weeks old when I saw it—"

My mouth seldom fell open in surprise. But now it did. "A few *weeks*? But, Miss Isabel, the time we were talking about was when the baby was *four months* old!"

Miss Isabel Barnett firmly shook her head. "Oh no, Emma, it

couldn't have been. That baby weighed so little and was so small, when that baby was born, the hospital had to keep it in an incubator for three weeks. The poor thing hadn't been long out, well, not more than a couple weeks, anyway."

"And you said it had that condition, Down's disease, or something?"

Her eyebrows rose. "You mean the Slade baby? Oh, I don't think so."

I just stared. Where had she come by all of this information, half of it conflicting with what she'd told me before? "Miss Isabel, are you sure we're talking about the same baby?"

She sipped her milk shake and frowned.

I don't know why I had expected her to remember back twenty years. I could hardly remember back twenty days, and I was a lot younger than Miss Isabel Barnett, whose mind was probably completely tired out from remembering things.

She hadn't seen Fay Slade at all.

"Thanks, Miss Isabel. I've got to be getting back."

I flew out of the Rainbow so fast you could have played cards on my coattail.

And I didn't even know where I was running to. I stopped to take a breath. The baby hadn't been seen by *anyone*. So my theory could be right—that the kidnapping had been staged. Gloria Spiker and Prunella Rice: they'd both probably been paid off. They both had to be in on it because they'd made sure the stories they told about the call were the same. Probably they'd practiced what they'd tell the police if they were asked. The Sheriff Mooma back then (Donny's uncle) was probably bought off by Imogen Woodruff's rich father. Paid not to investigate. Because there'd been no kidnapping.

Of course, I had to remind myself this was just a theory—that the baby hadn't been at the Belle Ruin at all. If so, what had happened to her that they didn't want people knowing about? Did they lose her? Did they leave her?

Now, had she come back? Was she the Girl?

My feet launched me toward the *Conservative* offices. I guess they thought Mr. Gumbrel would be a good person to talk to, since he had a kind of investigative mind. I pounded up the old wooden staircase and noticed for the first time the worn-away area in the center of each step, where there was a depression and the oak was worn nearly white. Imagine the number of feet it would take to wear away wood.

"Emma! You finish next week's installment?"

No more than I had since the last time he'd asked. "Not quite. But there's something I want to tell you about the *alleged"*—I emphasized that—"kidnapping." I went on to report my conversation with Prunella Rice and the conclusion I'd drawn.

Mr. Gumbrel had leaned back in his swivel chair, his glasses perched up on his head, twiddling his thumbs over his round stomach. "My Lord!" he said. "I'll be a monkey's—so you think the two of them, the Spiker girl and this Prunella Rice, were in it together?"

"Not that they were the main players, definitely not. The main ones had to be the family. If Mr. Woodruff was buying off police like Sheriff Mooma—"

"Carl Mooma, that would have been." He frowned and slowly shook his head. "Carl was a pretty good man, as I recall. . . ."

Nobody else did. "And the Slades could hardly *not* have known if the baby wasn't even there."

"You're saying that Morris and Imogen were parading around town with an empty carriage?"

"Yes. Don't ask me why. But remember, the baby's nurse wasn't with them at the hotel. It could be the baby was with the nurse all along. They could have told her they were going off for the weekend and the nurse didn't know anything was happening."

"Oh, but she soon would've found out."

I shook my head. "Not if Mr. Woodruff bought off the reporters."

He half laughed. "Easier to buy off police than reporters, at least around here. He'd never have succeeded with my dad, I can tell you that." He scratched his chin; the whiskers sounded as if they hurt.

I went on: "Even if he didn't buy off the reporters, how far would that story have gone?"

"Could've got picked up on the wire. The thing is, why would Lucien Woodruff want to halt an investigation of his own grand-child's kidnapping?"

I was getting really impatient. "That's what I'm *saying*. Because she never *was* kidnapped. It would have to be because the parents were guilty of something and he didn't want the family name disgraced or maybe his daughter to go to jail."

Mr. Gumbrel sighed. "I guess it's possible, Emma. It's possible. Trouble is, for newspaper purposes—I mean, your story—you can't speculate in print about the Slades and Lucien Woodruff. We could end up with a lawsuit."

"But I could still wonder what happened that night."

"You'd have to tread real carefully, though. Once you suggest a kidnapping never happened, that would be pointing a finger at the family."

"But—still, there might be something else that *could* have happened to make the Slades think the baby was kidnapped." Although I certainly couldn't think of anything.

I wished the Sheriff would come back.

I glanced at the big schoolhouse clock on the back wall and saw it was after five. I jumped out of my chair. "I've got to get back to the hotel to wait tables for dinner. Thanks, Mr. Gumbrel."

His voice followed me as I fairly flew down the stairs. "You remember to bring me your next installment, hear?"

I heard.

20

I t was five thirty when I slammed the door on Delbert's voice and ran up the porch steps. The cab took off and I think he was still talking to himself.

Ree-Jane was slumped in one of the green rockers with her feet up on the round green table; she was flipping through one of the fashion magazines in which she would be photographed in the coming years. I glanced over her shoulder at the models.

"You're really late," she said, "and Miss Jen's having fits." She delivered this news without looking up from the page of svelte summer dresses worn by girls with pouty lips and pointed elbows.

I wished I could have stopped for a moment, as I enjoyed listening to Ree-Jane talk about her future fame. There were so many kinds of it, seesawing back and forth, with Ree-Jane sliding up and down from marrying the Duke of Devonshire or other royalty to being a movie star, then marrying another movie star whose career wasn't quite equal to hers; then being a famous war photographer; then a tennis champion, coming to glory in the center court at Wimbledon.

I had told her she should start with our state tournament. A lot of the tennis players stayed here at the hotel. Nobody was busy during the tournament, except Mrs. Davidow making her famous mint julep bowl, where people stood around and drank minted Kentucky bourbon through straws. I told Aurora if I'd had a hose, maybe I could have run it up to the fourth floor.

In the kitchen, my mother, far from having fits, was measuring some infinitesimal amount of flavoring into a sauce with a pink tinge (her shrimp Newburg, possibly), holding up a tiny spoon like a scientist in a lab, then tapping the spoon lightly and observing the dusting of whatever it was that drifted down on her sauce. If Dr. Jekyll had been this careful with his potion, he might not have turned into Mr. Hyde.

Walter called hello. My mother studied the sauce.

I plopped lettuce leaves into bowls, six of them, so there must be a party of four coming, in addition to Miss Bertha and Mrs. Fulbright. I added onion rings and green pepper rings.

While I did this I wondered about Emily Dickinson and if she ever did housework. If she was home all the time (as Mr. Root had said), then she must have. He also said she talked to people from behind a screen. That would really be nice to do. If I could find a truly lightweight screen to carry around, I could set it up whenever I felt like not looking at the person I had to address. Imagine. I could place Miss Bertha's salad in front of her, unfold my screen, and ask her if she wanted anything else.

I did not realize my mother was at my elbow until she asked why I was lollygagging around. Is that what I was doing?

"Those salads don't look very interesting. Can't you give them a little more personality?"

(No wonder my brother liked drama.)

"Paprika would help," she said. "Chopped-up black or green olives or pimiento."

I moved over to the shelf of herbs and spices and took down the paprika and its kissin' cousin, the old, reliable cayenne pepper. I then shook paprika over five salads and red pepper over one, and set it over to one side while I thought. Black olives. Green olives. What looks like a plain green olive chopped up? My brain flickered, sending tiny neon pictures of dancing jalapeño peppers.

I moved quickly to the refrigerator and pulled out a jar of peppers that my mother had used for some Spanish dish, hot as blazes. I chopped green olives and sprinkled them on the five salads. Then I took out a small pepper and chopped it into tiny pieces. I tried one on my tongue. *Ow!* Call the fire department! I dropped a few bits on salad number six and added a few chopped green olive bits. That salad looked just like the others. I tossed on French dressing and the salads were ready to go.

Here came Vera. Or rather, here whisked Vera. She would be taking care of the party of four.

After serving Miss Bertha and Mrs. Fulbright, I was making Aurora's before-dinner drink when the yelling began.

My mother gave me a look. "Is that Miss Bertha?"

I was holding a tall glass full of Southern Comfort, brandy, and various juices and looked over my shoulder. "I'm just making Great-Aunt Aurora's drink." I was always to refer to her as "Great-Aunt" and did so only when my mother was around.

I had told Walter to get a glass of ice water ready. He was putting it on a small tray.

More yelling.

"Emma!"

"Finished!" I called to her, and set the drink on my small tray, not bothering to add a paper umbrella.

Miss Bertha was grabbing her throat when Walter and I sailed into the dining room with our fatal antidotes.

Aurora loved hers. She sipped and slurped and smacked her lips. She was not a tidy drinker. I hadn't been too careful in my measuring, but as long as brandy outsmarted juice, my drink was on safe ground.

"Good!" She sipped some more. "Where's the pineapple half, though?"

"You don't get pineapple in a Cold Comfort. You're thinking of a Pine Bomb." (This was a new concoction of pineapple and Bombay gin.)

"Oh, yes. I'm telling you, girl, you should do this for a living, get yourself a night job over to the Double Down."

"I'm twelve." Had Aurora ever actually been to that club? I didn't think Perry Vines had operated it that long.

I was leaning against the wall, my tray under my arm, as always. "Let's go back to the Slade baby, and don't say, 'What baby?'" She was wearing that fake, wondering expression.

"I wasn't going to say anything, miss, except this drink is one of your best." There was a wide display of her dentures in what Aurora thought was a captivating smile.

"Here's what I learned today from Miss Isabel Barnett. You remember I told you she said she'd seen Baby Fay in town that afternoon before she was kidnapped? Well, she doesn't remember that it was the Slade baby at all, it turns out. She was mixing up babies."

Aurora fiddled with her lace cuff. "Told you she's a liar, didn't I?"

"No, she's not; I think she just made a mistake. And she was the only one I asked who claimed to have seen the baby that weekend."

"I know what you're thinking: The baby wasn't there at all. Told you that too."

No, I had told *her* that.

Her remark was delivered to the tapping of her nails against the glass. My summons to refill it.

"You won't be able to eat your dinner if you drink another Cold Comfort."

"Oh, don't be such a stick! 'You won't be able to eat your dinner—'"

It was maddening. She sounded just like me.

"Just who do you think you are, girl?"

"The bartender. Keep your mind on the Slade case. If the Slades were just pretending the baby was here, well, why were they?" I asked.

"They might have wanted it known the baby was alive at that particular time. For example, say there's a will, and somebody left a fortune to a person who would get it only if the baby predeceased him. Now, say the baby had died on Friday night. This other person died on the Thursday night. So it'd be the relatives of that person who'd want to collect. They'd pretend the baby was kidnapped, not dead."

"I don't think that happened."

Aurora set down her glass long enough to fling her arms into the air. "I know it didn't happen, you ninny. I was giving you an example." She picked up the glass again and held it out. She looked hopeful.

"Give me one good reason for them pretending the baby was with them when she wasn't and I'll get you a refill."

Aurora stared at her glass as if enough concentration could make it walk down to the kitchen on its own. But I guess she was just thinking.

Then she lifted her eyes to me. They were gray and glittered as if their irises were a mix of steel and mica.

"Maybe they lost her."

I flinched. I nearly dropped the tray my armpit was holding up. "Lost her? How would you lose a baby?"

"Same way you lose a million dollars or a fish off your line or your way home."

When I just stood there being stupid, she tilted the glass back and forth. "Or a bet." Then she laughed in her crafty way.

Lost, I thought. I could hear Mr. Root's rough voice reading Robert Frost's poem about the orchard's plight when no one would come in with a light.

It was so sad. And it sounded like pure chance that anything would be saved.

It sounded, as Aurora said, like a bet.

21

It made me so sad I wasn't even careful getting the Southern Comfort from the back office. So sad I walked right past Ree-Jane without thinking up something to rile her. So sad I nearly cried tears into the orange juice. So sad I forgot my dessert. (I didn't forget what it was—pear and pecan tart with butter brittle ice cream—I just forgot to eat it.)

While I ate my dinner, Walter took the fresh Cold Comfort up to Aurora Paradise. I left my plate on the dishwashing counter for Walter and went out the side door and down the gravel drive to the Pink Elephant. The grass outside the door was uncut and thick and wet. The door was thick, and it creaked; I had to stoop to get through it.

The little room was underneath the dining room and housed only my few things, together with mice and cobwebs. The hotel cat liked to visit sometimes, either to sleep or to check out the mouse situation.

But the room's main purpose had been as a place for a cocktail get-together. Hence its name, the Pink Elephant. Its rough stucco walls were painted pink, of course. Once, there had been a painting of a pink elephant in a party hat, waving a bottle of champagne, but it was now gone.

There was a dark wood table and benches, something like a picnic table, but here the benches weren't attached. Around the room were bottles into which I'd stuck candles, now burned down to stubs. I also had a lantern that gave off enough light to read by and made interesting shadows on the walls. The room was something like a cave, but a pleasant one.

There was a Whitman's candy box on a shelf in which I kept a few things I especially liked, things like an old photograph of the Devereau sisters and Mary-Evelyn. There was a neckerchief Ben Queen had given me when we were at Crystal Spring.

I pulled out a gold locket I had found in the room where my mother's things were stored. She said I could have it. It wasn't hers; she didn't know where it had come from. Inside was a brown photograph of a man and a woman. My mother did not know who they were.

This set off a fresh wave of sadness in me, sadness for the unknown couple in the picture. She was wearing a straw hat between two dark wings of hair; he was unsmiling in little round glasses, with hair parted straight down the middle and damped down with tonic or rain.

I wondered, Was there a family or friends somewhere who still remembered them? My mother had acquired the locket, yet they were total strangers. I could tell the picture was decades old from the hat and the hairdo and the high collar of her dress and also from the way they didn't smile. Back then people did not smile at the camera. Now, you couldn't bribe a person not to smile in that phony way reserved for picture taking.

Who were they? It made me feel almost guilty, having this locket that someone had taken care to slip a picture into behind the locket's glass. It angered me that the locket had gotten mixed in with other pieces of jewelry, with scarves and gloves, with letters and documents, all scattered around the suitcases as if none of it mattered, as if my mother just hadn't taken the time to care.

Yet she had to take care of this whole hotel: cook, seamstress, furniture restorer. I guess when you have all that to do, there's not time to sit and be sorry about two people in a faded photo in a locket.

But it still made me mad that if I hadn't found it, the locket would probably have been lost forever. I felt sorry for anything that had to depend on me to find it.

I should have been able to discard Aurora's idea, but I couldn't. I tried to imagine a scene in which a baby was lost. Forgetfulness? ("Where did I leave that carriage? Surely it was right here.") A kind of amnesia? ("What baby carriage?") But if the carriage had been left outside the grocery store (as often happens), and the baby was taken, that would again be kidnapping.

I heard Aurora's insistent voice and its list of losses: a million dollars, a fish, the way home . . . a bet.

A bet.

That made me shiver. Surely, that would be impossible. It was the most shocking thing I could imagine. Then I heard Mr. Gumbrel's voice: "That boy was a gambler. He was forever at that poker club—'club' being what they called it. He'd bet anything just to stay in the game, anything. Had a lot of debts, I'd guess."

In the Western movies I'd seen on Saturday afternoons, men would play cards in a saloon and when they ran out of money, they'd bet crazy things like their horse, their house, their "spread"—anything. But I never saw a gambler bet a life.

I sat for a long time thinking about this wispy little life, this will-o'-the-wisp baby who floated between being there and not being there, like the deer emerging from the fog or mist that hung around the Belle Ruin and fading back into it. It was like having your life suspended between something solid and hard, like Miss Bertha at the dining room table, and something impossibly airy, like Will moving his lips and words only seeming to come out. A sound waiting for itself.

Then I remembered another word Aurora had used: changeling. That was where one person was exchanged for another, usually babies, I supposed, as it would be pretty hard to exchange one adult for another without people getting wise.

This led me to wondering, What if Fay Slade hadn't actually been theirs? I sat up straight. What if in the hospital Imogen's baby had been swapped for a different one and then the real parents found out and demanded their own baby's return? Morris and Imogen didn't want Mr. Woodruff to find out about the baby's identity and so staged the kidnapping.

But I forgot: Mr. Woodruff had not wanted an investigation. That would not have been his reaction if my new idea was right. But maybe he would not want anybody to know either. Why? Embarrassment? Humiliation? "You old fool. There you were thinking all this time the baby was your granddaughter, buying her things, giving her money." No, wait. I forgot Fay was only four months old when she disappeared.

I outlined the story to myself. Hospital: a mistake is made and two babies are given to the wrong parents. . . .

No. That would hardly have brought about a *staged* kidnapping.

Hospital: Imogen's baby is stillborn (whatever that meant) or it dies and Imogen steals some other woman's baby.

Stealing a baby is so bad that it would probably wind up with a violent happening, such as a kidnapping. How she took the other baby was a loose end I would tie up later.

Or: a woman with a newborn wants to put it up for adoption, so Imogen agrees to take the baby.

But there'd be nothing really wrong with that, so where did the humiliation come in for Mr. Woodruff?

Hospital: Imogen's baby is stillborn (that must mean "born still," dead), but they *don't want to tell Imogen* because she'd get hysterical. So Mr. Woodruff pays a nurse a lot of money simply to show Imogen a baby from the rows of babies you always see in a room with fathers outside tapping the glass. The nurse tells Imogen it's her baby, but that she can hold it for only a little bit, as it's weak or underweight or something. I don't know. That at least gives Mr. Woodruff time to track down a for-sale baby, or an orphan baby (although I really couldn't see how a newborn could be an orphan—yet).

Mr. Woodruff and Morris would let Imogen think it's her baby up until Fay is four months old, when something awful, something tragic, happens, and Morris and Mr. Woodruff are forced to think up some solution and hit upon this kidnapping scheme.

But what could have happened to make them stage a kidnapping?

The thing was this, and it was very important to me: Fay couldn't have died. She must have lived or else there was someone else walking around who looked exactly like Rose Devereau Queen and Morris Slade.

I hunted in my Whitman's Sampler box for the picture of Rose Queen and the one of Morris Slade. I set them side by side. Peas in a pod. I had found out that they were related as half brother and sister, that Rose's mother, who'd been a Souder, had married a Slade before marrying old Mr. Devereau.

Rose was murdered by her daughter Fern; then Fern was murdered by crazy Isabel Devereau. I put my head in my hands. What a horrible family history. It was almost as bad as ours, although in ours, no one had been murdered. Yet.

Right then the hotel cat decided to squeeze through the opening in the door that never closed right unless you pushed or pulled. The cat was gray and had a thick coat, so it was hard to tell if he was thin or fat.

He jumped up on the bench without seeming to move a muscle. I could have said he thought himself up to the bench. Cats were like magicians: They could levitate; they could suspend themselves in air; they could hover in silence.

The cat sat and washed himself as if the jump had rearranged the lay of his fur. He went on with his washing, paw licked and then rubbed over his face, then all of a sudden stopped and looked at me straight in the eye and blinked slowly several times. Maybe he had lost me and was just trying to blink me up.

Like I was trying to blink up that baby.

22

I woke up the next morning and thought better of it and clamped a pillow over my head.

I needed to talk to someone who could do something, like the Sheriff. Or I needed to talk to someone with good sense, like Dwayne.

Or maybe I needed to talk to someone with a foot in both worlds, the real one and whatever else was out there, like Mrs. Louderback.

What I did *not* need was to carry breakfasts on a tray up to the Big Garage.

"Why should I have to wait on them? Why don't they come to the kitchen like everybody else?"

My mother was grimly shaping Parker House rolls. "Because they won't. You know them."

"Let them starve, then."

"They would."

I fumed. "Well, where's Ralph Diggs? *He* should be doing things like this; he can certainly carry up a tray."

"He's driving to Alta Vista with Mrs. Davidow."

"It's not even nine o'clock; the state liquor store isn't open yet. Which is where they're going, of course."

"By the time they get there, it will be."

Plop! went another small folded roll onto the thin baking sheet. They looked like two dozen tiny smiles. I loved Parker House rolls and was distracted thinking of how they'd puff up soft and golden brown.

"Emma."

"What?"

She pointed to the white-porcelain-topped island in the middle of the room, where I did the salads. "The tray is there. I just have to add some scrambled eggs."

My mother always cooked scrambled eggs in the top of a double boiler instead of a frying pan. She whisked them over the simmering water, and in that way got a lot of air into them. Like the rolls, they came out puffy and soft and smooth. I scanned the tray: orange juice and buttermilk pancakes. The pancakes were on a plate under a dome to keep the heat in. Good grief. Sitting beside that plate was a pitcher of maple syrup so pure that Walter must have gone and tapped it out of a tree. I let the pancake smell waft around me.

"Put the cover back on or they'll get cold. Here—" She handed me a large plate of eggs.

"You've even put *parsley* on them?"

"I always do on scrambled eggs."

"This is *Will* and *Mill* we're talking about."

"And that's parsley and parsley. Go."

I heard noises in the dining room. It was nearly nine o'clock. "I hope that's not Miss Bertha scratching around in there."

"I'll take care of Miss Bertha if you just stop whining and take that tray to the Big Garage."

Not wait on Miss Bertha! I'd take the tray down to hell for that. I whisked it up on my palm and was out through the back door before my mother realized she was getting a raw deal.

I crunched along the gravel drive past the cocktail garden to the Big Garage. My hands being full, I had to knock at the door with my foot. As always happened, half of Will's face materialized between door and doorjamb.

"What?"

"You *know* what." I tapped the tray.

"Oh. Yeah." He opened the door and then walked away, not offering to take the tray. "Breakfast, mate!" he yelled to Mill.

Mate? And it was said with a phony British accent. I set the tray on a red-spattered stump left over from *Medea, the Musical.* A lot of spray paint had been used in that production, especially red for blood. They loved the blood and speckled a lot of things with it. I came in once and saw Paul was a mist of red. Or, who knows? It could have been real blood, when it came to them and Paul.

Mill gave a blast on his trumpet. He played everything—horn, piano, clarinet, drums. He was the most talented person I'd ever met and probably ever would. He flung down the trumpet as if he had a hundred others and came over to join Will, who was pouring a ton of maple syrup over his pancakes.

"Where's Paul?" I asked.

With his mouth full and his fork pointed upward, he said, "Rafters. Tying clouds."

Tying clouds. "Paul!" I yelled.

"Hello, missus." His white-blond head appeared for an instant and then vanished.

"Breakfast!" I wasn't going to let them devour it all. "Come on down!"

"Hello, missus!"

"Have you got him tied down?"

Will was forking eggs into his mouth. He shook his head. "No, because he needs to let the clouds down. There's a rope around him, though."

Around his neck, I wouldn't be surprised.

Mill folded a pancake and said, "I gotta get back."

To what? To where? I watched a cardboard cloud being lowered to within a few feet of the plane's cockpit. Then another cloud hung over the cabin.

There was a knock at the door and Will went to it. I noticed he opened it in a perfectly normal way and actually greeted whoever was outside.

A couple of mismatched girls walked in, one short, one tall, maybe around eight and ten years old. They both wore the same dopey expression, so they were probably related. There are looks that sisters and brothers pick up from one another just from being around one another.

Will told me these were "the Evans girls" (as if they'd come directly from a stint in a Broadway hit). Then he told them to follow him up to the stage. They climbed the three steps to the stage and stood looking at Will in a double-dopey way.

"Okay," he said, pointing both to the girls and to Mill at the piano. "Hit it!!"

Mill did: his hands came down on the piano keys like a starburst and rippled away.

"Come on, girls, go!" Will clapped his hands, tapped his feet, then waved his pancake like a baton. They apparently didn't know where to go. "Do what we practiced—legs up, legs kick, kick, kick."

They kicked, but not together, and one was a lot higher than the other.

"Mill!" Will waved him over and the two gave the Evans girls a demonstration: "Left, right, left, right, kick, kick, kick." Will and Mill were quite expert at it.

The Evans girls watched and learned nothing. Their next attempt had them kicking sideways, as they seemed to have no sense of direction.

"Okay, okay, take a break."

A break from what?

The girls broke and sat down in a couple of the old Orion theater seats that had been discarded.

Will turned and threw his hands up in the air. "It'll all come to tears."

"Where'd you get that expression?"

"The Brits say it—you know."

"No, and neither do you. What's all the Britspeak for anyway?"

Will was making up his "book" some more. "The play's set in England."

"England?" I got my face right up to his. "It's set in the *sky.* That's half of a plane you've got up there." I pointed to their half of an airplane. "It's called *Murder in the Sky,* remember?"

Will was unperturbed by my attempt at reason, and he was joined by Mill; they were now equally unperturbed. They were always willing just to take any old partly hatched idea and hatch it all the way.

The Evans girls had now crawled into the cockpit as pilot and copilot and were pretending to fly the plane.

I said, "Did it ever occur to either of you there's a lot *really* going on right around here, in Spirit Lake and Cold Flat Junction and Lake Noir, including murder, *three* murders to be exact, and one attempted, enough to keep you in material for the rest of your *lives*?"

Will looked up from the production book and they both stared at me, so I ticked the murders off: "Mary-Evelyn Devereau, Rose Devereau Queen, Fern Queen. And me, nearly." It was truly mind-boggling when I thought of it.

But they looked mystified. Will said, "So?"

So? "Well, there's your story. Call it *Murder in Cold Flat Junction* or *Murder at Mirror Pond* or *Murder in Spirit Lake.* As a matter of fact, you could do a . . . trinity. Three plays. You'd have the whole summer wrapped up."

They both folded sticks of gum into their mouths in the same synchronized way they'd kicked their legs. Will said, "For one thing, why would we want to bother with something that really happened?"

What?

Mill said, "For another thing, who would we ever get to play you?"

23

Lunch wasn't very interesting. I had managed only to put a tiny piece of garlic clove inside one of Miss Bertha's strawberries. Of course, there was the usual fuss about poisoned food, but as she'd swallowed the evidence, the fuss soon gave way to raised eyebrows and head shakes.

Mrs. Louderback said she'd be glad to see me. She had only the one appointment at two o'clock and I was to come afterward.

So after being admitted by Mrs. Louderback's strange friend, I sat in the anteroom outside the kitchen waiting, along with a starer. A starer is a person who won't look away until she has you bolted to the wall with her awful eyes. Even staring back does no good. I tried it with this woman, to no avail. I was tempted to pass my palm across the bridge of air between us, but didn't.

It was truly unnerving. I was about to say something when the kitchen door opened and a small woman, thin as a leaf, drifted out. Mrs. Louderback said good-bye to her and said hello to me, then turned to the starer and said, "Miss Jo, please come in."

Then it was I saw the cane and observed this Miss Jo person kind of struggling up, eyes seeking nowhere and nothing. I was embarrassed by my earlier reaction. The poor woman was blind as a bat.

Since I was supposed to have been next after the two o'clock appointment, I figured Miss Jo's visit was not scheduled. So there must have been an emergency. I wondered what it could be. Could she have just gone suddenly blind? Now, that would be interesting and even good for an interview. I thought for a while and decided that would be good for a series of interviews: how things look from the standpoint of the suddenly disabled—the suddenly deaf, the suddenly completely paralyzed, the suddenly speech-impaired (which I only thought of because of the Wood boys, but they'd been that way all their lives), the suddenly amputated. There was a really good movie where the hero was hated by an old doctor who revenged himself by amputating the hero's legs—both of them. It was pretty horrible. His girlfriend kept telling him to buck up. How? I wondered. Should he learn to walk on his hands? The movie was good, though; it had Ronald Reagan in it.

I wondered if Miss Bertha had been suddenly humpbacked. If lightning had hit her, for instance. No, that posture took years of practice. I tried bending at the shoulders like Miss Bertha, but couldn't do it. Then I stopped, for I should be thinking about what to ask Mrs. Louderback or her cards. I hoped I didn't get the Orphans in a Storm card again. It was some kind of bad news. The Hanged Man, another card that followed me around, was supposed to mean good news. If you can imagine that. He hung from a branch by his ankle with the other leg bent across the first leg. (The Ronald Reagan character might have seen good news in that, but who else would?) Things are pretty bad if a hanged man is good news.

I realized these were stupid thoughts and extremely unsympathetic. I should learn to be more sorry for people who didn't have the great advantages I had, like my mother's chicken pot pie, which I think was on tonight's menu. It wasn't thin and watery like Banquet frozen; my mother's had big chunks of chicken in it.

I'd discovered a rubber band between my chair cushion and the arm and was about to snap it across the room when the door opened and the blind lady, Miss Jo, came out of the kitchen. A ton of adrenaline got dumped around my insides.

"Emma!" said Mrs. Louderback, sounding surprised, as if she hadn't seen me fifteen minutes ago. I was busy watching Miss Jo maneuver around a footstool in her path. I could have got up and moved it, but I thought it was probably better to let the handicapped fend for themselves. It was certainly more interesting.

I jumped out of my chair and went into the kitchen, still unsure as to how to approach the subject of the kidnapped—rather, the non-kidnapped baby. Mrs. Louderback had known the Woodruffs, for they had spent summers here in Spirit Lake. They owned the biggest house around; it sat on four town lots.

I stared at the deck of cards sitting neatly in the center of the table, keeping its secrets.

"Well, Emma," said Mrs. Louderback, sitting down across from me and pushing back a wisp of hair. "How are you today? You sounded a little distraught over the phone." She rearranged the cards, cutting them like a casino dealer.

"No, I'm okay."

She turned over a card: the Two of Cups, in which I had no interest at all. The cups just reminded me of having to wait on tables at dinner.

Next came—I just knew it!—Orphans in a Storm. Though it wasn't called that.

Mrs. Louderback shook her head. "They really do seem to follow you around." We pondered the card. "I think you must have a long-standing problem."

"Well, this card isn't helping me solve it."

"No, but I suppose you could say solutions lie within us."

That was bad news. "I don't see it lying inside *them*." I tapped the card. "They didn't bring the wind and weather."

"You know, they're not really orphans; it isn't really a storm."

"Then what's all that snow flying into their faces?"

I thought she could have told me that before. Maybe Miss Jo couldn't, but that was all the rest of us had—our eyes, ears, noses, and mouths.

Mrs. Louderback said, "Do you believe everything you see?"

"More than I believe everything I don't." I hoped she wasn't going to bring up God and angels and all the rest. I had a hard enough time with Father Freeman.

"What I mean is, how do you interpret what you see?"

I wondered if I had come to the right place after all. I said, "If I see a cat walking by the door, then my mind sees, you know, a cat walk by the door."

She nodded and reached behind her to a blue cupboard and pulled out a book. She leafed through it and turned it around so I could look at it. I'd seen this trick-picture several times: the vase and the silhouettes of two faces, depending on what your eye did with it. Mine went back and forth between vase and faces. Before she could ask the boring question, I said, "It's either a vase or the outlines of two faces."

"That's right. Which do you see?"

"Both."

She shook her head. "Not both at once. I don't think the eye can take both in simultaneously."

Suddenly, I thought of the artist and his Fadeaway Girls: there was the red coat of one becoming part of the red background, or the white coat of another girl melting into the snow. You had to supply your own lines for the missing sections of coat.

"Yes, you can." Maybe someone my age should not directly contradict an adult, but I didn't want to fool around with that. "Did you ever see covers of magazines with illustrations of Fadeaway Girls?" When she shook her head, I described them. "You can see it all at once, the background and the girl. It's because the girl is part of the background. If you see what I mean." I looked at her hard, eyes narrowed, as if I could force my images of the Fadeaway Girls into her mind.

But she only shook her head again.

It was up to my mind to tell my eye—or was it the other way around? This was too complicated. "I keep seeing this girl—" I hadn't meant to say it; it just popped out. "Remember? I told you." Had I?

"A girl? No, I don't recall that."

"She keeps turning up where I am. Here and in Cold Flat Junction."

"You don't know who she is?"

"No." But I thought I did, didn't I? She was Fay Slade, wasn't she? Wasn't there evidence to point to that? "She *could* be the Slade baby— I mean the baby that disappeared twenty years ago. The one that was allegedly kidnapped." Mrs. Louderback had known the Woodruffs and Morris Slade back then.

"But the baby was kidnapped and no one around these parts ever heard anything after that. Why do you think it's her?"

"Because she looks like Morris Slade, or pictures I've seen of him. She looks like Rose Devereau Queen too. Because she and Morris looked alike; they could have been twins, the way they looked, only Rose would have been a lot older than Morris."

Mrs. Louderback looked doubtful. "I don't know, Emma. You'd think, if it was the Slade girl come back, she'd make more of an effort to find out what had happened, wouldn't you?"

Of course, that seemed true. "Then who is she? Why would she keep turning up where I am?"

"Don't our eyes sometimes deceive us?"

I sighed. "People always say that if they can't explain a thing."

She smiled a little. "I expect you're right." She was laying out three more cards.

I didn't know why, since the first three hadn't done much good.

First was the moon, or a sliver of it, and two big pillars, and wolves, or I guess they were. Then—I just knew it!—the Hanged Man, and after him the Three of Cups, not more interesting than the two of them.

"The Hanged Man," I said.

She riffled the cards a little, back and forth. "It's a long, complicated story, you know. The Fool is sometimes considered the Hanged Man. Now, the Moon—the Moon controls the Fool. He walks a watery path and that becomes a river. He's left with either staying with the wolves and hunting with them or taking his chances in a little boat; that is to say, on his ability to row a boat."

She looked at me; I looked at her.

"You're saying I'm the Fool?"

She riffled the cards again and smiled. "Well, are you?"

24

Miss Flagler was arranging items behind her small bow window in the Oak Tree Gift Shoppe. The things she sold, like the silver pillbox she had just placed between a tiny baby's bracelet and a little silver frame, were very small. The shop itself was so narrow that no more than two people could have stood in it shoulder to shoulder. Miss Flagler herself was proportioned like the shop, tall and thin as the edge of the silver frame.

The bell over the door jingled when I entered.

"Emma! You're just in time. Miss Flyte is on her way here for tea."

"On her way" sounded as if the person were coming from distant blocks away, when actually Miss Flyte's shop, Candlewick, was separated from the Oak Tree by only a narrow alley. Two side doors faced each other across the alley, and it was by these doors that Miss Flyte and Miss Flagler visited each other for morning coffee and afternoon tea.

Tea, I thought, was an excellent idea, as I had walked the two miles from Spirit Lake rather than contend with Delbert, because I wanted to think. I hadn't thought of anything helpful.

I followed Miss Flagler through a curtained alcove and into her kitchen. Tea was already steeping in the big brown pot, covered with an embroidered cozy. A wonderful smell was coming from the oven.

Her cat, Albertine, jumped up on the table and from there to a shelf above the chair I always sat in. Miss Flagler unhooked a pot holder and pulled a tray of sticky buns out of the oven.

Just as she did this, Miss Flyte entered through the alley door. She said hello to both of us, looking happy to see me. I don't know why they liked having me around, a twelve-year-old, but they did.

Sitting in my chair now, I felt Albertine's soft paw selecting a strand of my hair to chew on. Albertine really liked my hair.

As I surveyed the sweet buns for the ones with the most nuts and caramel, Miss Flyte asked if that Wednesday's paper would carry my next installment. It had been two weeks since the last one.

I cut my bun in two and said, "I hit a snag in the story."

"Oh? What's that?"

"Well, I'm trying to describe my state of mind when Isabel Devereau forced me into that rowboat." As if I could ever forget. "You recall, she had a gun." I shouldn't have to remind anyone of this.

Miss Flagler put her cool-looking hands to her warm-looking cheeks. "Awful, how awful it must have been."

Not as awful as you might think, what with the fame it had brought. But then their interest turned to Will and Mill's next production. Which was pretty irritating.

"Is it to be another musical?" asked Miss Flyte.

"Maybe. They haven't gotten it together yet. There are a lot of loose ends." I didn't mind Will being famous; I just didn't want him to be more famous than me, or famous at the same time.

"Well, they'll straighten it out, I'm sure. That brother of yours can do anything."

Except walk from the Big Garage to the kitchen for his breakfast. "I think maybe it's deliberate."

Twin frowns confronted me.

"What's deliberate?" said Miss Flagler.

"Loose ends." I pondered this, since I didn't know what I had meant. Then I thought of something. "I think sometimes Will doesn't really want to solve a problem." I was, of course, talking about myself.

Miss Flyte was an especially intelligent person, so I thought she might come up with something helpful.

Miss Flagler spoke first. "Why on earth would he deliberately hurt his own project?"

"Well, I can think of one or two reasons," said Miss Flyte, stirring her tea.

Good. Let's hear them. Albertine pawed up another strand of hair to chew on.

"One could be he's afraid that this play can't be as successful as the last one, so he's stalling."

No. Will and Mill afraid of anything but maybe a grizzly bear coming through the door with their dinner tray would surprise me.

"Or," Miss Flyte continued, "perhaps he's worried it will be even better and then he'll have to keep turning out productions that are always stunning."

No to that too. Will is not nearly as happy to stun people as I am. He's happy with applause, but that's because he's such a ham. For lingering celebrity he doesn't care.

Miss Flyte went on: "Or maybe he doesn't want it to end."

What? That caught my attention.

"Once I had a friend—Zelda Bittner her name was—who had several novels sitting around that she'd read most of but never finished. I mean, she'd be twenty pages or so from the end and just snap the book shut. And some of the books she really liked. Two of them she'd even read nonstop until those last twenty pages and she just quit. What really surprised me was that some were mystery novels, and that meant she didn't get to the solutions!"

I said, "Then did she finally? Did she read the endings?"

"No. She died." Miss Flyte picked up her cup of tea as if she hadn't just said what she'd said.

"Oh." Miss Flagler fell back in her chair as if she'd been pushed. "She never did find out."

Miss Flyte nodded. "She never did, no."

"What did she die of?" I was trying to be practical. The death might have been what they call lingering; if that was the case, she *could* have read the endings. Or even, say, if the doctor had told her: "I'm sorry, but you have only two or three weeks, Zelda." (I liked the name and considered telling people it was my middle name and I'd like to be called by it from here on in.)

Of course the dying Zelda would first have to spend time going around telling friends and family the news, and maybe writing a quick will if she didn't have one, but then she could collect all of her books and read the endings.

"She had a stroke," said Miss Flyte.

I said, "You mean she was struck down dead immediately?"

"Well, she went into a coma before she died."

"Did she come out of it at all? Even for a little while?"

"No. You know what a coma is like."

Sometimes, looking at Ree-Jane, I thought I did. "I mean, not even for"—I calculated how long it would take to read twenty pages—"fifteen minutes?" If she was a fast reader.

Miss Flyte shook her head, looking at me with a small and lofty smile, as if she were just becoming aware I was dim. I shrugged as if I really didn't care about all of those unread endings wasting away. I didn't want to appear overly concerned, but I had to know, and asked, "Didn't you see any of these books? I mean, don't you know even one?" I tried to match her lofty smile, but I think I just looked like my nose was stuck in the air.

"Let me think." She thought. "Yes, there were several of Agatha Christie's." She pondered. "She especially liked Miss Marple."

If I asked which ones, I would sound much too interested. "Was there a church funeral? And did people get up and talk about her? About Zelda?"

"Yes. It was quite a large funeral. Her family did say words about her. Why?"

"Nothing." I was thinking it could have been a good opportunity to read an ending—in the church or over her grave.

Of course, I did not say this.

"Agatha Christie was an enormously interesting person, I've always thought," said Miss Flagler. "She disappeared, you know."

My eyes might have been on stalks the way I swiveled them toward Miss Flagler. "Disappeared?"

"Yes, it was in the baths at Harrogate. That's in Yorkshire, I believe. It was quite a big scandal. Then she just, well, reappeared, and to this day no one knows exactly what had happened."

I sat there trying to take this in as Albertine chewed on my hair. In a little while, I left. Albertine didn't like that.

I needed a chocolate milk shake *now*.

25

Shirl was sitting on her stool behind the cash register, smoking. She had been to the Prime Cut to get her hair done, but the only way you could tell was that a little hair had been feathered over her forehead. The stylist at the Prime Cut always did that, but it was a waste of time, for the feathering lasted only a few hours and then it blended into the rest of the frizz.

Shirl grunted a "Hello" at me. I said, "Hello," back and managed to ignore Helene Baum, the doctor's wife, who was standing before the glass pastry case deciding which pie or cake to buy. She gave me a sour look, which I pretended not to see, and I walked behind her and the customers at the counter.

Maud was giving coffee refills all along the counter, where the cups were lined up like my mother's dinner plates, each plate waiting for a spoonful of something, and that reminded me of a communion service at St. Michael's. I seemed in a religious mood today. Maybe I was about to be saved; I hoped not.

I waited for Maud and this gave Dodge Haines and Bubby Dubois an opportunity to be funny. Bubby said, "Anybody else made you walk the plank lately?" He hit the counter with the flat of his hand and laughed like crazy and got the mayor beside him going as if being forced off a dock into a rowboat at gunpoint was just the funniest thing they'd ever heard. I looked at Bubby Dubois, at his sandy lashes and hair like meringue, slicked up and coming to a little point near his forehead, and didn't answer. I wished Maud hadn't come along at that very moment, as I'd have liked to go on not answering.

"Hi, hon," she said. "Want a Coke?"

"A chocolate milk shake, please." I made a point of putting a dollar on the counter, though I knew Maud would give me one for free. But I could see Shirl up on her stool, smoking and watching, and Shirl never gave anything for free, unless she was in a really generous mood, which she hardly ever was.

The milk shake can jittered away, then stopped. Maud poured the shake into a ribbed glass into which she plunged a straw. The milk shake looked really thick and I knew she'd added extra ice cream. I took it back to the last booth, which always had a RESERVED sign on it. It was for the Rainbow's employees. I especially liked the booths; they were dark wood and so high-backed that you couldn't see people coming unless you leaned a little toward the aisle.

I had drunk the milk shake halfway down when Maud slid into the seat across from me. Right away I put the question to her: "Here's a kind of problem. Say you've got three people who are friends. A, B, and C. You're C. B tells you something about A that you find hard to believe. What's the most obvious way to find out the truth?"

She looked puzzled and got the pack of Camels from her pocket. "Ask A, I guess."

"Yes. If C doesn't, but instead goes all the way around Robin Hood's barn"—one of my mother's favorite expressions—"to find out the answer—I mean, like asking other people who might know but might not—then what does that tell you about C? Anything?"

Maud lit up a cigarette, exhaled a stream of smoke, and said, "Maybe C thinks A's feelings will be hurt?"

"But what else?"

Maud smoked and thought. It occurred to me then that all this A, B, C stuff was just another of my roundabout ways and that a lot of people would reach across the table and strangle me. So I told her what Miss Flyte had said about not wanting to know the answer.

"Ah. So C doesn't ask A because C doesn't really want to know, even though she thinks she does?"

I nodded.

She smoked. She said, "That's pretty good. I mean, I think Miss Flyte is probably right."

"It's called denial."

Where had he come from? How had the Sheriff managed to just *appear* that way?

Maud said, "How did you manage to creep up on us?"

The Sheriff sat down beside Maud.

I said, "What do you mean, 'denial'?"

"That happens when you hide something from yourself. Alcoholics are masters of denial. They hide from the fact that they're alcoholics."

"You sound," said Maud, "like you just came from an AA meeting. Was it helpful?"

"Funny." He turned back to me, as if I were the adult here and the only one he could talk to. "It's actually a complex state, denial. But let's simplify it by saying there's something a person just doesn't want to know or admit to or find out about himself."

"Like if there's an obvious person to ask something—I mean, a person who'd be most likely to know—but I don't ask him, but just ask a dozen other people instead."

"You mean, you pretend to want to know?"

I frowned. "I guess."

"For instance"—the Sheriff had removed his cap and was loosening up his tie—"if you keep pretending to want to know, you'll throw people off? Which is often what alcoholics do."

"Well, but it's not so much trying to throw *other* people off, since they don't even get what you're talking about. No, it's more yourself, just yourself."

Maud blew out another thin stream of smoke. "I have a copy of the Big Book under the counter if either of you need to consult it."

The Sheriff smiled at me. "You have a perfect understanding of denial. So what are you denying?"

"Me?"

He nodded. "You."

I played with my straw, bending and rebending it. He just sat there, fixing me with his cool blue eyes. The Sheriff definitely didn't move in roundabout ways.

He said, "I went to Cold Flat Junction and talked to Gloria Calhoun and her friend Prunella Rice. You were right about that phone call. It was planned in order to give Gloria an excuse for leaving the room. According to her—and it wasn't easy getting her to admit this, obviously—Imogen's father gave her a hundred dollars to leave the room for twenty minutes. She could say she'd had a phone call. She arranged to call Prunella Rice at exactly nine thirty, while the dance was on.

"They didn't know the reason for this. They thought it was some game, some joke he was playing on the parents, or some surprise he'd arranged for them. But after the police were called, Woodruff told Gloria not to say a word or she might get in trouble with the police too. It sounded like a threat."

I started to say, "Then they were—"

The Sheriff held off my voice with the palm of his hand out, pressing against my words. "As you can imagine, Gloria was flabbergasted when she got back to the room and found Morris Slade there and little Fay gone. It was right after that when Mr. Woodruff told her to keep her mouth shut. She was scared to death—both of the girls were scared. Lucien Woodruff was a formidable man."

I said, "Then the three of them were in on it?"

He shook his head. "Not the three of them—the two of them."

"Morris Slade," I said, for some reason, disappointed in him, although I didn't know him. "Everyone thought he was no good."

"Not Morris. Imogen."

This did make me gasp, although ordinarily I'm not much of a gasper. "Imogen! The baby's mother!" I should have been enough into the Greeks and Medea not to be surprised by this.

He nodded. "Imogen and her father planned it."

"Gloria Calhoun told you all this?"

The Sheriff's smile was a little sour. "She didn't have much choice. But no, she didn't tell me all of it. Carl Mooma told me some. He was the sheriff back then. Donny's uncle."

Carl Mooma. I thought he was dead.

"Go on," said Maud.

"Sheriff Mooma was pretty tight-lipped."

I don't know why I felt oddly relieved.

"But there is more." He looked at me.

The way the Sheriff said that, my insides started jittering away like the milk shake container. I wanted to slap my hands over my ears. He was going to tell us what had happened that night; he was going to tell the end of it, the dazzling truth, the end of the story.

But he didn't.

It was a dazzling something else.

"Morris Slade's back in town."

26

Morris Slade.

The Sheriff said he didn't know why he'd come back, but that he was staying in the Woodruff house in Spirit Lake.

I had an hour before I had to be at the salad table, which was so boring I would almost rather sit in Miss Bertha's lap. I stopped in front of the Marigold Flower Shop and thought about the Woodruff house. Would I have time to investigate it before I had to serve tonight?

I was still trying to work out reasons for a put-on kidnapping, a staged kidnapping. Will and Mill might have some ideas about kidnappings, considering the way they kept Paul up there in the rafters and how Will had whisked little Bessie off the croquet court.

I moved on to the Prime Cut, where Bobbi, the owner, was putting rollers in Mayor Sims's wife's hair. She was trapped there behind the window; she couldn't get up and walk away or turn away, as Bobbi had possession of her hair. I frowned deeply to show I thought she really looked bad, shook my head, and made a pained face to be sure she got it.

But then I grew tired of that and walked on and puzzled over the kidnapping. Why had Imogen and Mr. Woodruff done it? Was it some kind of revenge against Morris Slade? Why? Every question began with Why? and went unanswered.

I passed Axel's Taxis and waved to Wilma, the dispatcher, and she waved back. So did Delbert. My wave was not meant to include him, but he was getting in on it anyway. I guessed I'd have to take a cab to the hotel in fifteen minutes, so I went in and told Wilma I'd be back at five. I wasn't even looking at Delbert, who was reading a comic book, but he put it down and looked at his big turnip of a watch, then from it to the clock on the wall, and back again. He gave the watch a wind, as if General Eisenhower had told Delbert to wake him up at exactly five a.m. so he wouldn't miss D-day.

"Fifteen minutes. That'd make it right at five o'clock is what I figure."

I rolled my eyes. "Yes, Delbert. Five."

"It's fifteen to right now, you realize that. So if my watch is right—"

I left him talking to his watch and went down the three wooden steps.

Revenge against Morris Slade. I thought about this. But for Imogen, from what I'd heard about her, it was just too complicated a plan. If she wanted revenge against her husband, she'd just hit him over the head with the fireplace tongs or something. As for Mr. Woodruff, I had the impression he was smart enough, only he wouldn't put in all that effort just for revenge against Morris Slade. He'd just get rid of him somehow. Morris Slade could be bought off, he would think. I suppose almost anyone could be bought off. I know I could.

Now I was in front of Forbish's Shoes (SHOES FOR BUSY FEET, the sign said). Mr. Forbish was fitting shoes on Helene Baum, who had a pie box sitting on the chair beside her. The store was dusk dark inside, as if it belonged in another solar system, but I could still pretend I saw how big Helene Baum's feet were. When she looked my way, I made my mouth into an O of surprise. But she was sitting too far in for me to tell if she could see my shocked face. Maybe we'd meet on the street one day and she'd pass me a few folded-up bills, saying that was for my not telling her shoe size.

I found an old stick of Doublemint gum in my pocket and stuffed it in my mouth and walked on. I thought probably I knew a lot about people they'd pay me not to tell. I walked up the other side of the street and then decided I had better get to the taxi rank and put in my time with Delbert.

Delbert made a big deal of the time: "Five p.m. on the nose!" as if he were responsible for my punctuality. As we drove out of town with the friendly faces of Braeburn's Tourist Home and Arturo's Restaurant sliding by, I wondered, If Delbert were to kidnap me, how much would some people think I was worth, and what would they pay to get me back?

I always sat behind him where he couldn't see me in the rearview mirror unless he craned his neck. He hunted my face out in the mirror the way I'd heard a pig goes rooting for truffles. He wouldn't last five minutes with Emily Dickinson—that's for sure—not with that screen between them.

"Do anything interestin' today?"

"No." I hated open-ended questions like that; the questioner didn't care about the answer, only that the burden of conversation got to the other person, so the one asking could sit back and not do anything (and then call himself a good listener): *You're a mountain climber? Tell me about it!* "You play the oboe? Tell me about it." "You murdered your children? Tell me about it!" Here I pictured the questioned one, Medea, plunging a knife into the questioner's chest and answering, "That's pretty much it."

"That brother o' yours," said Delbert, up and running again, "he puttin' on any more plays? That last one was a corker!"

"You mean you saw it?"

"Nah. I just heard. I ain't got time for stuff like that."

I watched the scenery wander away and thought for a moment. "Gee, that's too bad because you were one of the characters."

That got him going. He almost ran off the road. I guessed there wasn't a lot of drama in Delbert's life.

"What? What do you mean?"

"You were Creon."

"Cre-un who? Who's he?"

"A cabdriver." I was afraid he was so excited by all this he was going to stop the car. But he just flailed around, searching the mirror.

I said, "This was back in the old days of the Greeks."

"The Greeks, they had cabs?"

"Chariots."

"So this guy was drivin' a chariot? With horses?"

"No. You were driving a cab. It was right onstage, or part of it was, the front end that Will put together from scrap metal. It was cab number eighty-two. Medea took it to go to the Games."

We were passing Britten's store then, and I waved to Mr. Root, but he was too busy with Ulub's recital to notice.

"So how'd people know it was me if I wasn't there on the stage?"

I considered this as the cab neared the Hotel Paradise driveway. "Because the character talked like you. And he worked for a Greek named Axel." I had a sudden inspiration. "Listen: Don't turn into the hotel yet. Turn right up here on Pine and then go along E Street."

It was almost too much for Delbert, this shift in the usual route. He nearly tossed me into the trunk, braking like that. "What? What in God's name you want to go to E Street for?"

"Just do it, Delbert."

He grunted, then sped up a little. "Cost you more; this here's a detour."

We passed the Custis place and Mrs. Louderback's. The old Woodruff house, looking spick-and-span as always, sat on the next corner. The house hadn't been lived in for years, not since the Belle Ruin days. But it had been kept up; the grass was mowed and the house aired out by whomever Mr. Woodruff hired to do it. I only knew this because I saw old Mr. Bernhardt trundling slowly behind a mower and his wife, who did cleaning, going in and out. It was a beautiful house, with long windows right down to the floor, and a wraparound porch. The house was painted white, of course, with green shutters.

There was a light on inside. Several cars were parked along the street and one of them I'd never seen before. It was a red convertible with a black top and looked like one of those snappy foreign models. With all the time I spent in Slaw's Garage, I should have been able to name it, but I couldn't.

"Okay, go to the hotel."

I thought I'd never hear the end of this detour. It even overshadowed Creon for five minutes.

I handed over the fare plus the "detour charge" and a twenty-five-cent tip.

"Thanks, only I wish you'd've told me about that play. I definitely would've gone."

"That's too bad. Well, don't worry. You'll probably be in the next one too."

With Delbert excitedly hurling questions at my back, I was up on the porch and through the door. I knew I'd set myself up for years of questions by making up that story and taking that "detour," but some stories are, well, irresistible. And so are some detours.

Mrs. Davidow was back in our kitchen, martini in one hand, ladle in the other, stirring the salad dressing. The ash of her cigarette was dangerously positioned over the brown crock. When I saw the iceberg lettuce quarters arranged on nine salad plates, I assumed there was a dinner party and asked whose.

"Was. They just canceled. It's the Browns. I told Bruce Brown it was too near dinner to cancel, that your mother had spent hours over the dinner and that our cancellation fee was thirty percent."

"What cancellation fee? We've never had one."

She tapped the ladle against the stone crock as if she were calling up spirits. Her face was red, half from martinis and half from anger. "We do now."

"What did they order?"

"Surf 'n' turf. The lobster tails were half defrosted when he called."

"Then who gets the salads?"

"There's a party of four coming at seven. Bringing their own wine. Vera's waiting on them."

Seven. That meant they'd be sticking around until eight thirty or nine—if they were drinking. The hotel didn't have a liquor license; we weren't allowed to sell it, but guests were perfectly free to bring their own. But that way, the hotel didn't make any money on drinks. So Lola Davidow got around that by charging for setups—ice, soda, ginger ale, and so forth. I could see she was trying to think of a way to charge for wine.

"Who else?"

"Only a couple staying the night. They'll be in around seven thirty. Vera will be waiting on them too."

I wasn't good enough for the new people, but that was okay with me; it meant all I had to do was take care of Miss Bertha and Mrs. Fulbright and Mr. Muggs, who was staying overnight.

Mrs. Davidow said she was going to the office, which meant I wouldn't be able to get at the liquor supply.

I would have to use my emergency drink. I'd started hiding an extra drink behind the block of ice in the icebox. It was called a Jack Frost, made from Jack Daniel's and brandy and orange juice, and as it wouldn't have time to defrost completely, that explained the "Frost" part. I took it out now, making sure no one was looking, and set it behind the Waring blender.

Of course, there was a chance my mother would find it back there if the ice melted, but Walter and I were ready to say it was Lola Davidow's. She'd say she hadn't put it there, but we'd say she just forgot, which wasn't true, but it sounded that way.

Dinner was roast lamb with brown gravy or mint sauce. Miss Bertha always wanted her lamb very rare; my mother always refused to serve rare lamb. Tonight the same request was made, the same refusal given. "If she likes, Walter could go out and kill a rabbit for her. I could serve that with a nice tularemia confit."

Walter hee-hawed. Miss Bertha refused to eat. That was fine with me.

While this noise went on, I served Mr. Muggs his dessert. We both looked at it with respect. It was Neapolitan tart, one of my mother's masterpieces, half of it a caramel-ribboned ice cream, half flaky pastry, all in a crushed almond shell with hot caramel sauce.

I went to the kitchen and collected my Jack Frost and hurried it up to Aurora's room.

27

"What if she died that very day?" said Aurora, eyes glittering.

"You mean died, or was killed?"

"Either. Both." Her hand waved my question away. "I don't know what I mean, tryin' to fly on one wing. Here—" She held out the glass.

I didn't have another Jack Frost on ice. "I can't get at the whiskey if Mrs. Davidow is in the office."

This had no effect on the outstretched hand. She said, "More likely she's out at her still. Go on. You'll think of something."

"I'll think of something later." I wasn't moving. "You're saying you think maybe the baby died or was killed and Mr. Woodruff and maybe Imogen thought up the kidnapping as an excuse? But staging a kidnapping wouldn't be easy."

"Well, it'd be a lot more trouble to explain a dead baby, wouldn't it?"

"She's not dead."

Aurora was now pretending not to hear, since I wasn't running to get her refill. She started humming tunelessly and fiddling with the pearl button of her crocheted glove.

"I've told you about a girl I keep seeing who's the very spit of Morris Slade. She has to be related."

She stopped then and looked at me. "You mean just because you saw someone who looked like him, you're saying it has to be that baby? Don't be daft. What makes you think she was the only one?"

I looked blank. I felt blank.

Aurora took my silence as an opportunity to hold out her glass again. I was in such a blank state, I took it.

Lola Davidow was in the back office, and I heard ice cubes clinking against glass, so I guessed she had her ice bucket there. There was no chance of getting to the liquor supply, and I walked on back to the kitchen.

Walter was by himself, back in the shadows, drying a big platter. I sighed and set down Aurora's glass. "Mrs. Davidow's in the office, so I can't get Aurora another drink." Not that I cared much; I was too tired to care.

Walter dried his hands and said, "I'll be back." He took the kitchen shears off a nail and went out the side door and the porch and stairs that led down to the gravel road that circled the hotel.

I went out after him, letting the screen door bang. It was dark by now and I stood looking at him below, seeing his light shirt moving across the dark grass. He was cutting something with the kitchen shears, but it was almost as if he were scything, the way his arms moved back and forth. It put me in mind of a painting in the library of men with scythes, rising or falling, cutting wheat. It was painted by a famous artist. He painted a lot of other pictures too, a lot of boats and seas, but I liked the one on the farm. I couldn't remember the artist, even though he was famous. It depressed me, to think fame was so fleeting. Of course, if he had only people like me to remember him, no wonder it was fleeting.

So I watched Walter bending and moving, bending again, and heard the occasional snip of the shears, and it suddenly struck me that this was more real than anything else that had happened that day. The rest of it now seemed weightless as cornsilk, words and events blown about like the seeds of puffballs, colors that were as filmy as the way sun reflected on water.

I might have said, as people do, "It really opened my eyes." Or as Father Freeman liked to talk about "seeing through a glass darkly," though he didn't say it again to me after I told him to get a window washer. There's a word for things coming together, but I don't know what. It was a little like the rush of colored splinters you see when you turn a kaleidoscope and then the splinters rush to form a pattern.

What was the pattern here?

Then pretty soon Walter was clumping up the stairs holding nothing more than a big bunch of mint.

"Walter, you were out there long enough to cut an acre of corn."

He laughed his slow laugh. "I was tryin' to find the good-leafed ones. Anyways, don't bother yourself no more; I'll get it."

With that peculiar message, Walter swept by me and in through the screen door. I watched him walk over to the door on the other side of the kitchen and go out.

I went down the stairs and along the gravel to the Pink Elephant. I needed a place to think. The hotel cat materialized out of the darkness and pushed in after me. His smoky fur was damp from maneuvering through the same grass and mint Walter had been moving through, but the cat would have been searching out field mice. In a way they were alike; they had an object; they had a purpose. They just went and did. They didn't have a story.

The cat enjoyed lying on the table beside the hurricane lamp after I lit the candle. His pale eyes would flicker like the flame. He settled down now, paws battened to his chest, eyes slowly blinking, looking as if he'd come in for the purpose of sending me a message: *"Your thinking is murky."*

I was so downcast because I just couldn't take on the burden of this new complication—that Morris Slade could have had other children. Why would he? I frowned. And was it to do with his being a "playboy"? I had to admit I wasn't completely clear on the whole subject of sex, but whether I was or not, babies were still being born.

But then I told myself that Aurora just tossed this out about Morris Slade the way she tossed the comment out about Miss Isabel Barnett being completely undependable. For Aurora, it was just something to say.

The story had already gone down four different paths, none of them, apparently, right. First, the Girl was Ben Queen's granddaughter, meaning Fern's daughter; next, she was the Slade baby, Fay; next, Baby Fay wasn't even *at* the Belle Ruin that night—or any night—and so hadn't been kidnapped; next, the baby was there and there'd been this bogus kidnapping.

And now there was a fifth possibility: Fay hadn't grown up to become this girl at all.

The Girl I saw was somebody else.

And the awful question: Was she there at all? Or was I seeing things?

I just didn't know anyone to ask because I didn't know any crazy person, except Ree-Jane, and she probably wasn't really, but then what was all of her talking and laughing when no one was around—what was that about? She acted as if she were talking to some invisible person, smiling and sometimes outright laughing. Well, it made no difference. I could imagine asking Ree-Jane's advice; it would delight her no end that I thought I might be seeing things and she would certainly assure me that I was.

So it was better to go back to thinking that the Girl was not the person I'd thought she was, that she was just a girl, a visitor, a person who came and went, who appeared and disappeared, a pretty girl in a milky blue dress; or in red velvet, mailing a letter; or in black cotton, kneeling at a keyhole. A girl who melted into the canvas, a Fadeaway Girl.

28

The hand holding the hat was fine and manicured, the nails smooth and squared off; the hat was straw. I don't think I'd ever seen a man with a straw hat before. This one was as fine as the hand holding it.

The suit was white and seemed to go with summer. That's what he made me think of, summer and the sea.

He was leaning against the first of the dark wood booths in the Rainbow, his back to me, so that I could study him for many minutes without seeing his face. He was talking to someone sitting in the booth; I couldn't see who. I wondered why he didn't sit down. Well, no, I didn't; he didn't seem like a Rainbow Café kind of person.

He was tall, about the Sheriff's height, and probably handsome. I wondered if my life was to be filled with only handsome men, but then my eye fell on the regulars at the counter, Bubby Dubois and the Mayor, and I stopped wondering.

I was drinking a chocolate soda and trying to write the next installment of my *Conservative* piece. But I kept looking at the man with the straw hat. His arm was up and resting along the edge of the high-backed booth; his other hand turned the hat slightly, this way and that. The hat had a dark blue band around its crown. His ears lay flat against his head and his hair was different shades of light. His clothes and his whole back looked elegant.

I hadn't written a sentence and was pulling not much more than air up through my straw when Maud slid into the booth.

She whispered, "You know who that is?"

I stopped blowing through my straw and shook my head. "No, but I'm guessing it's Morris Slade."

She nodded. "Mayor Sims told me it was." She gave a little nod of her head, backward as if toward the counter.

"Who's he talking to?" I still was having a hard time believing he was here, in La Porte.

"Isabel Barnett." She scrunched over to the end of the table so that she could take a look at him, or his back.

He'd been standing there a good ten minutes, so it was more than a "Hi, nice day" kind of talk. What could she have to say of interest to Morris Slade?

"Why do you suppose he's back?" said Maud. "He hasn't been here since their baby was kidnapped."

"Or at least that's the last time we knew of."

"Don't complicate things," she said.

Why not? I wondered, watching her tapping a cigarette out of her pack of Camels.

"Lord, but he's handsome."

"I'm going to the courthouse. Excuse me." I slid across the seat and pushed out. He was two booths ahead, and as I passed—making sure I crowded him a little—I dropped my change purse, bent down to get it, then got up and said excuse me to him and hello to Miss Isabel. But I still didn't look at him because I was sure he'd know how hard I was trying to.

I trotted on and out, not failing to notice that most of the men at the counter and Wanda Waylans were snatching looks at him. Shirl didn't even give me her usual glum look as I walked out.

"He ain't here," said Donny Mooma, shifting his feet off his desk and standing up for the express purpose of sticking his thumbs in his big belt and thrusting out his chest as if he had one. "Sheriff's out on police business."

Maureen finger-waved a hello to me and I waved back. You would have thought we were worlds away instead of just across the room. It was a big room. She went back to her rat-a-tat typing.

Donny said, his tone sly, "Someone new in town we're all interested in."

Knowing he wanted me to ask, I didn't.

"Yeah, someone I ain't seen around these parts for a good twenty years. Back when my uncle was sheriff. Yeah, sheriffing talent runs in the family, I guess." He gave me a smile that was supposed to look know-it-all. "Caused a sensation, this fella did."

Maureen more or less sang out, "Morris Slade's who it is," and hit the typewriter carriage—*zzzzzzing*.

Donny turned on her. "Now, Maureen, you're not to go givin' out police details."

"Sorry." *Zzzzzing!* "I thought maybe you forgot his name."

"Ain't forgot nothin'. I just don't tell every Tom, Dick, and Harry walks in here po-lice business, that's all."

I said, "What's Morris Slade doing in town?"

The smirk. "Wouldn't you like to know?"

Yes. So would you.

Knowing there was no point in asking Donny where the Sheriff was or when he'd be back, I left the courthouse. It was only after leaving Donny that I thought of Dr. McComb.

Dr. McComb was retired and lived out on Valley Road. He was one of my favorite people and made the best brownies except for my mother's. The thing was, he'd been around back when Baby Fay had been kidnapped and must have known the Slades and the Woodruffs. The hotel might even have called a doctor when it happened in case the parents were hysterical or something.

"Valley Road." Delbert said this in a puzzled way. Tapping his thumbs on the steering wheel.

"Delbert, you drove me there a couple of weeks ago and another time before that. You know perfectly well where it is. Dr. McComb lives out Valley Road."

"Yeah, I *know,* I was just thinking: What's the best route?" He started up the cab, finally.

"There's only one route. You go to Red Bird Road and that leads to Valley Road."

He drove along Second Street so slowly you'd have thought there was a series of red lights down the block. "There's more'n one route I could take, like out around the country club—"

I should've walked; it would have taken me over an hour, but so what? "Just go as you did last time."

"Now, last time . . ."

I slid down in my seat and stayed there until we were passing Country Club Road. I wondered what La Porte and the area around were doing with a country club.

29

nstead of Dr. McComb, a strange woman I'd seen here before came to the door. She was even stranger than Mrs. Louderback's friend, or at least the experience was. She asked me what I wanted in a voice that sounded rusty, as if she didn't use it much. I know the first time I'd been here, we just sat and she didn't say a thing.

She did not answer my question about Dr. McComb's whereabouts, but just waved me in and sat down. She sat in a slipper chair and indicated I should sit across from her on the sofa. I did not know why.

But then I thought this might be my opportunity to find out about craziness. So I made my face look thoughtful. After a few moments of thoughtfulness, I said, "Did you ever know anyone who saw things that weren't there?"

She gave the merest inkling of a smile, as if she knew how but chose not to. It was worse than no smile at all. It was kind of eerie. "Things that weren't there," she repeated, as if it were a lesson.

I had the uncomfortable feeling that the things *were* there and maybe hanging around behind me, so I turned and looked. Then I turned back and said, "I have a friend, and she sees people that I don't think are really there."

She nodded, the ghost of a smile still in place, as if she knew the same people as my "friend." If she did, that was very bad news to me. I twisted a strand of my mousy brown hair around my finger and drew it through my mouth. This wasn't a habit of mine; I somehow felt I was keeping some distance between us, some space.

We stayed like that for some moments, so that I jumped when I heard a voice behind me. "Emma Graham!"

Dr. McComb came into the room with his butterfly net. His smile was the sort that knows it's a smile and means it. "Didn't know you were coming." He said this as if it were his fault.

"Hi, Dr. McComb." I jumped up and breathed easier.

"Talking to Betsy, are you?" He turned to her. "Betsy, how about you putting the kettle on?"

Betsy nodded and rose, giving me another memory of a smile on her way out. I'd never seen Betsy in the kitchen when Dr. McComb and I were in there having brownies and coffee.

"Come on, Emma. I've got my eye on a clouded yellow out back."

"Okay!" I wanted to sound really interested in butterflies, which I wasn't. Not that I disliked them, of course not; I just thought that hunkering down in tall grass and waiting for an hour wasn't time best spent.

But butterflies were Dr. McComb's first love. He had even written at least one book, which I had taken the trouble to read in the library. Also, I'd skimmed over other butterfly books and was grateful there were a lot of pictures. Studying up on someone else's hobbies is the best way to getting them to help you. You make it look like what they do is what you would have done too, had your life not taken a wrong turn.

We were out and around the corner of the house when he pulled up. "Wait. Kitchen. I was just about to put in the brownies. Lucky thing, you turning up."

Lucky is right. He was in and out of the kitchen in two winks and we proceeded along the path through the junglelike acres behind the house. The grass in some places was as tall as I was. I plowed after him down a path beaten from many years of his footsteps.

"I was just wondering—who's Betsy?"

"Sister-in-law." His eyeglasses slipped down his nose as he bent to inspect something. "My brother died ten years back and Betsy came to live with me. She's no trouble at all."

"Oh, I can see that. She's very quiet."

"As more people should be."

I didn't know about that. "She's quiet like someone who misses somebody a lot. Now, I have a friend like that and she makes up people, you know, the way kids do."

"Betsy's spent time in a mental institution. Broke down after Joe's death—that's my brother—and was in one for a year. You're pretty smart, figuring that out."

"Oh well, you know. If a person's grieving, it shows." Maybe it did, but not in Betsy's case.

We moved farther along the path and I swatted away a couple of butterflies. There was a school of pale yellow ones banking around Dr. McComb's head, and he looked as if he were bathed in light. "I wonder, did Betsy ever come across patients there who, well, saw people who weren't there?"

Dr. McComb swooped with his net and a dozen butterflies took off. "You mean hallucinating? Imagining you see something that's not there? Damn but I think that's a clouded yellow. Look."

I sighed and bent down and saw a butterfly that looked like all the other butterflies. "Hm. I don't think so."

He gave me a comical glance, surprised.

No wonder. "Because a clouded yellow's color isn't as bright as this one's." Clouded, in other words. A rule I tried to live by was that if you're going to pretend to know something you've really got to sound sure you know it. If you're wrong, at least it isn't a wishy-washy wrongness and you've given the impression you must know a lot more about the field. "Now, *that* one"—I was looking at the empty air—"too bad, you missed it. That one I think was your true clouded yellow."

He still turned to look back, but saw nothing.

"Of course," I said with a shrug, "I might be hallucinating."

He grinned and shoved back his cap and scrubbed at his head. "I doubt it. You're the last person on earth to start hallucinating."

What? "I am?"

"You got too much good sense; you got your feet so firmly on the ground they're practically in it. You're a tree." He pulled his cap straight.

I wasn't sure that last bit was a compliment, but I felt hugely relieved that he didn't think I was seeing things. "What if I saw someone several times, saw her more than *once,* see, that maybe wasn't there."

He frowned. "What makes you think she wasn't? Come on, time for brownies."

We moved fast along the path, followed by deep breaths of clouded yellows. Or some kind.

Brownies could turn a bad day around very fast, as if a day had two doors and I could walk through the bad one and out the good one with a brownie in hand. What I liked about Dr. McComb was that he would sift confectioners' sugar on them; it would fall soft as snow. My mother did this too, on cakes, using paper doilies to make designs. The cake would have a snowflake pattern on top. They were beautiful cakes, layers and layers of light sponge held together by a chocolate or vanilla cream filling.

Dr. McComb and I sat at the kitchen table eating brownies and drinking coffee. My coffee was mostly milk, but being offered any coffee at all was a new experience. There was no sign at all of Betsy. I wondered if she ever ate brownies.

As usual, we kept an eye on the brownie pan, "reserving," you could say, our second brownies. Almost always, our eyes went to the same one, but we were always polite about not taking it. I should say Dr. McComb was polite. As I was the guest, I naturally got the pick of the second brownie. But I gave him the pick of the third.

Just now we were on our first brownies. I continued talking about the Girl and hallucinations. "The thing is, she always looks the same. I mean, she always wears exactly the same clothes."

His forehead furrowed. "I been wearing the same clothes for a decade or more. The same clothes doesn't signify."

I had almost forgotten about Morris Slade. I hadn't come to talk about the Girl—indeed, I was surprised I'd talked about her at all. "Do you remember the Slades? Especially Morris Slade?"

"The one that married the Woodruff girl; of course I remember. They were the parents of that baby who was kidnapped out of the Belle Ruin hotel. Couldn't forget that, hardly. They went back to New York and we've not seen them since. Stands to reason they just wanted to put this place behind them." He paused. "What happened to that poor little child to this day remains a deep mystery."

"Morris Slade's in town. I saw him in the Rainbow Café."

Dr. McComb set his cup back in its saucer. "Well, now, that's news. I haven't laid eyes on Morris for over twenty years."

"Did you know him when he lived here? I get the impression that people think he wasn't much good. You know, the playboy type."

He chuckled the way you hear little kids do, but hardly ever grown-ups. Chuckles like that come from deep within a person.

"I guess that's kind of true. Morris was handsome even as a kid; in his teens he had every girl in town hot on his heels. As a man, he went with first one woman, then another and another. Not all La Porte girls, either. City girls. Had a job in banking, I think, in"—he studied the brownie pan —"Philadelphia, was it?" His hand went for a center brownie.

I had been thinking so hard I'd forgotten to make my brownie choice, which was the same as his. I picked the next best. "I thought playboys didn't take to work."

"Not much, I guess. Had a bit of trouble there. I think he was some kind of bookkeeper and money came up short."

"You mean he stole it?"

"There was talk, yes. Let's say, for instance, that, oh, Jane Davidow is employed as bookkeeper at your hotel—"

That was already a big fat zero.

"—so when, say, a guest pays a hundred dollars for his room, Jane enters eighty onto the books and keeps twenty herself."

Now that kind of "bookkeeping" I could picture her doing. "Did he go to jail?"

"Oh no. Nothing was ever proved."

"But did you know him personally? I mean enough to have some feeling about what he was like?"

"Yes. Morris struck me as a complete charmer. The most charming man I ever met."

"A playboy."

He smiled and polished off his third brownie.

30

Once again in the rear booth of the Rainbow Café, I wrote:

The story of the Devereaus doesn't end here; it doesn't even begin here.

I stopped. That had a familiar ring to it; it sounded like something I'd read or heard. Since the only writers I was currently familiar with were the author of the Perry Mason mysteries and William Faulkner, my guess was William ("Billy," as Dwayne called him) had said it. I was pretty sure Perry Mason hadn't. I would have to ask Dwayne.

So I read my opener again and decided to let it stand, as it was really good. It was hard enough writing like somebody else, much less making it all up myself.

I looked at the empty seat opposite me, at the empty air, at the ceiling, the walls. I heard the noises that came back to me, the rattle of dishes, the voice of Jo Stafford emptying out a pitcher of something sweet. All the emptiness.

"The Devereau sisters lived a life of great emptiness." No. "An empty life. Lives." I didn't know that. And Rose certainly hadn't led an empty life, nor Iris. I should speak only of Isabel, anyway. She was the murderer. Yes, a murderer could lead an empty life—in her case, that's what was wrong. Or it could be. "Isabel Devereau lived an empty life." I wanted to add, "and she took it out on me," but that sounded too . . . I frowned and tapped my pencil on the table. Too whining. It wasn't the point either. Even if she did take it out on me. I wrote, "and she had to take it out on someone." It was clear who, especially if I underlined *"someone."* It said the same thing without the whine.

How could I tie this to my point about beginnings and endings? I cupped my chin in my hand and listened to Shirl yell at somebody, probably Wanda, as "You Belong to Me" wrapped up on the jukebox.

All I wanted was to get to the next chapter. "The story doesn't end here, as I said." I crossed out "as I said," which sounded like filler. Suzie Whitelaw was always going on about "filler." Lazy man's writing.

"For the Devereaus had a brother—" But wait: what would he have been to Iris and Isabel? Step? Half of half? Morris's father was a Slade. Rose's was a Souder. I couldn't figure this out, so I wrote, "All families are complicated; this one was complicated in its own way." And *that* had a familiar sound too. William Faulkner again? No. A Perry Mason case? Well, I'd think about that later. But the half brother, Morris, was *Rose's* half brother. Morris Slade and Rose had the same mother, but different fathers. So what was Morris to the other Devereau sisters?

My head was in my hands. This was taking me *hours,* it felt like. There were people in this world who got paid for figuring out families, and I wasn't one of them. So I'd just move on.

"The handsome and charming" (in case he read this) "Morris Slade married into the rich"—no—"well-to-do Woodruff family of New York City. Morris"—no—"Mr. Slade married Lucien Woodruff's daughter, Imogen. They had one child, Fay, whom they brought as a baby to La Porte one summer. . . .

"And here begins the tragedy of the Belle Ruin."

There! Now all I had to do was tell the tragedy. I'd take this to Mr. Gumbrel just so he could see I was really working, and then finish it later. Maybe, just *maybe,* he would even use what I had here as a kind of "watch this space" sort of thing. "To be continued in the next issue," or something.

I had put in a good morning's work and was quite satisfied. Maud came back with a cup of coffee and sat down, and I asked her what time it was.

She glanced at her watch. "Eleven twenty-three."

What? Did this mean I'd been writing for only *twenty minutes?* Twenty minutes? How did writers stand it if they put in a whole morning doing this?

"What are you working on?"

I was still irritated with the twenty minutes. "My story. This is a new part."

"Good. Everyone's waiting to read it, I can tell you."

Even with the compliment, I felt grumpy. "Do you think there's any connection between what you write and how long it takes you?"

"No."

Ah. *"No?* In other words, you could write something very good in, say, twenty minutes?"

"Of course. Did you ever hear of Trollope's working habits?"

Since I'd never heard of Trollope, I didn't know his working habits. "No."

"He put a watch on his desk. He forced himself to write two hundred and fifty words or somewhere near that every fifteen minutes."

I just stared. "How many fifteen minutes did he write in a day?" That, I thought, was key.

Maud thought about it, looking at my page, which I covered up by leaning over it. "Well, probably four. That would be an hour. He'd have a thousand words then. But that was Trollope. Think about Flannery O'Connor."

"How much did he write?"

"She. The thing is, she would sit down at her desk and stay there for four hours even if she couldn't write a word."

Talk about mouths dropping open. If I had ten mouths, they all would have hit the floor. "You've got to be *kidding*."

Maud drank her coffee. "Or she's got to be lying."

We both laughed.

Then we began talking about the kidnapping and what the reason for it could be.

I said, "What about the baby's great-grandfather—I mean, Mr. Woodruff's own father? I think his name was Raphael and he was really, really rich and he wanted his money left to his great-grandchild, Fay—"

"Why not just his grandchild Imogen?"

"Maybe he thought she was useless. It sounds as if she was really spoiled."

Maud was toying with a cigarette she couldn't decide to smoke.

I said, "Another reason could be Imogen hated the baby."

"Why would she?"

I thought of my hospital scenarios and frowned. I was missing something obvious. I raised my frown to take in Maud.

"What's wrong? Did I say something?"

"No. I did, but I don't know what."

"You said maybe Imogen hated Fay."

I nodded. But whatever notion had been lurking at the back of my mind had now escaped me. "Maybe Fay had something wrong with her." I remembered Miss Isabel Barnett's remark about Down disease, although she had the wrong baby. "Maybe she was deformed or would never grow beyond four or five mental years, or something."

"How horrible—to get rid of a child just because she wasn't perfect."

This could be tiresome if Maud was going to get preachy about everything. "Well, but we're not judging here; we're just trying to work out what happened."

Maud lit the cigarette, waved out the match, frowning in thought.

I said, "There's another possibility: it could have been an accident."

Maud blew out a stream of smoke, still frowning. "No. If it was accidental, why go to such lengths to cover the death up? Staging a kidnapping is pretty extreme. And if you're bribing or paying off other people, that makes it even harder to keep control. You're leaving a string of witnesses behind you and one just might talk—as one did: Gloria Spiker."

"But there's other kinds of accidents where people—in this case, parents—are to blame, where the law says they're negligent. For instance, mothers who leave their children in cars while they shop. Or leave them alone in the house."

Maud just looked at me, her frown deepening. "But any kind of accident would mean Morris Slade was in on it, and Sheriff Mooma didn't think he was."

Shirl was calling her name again, and she said, "I've got to scoot, Emma. We'll talk later." She tamped out her cigarette and slid out of the booth.

I sat for a few moments, then gathered up my paper and pencil and scooted too.

31

Mr. Gumbrel was sitting at his desk in the back of the newspaper office.

"I just wanted to run this by you. I called a couple of times, but you weren't here." No, I hadn't. As if the only thing holding up the installment of the story was his not answering the phone. "I need to know what you think of this story line."

"Shoot."

When I looked at the little I'd written, I felt disloyal.

"I'm all ears; go ahead." As if to prove his point, he cupped his hand behind his ear.

I cleared my throat and went ahead: "'The story of the Devereaus doesn't end here: it doesn't even begin here.'"

Mr. Gumbrel brought his fist down into his hand. "Now that's good!" He paused. "Sounds a little familiar. But go on."

I continued with my diagnosis of the Devereaus, not contributing much beyond their "empty lives," which I repeated in three different ways, at least.

Mr. Gumbrel nodded seriously. "You're right there. Isabel Devereau—hell, probably none of them had inner resources. That's what gets you in trouble. That accounts for all this emptiness."

I was pleased mostly by his interruptions, which made what I'd written sound several times longer than it was. "Now," I said, "this is where it gets interesting—the Devereau sisters' relation to Morris Slade."

His reaction was pleasing. Mr. Gumbrel apparently didn't know there *was* a relationship, as his next words bore out.

"Morris *Slade*? What's he have to do with them? He'd have been only a kid, wouldn't he? Much younger than them."

I told him what Miss Flyte had said.

"Well, I'll be a monkey's. So he's a half brother of theirs."

"Of hers, I mean of Rose Devereau's. Not of the other three." I was about to say he looked just like Rose Devereau Queen; then I thought of the Girl and Fay and wondered if they both were gone.

A sadness washed over me. "What I'm thinking is that they got rid of her. The baby. Not necessarily all of them were in on it. Maybe just the mother or maybe Mr. Woodruff." I heeded the Sheriff's warning.

That shocked him. "You mean killed her?" He flattened his hand against his forehead, then started, but didn't finish, a laugh. "Emma, you've got murder on your mind."

"I'm not the one doing them."

"Now, you're not thinking of writing that up, are you? What you just said?"

"Of course not. Not without evidence." Of which there was none, as the Sheriff had pointed out.

"And with Morris Slade in town, I don't think he'd take to such a story."

The interview! I'd almost forgotten. That could be the rest of the story, or, rather, the last of the "Aftermath" and the first of "The Belle Ruin Tragedy."

"Mr. Gumbrel, what I'm thinking is that the part I just read to you could introduce the three interviews. The eyewitness accounts of that night. The alleged kidnapping." I sat back and tried not to indulge in the childish habit of kicking my feet back against the chair rungs. I only did it a few times, for I was beginning to feel flyaway, as if I weren't pinned to the chair and the chair not anchored to earth. It probably all came from too much thinking.

I slid off the chair and said, "I think I'll have a look in the archives if that's okay."

Mr. Gumbrel patted my arm and told me to go ahead, and if he'd known what a hard worker I'd turned out to be, he'd have fired everyone else "including myself"—we both laughed—"and just let you take over."

I thanked him for saying it, knowing he was exaggerating, but not by much, having watched Suzie Whitelaw at nonwork.

It wasn't really old accounts in newspapers I wanted to see, but the magazine covers of Fadeaway Girls. I looked in the tall piles on the table inside the door and found five of them.

I lined them up and sat down to study them, beginning with the Christmas issue, the girl in the red coat, trimmed in white fur. It was the white fur that kept the coat from being absorbed completely into the background.

Sometimes the fadeaway trick was done with color, sometimes with pattern or texture. There were white birches in gold and amber woods, with a girl dressed in amber and white taking long strides through the autumn, and a collie dog with a white and amber coat running beside her.

I liked the maid in black, down on one knee, peeking through a keyhole. The uniform reminded me of Vera, but certainly not the face, which was young and pretty. The black uniform was all but blotted up in the black background, revealing its lines by means of the white apron tied in back and the white cuffs. I liked her nosiness, as it matched mine, except there were no keyholes around the hotel big enough to see through. If there were, I'd spend most of the day down on one knee, I'm sure.

I sat there with my chin in my hands, my elbows on the table, and tried to see the line where the white dress met the snow-covered pine, the coat of the collie met the leaves, the connecting lines, but there weren't any. That was the point, wasn't it? If the artist had made the dress or coat or collie all one color, all of the Fadeaway Girl would be gone except for the head and perhaps the hands.

It was as if they were drowning in color.

32

I got back to the hotel in the afternoon; to avoid Delbert, I had walked. I stopped in the Big Garage to see how lunch had gone and if my mother was angry with me for missing it.

Will was doing something with colored scarves; it looked like he was pulling them out of nowhere, as in a magician's book of tricks. "Where'd you learn that?"

"From Ralph. It's not all that hard."

I was glad at least he wasn't calling him "Rafe."

"Hello, missus," said Paul, jumping and breathing hard; he was out of the rafters for a change. Not much of a change, for now he was jumping on a trampoline, a big one I'd never seen before.

Will yanked him off it.

"What's the trampoline for? And what are you doing with those scarves?" It was hard to keep up with them.

"Practicing tricks. We decided there should be a magician in this play."

He was so pleased with himself, he forgot they never told people anything about their productions if they could help it.

"Who's the magician?"

"I am."

"Wait a minute. You're the pilot. Why is the pilot a magician?"

"Maybe the copilot."

I heaved a sigh. Sometimes talking to Will I'd sooner have kneeled on the driveway and eaten gravel. "So who plays the *copilot*?"

"I do." He pulled a sapphire blue scarf from the vicinity of Paul's ear. "I'm both." He started winding the blue scarf around Paul's neck.

"*Both?* You can't be both the pilot and the copilot."

It was Will's turn to heave a sigh. "For God's sake! I mean the copilot and the magician." He pulled on the ends of the scarf. Paul made a gurgling sound. "Look, who wrote this play anyhow?"

I shrugged. "Walter?"

"Ha-ha. Me. I did. Mill and me." He generously corrected himself. "Haven't you ever heard of imagination?"

Mill was back at the piano, picking up Will's word:

> *Imagination*
> *Is silly,*
> *You go around willy-nilly—*

Long ripples of the notes came here.

Willy-nilly was right, and I was standing between them: Will and Nill.

Will forgot about suffocating Paul and joined Mill at the piano.

> *For example, I go around want-ing yoooouuuu—*

They harmonized, as if life were just one long duet.

I tried to plug in the here and now. "So why don't you have this Ralph be the magician?"

Mill stopped running ripples and they both turned to look at me as if I hadn't been there all along. This wasn't surprising, since people kept popping up out of nowhere these days.

The door to the garage actually opened—I mean, it wasn't locked up as it always was when I came up here—and in walked Joanne and Peggy Tree. They had come just that morning with their mother,

Priscilla. Their father never came, and I can't say I blame him. I wondered how many sets of girls there were around here, having just met up with the Evanses yesterday.

The Trees were the prissiest girls I'd ever run into. They were eleven and thirteen, which meant I was in charge of whatever fun they'd have (according to my mother and Lola Davidow, since I was twelve). If Peggy was what it was like to be thirteen, I would just go to sleep for a year and wake up fourteen.

They were both insufferable, but Peggy more so, since she thought being in her teens made her queen of everything. She lorded it over me and even tried to hang out with Ree-Jane, who was nearly seventeen by now. For once I admired her horrible manners: every time Peggy came around, Ree-Jane walked the other way.

Joanne wasn't quite as bad as Peggy, but that was only because she hadn't lived two years longer.

They took lessons in everything: horseback riding, tennis, iceskating, piano (which gave Mill a few laughs), and ballet. They came into the garage dangling ballet shoes of pink satin. They weren't wearing that tulle-stuff ballerinas do, but their dresses were still flouncy. Priscilla claimed to be a children's clothes designer. I said if Mrs. Tree was a designer, I was Jim Beam. That got a big laugh out of Mrs. Davidow.

Priscilla joined in the cocktail hour, but she wasn't any fun. Mrs. Davidow was always rolling her eyes at Priscilla, who insisted she was an expert cocktail maker and once asked Lola Davidow if she knew how to make a "truly dry martini." That was like asking John Dillinger if he knew the way to Chicago.

Even Miss Bertha mocked "the stuck-up Trees," as she called them. She went so far as to straighten up and put her nose in the air, which, considering her hump, took a lot of grit.

I watched the Tree girls strapping on their satin toe shoes, and then the two started pattering around and waving their arms in the air.

"What are they supposed to be doing?" I asked Will, who was

now sitting by Chuck in the so-called cockpit of the plane. Chuck was their lighting expert.

"We haven't decided yet."

"You've got a couple of toe dancers on an airplane with a dead body and you don't know why they're *there*?"

"Well, we know one thing," said Chuck, snuffling a laugh around in his nose.

Will joined in. "Yeah."

Mill was down at the piano riffling away at "Paper Moon."

Peggy and Joanne were circling around with their eyes closed, bouncing up and down on their toes to some tune in their heads that wasn't Mill's.

Paper moon. Trampoline. Toe dancers.

I could just imagine.

BYE, BYE, BLACKBIRD

33

I considered the best time to approach Morris Slade and decided on the cocktail hour, when people always seemed to be less on guard. That is, drinkers were. I certainly assumed Morris Slade was one. He had, after all, been a playboy.

I would present myself as working for the *Conservative* and wanting an interview for the story of the Belle Ruin. This had the disadvantage of being the truth. I'd rather have pretended to be selling Girl Scout cookies (the Girl Scouts being a bunch I would drop dead before joining). But here I was stuck with the truth.

Usually, a cocktail hour went from around five to six, although Mrs. Davidow could stretch that at either end, as could Aurora Paradise. It was not a good time for me, as I was supposed to be in the kitchen at five thirty.

My work for the newspaper, however, gave me leeway. So I asked Walter, who was always in the kitchen, to tell my mother I'd be a little late, as I was interviewing someone for my article. I also told Walter to take a drink up to Aurora Paradise at five o'clock. It was ready in the icebox behind the big block of ice.

"What kind is it?" Walter was always interested in my drink menu. He was wiping a big platter. Doing dishes was a continuous process—washing, wiping—so Walter was always doing them.

I shrugged. "I just made it out of scraps. Some Jim Beam, some Gordon's gin, and some orange and pineapple juice."

Walter thought about that at length. "You can call it a Gin Beam."

"Good, Walter!" I clapped. "That's really good! She'll like that!" Aurora would like anything in a glass that could walk on its own.

I had the night before prepared my questions carefully and would not ask anything in a way that would put Morris Slade off; that is, not ask anything in an accusing manner the way police always did: "And where were you between nine o'clock and eleven o'clock on the night of the murder?" Would the person who'd done it answer, "I was in the room with the victim"?

I wanted to look businesslike, so I searched my wardrobe for something ironed. I found a plain blue-and-white-checkered dress.

Usually, I looked wrinkled, even my hair. Even my face, if it had been lying against a pillow, as sometimes it was when I watched *Perry Mason*.

I sat at my makeshift dressing table, a painted board balanced across twin dressers, and brushed my hair a lot. It was straight and hung to my shoulders and looked completely businesslike. I wanted to leave the flowery barrettes out, but then my hair would be flopping around and getting in my eyes and not like Veronica Lake's, either. My ears wouldn't hold it back the way I have seen women's ears do, like models and movie stars, as if their ears were made for that purpose. I pushed the barrettes back in. I then tried out several smiles and was satisfied with the one that looked friendly, but not overly.

It was half past four when I left the hotel grounds, and I took my time walking across the highway to the other side of Spirit Lake. The Woodruff house sat a few houses down and across from Mrs. Louderback's.

The single car parked at the curb was the red convertible I had taken for Morris Slade's when I'd driven by with Delbert. I decided I would stroll by once or twice, just to see if there was any life going on inside. Since it was not yet dark, I couldn't tell by inside lighting if any of the houses were occupied. Windows merely squared off interior darkness.

There were a few people here and there sitting out on their porches, fatly bunched on creaking metal gliders or glued into rocking chairs. They were extremely interested in me, as I was the only thing moving out here at the moment.

So here I now stood on the Woodruffs' porch, pushing a bell which chimed distantly inside as if church bells were ringing in another town.

Here I was, my questions prepared, my clothes, my hair, my smile prepared.

What I wasn't prepared for was Morris Slade himself.

34

He opened the door and said, "Hello," and I just stood there like a scarecrow, only ironed. Birds could have nested in my brightly brushed hair or perched on my barrettes, and I wouldn't have moved.

He said it again—"Hello"—with an even bigger smile, as if my silence amused him, although he didn't give the impression he was laughing at me.

I cleared my throat, which at least showed I could make a sound, balled up my fist in front of my mouth as if I were about to cough, rehearsed the word "hello" in my head to see if it was a real word, then blurted out: "My name is Emma Graham."

My mouth snapped shut like Ree-Jane's silver compact. I would even have been glad—unbelievable!—for Ree-Jane's presence, if only to take up the slack.

Morris Slade took it up himself. "Emma Graham. That sounds familiar, for some reason. Please come in."

I walked into a room full of shadows and plants. It was cool; it smelled green and somehow drenched. The silky rug I was standing on might as well have been water. I thought for a moment it had started to rain outside, but the whispery sound came from the turning palms of the ceiling fan.

I could have been in the Florida Keys with Humphrey Bogart in a hurricane, but I was in Spirit Lake with Morris Slade in air stirred by a fan. Either way, it had to be a movie.

He picked up an elaborately cut martini glass (one thing I can always identify), raised it a bit, and said, "Would you like something to drink?"

I almost said, "Whatever you're having," but caught myself. "Yes, thank you."

He turned to a highly polished table, walnut, or maybe cherry, that the fan veiled in moving shadows and which held a lot of bottles and an ice bucket (another familiar item).

"Coca-Cola? Root beer? Scotch?" He smiled.

I smiled back. "Coke, please."

He picked up a glass, not a squatty, ordinary one, but one like his own, dropped an ice cube in it, and filled it with Coke. Then he set it on a table beside a rattan chair across from a matching sofa. "Sit down, why don't you?"

Why didn't I? I did.

So did he, on the sofa. "You've got a journal there." He nodded at my spiral notebook. "You're a writer?"

I was astonished that he would say this, and more that he would say it without a hint of sarcasm or teasing. I was astonished right out of my trance. This person had had a lot of practice being wonderful.

"Well, yes. I mean I'm writing this long story for the *Conservative*. You know."

He nodded. "The local paper."

"I'm interviewing people." But I didn't know how to get to it: the Belle Ruin. The kidnapping. I wondered, as I hadn't before (since I was too busy being me), if it might be truly upsetting for him. If he wasn't involved, if his baby had really disappeared . . . Why hadn't I considered his feelings before? Where was all of my smooth preparation? I looked down at my notebook.

Morris Slade had taken a cigarette case out of his jacket pocket and was tapping a cigarette against its silver surface. "I'm a person of interest here?"

I nodded. "See, this starts forty years ago, with the Devereau sisters." I felt like I was walking a minefield. "There was Mary-Evelyn, first."

"First?"

"The first death. They said she drowned. But she was murdered by her sisters."

"My God." He stopped in the process of bringing his lighter up to his cigarette. "This isn't just gossip? I mean, you're sure of it?"

I nodded.

"Rose Devereau was my half sister, but I hardly— I was a lot younger than Rose." He lit the cigarette, inhaled, exhaled. "It wasn't long after I was married that Rose was killed by her husband—or so it was assumed."

"Ben Queen. No. Her daughter Fern killed her."

The cigarette stopped on its way to the ashtray. Something jarred him here. "What? I didn't hear about that."

"Well, nobody did. It's only recently been discovered." I'd have liked to add *by me,* but didn't. "Ben Queen, Fern's father, knew it. He took the blame."

"Good Lord. How do you know all this, Emma?"

"It's the story I'm writing—well, part of it." I picked up the gorgeous glass that held my Coca-Cola. It tasted a lot better than Coke usually tasted. Cold from the melted ice cube, the drink revived me a little. I moved into my smoothly prepared questions. "Now. You used to live in La Porte, didn't you?"

He smoked and seemed to be watching me through narrowed eyes.

I was twelve. What was to watch?

"I did, yes. I was born here, as a matter of fact."

"But you haven't been back in twenty years. Well, I was told that."

His smile was slighter. "You were told?"

"Someone said he was surprised to see you, that you hadn't been here in a long time. Since"—I went for it —"the Belle Ruin."

He paused. He smoked again. "How does the Belle Ruin fit into this story about the Devereaus?"

Because I'm fitting it in, I wanted to say. "I'll tell you how: Too many bad things happen around here. Three murders, an attempted murder, a kidnapping." I paused, feeling sorrowful. "Your baby."

Then I knew why I was fitting it all in. "I'm calling it 'Tragedy Town.'"

35

I t had just come to me, and I wish it hadn't.

Tragedy Town.

It was from that point, from the point of my merely saying it, that things began to change. I don't mean change in the sense of weather changing or fortunes being lost or made, or even luck turning. It was more in the way the world looked.

I stood on the pavement outside the Woodruff house after Morris Slade had driven off in his red sports car, and I sort of seized up, the way an engine does, the way the engine of Dwayne's truck did once. Or it was like getting a muscle cramp. I could not seem to get to the next thought. Maybe this was really writer's block, even though I wasn't writing.

I just stood there staring into the gray light. Everything looked rinsed by rain, not clearer and brighter, but sadder. When a thought did come, it was of the Waitresses. It was strange to me I could not remember how many there were. Usually I saw three of them. But it could have been four or five. They probably did not all come at the same time, yet I always saw them together, a flock of bright birds, flying into my small life and then flying away.

I had to get my feet moving toward the hotel. When my feet did move, it was with an old person's shuffle. I just didn't want to go much of anyplace. I wanted to lie down in the grass or lean against the fence and do nothing, except think over what Morris Slade had said. Or not said.

"That's pretty terrible, Emma. When did all of this happen? And to whom? The little Devereau girl was drowned, you said. Ben Queen's daughter. And Rose." He looked away at that, his cigarette busy with an ashtray that stood on a tall brass pillar. "An attempted murder? Whom did that happen to?"

"Me."

I told him the story, in every bit of detail I could think of. I must, he said, have been terrified, and yet I'd been almost unbelievably self-possessed.

I agreed.

"And Ben Queen saved you?" Yes. He thought for a long time. "Ben Queen is a good man. I never did think he killed Rose. He loved her too much."

When I say he fell silent, falling is a lot like what it was, as if he had been up here in the half-light and then suddenly dropped into something murkier and far more troubling.

"That's what I thought too," I said, and then found myself in the same troubled waters. I felt things were hard for him, and couldn't bring myself to mention the Belle Ruin again.

But he did: "The Belle Ruin. Is that part of your story?"

My mind quickened, and I said, "Yes," before he could change his. "A big part. It's the most mysterious thing that's ever happened around here."

He smoked and looked at me for a while. "You've got a theory, haven't you?"

"Well . . ." I looked off through one of the long windows where I made out the thin silver threads of a spider's web. Where were my roundabout ways? Why weren't they helping me now? A tiny spider dangled from the end of a thread. My vision seemed to have increased by about a thousand percent.

He said, "There were a lot of theories. One was certainly that the kidnapping never happened." For the first time he picked up his glass and drank.

All that came to mind was that Lola Davidow would never have let a martini sit idly by that way. "I know; I heard that too. And that Mr. Woodruff paid off the police not to investigate."

He just looked at me. Then he said, "It really did happen, though."

"There was never any ransom demand?"

"No."

We sat for a little bit in silence and then he glanced at his watch and apologized and said he had to go; he had an appointment.

I realized, after the car drove off, that I had missed my golden opportunity. Why hadn't I asked him why he was back in La Porte? What had brought him here? Oh, he said he'd be glad to talk to me again, that, very briefly, he and his wife had never found out what happened to their child and it had been awful, the worst thing that had ever happened to him.

So I plodded along, irritated with myself.

But then I thought, Morris Slade hadn't really wanted to talk about the kidnapping or about Baby Fay.

You can't hang around in Tragedy Town for long or you might never leave.

36

next tried out the idea of "Tragedy Town" on Miss Flyte and Miss Flagler.

Miss Bertha and Mrs. Fulbright were the only guests for dinner that night, and they were done by six thirty. I phoned for a cab ahead of time and was climbing into it before seven.

I had told my mother I wanted to see the movie at the Orion. What movie? she asked, trying to keep a grip on my movie education.

"Public Enemy," I said, "with James Cagney."

"That's an old movie, isn't it? It's much too violent."

You'd think she'd never spent a day at the Hotel Paradise. Ten minutes up in the Big Garage would make James Cagney look like her best pal.

"I guess it is," I agreed, and went into town anyway.

I told Delbert to drop me off at the Orion Theater. Delbert (as always) wanted to know what I was doing going into town in the evening.

"If I want you to drop me at the Orion, what do you think?"

"You gonna see that James Cagney movie? That's what I want to see. I like them gangster shows."

"I like men with guns." I said this despite my vow never to give

Delbert any information to chew over. My world had altered; things were just popping out. I'd have to watch myself.

Delbert liked the "men with guns" comment; he hee-hawed and slapped the steering wheel as if I'd just said the funniest thing.

I don't know why I'd said it, unless men with guns seemed an obvious part of my sadder worldview.

When I piled out of the cab in front of the Orion, Delbert asked me what I was going to do until the movie started, which wouldn't be for another half hour.

"Shoot up the place," I said, and slammed the door.

As well as their morning coffee break, Miss Flyte and Miss Flagler often had dinner together in Miss Flagler's kitchen after their work-day was done. Their shops were dark in front, their living quarters lighted behind.

However, Miss Flyte's plate-glass storefront window was never completely dark. She owned the Candlewick, and there were always candles burning in it after dark. Not real ones, of course, but electri-fied ones; still, their small lights gave the impression of flickering flames.

The two of them were always glad to see me. I guess I did have a kind of entertainment value, what with all the murders and near murders, and *Medea, the Musical* updates, and reports of the people who'd come to town. Which was what we were talking about now as I blew on my cocoa and they blew on their coffee.

"Morris Slade! I can't believe it," said Miss Flagler.

Miss Flyte said, "Now, why do you suppose he's back? And in the Woodruff house?"

They both looked at me, thinking I had the answer. "I guess be-cause it's their house," I said. "Did you know him well?"

"Yes. Back as far as when he was a boy and later when he was a teenager and pretty wild."

"Isn't it hard to be wild around here?"

Miss Flyte laughed. "There were girls around here, after all. And he went away several times; he went to work in Philadelphia, didn't he?"

I knew all of this.

Miss Flagler nodded. "He worked in a bank. Something happened there, but it was never clear what. To do with bank money, I think."

"Embezzlement," said Miss Flyte, "is what I understood."

"It was never proven," I said. When they both looked surprised, I said, "It's just that I was doing research for my story and I came across an old newspaper." I took a drink of my marshmallowy cocoa.

Miss Flagler said, "Then there was that scandal with the girl."

I stopped chewing my marshmallow. "What scandal?"

"Well, while Morris was engaged to Imogen Woodruff, they discovered that Morris had another girlfriend." They glanced at each other and both dropped their eyes.

They were afraid of talking about sex, I guess. I would have been more curious but I didn't have time. I had too many things on my mind. Breezily, I said, "Don't worry. I know all about that. What girl?"

Miss Flagler had retrieved the coffeepot from the stove and now filled the cups. She picked up the enamel pan of cocoa and poured me some more. "All we know is that Imogen's father paid someone"—here her eyebrows danced wickedly for Miss Flagler—"to break it up."

I was all over this bit of news. "Paid Morris, you mean?"

"Or the girl."

I don't know how he had any money left, Mr. Woodruff was so busy paying off people. I wondered why I hadn't heard about this other girl and said so.

"She wasn't a local girl. It happened in Philadelphia, I think, where she was from. The only reason we know about it is Betty Sue Crouch—you know, she lives over on Red Bird Road—"

I didn't but I nodded, so as not to get off the track with Betty Sue Crouch.

"Well, Imogen asked Betty Sue to take some wedding presents to Morris's apartment in Philadelphia—Betty Sue was going there to do some shopping. She did it, showed up at the apartment, and there was Morris with this girl."

"In his apartment?"

"Most definitely in his apartment."

Another swift sex-glance was exchanged. But I didn't care about the details, only about him having this other girlfriend. "So they broke up?"

Miss Flagler nodded hard.

"And Imogen stood for this?"

"I think she just had to have Morris Slade. He was quite a catch: the looks, the charm, the talk." She sighed. "I think Morris could talk his way into or out of anything. He was never a faithful boy, Morris."

Sadly Miss Flyte said this, as if Morris Slade had broken faith with her too. "Morris could really draw one in. I think it was the way he seemed so *interested*. That's a rare quality."

I knew what she meant, but I didn't like thinking he hadn't really meant his interest.

I went to scratch my head, but the cat Albertine did it for me. She was up there lounging on the shelf. "I think he's here because of his kidnapped baby, really."

As I had done with Dr. McComb, I told them the theory involving Imogen and her father.

"I just don't see how that's *possible,* Emma! To put your own child through all of that? But that's—depraved." Miss Flagler shook her head.

As did Miss Flyte, generally better able to accept unpleasant news, but I guess not in this case. Then I told them my idea for my newspaper piece.

"'Tragedy Town'? La Porte?" Miss Flagler nervously spooned extra sugar into her coffee and stirred.

Miss Flyte had her cup raised and smiled at me over it. "Not a nice sobriquet, I think."

Whatever that meant, she didn't mean the smile. I said, "I didn't mean it to be nice." I looked from the one to the other, wondering why this upset them, and could only think that I was ruffling waters they were used to seeing as smooth, even glassy.

"But, look, it's not La Porte only," I added. "There's Spirit Lake and Cold Flat Junction and Lake Noir and Soldiers Park, where the Belle Ruin was. See, it's all of those places together." I grew excited by this as I spoke and spooned what was left of a marshmallow out of my cup. "It's like all of those places are one place—no, all of those places are . . . What's the word?" Was there a word? "You know, the way you make moonshine liquor."

"In a still, you mean? Oh, you mean *distilled*."

I nodded. "All distilled into one place. One town."

"It's just so unpleasant." Miss Flagler shivered a little.

More unpleasant than what happened to Mary-Evelyn Devereau? "It's just a theory."

"The thing is, Emma, when you work with things like wax"—for Miss Flyte not only sold candles, but also made them—"that is, when you get creative and start, well, *re*inventing something, the wax sticks to you, gets under your fingers, you know."

What was she saying? What were *they* saying? It was almost as if they thought I was some kind of danger to them.

Me. Emma Graham. Age twelve and dangerous.

It was seven forty-five when I left Miss Flagler's, so the movie had already started, but I didn't mind that. You could always lose the first fifteen minutes of any movie and still understand what was going on.

Even though I was missing the movie's beginning, I stood before the poster of James Cagney looking squint-eyed and grim, as he always did with a machine gun in his hands; it was like a wild thing he couldn't control. I wondered if the movie would make things more dangerous for me or less. Would James Cagney's snarl wear off on me? I could see why Dillinger was dangerous, but why was I?

I must have taken on some of James Cagney's grimness as I stepped into the lobby, for Mr. McComas, who owned the theater and often sold tickets from a big roll, looked concerned.

"You okay, Emma?" he asked as he tore off a ticket.

I guess I unclenched my teeth satisfactorily, for he smiled. "I'm fine. I just need some popcorn." I handed him a dollar, or tried to.

"You missed over fifteen minutes of the feature. Be my guest."

He was a very nice man; he and Mr. Gumbrel were good friends, and I could see why.

Popcorn was overflowing its metal kettle, and Cora Rooney caught it in a red and white box. I insisted on paying for that, and Cora gave me back change. I could hear loud and brittle rat-tat-tatting machine-gun fire and the whipcrack of bullets from hand-guns. Then a scream, a call, more gunfire. Heard from out in the lobby, it was quite a symphony.

I took my popcorn through the swing doors and stood for a moment in the weighty dark that felt like a hand against my chest, holding me back. Everything was silver up there on the screen, from the gun barrels, to the slick dresses on the actresses, to their hair and jewelry. No wonder they called it the silver screen.

I liked standing in the dark, munching popcorn, waiting for my eyes to adapt and I could see the empty seats. I stood longer than I needed to. Sometimes I wondered if I really came for the movies themselves; I believe I came for the comfort.

For it was nice to be in a crowd of people who were still as stones. When I sat down, I could steal glances across an aisle and see their faces, all looking up toward the screen in a wondering way that made me think of rows and rows of little children. They seemed to have entered their own secret garden, which in this case happened to be Chicago.

I didn't really care what the story was; I just liked looking at James Cagney, with his rapid, jerky movements, looking as hard and fast as a bullet himself. Yes, they were mowing each other down, left and right, but not aiming at me.

I found their company comforting; I felt, almost, as if we shared something, Jimmy up there on the screen blistering the air with bullets, and me, Emma, down here, unarmed, undangerous.

37

The next morning, I took Aurora's breakfast tray to her: a fried egg, bacon, toast, and tomato juice.

"'Bout time. I'm famished!" she said, getting up her temper for the day ahead.

I stood beneath a faded photo of the Hotel Paradise and said, "Morris Slade's back."

She stopped cutting off a small section of egg white and looked at me. "What? That young devil? What's he back for?"

I shook my head. "I don't know." I didn't tell her I'd talked to him, because she'd ask too many questions.

She broke her egg yolk with a corner of toast. "Uh-huh. He's back to destroy evidence. A little gin in this tomato juice would sure get it up and going."

That wasn't even a real request, and I ignored it. One thing I'll say for her, Great-Aunt Aurora was never afraid of a wild guess. "What evidence could there possibly be after over twenty years? And after the place it happened burned down?" I said.

"Oh, there's some evidence stays around forever, even in burnt places, even in embers. You get a private detective on him, see what he's up to."

Did she know how absurd this sounded? Probably not. She always had this way of pretending I had the money to do things I didn't. "I don't know any private detectives, much less can afford to pay one."

She was nibbling her bacon and didn't choose to answer.

"Did you know Morris Slade well?" This was a dumb question, for she knew everyone well, or claimed to.

She was dabbing her mouth with the linen napkin that accompanied all room-service food, food carried, of course, by me. "Well of course I knew him. He was a rascal, that one."

If Morris Slade struck me as anything, it was not rascally. Of course, rascals are younger than he was now. Maybe his rascally ways had left him when he discovered life was hard. Anyway, he was much too dignified now to be called a rascal.

"He ain't still married to that dust bunny, is he?"

"Imogen Woodruff? I guess so." That had not come up.

"They never divorced?" She paused. "Scene of the crime."

"What?"

"Scene of the crime's where he'll go."

"The Belle Ruin? But he might go there anyway if it's where he last saw his daughter." It kind of pained me to imagine him standing there, in what was left of the hotel, maybe trying to search out the room from which she was taken.

Aurora barked out a laugh. "You mean it'd be like a sentimental journey?"

"I still don't see what would be around that he could find after twenty years."

"It doesn't have to be a speck of blood or a fingerprint. Maybe it's not at the Belle Ruin. Maybe it's a person. Maybe it's information." She picked up a half slice of toast and said with distaste, "Burnt."

No, it wasn't. "Did you ever know my mother to serve burned anything?"

Her eyebrows danced around as if that were an answer as she set the perfectly browned toast back on her plate and folded her hands (in their lavender lace mittens) across her belly. "I used to know one name of Oates."

I had no idea what she was talking about. "What?"

"Private detective. Ain't you been listening? Yes, Larry or Barry, no, Harry Oates. We went dancing together under the stars."

Pushing away from the wall, I decided to leave before she remembered that scene too well and got out of her chair.

38

The best choice probably wasn't the Woods and Mr. Root, although they were plenty glad to see me.

As if he hadn't even sat down since I last saw them, Ulub had the same poetry book in his hand and was declaiming what sounded like the same poem. That is, as well as I could make out. It was the same process—Ulub getting out a line—"Ah owe ah nace er"—and Mr. Root slicing the air with his fingers, and Ubub tapping his foot like a metronome.

I arrived at the bench, saying, "Ulub needs a break, Mr. Root. Let's go in and get sodas. Then I have something to talk about."

All three looked happier as we trooped into Britten's store to look at the candy counter and the big dispensers of cookies while Ulub went to the cold-drink bin. This all made Mr. Britten unhappy. Or unhappier, for he always looked unhappy.

"You all be careful now," he called out the moment we were through the door.

"God's sake, man," said Mr. Root, "we only just come in for a cold drink."

Mr. Britten mumbled some reply. Or maybe curse. There was something about all of us together that looked to Mr. Britten as if we were John Dillinger, Al Capone, and Pretty Boy Floyd all bunched together, and his was the last club in Chicago still standing. I wished we had been; I could think of nothing better than clearing out a dim-lit, smoky Chicago club.

Ulub called out the drink choices: "E-hi gape, E-hi ownge, Co-cola, E-hi oot eer."

I wondered why he put himself to the trouble of repeating "Nehi" before each flavor instead of just saying them all at once. Do people who have a special difficulty keep calling your attention to it, though they don't mean to? Ubub and Mr. Root wanted Nehi grape and I asked for a Coke.

Mr. Britten stood watching us with his hands clasped under his apron as if he might at any moment whip out a gun. I offered to pay, but Mr. Root and Ubub said no, no, it was their treat, and as we were standing directly in front of Mr. Britten, I insisted again on paying just to let him know what good manners and concern for others looked like. But he just took Mr. Root's money with a twisted lip.

Then I purchased two packets of Sno Balls, which came two in a packet, and we left to take over the bench again.

Each of us had one Sno Ball and a drink. I told them my plan (which wasn't a plan at all). I mentioned Great-Aunt Aurora's sugges-tion I hire a private detective, knowing they would pooh-pooh the need to hire one, Mr. Root in particular.

"Why'd you have to go pay a private detective when we can do it?"

Ulub and Ubub appeared kind of doubtful, but after consulting each other with a look, they nodded. I really admired this quality in them—all three of them—how they were willing to take on a project without rhyme or reason just because we were all friends. For a mo-ment I wanted us all to hold out our hands and make a deck of fists in that all-for-one gesture.

"Now," said Mr. Root, "you two got your trucks and I got my old Ford, if you're thinkin' along them lines."

I wasn't thinking along any lines; I was just hoping we could come up with a private detective. Since I didn't know what Morris Slade was looking for, I didn't know how he'd look for it.

To Mr. Root, I said, "We'll see." I thought and ate my Sno Ball. I loved these cakes because they were deep chocolate on the inside and marshmallow white with coconut on the outside. They were nice and mushy.

My mind could not come clear about following Morris Slade, and I thought I would go into La Porte and see the Sheriff and find out if he knew of anything that would account for Morris Slade suddenly turning up. I did not expect much, though.

Just then, down the highway, I saw a cab coming. As it got closer, I saw it was the one Axel drove, the maroon Chevy. I shaded my eyes and peered from under my hand. The cab was empty except for the driver, and it was indeed Axel. Axel! I ran down the embankment toward the highway, waving wildly, gesturing in what I thought clearly meant "Stop!"

Axel tooted his horn. I jumped around. Axel waved and drove by me, tapping his horn again. He must have thought I was just giving him a friendly wave hello. I couldn't believe it. It was as close as I'd ever gotten and would no doubt ever get to riding in Axel's cab.

I said good-bye to my three friends and set off walking the two miles into town.

I felt beleaguered; I felt a lot was riding on my shoulders. But what? There was nothing riding on my shoulders except my head and what was in it, and what was in it was Morris Slade.

39

On my way back into town, I passed Arturo's with its faulty neon sign. The dead letters didn't make any difference in the daytime, since the lights didn't blink then. ART—EAT—ART—EAT. I liked the message and hoped he would never fix it.

It took me another fifteen minutes to get to the courthouse. I trudged up the steps. It was after noon and the Sheriff might be at the Rainbow, but I seemed to remember he said he didn't eat lunch; he didn't like it. I wondered how a person could not like a mealtime.

I tried to see through the pebbled-glass door of the Sheriff's office, but couldn't make out the figures in there. If the Sheriff wasn't there, that was all right, for I'd actually come to see Donny. For once.

I wanted to know where his uncle lived. The Sheriff hadn't said, and I hadn't asked. If I had asked him, he would have figured out the reason I wanted to know and would've told me not to.

There were a lot of Moomas in the phone directory, but no Carls. There were two C's, and I called both numbers. I pretended to be selling magazine subscriptions, and one said his name was Charles, and he nearly talked my ear off, and the other hung up. I couldn't find out from the operator, because she didn't see a listing for a Carl Mooma.

Donny, of course, wouldn't tell me on general principles.

I stood thinking for another moment, then went in. "Hi."

Maureen said hi back; Donny curled his lip. "Sam ain't here."

I yawned and said I was going to the Rainbow for a doughnut and did they want any?

"You buyin'?" Donny snickered, as if I couldn't possibly be.

I shrugged. "Sure, why not?"

Maureen said, "That's mighty nice of you, but you don't—" She started rooting in her purse.

Donny said, "Why not? Seems to me she owes us one, Maureen."

"I'll be right back." I hurried off.

Donny was calling "—with sprinkles" before I got to the staircase.

It was lunchtime, so the Rainbow was crowded. All the counter seats were taken and the booths in back were filled, except for the "reserved" one for the waitresses' coffee breaks.

But I didn't care, as I didn't want to sit. Wanda Waylans was behind the baked goods shelves, friendly as ever.

"Well, hi, Emma. You after a doughnut? We got some good cinnamon buns today."

I thanked her for the suggestion but ordered the doughnuts: two with chocolate sprinkles, two chocolate frosted, one strawberry frosted with multicolored sprinkles. It just looked festive. Glad I'd brought enough money with me, I paid Shirl, who looked at the dollar suspiciously, grunted, and gave me change. Then I thought of coffee and asked Wanda for two cups to go, sugar and cream on the side. Wanda set the cups in a four-cup carrier that looked kind of like an egg crate, and I paid Shirl for the coffee.

It was a lot to maneuver with, the coffee and the cardboard tray with the doughnuts. I went as fast as I could without spilling, back to the courthouse.

Donny was pacing and dictating. Maureen was typing, or would be if Donny could get going on with what he wanted to say.

"Dear Mr. uh . . . No, 'Councilman' . . . That ain't a 'Your Honor,' is it?"

Arms folded, Maureen shook her head and tapped her fingers on her forearms. "Just say 'Mr.,' why don't you?"

Donny brought down his hand as if there were a flag in it and he was starting a race. "Okay, okay—"

When they saw the coffee and doughnuts, their eyes lit up, or hers did; Donny's just grew more bulbous.

"Why, thank you, hon," said Maureen. "That's awful thoughtful."

Donny half snarled, half smiled. "What'cha want? Probably, she wants somethin'," he said to Maureen.

Maureen just picked up her coffee and waved his comment off.

Actually, I was surprised he'd said something smart for once.

Maureen was enjoying one of the chocolate doughnuts and looking out the window. Donny was eating the strawberry-iced with sprinkles and looking at it cross-eyed.

I was trying to figure out how to get the talk to Carl Mooma. I remembered Miss Flyte talking about Agatha Christie, and when Donny was slurping his coffee, I said, "You ever read anything by Agatha Christie?"

"Hell, o' course. Ain't everyone? Read *And Then They Were Gone*." He was pleased with himself.

Maureen, whom I'd never put down as a big reader, said, "'None,' Donny. *And Then There Were None*."

But he was just eyeing the tray of doughnuts.

"You know she disappeared? Agatha Christie did. Nobody knew where she was."

"She did?" said Maureen.

I nodded.

Donny grunted and helped himself to another doughnut. "They find her?" he asked, obviously indifferent to Agatha's fate.

"She reappeared in a hotel somewhere, or was it in some baths? Anyway, she wouldn't say what happened." I grew fake thoughtful. "Speaking of disappearing—wasn't that your uncle that was in charge of that case twenty years ago about the baby disappearing from the Belle Ruin hotel?" My mouth was dry and I wished for a glass of water. I hadn't thought to buy a drink for myself, since I didn't have to bribe myself. "I think Great-Aunt Aurora knew Sheriff Mooma. Yes, I recall she mentioned him, first-rate policeman, Carl Mooma. Smart as a whip is what she said."

Donny gave a pleased snicker. "Gotta get up pretty early in the morning to beat Carl, and that's the truth. I tell you he's writing his memoirs? Yeah, he is. Got himself a publisher and everything."

Memoirs? This was better than I thought. "A publisher? Like in New York City?"

"Nah. Place in Cleveland—"

I frowned. "Cleveland? It has publishers?"

Irritated, Donny said, "Well, just you listen and you might learn somethin' for a change. This publisher, the author pays the cost of printing it up and marketing it and the author—in this case Carl—gets the profits. Pretty neat arrangement." He made that click-click sound, tongue against teeth, in the way people do when they're pleased with themselves.

"That's really exciting." I snapped my fingers as if I'd only now thought of it: "Listen, you know some of what I'm writing for the paper is about that baby disappearing; do you think Sheriff Mooma"—I wanted to sound respecting of his former position—"would be willing to be interviewed? I didn't even know he was still around; it's why I never thought of it, I guess."

Donny clearly thought any Mooma was deserving of attention, as I expected he would. He started pacing again, thumbs hitched in his Sam Browne belt, sidearm riding his hip. "He sure as hell is. Now, I can't answer for Carl, but no reason Gumbrel couldn't put out feelers. . . ."

As if the wire services were just waiting for a word from Carl Mooma.

Maureen was sitting back there, rolling her eyes.

"Oh, good," I said. "Where's he living now?"

"Over in Rawlins."

Rawlins wasn't much of a town, just a dirt-grooved little place made up of a couple dozen houses, a bar, and a gas station. The bar was in the station. Even Cold Flat Junction was more substantial. Rawlins was just before Hebrides.

Donny added, "Lives on Blackbird Road. Number fourteen Blackbird Road's his spread."

Blackbird Road! It seemed a sign. But "signs" didn't happen to people like me, only to ones like Romeo and Juliet, or Moses, or Ree-Jane. To hear her tell it, she was always getting "signs" as to her career or love affairs (of which she had neither), as if stars littered her path by divine command.

I wondered why I'd never thought of Carl Mooma as a source of information before. Well, I guess I had supposed he was dead. Probably because there was such a rich supply of events and detail, I hadn't really thought about him.

"How much of this book has your uncle written?" I wanted to know how long and hard he'd thought about the event. "Did he make notes at the time?"

Donny grunted in mock disbelief. Could I be that stupid? "Just shows to go ya how much you know about po-lice work. Course he made notes."

I dropped the note taking and repeated my first question: "Then how much of his memoir has Sheriff Mooma written?"

Donny considered. Then he winked and tapped his temple. "Got it all right in the old bean. You don't start writing all helter-skelter, just tossin' facts and details around—"

As far as I was concerned, helter-skelter was the only way any book got written, including the King James version.

"—no, siree, you got to have your material in order, marshal your thoughts, get 'em lined up like a dress parade, let 'em march one-two, one-two and salute!" He actually did. "Yes, sir, that's—"

Maureen said, "Oh, shut up, Donny." She'd lit up a Lucky to have with her coffee and was looking at him through the smoke. "You don't know any more about writing a book than fishing off a moonbeam."

He whirled around toward her quick as a dervish. "What? Now, just how in hell do you know, anyway?"

"I know it comes hard." To my surprise, Maureen held up the book on her desk. It was *The Great Gatsby.* "Ask him."

Donny corkscrewed his neck out, squinted. "Who? Gatsby?"

"No. F. Scott Fitzgerald."

Donny flapped his hand as if he were chasing away pigeons. "For God's sake, Maureen, he's one of the greats, him and . . . Shakespeare and them. Course, they work different."

"Well, there's Emma, who's writing for the paper. Why don't you ask her?"

No no no no. While Donny was looking at Maureen, I shook my head violently. For all I appreciated her being on my side, I didn't want her on it right then. "Well, but Donny's got a point, Maureen. I think you write better if you 'marshal' your thoughts first." I'd have batted my eyelashes at him if I'd had battable lashes.

Donny just hitched up his pants and gave her the pigeon wave again.

I could tell, though, that he was somewhat appeased by my words. I said, "I'll talk to Mr. Gumbrel about the interview. Thanks, Donny. This is going to be a really good piece. Do you think you could let Sheriff Mooma know the *Conservative* will be in touch?"

Donny scratched his neck. "Well, yeah. Yeah, Carl, he'll need to work it into his schedule."

I nodded. "I'll talk to Mr. Gumbrel right away." I got up and tossed my crumpled napkin in the wastebasket.

"Yeah, once we get the ball rollin'," said Donny, "I wouldn't be surprised if the big newspapers didn't pick up the story."

It was becoming, already, Donny's own success story.

I said good-bye to him and Maureen and let him dream on.

In case Donny called Mr. Gumbrel, and he probably would, just to jaw about his uncle's book, I headed for the newspaper office.

There were several people there, including Suzie Whitelaw and the freelance photographer, but not Mr. Gumbrel. I left my message with the girl in charge of want ads, since I knew her to be the most reliable person there.

Then I was ready for Rawlins.

40

The train didn't stop in Rawlins, it being such a no-account little place, so I had to take a cab from Hebrides to get there.

It was a town I'd never been in and I wondered why I thought Cold Flat Junction was a much better place, when the whole point of the Junction was its unconnected life. It was lonely; it was silent; it wasn't on the way to anywhere, despite its famous railroad station. I thought at times Cold Flat Junction, unattached to anything, floated in my mind. Yet it didn't have this strange quality of Rawlins; Rawlins felt more like it was the tag end of nowhere; it was, actually, where the Hebrides road ran away to a mere trickle.

Blackbird Road was a treeless street with only thinned-out hedges defining properties, the dark little shingled houses studded about like cloves. Number 14 was at the end.

It was a brown-shingled bungalow with a shadowed, white-pillared porch up a narrow walk. Thin rows of red and orange geraniums were planted evenly along each side.

A man sat on the porch and I wondered if this was Carl Mooma, sitting in a rocking chair in the deep shadows, smoking a thick cigar.

" 'Lo," he said, in a quite friendly tone.

"Sheriff Mooma?"

He laughed, a dry sound, forced as if his chest were resenting the effort. "Been a long time since anybody called me that." The chair creaked a little as he leaned forward to see me better. "You look kinda young to be looking for a sheriff."

I was walking up the three butterscotch-tan-varnished steps. "My name's Emma Graham; I live in Spirit Lake. I tried to call, but couldn't find a number for you."

"Don't have a phone. Hardly anyone calls." He cocked his head to the right. "Fella next door takes messages for me."

"Oh. Then you haven't heard from your nephew Donny about the interview?"

"No, ma'am. I ain't heard from Donny, but then, he never was Mr. Reliable. Go on, sit." He indicated the rocker next to his own.

I thought about defending Donny here, given the little time that had passed since I'd talked to him. But I managed not to. As it was, Carl Mooma was turning out to be a lot different from what I'd expected. But then I remembered I'd gotten most of my information from Aurora Paradise, and she never was handy with the compliments.

I sat. We rocked. Everything was mournfully peaceful. I looked out over Blackbird Road and felt the failure of the place. It was where you ended up if you were not awfully careful. I had no doubt but that it was where I would end up, being about as careless as they come.

Blackbird Road. I looked for something wheeling across the sky, but there was nothing. The sky was cloudless, a slab of slate gray.

"So now, what's this interview you said?"

I explained about the story I was writing, the several murders, the kidnapping, my own near murder.

"Jesus H. W. Christ! I was going to say you're pretty young to be writing for a newspaper, as well as seeking out a sheriff, but I guess you've had a lot of life experience."

"I guess," I said, modestly.

He just kept shaking his head and giving Jesus Christ the same initials. I wondered what they stood for.

"Okay, so Donny told you I'm supposed to be writing my—

what?—my 'memoirs'?" he laughed. "Well, it's not the first time Donny was full of hot air. We was talking about this once and he said I should do it, should write up this alleged kidnapping of that poor Slade child and that he could be my agent and there were publishers who got your books printed for a fee. So I asked him, 'Who's got the money for a fee?' He says, 'Never mind, I can talk them down.' I says, 'Talk who down?' He says, 'Why, publishers, of course. There's places that print up your book and then sell it.' He goes on talking about it like it's a done deal."

I laughed. I liked the way Carl Mooma talked. "You talk really well, Mr. Mooma. I bet you *could* write a book. Maybe you ought to try it."

He smiled. He had a square head with thinning gray hair set on a thick neck and heavy shoulders. He did have steady dark blue eyes that had probably helped him when he was questioning suspects. You wouldn't want the eyes trained on you for too long.

"It's true," he said. "That whole business is worth being writ about, and maybe you're the one to do it. I can't write worth a damn."

I thought for a moment about the police investigation, or lack of it. "There doesn't seem to have been much of an investigation into that kidnapping, or disappearance, or whatever happened to that baby. I don't mean to offend, but there was talk that Mr. Woodruff bought off the law."

He only laughed. "Yeah, I'm familiar with that talk. No money changed hands." As if to make this understood, he wiped his hands down his thighs. "No, I agreed to hold off for a bit because he was a friend, that's all."

"Why did he want you to?"

"Because he was afraid his son-in-law done it and he wanted time to get it out of him. I shouldn't have done that, I know, but the man was so overwrought." His smile was slight. "And he also knew the Governor." The smile turned sly. "But he never tied Morris Slade to the kidnapping."

"So the trail went cold," I said, helpfully.

"You seen too many movies, little girl." He grinned. "Trail was always cold. I was sliding on thin ice, and I knew it."

I frowned. It sounded as if Carl Mooma almost knew before he started it was hopeless.

He went on. "Whole thing was fishy, I finally came to realize."

"Fishy how?" I wondered if he'd come up with the same fishiness I had.

"That babysitter, for instance. What was her name?"

"Gloria Spiker. Now it's Calhoun."

"Yeah. She said—finally, after I asked the girl a hundred times, for I knew she was holding back—"

He chose this moment to start in coughing and waved his cigar smoke away. "Bad lungs—" The coughing went on.

I hoped he didn't die at my feet before he finished his story. I pounded him on the back. I was surprised I felt free to do this, as if Sheriff Mooma and I had known each other for an age. Finally he quit.

"I gotta stop these things." He held up the cigar.

"Later," I said, unsympathetic as usual. "Go on about Gloria Spiker. What was she holding back?" I knew, but he might know more.

"She said the mother didn't like that baby. That was Imogen Woodruff, then Slade. The Spiker girl said she could tell in just the way the mother gave her directions, it was more like she was talking about a sick dog. She—Imogen, the mother—said to leave the baby alone, not to wake it up or do anything. Well, she'd never heard any mother be so cold toward a child."

Well, I thought. "How about the father, Morris Slade?"

"Oh. Gloria never said anything about him, much, except he was pretty nice. But I don't think he had much to do with telling her her duties. He wasn't in the room, if I remember right."

Rain had started, a fine mist blowing onto the porch, but we stayed put and looked at it as though from another country. Bullets of rain could have peppered the porch, and us with it, and I wouldn't have moved.

"What about the friend, Prunella Rice? I guess you talked to her too?"

He nodded. "Sure did. She verified they were on the phone for around twenty minutes."

"I talked to her. They told exactly the same story about the phone call, word for word."

He waved the rain away like smoke and looked at me. "It was a put-up job; it had to be."

"There never was a real kidnapping, was there? It was all an arrangement, wasn't it?"

He gave me one of those up-and-down looks people do when they're trying to figure you out. "You're pretty smart if you worked that out."

"I didn't. Someone else did." At this point I didn't know who, or care. I just wanted to get on with the story. "Go on."

He started up rocking again. "This is where a kid named Robby Stone comes in. He worked there as both waiter and bellhop. What I think is Woodruff and his daughter paid him to take the baby away. Robby Stone's car was found just over the state line, in Pennsylvania. Accident, a bad one. The boy was killed. Whether the baby was thrown from the car or not in the car when it happened we'll never know." He paused and looked at me. "Why am I telling you all this? And have you broadcast it in the paper? Maybe because you look so damned harmless. Pardon my French."

It was nice to be seen as harmless instead of dangerous. "I am. I won't tell anything you don't want me to. We're off the record. Could he have taken the baby somewhere? Maybe also arranged?"

"Sure he could have. He was working at the Belle Ruin earlier; then he left. Woodruff paid him to take the baby with him."

"And there was never any trace of her. But she still could be alive somewhere."

Carl Mooma turned to stare at me. "She? It wasn't a girl; it was a boy."

"*What?*" I felt the rain then like ice on my skin. "But her name was 'Fay.' That was in the police report. I saw it when—" I didn't want to add when I stole the folder out of the sheriff's office.

He smiled. "Yeah, well, a lot of people made that mistake. That was his name all right, but spelled f-e-y. It was like a nickname. The kid was named after his great-grandfather, named"—he studied the porch railing for a moment—"Raphael?"

I couldn't answer him; my mouth was dry. *Raphael.*

41

Carl Mooma gave me a ride back to the hotel, as he had to be in La Porte around six o'clock. He'd promised Donny he'd see him for supper and a few beers after.

I was just too stunned to talk. I asked Mr. Mooma to let me off at the bottom of the hotel driveway, since that would save him some time.

"If ever you're in my neck of the woods again, drop by." He tipped up the bill of his Mail Pouch tobacco cap and drove off.

I stood there in a cloud of dust and gravel until his truck disappeared around a curve. Then I ran up the drive.

For once, I was sorry Ree-Jane wasn't gloating on the front porch, because Ralph Diggs would have been with her. I supposed I might as well call him that temporarily. Ralph Diggs. Rafe Diggs. Raphael Slade. "Fey" Slade.

The newspapers had called the vanished baby "Fay," so naturally people assumed it was a girl. I thought about Gloria Spiker: she'd said "her" when speaking of the baby. That she'd been told not to wake "her" up—or had she? Maybe she'd said "it." Had either of the parents actually said "her" or had they said "Fey"?

I set out to find him, although I wasn't clear as to what I'd do once I did find him. First I tried his room. He wasn't there and I resisted the temptation to look around. I went down the back stairs to the kitchen and asked Walter if he'd seen Ralph.

"Up in the Big Garage I seen him."

The door was open, not all the way, not even half. More like a quarter. But to find it open at all was an occasion. I went in. The Tree girls were back with their satin slippers tied on. This time one was in a tutu, pink like the slippers. The other was in her regular clothes, a skirt and sweater, and looked enviously at her sister as they both twirled. Probably mad she didn't have a tutu. I could have told her that her sister looked pretty stupid in hers so not to mind.

He was standing talking to Will and Mill and seemed right at home. I gave Ralph Diggs a closer look now that I knew who he was, or at least was pretty sure I knew. Tawny hair, like Morris Slade's, and his skin was as fine as my mother's blancmange. Skin like that was wasted on a man; it was a girl's face, a soft face.

"That was the most spoiled girl I ever knew," I heard Miss Flagler say once about Imogen Woodruff. *"Everything about her was spoiled. Even her face."*

A handsome, spoiled face. As if Morris Slade's face had been tampered with, pulled about out of true.

Will just jerked his head at me. He was looking down at something he seemed to be whittling. "Ralph's helping with the production."

You mean Raphael. I was dying to say it, but of course I didn't.

Ralph Diggs's eyes turned to ice. I think it must have been just a trick of the light. I hoped it wasn't because he was reading my mind.

He smiled, I guess you'd say "winsomely." "Hi, Emma."

I did not "Hi" him back. I tried my own winsome smile, which was probably not at all winsome, just crooked.

"Doing what?"

"Magic. I told you."

"You're the magician?"

I tried to make my tone flat and unimpressed.

He nodded.

"What kind of magic do you do, then?"

"Nothing extraordinary. I'm pretty much an amateur." He laughed abruptly.

"Well, you've come to the right place." I laughed abruptly too. "Can you disappear?"

Ralph looked at me uncertainly. Then he took a step toward me, put his hand behind my ear in a quick smooth motion, and pulled out a quarter. "What's this?" he asked, as if surprised.

I was supposed to be pleased and surprised. I will admit to being surprised, but I tried not to show it. Calmly I asked him how he'd done it.

Slyly, he shook his head. "Sorry."

"The thing is, see, there wasn't a coin behind my ear, so if you found one, that means you put it there."

Will was actually looking at me with interest. "How'd he put it there?"

"When he reached there supposedly to find it."

"I had nothing in my hand."

"Of course you did. You've probably got hands as nimble as Mill's." I nodded toward the piano, where Mill had gone to play some tune for the Tree girls to twirl with. "The quarter was hidden some-place, that's all. You palmed it."

"She doesn't know what she's talking about," said Will, who'd gone back to whittling whatever.

"I've got to go."

"Good-bye, Emma," he called out when I was at the door.

I didn't "Good-bye" him either.

I was almost looking forward to taking Aurora her tea. We'd certainly have something to talk about.

Rafe Slade.

What I couldn't figure out was why he was here at the hotel. Why wasn't he over at the Woodruff house? Unless he was picking a par-ticular time to see Morris Slade. But that still didn't say why he was here in the Big Garage hanging out with a couple of kids.

Morris Slade and Ralph Diggs; Morris Slade and his son. Surely both of them turning up at the same time in Spirit Lake wasn't a coincidence.

Or was my imagination just running wild?

I stopped outside the kitchen door. I finally agreed with Will about something: I didn't know what I was talking about.

42

I t was after five and Lola Davidow would be either in the kitchen stirring up a pitcher of martinis or in the back office drinking them. I first tried the office. It was empty. I grabbed up a bottle of whiskey and slipped out again, around the front desk and down the corridor to the back door. Then along the wooden walk to the door of the kitchen. I checked the bottle to see what I'd taken. It was 100-proof whiskey called "Apple Hollow" and according to the label was "cured in the keg." I bet.

I called "Hi" to Walter, then went to the refrigerator for a couple of ice cubes. Over this I poured a large measure of whiskey and topped it off with apple juice. I dusted some cinnamon over the top, then stuck in one of Lola's swizzle sticks. I studied the drink for a moment and called it a "Hollow Leg."

"That's good," said Aurora, "real good. 'Hollow Leg.' You outdone yourself." She took another mouthful, seemed to be turning it around as if it were a great wine.

"It's only apple juice."

She shook a bony finger at me. "Don't forget the cinnamon. Gives it a bite."

"I'd say the bite comes more from hundred-proof whiskey."

"Lola Davidow ought to open a bar, make you head bartender."

"You've suggested that before. It'd really go down well with the vice squad." I didn't know if there was such a thing (certainly not in La Porte); I thought I'd heard Perry Mason refer to one. "Listen, remember about the police coming to the Belle Ruin the night of the Slade baby kidnapping?" I was holding off telling her about Ralph Diggs.

"Yes, since you don't let me forget it for as much as fifteen seconds."

"It was Sheriff Mooma. Why'd you say he was such a big fool?"

"Did I say that?"

She didn't care whether she'd said it or not. Her face was tilted over her glass as if she were seeing treasure from the *Titanic* down there.

"He's not. I talked to him today for a long time. He's no fool."

She held out her glass; it was still half full, but I guess she was preparing for the future. "Ready for another!"

"I'm not. The baby's name was Fey. How do you spell it?"

She gave me a squinty look. "What? How do you spell 'Fay'? Now there's a hard question. The hotel cat could tell you that."

The ice in her glass rattled as she took another drink.

"The name was f-E-y, not f-A-y. It was a nickname for Raphael. A boy."

This surprised her as much as it had me. She actually gave some thought to it, actually set her glass on the table beside her chair. "Well, it'd make an investigation pretty hard if they didn't even know the sex."

"There wasn't really an investigation, remember."

"Told you that Mooma was a fool."

"No, he wasn't. Isn't. Mr. Woodruff asked him to hold off for several hours because he wanted to find out if his son-in-law was involved."

"You mean Morris Slade? Police ain't supposed to do favors for people."

"You do if the Governor asks you to."

"Lucien Woodruff was friends with the Governor? Nothing but corruption city." To irritate me into getting her another drink, she took her worn deck of cards out from her box of odds and ends. She also took out two little black boxes of tiny matches and slapped those down on the table.

I picked one up. The top was shiny black with a French word— *L'ennui*—printed across it. "What are these?"

"Matches. We can bet with 'em, seein' you don't have any money." She started shuffling.

"But what's it mean?"

"*L'ennui?* For goodness' sake, you don't know that song about fighting the old on-weeeee?" She sang the line. "Means weary. No, world-weary. Sick of life. Seven-card stud or spit in the ocean?" She riffled the cards and looked at me like the card shark she wasn't.

"Raphael," I repeated. "Does that put you in mind of anybody?"

"No." Slap went one of the cards.

Her lack of curiosity, after her initial surprise, was beginning to rankle. "*Raphael* was the name of Mr. Woodruff's father."

That made her look up, again with that squint. "So? What's he got to do with anything?"

"There's more obvious nicknames than Fey. Like Rafe, for instance."

She stared. "Now, wait. Are you sayin' this good-for-nothing fella Lola Davidow just hired—?" She waved that away and went back to shuffling.

"That's what I'm saying. Ralph Diggs is Morris Slade's boy, the one who was kidnapped. He was taken somewhere as a baby, but apparently no one knows where or to whom. Now he's here. And maybe that accounts for Morris Slade being here too."

Aurora shook her head. "Girl, you got a wilder imagination than your crazy brother." She started dealing out two hands.

That was truly annoying. It sounded like Dwayne and the Sheriff.

I picked up her glass and palmed my box of matches and marched down the stairs. Halfway down the long hall I heard her raspy voice singing about the old *ennui* and battling it by going on a spree. Aurora was out on a spree every day of her life.

I looked at the stolen box of matches: *L'ennui.*

That had a definite Emma-ring.

43

Except for the Sheriff, whose schedule was always changing according to the comings and goings of lawbreakers, the person who could best bring reason to bear on this story was Dwayne. Unfortunately, he also brought a lot of sarcasm.

So the next morning, following my peach pancake breakfast, I was once again sitting on the tire tower, my arms hooked around my washed-out blue pedal pushers, my chin on my knees, waiting for Dwayne to come up for air.

"I'm not going to tell you while you're banging away on that engine or exhaust pipe or whatever." He was under an old blue Chevy.

"Okay," he said.

He did not mean, *Okay I'll roll out from under;* he meant, *Okay, don't.* He enjoyed taking things literally to annoy me.

Yet I had already told him most of it, since I could not resist the telling, even if he could resist the listening. Yet, he was listening, I knew. There were times I thought he was even anxious about me.

At last Dwayne stopped what he was doing under the car and rolled out.

"Sometimes I think you save underneath-work for when I come around."

The oily rag was out and he was wiping down his fingers. "Me too."

"Ha-ha." I hated when he reduced me to ha-ha's. It's a typical Ree-Jane response.

"Okay, what's next?"

Narrowing my eyes, I looked closely at his face for a sign of amusement at my expense. I found it too, his mouth kind of twitching away from a smile, as if he were holding it back. "The baby's name was Fey." I had tricked Aurora with this. "How would you spell it, if asked?"

"F-a-y. Same as if I wasn't asked. That's how you spell 'Fay.' You, of course, are about to spell it different."

"There's a point here, you know."

"I hope so." He stood with arms crossed, leaning against the Chevy, looking at me.

"The *point* is, it's spelled f-E-y. It's a nickname. The baby's real name was Raphael, according to Sheriff Mooma."

"That's a boy's name. You mean this kid was a boy?"

Eagerly, I nodded.

Dwayne thought this over. "First it was: She's back. But that doesn't work anymore, so now it's: *He's* back." He looked at me. He was chewing gum that I didn't even know he had in his mouth. Dwayne was subtle that way. "My God, girl, but you got enough ghostly characters roaming around to stage a production of *Hamlet*."

"What? They're not *my* inventions!"

"Uh," he grunted. "And everyone thought the vanished child was a girl?"

I said, stumbling about for meaning, "There weren't that many 'everyones' to even have an opinion. The baby was only here for a day. His importance was born with his kidnapping. That's what I'd bet. The baby didn't mean a thing to anyone; he was invisible till he got kidnapped."

He was silent. Then: "Sorry. Did I miss something? This Raphael— that's supposed to mean something to me?"

I guess it didn't, since he hadn't known about Mr. Woodruff's father. So I told him, adding, as I had for Aurora, "Fey they called him as a baby. There's a more familiar nickname than Fey, though, for Raphael."

"Ralph, I'd say."

"Or Rafe."

He chewed so slowly you could hardly see his jaw move. "You're not supposing that this new guy you've got working at the hotel is this vanished child?"

The vanished child. The disappeared baby. It was as if this defined them, as if they had no existence without the vanishing or disappearing. What did I mean? And why *they*? There was only one. "Yes. I think Ralph Diggs is who people thought was Fey Slade."

Dwayne was stock-still. It made me nervous. I thought he was about to say something, when Abel Slaw walked in with You-Boy. I jumped down from the tires when I saw Abel was working his way up to giving me a verbal licking about how a garage could be a dangerous place.

I left before I gave *him* a verbal licking about danger.

44

I didn't want to walk into town or even back to the hotel to call Axel's Taxis. I was not about to ask Mr. Slaw if I could use his telephone, so I went to the pay phone next door, just in front of the lumber shop. Then I sat on the bench outside and waited for Delbert.

Naturally, he wanted to know why I was at Hanna's Building Supply, and I told him because we were building an ark at the rear of the hotel grounds and were charging fifty cents for anyone who wanted to bring his pet to get blessed.

Anyone else would have been questioning the whole ark-building plan, but not Delbert, who instead had to comment on Noah: "Now I don't think he blessed the animals; I think his job was just to get 'em on board, march 'em up the ramp and inside the ship and that was all."

I slid down in my seat and did not contradict him, because that would encourage conversation. Probably, it served me right for the ark story. And I forgot that silence could encourage conversation as much as speaking.

"So who's doin' the blessin'? I mean, who's qualified? Who's got the papers?"

Delbert had been referring a lot to "the papers" lately, and I wondered why he'd got that bee in his bonnet; what he meant by it I certainly wasn't going to ask.

"Walter," I said.

Delbert's neck was going to seize up if he didn't stop turning it so fast. "Walter? You talkin' about Walter Knepp? Him that works at the hotel?"

"If you mean the Hotel Paradise, yes." It irritated me I'd forgotten Walter's last name was Knepp.

We were driving by Arturo's with its busted neon sign.

"Don't kid me," said Delbert. "Walter ain't got the qualifications for givin' blessin's."

"You mean the papers?"

"What? What d'ya mean?"

"Nothing." When we came to the corner of the street where the Rainbow Café stood, I suddenly thought of something. "Delbert, have you driven anyone new lately? New to town?"

"Like who?"

I gritted my teeth. "If I knew who, I wouldn't be asking, would I?"

"Well, you could. It could be somebody you know and you're keeping tabs on." He pulled up to the curb and gave the transmission stick a smart little push upward, pleased with himself.

If I didn't get out of the cab quickly and bolt into the Rainbow, I'd strangle him.

It wasn't lunchtime yet, but the usual row of counter sitters were there silently studying the same menu that had been in effect since before I was born.

Maud was racking glasses, and Wanda Wayans was placing fresh doughnuts in neat rows on a tray on one of the glass shelves. I asked Maud if the Sheriff had been in yet for coffee. She said no, and looked toward the door.

"He's just coming. Go on back."

I did, and turned to see the Sheriff talking to Dodge Haines. Not one of the men sitting at the counter really liked the Sheriff. The Mayor was afraid he'd be out of a job if the Sheriff ever ran for public office; Bubby Dubois had been caught with the Sheriff's wife; Dodge Haines was in fear of losing his dealership license; and Melvin Creek was a crook whom the Sheriff had arrested a bunch of times. But at times, to see them all glad-handing him, you'd think the Sheriff had just deputized them all and handed out keys to the courthouse.

Then he was at our booth. "Emma," he said, with an unsmiling face and in an unsmiling voice as he slid into the booth. "What's this about you going to see Carl Mooma?"

My mouth, open to say hello, said instead, "How do you know that?"

"Carl told Donny a reporter girl came to see him. You got Donny to tell you where his uncle lived."

"Where he lives isn't a secret, for heaven's sake."

"No, but I don't like the idea of you going off on your own and talking to strange men."

I threw up my arms in what I hoped was a dramatic gesture of disbelief. "Sheriff Mooma was there at the Belle Ruin the night the baby disappeared."

"I know that."

"And I'm writing a story for the paper, re-*mem*-ber?"

"You can get your information without going around talking to strange men. You've knocked on more doors in Cold Flat Junction than the Fuller brush man."

"Oh, really? I guess you think Gloria Spiker's dangerous, then."

No need to bring up Jude Stemple and Reuben Stuck and Morris Slade. "And you don't know a thing about reporting. Mr. Mooma was an eyewitness! Eyewitness—doesn't that mean anything to you? In other words, it wouldn't be hearsay, what he says, like it was for me about Isabel Devereau."

As if by magic, Maud appeared and set down a cup of coffee for the Sheriff and a Coke in front of me. "What're you on about?" This was directed to the Sheriff. She shook a cigarette out of her pack of Camels.

"He's telling me not to go 'Talking to Strange Men.'" I was seeing it now as a movie. Starring me.

"Are there some strange men? I wouldn't mind talking to them
myself." A long look at the Sheriff made him turn and look grimly at
her.

"You're not concerned that Emma goes off on her own hook and
into houses she doesn't know anything about and starts jawing off
about a crime being committed?"

"I don't 'jaw off.' I'm good at disguising why I'm there."

"'Disguise,' I can believe. You've got to stop playacting, Emma.
That's what you think life is—a play or a movie."

Having just turned "Talking to Strange Men" into one, I was a
little embarrassed. "No, that's what Will does. He thinks life is—"

The Sheriff shook his head and bummed a cigarette off Maud.
"Your brother stages plays. So did Ziegfeld. He doesn't think he *is* the
play. He can tell the difference between fiction and reality."

"What? What?" I was leaning so hard up against the tabletop that
my "what?"'s came out in breathless spurts. "The difference between
fiction and reality? Will can't tell the difference between his own two
feet. I'm the one that knows the difference. I have to look at things as
they are to be a newspaper reporter." That was a terrific answer, I
thought.

The Sheriff didn't. He too shoved himself up against the tabletop.
"There are dangerous people out there, Emma—"

"Like Ben Queen?" I hoped my voice just dripped with sarcasm.

"You didn't know Ben wasn't dangerous."

Well, I guess I had to admit that when I ran into him with a gun
in his hand, I probably thought there was some danger involved. I
didn't know what to say, so I just made something up, having no idea
what I meant. "Danger is what you make up to be danger."

"Oh, well, then I'll just turn in my badge and my sidearm."

Maud shook her head, annoyed. "Oh, why don't you two just
give up? You're always fighting."

This shocked me, for we didn't used to. Didn't used to fight, I mean. I felt suddenly sad. He was right, I knew. I'd always known I shouldn't go around knocking on strangers' doors. And it wasn't reporting either. I wasn't working for the newspaper when I started investigating the old Devereau house. And look what happened there. Even though I thought he was being bossy, telling me what to do, still, I guessed he was really worried that something might happen to me.

"I think I'll have some chili."

"Me too," said the Sheriff.

He never ate chili. I don't even think he liked chili. So I guess this was a kind of truce we were calling.

Maud brought the chili and we ate it, happily making small talk.

And I completely forgot to tell him about the Slade baby, that it had been a boy. I also didn't tell him about Ralph Diggs or Morris Slade, which I think I would've in better days.

Talk about talking to strange men.

I had missed serving lunch. When I realized it was noon by the time I finished my chili, I raced out of the Rainbow and around to the taxi stand, where Delbert was reading a comic, and Wilma, the dispatcher, was putting bright coral polish on her nails.

Delbert grabbed up his keys and we left.

Even while he was pulling away from the curb, he started in: "They have to come two by two? If they don't, why build an ark? I mean you could just put up a tent for cover if you needed it."

Being full of chili, I was pretty dozy and closed my eyes, if not my ears. Here was someone who didn't give a hoot about reality sitting up there, driving.

That really miffed me, that the Sheriff thought my brother lived more in the "real" world than I did. Had the Sheriff ever visited the Big Garage? Every day, dawn to dusk, Will and Mill were in there giving the real world a run for its money.

Mrs. Davidow was in the kitchen, cigarette in one hand, some pale drink in the other, waiting apparently for her lunch, some version of her beef and grapefruit diet, to be served up. My mother was strangely unmoved by my excuse that I had had to wait forever for a taxi.

"You never have to wait for a taxi. Miss Bertha and Mrs. Fulbright have already eaten."

"Fortunately, Ralph was here," said Mrs. Davidow.

" 'Fortunately'? You're *paying* him to be here." Then I remembered that wasn't strictly true.

There was a laugh behind me, a deep one. I hadn't seen him, sitting in the shadow at the round table where I ate my meals, joined sometimes by Walter, there by the rear door. I didn't like him sitting at our table.

Mrs. Davidow looked toward him with a simpering smile. "Well, he's certainly earning whatever he gets." My mother put two very succulent-looking hamburgers on the two plates, and Mrs. Davidow carried them over to the table *herself.* I'm surprised she knew how to carry anything but a glass. She was actually *lunching* with Ralph Diggs.

I smiled in Walter's direction. "Well, I've always said Walter *Knepp* is as good as any waiter we've got. He can have the tip too, when he takes my place."

Walter said, in his drawly way, "Miss Bertha don't leave no tips."

"I meant at the end of summer, when they go." I hadn't meant anything at all; it was just empty talk.

My mother had turned to take a plate down from the shelf over the stove. "Well, now that you're here—finally—you can take your great-aunt's tea up to her."

Lucky me.

45

Aurora raised the little lid and looked in the teapot as if looking for more than tea leaves, set it back down and looked at the milk in the pitcher, raised the lid of the sugar bowl and frowned into it. She reminded me of a squirrel looking for a hidden acorn.

Then she picked up one of my mother's lace cookies and studied the holes and tiny slits made by its stretched thinness.

I slouched against the wall and asked a useless question. "What are you doing?"

"Checkin' out my tea. What's it look like?"

"Why are you having tea? You never have tea."

She shrugged and bit the cookie. She plunked four cubes of sugar into her cup. "Milk's cold. Must of come straight out of the icebox."

"I'm so sorry. Next time I'll milk a cow. Now: Raphael Slade." I guessed she was thinking with that blind stare.

She actually rose up out of her chair a few inches, then fell back. The exertion had her munching another lace cookie. Through the crumbs, she said, "Why?"

"That's what I've been asking myself."

"Well . . . All right, the Slade baby gets kidnapped the night of the ball at the Belle Ruin. I was there, did I tell you?"

"A lot of times."

"The belle of the ball, that was me."

Aurora was ninety-one. She would have been around seventy. I guess if you're not dead by then, you're the belle of the ball. I didn't want her to get caught up in that. "You told me before that you were there when Sheriff Mooma came."

"Indeed I was."

"Okay: So Gloria Spiker told him she'd just stepped out to make that phone call and was gone for twenty minutes."

She nodded and bit off another piece of cookie and studied the rest.

"She was lying and so was Prunella Rice. They were both paid to set up that phone call, so when Mr. Woodruff told Sheriff Mooma he just needed some time to work out whether Morris Slade had something to do with the kidnapping, he was lying too. Obviously, Mr. Woodruff knew what was going on and who was responsible, because he knew the phone call was bogus."

Aurora was rocking now with both hands on the arms of her chair and a glint like splinters in her eyes. "That old Lucien Woodruff paid somebody to take the baby away."

"Robby Stone. He was the bellboy that had the car accident."

"You said they found his body, but not the baby's."

I nodded. "So I'm guessing Robby had already delivered the baby to someone."

"Could've killed and buried it."

I did not want the notion of a baby being murdered to hang around in my head too long. "Hardly. As the baby turned out to be Ralph Diggs."

Now she stopped rocking. "Delivered, but nobody knows where." She clucked her tongue. "Ain't that the limit?" She took her deck of cards out of the pocket of her dark blue cotton dress. It was sprigged all over with tiny flower bouquets. She started slapping the cards down, probably more to help her think than from a desire for solitaire. "Why don't you ask him?"

"Ask him? As if he'd tell me. Anyway, I don't want him to know I know. I think Morris Slade was meant to be the guilty party in that so-called kidnapping."

"Framed? God, I think maybe you're gettin' ahead of yourself. You haven't got one speck of hard evidence. Did you get hold of that Oates fellow?"

I think Aurora was getting addled. "Get *hold* of him? How? That was back in your day. I told you I can't pay a private detective." I saw no reason to add that the Wood boys and Mr. Root were on the case.

After serving Aurora's tea, I had a couple of hours until her drink serving. I decided to make a quick trip to Britten's, to see if Mr. Root and the Woods were back.

They were. The three of them were standing together, smoking, or at least Mr. Root and Ubub were. Ulub and Ubub had their old suit jackets on, collars turned up. The collar of Mr. Root's jungle plaid shirt was turned up too. They probably all thought they were searching for the Maltese Falcon. At least it was an improvement over poor Ulub reciting Emily Dickinson. The way they were huddled you'd think there was a dead body at their feet, or else a pile of money.

When they saw me, they made furious motions with their hands, waving me over to the conference.

"Hi. Did you find—?"

They all started talking at once, but Mr. Root was the only one I could understand.

"That Slade fella? We sure did. He—"

"E en at ow fat union—"

"Now, just you wait, Ubub; I'm tellin' this."

Ubub looked crushed. He had very large chocolate brown eyes, and looking crushed was one thing he did well.

Mr. Root backpedaled a bit. "I mean, just the beginning, you know, to put Emma here in the picture."

"Ah en up er n a eur."

We could stand here all day and all night at this rate. I said, "Let

Mr. Root give me the facts, Ubub, and you two can interpret them."
Whatever that meant. But it seemed to mollify them. Sometimes I
wondered at my able diplomacy. I think I was the only one who wondered at it.

"Right," said Mr. Root. "You know where the son of a gun done
went? Cold Flat Junction."

That did surprise me. I don't know where I thought he was headed
for, but that wasn't it. "Where?"

Mr. Root looked as if he'd invented the whole story, pleased as
punch. "Queens' house."

I frowned. Then I remembered, of course: Rose Devereau Queen.

"We sat in the truck—at a distance, mind; he never saw us—and
waited. Whoever came to the door stood talking to him a minute.
Then he went inside and never come out for over an hour."

Ubub blurted, "E usta ha omin a alk out?"

"Indeed," said Mr. Root, nodding. "They musta had somethin'
to talk about, is right."

Ubub looked pleased at his interpretation. Then he said, "En he
c'm out, e ooked ad."

"Mad? Bad?"

All three shook their heads. "Sad," said Mr. Root. "Real sad."

They would have talked about the death of Rose Queen. "Where'd
he go then?"

It was Ulub's turn. He spoke a shade more clearly than his brother.
"En he ent t' the iner."

"What? Did you say the *diner*?"

"Sure did, and we was hot on his heels. Now, diners, that's a place
I feel right at home. Right, fellas?"

I thought for a moment Mr. Root was going to snap his suspend-
ers like Walter Brennan. Morris Slade in the Windy Run Diner. Oh,
how I wish I could have seen it.

"He was havin' coffee. Havin' coffee and smokin' a cigar. Tell you
what: That was the best-smellin' cigar I ever encountered. Looked
expensive too. He clipped off the end with a gold thingamabob and

just smoked away. People in there, hell, you'd've thought he was some foreign official or some member of royalty or other."

Mr. Root went on: "So we had ourselves some coffee and some coconut cream pie—"

"Ah ate appa'." Ulub wanting to set the record straight.

"Good pie," said Mr. Root.

By now we were all sitting down, crowded onto the bench that could comfortably hold only three, listening to this story, Ulub and Ubub listening right along with me, as if they hadn't actually been there and were hearing it for the first time.

"Now, the lady behind the counter that waited on us all, you could see she was all agog, seeing the likes of him in there. Well, you got to admit, Morris Slade looks pretty good."

I had to admit Morris Slade looked pretty good.

Morris Slade and the Queens.

Added to the mystery of why he was here at all was what business he could have in Cold Flat Junction.

"Fey" Slade. It was a peculiar nickname to draw from "Raphael." Why not "Ralph" or, even more likely, "Rafe," as he was calling himself.

According to the police report, he was no more than four months old when he was taken. That's if Sheriff Mooma was to be believed, and I saw no reason to doubt him.

I had just delivered Aurora her before-dinner drink and pondered all of this as she pronounced the Hollow Leg the best one yet. I'll say this about her. She can be quite complimentary. But then I guess even Mrs. Davidow would be paying me compliments if her glass were three-fourths whiskey and one-fourth apple juice and, in this case, a tiny bit of crushed-up red chili, which gave it its kick. I mean, whatever kick the whiskey didn't provide.

I studied the posters on the walls. Aurora had been a big traveler in her youth, sailing off on the *Queen Mary* and "almost" on the *Titanic,* she said, "But I canceled that. I knew something bad was going to happen." Like the captain knew, when he saw that iceberg, I didn't bother adding. The only second sight I can put up with is Mrs. Louderback's.

The posters were not framed, but just put up with a sticky gum-like material behind each corner. They showed slim men and women looking rich and being gay in Brittany, the Côte d'Azur, Deauville, Capri, and places such as that. Above the beach in Deauville, where brilliant umbrellas fluttered in what must have been a warm breeze and a golden sun, a woman in a bathing suit waved to her friends farther down on the beach. Rich and happy people waved to other rich and happy people in the distance. Did women really dress like that in those airy-looking gowns, so thin and flat they looked like ocean waves themselves? And men in boaters and striped jackets happily handing these women down to patios covered with plum trees. Hanging around a chauffeur-driven car, a woman wrapped in white fur waved at someone else out there, dancing under the stars.

They all looked so fortunate that I had to wonder if it was really this life they were living, or if they were waving to me from latitudes I probably would never be lucky enough to share.

I was snatched back from Deauville by ice rattling in Aurora's glass as she held out her hand and demanded another Hollow Leg. I didn't protest; I couldn't be bothered. I was making plans for tomorrow.

46

I was glad I was wearing a sweater because there really was a wind coming down Windy Run Road and it just about blew the metal-framed door of the diner back out of my hand. I knew the first comment would be of the just-blew-in variety.

"Well, look what that wind out there just blowed in!"

This was Evren, sitting on his usual counter stool between Don Joe and Billy.

For several boring minutes, while I studied the pies in their glass case, they all talked about the weather. Then Mervin came in without his wife (I was glad to see) and said hello to everyone and slid into his usual booth.

Louise Snell smiled and asked, "You want lunch, Mervin, or just coffee?"

"Coffee, thanks. Too early for lunch." Then he thought better of it and said, "Maybe a waffle, Louise, to hold me over." He kind of laughed, then smiled at me, tipping his head in greeting, as if it were a hat. "How are you, Emma?"

Evren answered for me: "She nearly got blowed to Alaska."

Don Joe put in, "One of our fifty states. The other bein' Hawa-ya, if I remember correctly." He stared at me.

I crimped my mouth shut. He was never going to let it rest that

I'd corrected him about the forty-eight states. I let "Hawa-ya" be, though I was sorely tempted. When Louise Snell asked me if I'd like a piece of pie I said no, I'd like a doughnut. I'd taken to heart what Mervin had said; it was a little early for lunch. It had better be, if I was to get back to serve it.

I tried to come up with some easy way of getting talk around to the stranger in the tan suit with a cigar.

"So what you up to this mornin', girl? You finished writin' that story yet?"

This came from Don Joe, to Billy's obvious displeasure, for he always wanted to be the one to ask first. It was the perfect subject, one that I'd almost forgotten about because I'd hardly worked on it for nearly two weeks. "No, I haven't finished. That's one reason why I came. I need to talk to the Queens again. And I'd like to talk to their cousin. I hope he's still around." I munched my doughnut.

Interest sparked. Here was a fresh topic. Billy waded right in. "Now he wouldn't be a tall blond fella, kinda citified type?"

"Citified? He probably is, as he's from New York."

Mervin said, "I'd not call him blond, Billy. No, his hair's more tawny, you know." He was looking at me. "All shades of blond and light brown."

Billy had swung around on his stool to face Mervin. "Mervin, is them specs you got on in need of cleanin'? 'Cause you don't see very well in 'em. That hair was blond hair if I ever did see blond hair." He swung back to face the counter.

Then Evren dared to say, "Well, now, I think Mervin's got a point there—"

Billy glared at Evren, and Evren drank his Coke. "Pretty soon you'll be sayin' the man was drivin' a Ford."

Don Joe got a swallow of coffee spewed out of his nose when he laughed. He said to me, "He was drivin' a Porch."

I wanted to say he drove a Porch all over Hawa-ya, but I held my tongue.

Louise Snell, who, like Mervin, had good sense, said, "Yeah, and all of you looked like you was six years old, gawking out of the window as he drove off."

"You got to admit, Louise, we don't get many of them kinda cars around here."

"Good thing too, the effect it had. And it's 'Porsche,' Don Joe."

"What is?"

"The car. You were callin' it a Porch."

"No, I never—"

Mervin said, "Wasn't a Porsche, anyway."

Billy fumed. "Now just where do you get off sayin' that, Mervin?"

Mervin shrugged. "It wasn't big enough. That was one of those Italian automobiles."

Before Billy could contradict this, I said, "Did he say anything about going to see the Queens?"

"No. We asked him—Billy did—if he was from around here," said Don Joe, interrupting himself to blow on the fresh coffee that Louise Snell poured into his cup.

Billy picked up on this. "Said no, that he was from over to La Porte. Born and bred there. But now he was living in New York City. Manhattan, he said. He just come back for a visit."

I was surprised Morris Slade would talk to them. But I guess their questions were just the usual ones, hardly what you'd call probing.

Billy went on. "He said he knew the Queens from when he lived here. In La Porte, I mean."

"He's related to 'em." This flat statement came from Mervin, who was now eating the waffle Louise Snell had set before him.

"What?" Billy swung around to confront Mervin, as he always did. "Now, Mervin, the man never said he was any relation."

"Emma just said he was a cousin. He looks like 'em." Mervin frowned a bit, his forkful of waffle suspended before him. "I mean like Rose Queen. He looks like her."

The counter sitters all looked dumbstruck by this comment. As a matter of fact, I felt struck dumb too, that Mervin would notice such a thing.

Anytime Mervin claimed a knowledge of Rose, Billy got huffy. "Mervin, we been over this before. You ain't exactly a Junction native; you're a newcomer—"

(I bet there weren't many of those around.)

"—and you never did know Rose Queen." Billy considered himself the expert on Rose.

"I saw pictures of her in newspapers. That man looked enough like her to be her twin."

Billy was completely discombobulated (a favorite word of my mother's) and just swung back and forth on his stool, trying to contradict this. "Rose Queen was murdered twenty years ago. You wasn't even here. So you saw a picture in an old paper. Now, are you sayin' your memory's that good you can see her face enough to compare it with his?"

"It's not my memory that's that good. It's her face. You'd not forget her face."

The suggestion that Billy had forgotten her face nearly sent the man flying off his stool. He was red in the face and balling up a fist.

Louise Snell said, "Oh, for God's sake, Billy. Mervin just has an eye for things." She was wiping down the counter.

"You don't think I got an eye? Sure, I noticed he looked like Rose. Of course I did." He muttered something else over the rim of his coffee mug.

They were irritating me. "Why didn't somebody just ask him? Why didn't you say, 'You wouldn't be related to Rose Queen, would you?' Or Devereau. It'd be Rose Devereau Queen, wouldn't it?"

This was something else to mull over. Now they all looked discombobulated, even Mervin, a little. So I gave them an out. "You probably didn't want to appear nosy, that's why." No, it wasn't. They were some of the nosiest-appearing people I'd ever known. But they had their roundabout ways, just like me. We were like jays that would rather have to crack open a sunflower seed than be presented with the nut inside. Maybe that's why I liked to come here, to be with people with roundabout ways.

I could tell it annoyed Billy that somebody else was accounting for Rose Queen. He shrugged and again muttered something I didn't hear.

I had my stub of a pencil, but I'd forgotten my notebook, so I took a couple of paper napkins from the holder. I put money down for my doughnut, swung down off my stool, and said good-bye.

"Well, how are you, Emma?"

I was glad it was George Queen who came to the door instead of his wife, Sheba, who didn't especially like me, although she did serve me cookies when I was here before. I'd managed to get rid of them. My mother's cookies had spoiled me for anyone else's. I think I crumbled up Sheba's and tossed them off the porch.

"How are you, Mr. Queen? I'm real sorry to bother you again."

He held wide the door. "No bother at all. Come on in."

I did. Last time we had sat on the porch, which I much preferred. The walls of rooms hold you in more and hold in what you say. They're stricter.

The rooms seemed dark. The one we went into held dark brown and olive green chairs and a sofa—I think horsehair or something that had an ugliness to it—with thick arms and cushions that looked like no one ever sat in them, and all of them looking as if they were daring you to do it.

Mr. Queen sat down in one of the chairs and motioned me to another. I sat gingerly on the edge. The upholstery was rough and scratchy.

"You still being a reporter, Emma?" He smiled.

It was as if reporting were a holiday costume you put on and took off. But I had found most people didn't understand the writing life. However, his question did remind me that I hadn't finished, had barely started, my next installment.

"Yes, I am. It's why I'm here. You remember about the Belle Ruin and the kidnapping?"

He nodded. "That little baby. The Slade kid."

"I'm still trying to get details. . . . I'm looking for the backstory."
I loved that word; it was fast becoming my favorite.

"Backstory?"

"About Imogen and Morris Slade. You know—what their life was like. They lived in New York City, I think." It came to me there was no reason to be asking George Queen about Morris Slade. There was no way I should know Morris Slade had been here, or even that Morris and Rose were related. He'd be no relation to these Queens. But I had to keep on at this point. "And they lived here, of course. I mean in La Porte. I understand Morris Slade was brought up there. His wife's family had a house in Spirit Lake. All that, that's backstory."

"Well, now, this is a coincidence."

No, it wasn't. I breathed easier.

"It was only just yesterday Morris Slade came to see us—"

I made my eyes wide. "Really?" I took out the napkins and pencil stub. It didn't look very professional.

George Queen went on. "He seemed a nice-enough fella. I can't figure why people took against him so much. Like Sheba did." He inclined his head in the direction where Sheba must have been and I hoped would stay.

"She took a dislike to him years ago when she was a teacher and him a student at Colonel Henry E. Mott High School. It's out there on 219; you've seen it, I imagine."

I was trying to take notes, which was hard with just the napkin.

"Sheba said he was stuck-up and runnin' after every girl in school." He seemed to like the idea, for he smiled. "Then grown-up, he was a real playboy."

Playboy. That word again. "How was he? I mean, a playboy?"

George Queen scratched his head. What little hair remained to him was gray bristles. "Oh, chasin' after girls, drinkin', goin' to clubs." He lowered his voice. "It didn't help any that Fern had this terrible crush on him too."

Go on, I thought. He didn't. So I prompted. "Now, his mother. I think I heard she was a Souder?"

"Yeah, she was. Married old man Devereau after that Ralph Slade died. Rose was her daughter. Devereau was married before to . . . Hell, I can't remember. Anyway, those sisters of hers, they were the first wife's children. Guess she died too. Anyway, Rose and Morris is half sister and brother."

"So that's how you knew him, because Rose was his sister. Half sister."

George Queen shook his head. "I never did know him all that well. It was Ben knew him. And of course Rose more than Ben."

Oh, I thought, as if air had just whooshed out of me, or as if I'd suddenly sat on one of those trick cushions. "They were friends, you mean."

George Queen was fishing in his pocket for something, probably cigarettes, but not finding them. "Well, no, I don't know as they were exactly friends. . . ." He stopped talking, frowned.

"Is your brother Ben around here, Mr. Queen?" What could I lose, asking?

He shook his head. "I don't know where Ben is. All that prison stuff took a lot out of him."

That prison stuff would take a lot out of me too.

"Anyway, he's cleared of killing Rose, thank the good Lord. And will be of killing Fern, I'm sure." He sighed.

But apart from that sigh, there hadn't been much sorrow shown over Fern Queen. And I think there had been something terribly wrong—maybe Devereau wrong—with Fern, given the murderous Isabel Devereau. I could hardly blame them if they couldn't feel sorry Fern was dead, when she'd caused so much grief. I remember the Sheriff saying that a gene must have come down that missed her mother, Rose, but "blasted that girl to kingdom come."

I'd like to have asked about Fern "going off" for several months, but I didn't know how to introduce that.

I was even more sure than George Queen that Ben hadn't killed Fern, because I knew who killed her: Isabel Devereau. The police would like an eyewitness to it; apparently my testimony wouldn't be convincing enough, as it was hearsay. Hearsay evidence. Shot at out on the lake by crazy Isabel, and all the Sheriff could say was "hearsay evidence."

Unfortunately, Mrs. Sheba Queen chose to come into the room just then, standing hands on hips, looking as if she might be going to rearrange the furniture.

"You recall Emma, don't you, Sheba? She's writing up a story for the newspaper in La Porte."

Fiddling with one of the antimacassars on the sofa back that I guessed were there to protect the furniture from people's oily heads, she kind of nodded as she straightened it and then sat down. She said, "Well, I don't think Morris Slade is any proper topic for a child, George."

But George Queen hadn't mentioned Morris Slade.

Her eyes bored into me as if she were suspicious of my being a child. Was I possibly something else? An elf, maybe? Sheba Queen did not like me.

"Why not? What did he do?" I asked in my innocent, elflike way.

"Never you mind, young lady."

If there was anything I hated more than being called "young lady," it was not being told gossip. "It's just that I should put it in my account if it's connected—"

But she was wagging her finger at me. "We'll just leave that subject rest."

No, we won't. "Mr. Queen says you were one of Morris Slade's teachers at Colonel Henry E. Mott High School."

She pleated her skirt with two thin fingers. Her smile was as crimped as her skirt. "Tried to be." She sounded awfully self-satisfied for some reason, even more than Aurora Paradise when telling me of yet another suitor begging her to be his. I wondered if everything came down to love ("sex," I should say, but I didn't know enough to say it more often), love and money.

"Thing about Morris was, he wouldn't ever put his mind to anything for long enough to learn it. Oh, he was charming and all—"

Yes, Morris Slade was definitely on her mind. And I wondered where in heaven's name he'd come by all his charm, since I'd never seen any in the Souder branch of the family, at least not in Souder's Pharmacy, except for the Evening in Paris window display.

She went on. "Thought he was the bee's knees, Morris did."

Bee's knees! I wrote that down with such a wallop I tore the napkin. That was going into my account no matter what! She was still talking.

"—and you'd've thought certain females on the faculty would've demonstrated more sense than to let that boy pull the wool over their eyes with his little Christmas presents of cologne and such—"

Bought at a discount in Souder's or merely snatched out of the window, I supposed. Yet, somehow I could believe the opposite of this, of Morris chasing the girls and kowtowing to the teachers. I wouldn't be surprised if it wasn't the other way around: the girls doing the chasing, the teachers the kowtowing. If he was anything back then like he was today. My mind's eye caught at him for a few silent seconds and then let go.

"But they didn't see through him," said Sheba. "No, sir. I did."

And I knew in a flash that Sheba didn't get any Evening in Paris cologne or any other "little presents" from Morris Slade. That was what told against him. Well, it was kind of sad, or would have been if I'd felt inclined.

She went on: "And I told him he would not pass my course if he was absent again and not to give me any of his made-up excuses."

I'd noticed Mr. Queen opening his mouth to say something, then shutting it again. That Sheba Queen must have found Morris Slade near-irresistible was clear, even though she was fifteen or twenty years older than he. I tried to dam the flood of words: "So then, Mrs. Queen, what do you think happened to Morris Slade's baby back on that night at the Belle Ruin? That's mostly the subject of my story."

She shook her head. "I guess like most people, I think the baby was being held to ransom, seeing as how Morris Slade's father-in-law was so rich. That's what he married for: money."

George Queen chuckled. "Well, yesterday you seemed to think he was pretty nice."

"Oh, for heaven's sake, George. I was just being polite." A flush crept up her neck into her face.

Casually tapping my pencil against the chair arm, I said, "He might have just wanted to see you for old times' sake." I smiled unconvincingly.

"Him?" Sheba motioned with her hand, waving old times away. "Morris Slade never had a sentimental bone in his body."

I doubted if that was true. I was trying to work Ralph Diggs into the conversation. "Maybe he believes the baby is still alive somewhere, and he's trying to track it down."

"Hmm," muttered George.

Sheba just waved her hand again. "That's ridiculous. Why ever would he do that?"

George said, "He wanted to talk to Ben." He leaned forward in his chair, hands clasped loosely before him, as if this were deserving of thought.

His voice fell away and before he could get it back his wife had risen briskly and was now offering milk and cookies. She became, in little bursts, hospitable.

I thanked her but said no thanks, not to put herself to the trouble.

"Oh, it ain't no trouble." And she whisked herself away like a stiff broom.

"What did you wonder, Mr. Queen?"

He shook his head and looked at me as if he were surprised I was still there. "Now, is all of this talk necessary for the what-d'ya-call-it?"

"Backstory?"

"Yeah, that."

No, but it probably was for the understory.

It was time for me to go. Before the cookies.

Maybe Morris Slade had been drawn back by the murder of Rose and wanted to see Ben Queen because of that.

I frowned. And Ralph Diggs?

Somehow, he had found out about the events at the Belle Ruin. I knew I was getting ahead of myself to think this fellow knew he'd been kidnapped, or stolen out of the hotel, twenty years ago.

For how could he come to know that? He would first off have to discover the man and woman he always thought of as Mom and Dad weren't his parents. How? Was it as simple as an overheard conversation?

"Shouldn't we tell him."

"Why? Why should we?"

"Doesn't he deserve to know we're not his real parents?"

And so on.

For I knew he wasn't who he said he was, and that he'd taken this job so he could hang around us, not us at the Hotel Paradise necessarily, but around Spirit Lake. Or maybe La Porte. He wanted to be in this area. I knew he wanted to be able to stop awhile around here.

And that he had a spectacular motive for doing this.

47

Carl Mooma was probably a more dependable source than Gloria Spiker Calhoun; still, I wanted to clear up one little point, and I could take fifteen or twenty minutes to see Gloria before the train came.

The Calhoun house was the prettiest blue house I'd ever seen. Maybe it was just that the colors of houses in Cold Flat Junction were a relief from the white-wood-and-green-shuttered Victorians in Spirit Lake. (Spirit Lake, though, had a lot more money in it than the Junction.)

As I walked up the zinnia-brightened path to the blue house, I wondered if I'd ever see Gloria's husband, Cary Grant Calhoun. I still wanted to verify whether he looked like Cary Grant, the movie star his mother had idolized, or if he was as unattractive as the people in the Windy Run Diner had said. He was probably just ordinary-looking.

"Hi, Gloria," I said when she came to the door.

"Why, hello, Emma. Come on in. I'm just about to take a batch of lemon drop cookies out of the oven!"

As if that were great news. The housewives in Cold Flat Junction all seemed to think cookies were the high point of their day. I guessed I'd have to eat one to be polite. "Oh, swell," I said, walking with her back to the lemony-smelling kitchen that looked so neat you'd have thought nothing was ever baked in it. It was what you called "pristine": cleared counters, scrubbed sink, polished fittings.

Gloria had the oven door open and the cookie pan she slid out held perfect little circles of pale yellow cookies. I didn't like lemon except in my mother's lemon meringue pies. And she never made lemon cookies.

Gloria pushed nearly half the panful of cookies out on a glass plate the same blue as the house. Indeed, this place was as blue as Prunella Rice's was brown. Did they know they had a competition going?

She held the plate of cookies out to me.

"Oh, I wish I could have one, but you know I have sugar diabetes. I especially am not supposed to eat baked goods. Pastries and things."

Poor Gloria's hand flew to her face as if she'd been enticing me toward death.

I supposed you died if you ate a lot of sugar, but my thinking was fuzzy on the point. I knew that people had to get shots of something for the condition. "My! It's after eleven and will soon be time for my shot," I said.

Gloria looked as if she might be going to call for medical attention.

"Oh, don't worry. It can wait until noon." I sat down on a kitchen chair as if I might be going to be dizzy just from smelling sweetness.

"You have to take shots? You mean insulin?"

"Insulin shots, that's right for sugar diabetes, yes. But I just give them to myself." I smoothed my hands over my skirt. "I just wanted to ask you something."

She sat down too, in a scrubbed-to-death pine chair. "You still writing that story about the Belle Ruin?"

"That's right. You remember when you were in the Slades' room at the hotel? When they told you not to bother the baby?"

Gloria nodded. "It was she that told me. Said the baby was sick or something and would probably just sleep on."

"Think carefully. What you said was that Mrs. Slade told you not to bother her—is that right?"

Gloria frowned. She answered slowly, as if she feared a trap. She should have, but not from me.

"I guess that's what she said."

"All I mean is, did she tell you 'don't bother *her*'? Or 'don't bother Fey'? Or maybe just 'the baby'?"

Relaxing a little (the question seeming so innocuous, I guessed), she pursed her mouth thoughtfully and said, "Well, I think she just said not to bother the baby, or, no . . . 'It' is what she said. I remember now. She referred to the baby as 'it.' That's kind of cold, don't you think?"

I certainly did, but it served my purpose well. So I agreed with her about the coldness. I was sure that Gloria must have remembered every instant pretty clearly. Given her criminal part in it.

I thanked her and jumped up—my insulin shot, you know—and left hurriedly.

48

Why was it that Ree-Jane chose this particular time to go mad?

Although the mad ordinarily must have their fates chosen for them, with Ree-Jane conscious calculation had to be involved.

I'll say this: it was really attention-getting, the way she went twirling around the porch in her Heather Gay Struther tiny-pleated rhubarb pink dress, singing "Bye Bye Blackbird."

I had heard the singing before I reached the porch. She was both singing and laughing, holding up her skirt at the sides.

"What are you doing?" I asked this in a loud voice.

She didn't answer. But I knew she'd heard me because her eyes slithered sideways and her crazylike smile got wider. I stood and watched until she got through the part about no one loving or understanding her (while I thought, *How true*). Then I veered off toward the kitchen to fix the salads.

Vera was there, white-collared and -cuffed. She reminded me of pictures I'd seen of old English tombs, where the knight and lady were laid out in stone atop their stone caskets, their stone faces sharp and gaunt.

We must be having a dinner party. "Who's coming?"

"The Baums," said Vera, unsmilingly.

"How many?"

"Eight. I can handle it."

She could handle eight hundred, she was so efficient. That was fine with me. I lined up the salad plates, ten of them, two for Miss Bertha and her party.

My mother was concentrating on the electric mixer, adding oil drop by drop into the bowl, so it must be Roquefort cheese dressing. She could not be disturbed in this process, any more than Agatha Christie could, writing the end of one of her books that Miss Flyte's dying friend never read. So I waited until she was done before I asked, "What's the matter with Ree-Jane?"

She shrugged. "We don't know." She pushed the lever that released the big bowl of the mixer and poured the contents into two large mason jars.

The "'we' don't" told me there'd been discussion about it, so they thought it was more than just Ree-Jane being herself. I was about to pass on the information that she was on the porch whirling like a dervish (and hoping she'd keep it up until the Baum party pulled up under the porte cochere), when Mrs. Davidow slammed into the kitchen. For once the color high in her face wasn't from drinking. She shouldered my mother along to a corner out of hearing distance and her mouth started working furiously. Happily, I sorted through the olives, looking for a small one to hide under one of Miss Bertha's lettuce leaves.

Then to my great surprise, Lola Davidow headed toward me like a tanker approaching a pleasure boat. Was it to be all my fault?

"Emma, I want you to go out to the front porch and try to stop Jane singing."

I dropped the lettuce leaf. *My* help was being requested? *I* was to de-twirl Ree-Jane? Oh, but *what* a *great* assignment!

I figured, as I walked toward the front of the hotel, that if the act was to get attention, Ree-Jane would be happy to have people try to shut her up; on the other hand, if she was really going mad, nobody could stop her. In either case it looked fairly hopeless.

Just then, Miss Bertha was coming down the staircase and holding to the banister as if the steps were made of glass. "What is all this commotion?"

"Jane Davidow." I smiled.

She grunted as she maneuvered the slippery slope of the stairs and asked where Ree-Jane's mother was. I told her and she set off like a little steam engine, going pretty fast for her.

It was then that Ralph Diggs appeared, as he often did, seemingly out of nowhere, though of course it wasn't; he'd probably been walking down the hallway of the left wing, hidden by Miss Bertha on the stairs. Now he had come around and was here.

"What's going on?"

"Nothing." I flopped down in an armchair and picked up a magazine. "Nothing" was hard to believe, what with Ree-Jane dancing and singing past the front screen door.

He walked to the door and watched and listened. He was wearing his linen "bellhop" jacket, probably ready to open car doors for the dinner guests. He plucked the cigarette from behind his ear and lit it with his Zippo, which he let fall again into his jacket pocket. He made no move to go out onto the porch.

In another few minutes, Lola Davidow was coming through the hall from the direction of the dining room, looking determined and ruddy-faced.

Lola saw Ralph and immediately nodded him over to join her. That annoyed me. I was angry with myself for letting him detour me away from going out on the porch, but what chance would I have anyway to try to stop Ree-Jane's nutty behavior, what with her mother here and now Ralph on the job.

I could not imagine why he would be taken into anyone's confidence, or be included in any plan to calm Ree-Jane, who was singing louder than ever.

Of course, they didn't know what I knew—or thought I knew— about him, but couldn't Mrs. Davidow see through the flattery and smiles enough to realize he was putting her on? She wasn't what you'd call a "student of human nature," but she wasn't stupid about people either. I'd heard enough talks between her and my mother that showed she could cut some people open like a watermelon and count the seeds. At the same time, I thought Mrs. Davidow might at times be starving for flattery and would take compliments any way she found them and from anyone. I mean, how long could I put up with Dwayne, do you think, if I didn't have the hide of a buffalo?

Will could put something over on her, but then, Will, even at his age, was smoother than Ralph Diggs. He just wasn't as insinuating, you could say. Will's smoothness came partly from being raised in a hotel, and partly because he'd been born smooth. I pictured him as a baby being picked up by a nurse and gently sanded down until there were no sharp edges anywhere.

But Rafe Diggs was all sharp edges.

Mrs. Davidow was putting keys in his hand and I heard her telling him to bring the car around. I wondered what car and why he was to drive it. Then she said something about a hospital and Cloverly. Cloverly was twenty-five miles away, and twice the size of La Porte. I hadn't known it had a hospital.

Then Ree-Jane came in. No: I should say she *entered*. She made an entrance, her face bright and flushed, her eyes nearly sparking from all of this excess energy she'd found. She fairly flew across the lobby and up the stairs.

I watched Ralph watching her with that little sideways smile of his, not a smirk, exactly, but not far from it. Was that car key in his hand a good idea?

When Mrs. Davidow separated herself from yet another phone call and headed toward the back office, I followed. Probably my opinion didn't count for much, but I said, "Ralph Diggs driving Ree"— I caught myself—"driving *Jane* anywhere. You can't trust him."

She stopped and looked at me. "She won't go with me and we have a dinner party, so your mother can't drive her. Who else is there?" She had poured herself a measure of Jim Beam and now tossed it back, neat.

Well, I had to admire her, in a way. I guess for not flying apart, for not yelling and making a scene. And what scene could ever follow Ree-Jane's act? For it was an act, surely?

I said at least someone else should go along. I was thinking of Will. But she said no; Jane thought everyone was against her.

I left the back office just in time to see Ree-Jane more or less waltzing down the stairs with a small suitcase. She had dressed up the rhubarb by winding a blue silk scarf around her neck.

Ralph said he'd be back in time for the Baums' party. Easily. It was only a little after five and Cloverly was only twenty-five miles away.

With her suitcase and her merry face and her devil-may-care attitude, you'd have thought they were a happy couple dashing off on their honeymoon, not going to the loony bin.

We stood on the porch, we three, and watched the white convertible bucketing along down the gravel drive, Ree-Jane's sea blue scarf whipping back in the wind, her arm raised and her hand waving, waving like one of the happy, rich women above the beach at Deauville, in one of Aurora's travel posters. Waving whatever was left of the sane world farewell.

Ralph Diggs did come back, as he said, inside of two hours. He was there to grace the front steps when the Baums arrived. I did not hear what he told Mrs. Davidow and my mother later, in the kitchen, even though I got my tray as close to their little group as I could where they were gathered by the salad table; or even though I hung around the crock of salad dressing as long as I could. Strangely, I kept reminding myself of the maid in her black uniform, kneeling at the keyhole on the magazine cover, even though Vera was the black-uniformed, white-cuffed one among us.

After dinner, I hung around the long hall where Ralph's room was. When I heard someone coming up the stairs that led from the dining room to the second floor, I walked quickly into the hall bathroom, and when I heard the steps in the hall, I came out, casually flicking off the light switch as I left.

"Oh, hi."

Ralph Diggs nodded, but didn't say anything. Yet he stopped as if inviting conversation.

I accepted. "Well, that must have been pretty hard driving all the way to Cloverly and back in time for dinner, wasn't it?"

He leaned against the wall in that lounging way of his and took the cigarette from behind his ear. It was like the way he'd drawn the coin from behind mine, the magic gesture. He almost always had that cigarette behind his ear. It reminded me of Dwayne with his oily rag. It had never occurred to me before that maybe the rag was a comfort, something you could depend upon, something always by you. So maybe the cigarette was a comfort for Ralph. I wondered if my roundabout ways were like that.

Finally, he answered. "I'm a fast driver."

"Still, you had to take Ree-Jane—I mean, Jane—into the hospital. I mean, you didn't just drop her off and say, 'See you later.'"

"No. I went in with her to the admitting desk."

"What happened?" I asked directly.

"Someone, a woman, came and got her. She took charge."

He was still for a moment. Then he said, "She didn't look back. Jane, I mean."

He said this as if he'd thought about it, as if it were important. I never thought of Ree-Jane as doing anything important in all the time I'd known her.

He said, "I guess you have to feel sorry for her."

No, *I* didn't have to. I found this annoying, really annoying that he should be telling me how to feel. I'd been doing a perfectly good job of feeling for myself before he came along. I said, in a more irritated way than I actually felt, "You think she's really, you know, mentally ill? I think it's just a big act, all of that dancing and singing, trying to make people believe she's, well, interesting, because she's crazy."

He was silent for an uncomfortably long moment. The thing was, his silences carried a weight of words I didn't get. It wasn't exactly silence; it was more as if there were another language running beneath his words. It was as if he came from somewhere with a separate language, a language I would never speak and a somewhere I would never see. Finally, he said, "You'd still have to feel sorry for her. I mean, to be so driven you'd have to go that far."

This was so intensely sad, I would have taken a step back if the wall hadn't been there. I tried to rid myself of the feeling with a little sarcasm: "Well, I'm sure you didn't come here with the idea of having to drive someone to a *mental* hospital." I also thought this was a way of getting the subject around to why he was here.

He didn't speak. He looked at me as if I were something alien to his world.

I added, "You said you were just passing through. What made you stop here and look for a job?"

"I needed a place to stay and I'm low on cash. A hotel, I thought, would be a place that could use somebody."

It sounded reasonable. Almost.

"You're not getting paid."

"No, but I'm getting a room and food. Some food."

It was the first subject we could talk about without being so guarded. "Yes, it's some food, all right."

The cigarette was nearly smoked down by now. A long ash hung from it; I wondered why it didn't fall. It seemed to levitate. Another bit of magic.

I was not doing a very good job of extracting information, so I said good night and shrugged myself away from the wall and from him.

That night in bed I let my mind drift back over the last few weeks, looking for hints of Ree-Jane's serious craziness. But all I could see seemed to have been there ever since I'd known her: talking to herself, or, more disturbing, to someone else that no one could see; the awful silent laughter that was meant to suggest to me I was an idiot; acting generally like a six-year-old. I had been sure she was just putting on an act, but that night, I was less sure. And after listening to Ralph Diggs, I wondered, Wouldn't putting on an act like that be crazy in itself? Then I thought of the picture of the black-uniformed maid kneeling by a door and wondered if maybe I was looking at Ralph Diggs through a keyhole. I turned on my side and watched a shadow on the wall made by the dim hall light coming in through the transom and wondered if I lived a keyhole kind of life.

49

"I t's some mental condition," said my mother the next morning, lifting my perfectly done eggs over easy with a spatula from an iron skillet.

"We all have *some* mental condition, don't we?"

"Don't be amusing." She put the cast-iron skillet back on the stove with more force than seemed necessary and took up the flat one with its three pecan pancakes and slid them onto my plate. "I can tell you it's thrown my morning into a cocked hat."

I assumed she was talking about Lola Davidow's nonstop telephoning, mostly to the Tri-State Hospital outside of Cloverly, before and after her own sturdy breakfast. Ree-Jane's condition hadn't had much effect on her appetite. But then, it was my mother's cooking, after all. People would eat it on the way to a hanging.

I ate my eggs and pancakes in the company of Walter, who was drowning a stack of cakes in maple syrup. Walter looked less crazy by the minute.

Following that, I called Axel's Taxis and asked for Axel to pick me up and waited on the porch, rocking away, until Delbert came.

You would not think of madness, murder, and kidnapped infants if you drove along the main street of La Porte; or if

you walked around Spirit Lake; or stood in the old train station of Cold Flat Junction. Yet that is what has happened in
these tragic places.

Mr. Gumbrel was reading aloud what I'd written for my next
piece in the paper.

You have already read in this paper about the drowning of
Mary-Evelyn Devereau in Spirit Lake forty years ago. This
was always counted an "accident." But *accident* is not what
it was. No, it was a cold-blooded murder. Mary-Evelyn was
drowned by her own sisters who were also insane.

Mr. Gumbrel stopped reading, made an "um–hmm" sort of sound,
and said, "You mean all of them? All three of them were insane? And
drowned that little girl?"

"I wanted to avoid calling attention to any one of them." No, I
didn't. I wanted to avoid writing any more than I had to. "According
to Isabel, when she was pointing that gun at me, 'Elizabeth was the
first.' Meaning, the first one to hold her under, I guess. The only sister
I'm not sure about was Iris. She might have been pretty sane."

"I'll tell you one thing that's real good about this, Emma: It's
leisurely."

Leisurely. That didn't sound too good to me. "Do you think that's
good when I'm telling about three murders and a kidnapping? And
an attempted murder?" I kept forgetting my own hairbreadth
escape.

"Of course I do. If you've got all that in the story, you wouldn't
want the reader to be hurried along, forced along like a train wreck."

I pursed my lips. I wished there *had* been a train wreck. "Well,
okay. I just don't want to get in the habit of being overwordy. Sometimes I'm afraid I go on. . . ."

"No, sir. You're creating context, that's all. And atmosphere.
Now, listen, this is really good: Police Pursue the Wrong Person.

That grabs you right off. For the reader to find out that baby was a boy, not a girl! My God, you really do have sources, girl!"

> It happened one warm summer night at the Belle Rouen hotel, popularly known as the Belle Ruin.
> There was music. There was moonlight. There was dancing. There was a ladder placed up against a window.

Mr. Gumbrel was not reading aloud; I was reading over his shoulder. If I say so myself, I really liked the music-moonlight-dancing-ladder construction. It all sounded dreamy. And sinister. What was that ladder doing there? Well, I know now: nothing.

I had not named Gloria Spiker as the babysitter, thinking she certainly didn't need the bad publicity. Anyway, everyone knew who the babysitter was.

And I did not name Carl Mooma as my source, for the same reason.

50

She was back.

Less than twenty-four hours later and here she was.

When I returned around one p.m. from my visit to the *Conservative,* Ree-Jane was sitting on the front porch, rocking away, smiling in her huge, vacant way at nothing unless it was me getting out of the cab.

Only now the smile was beating down on me with a kind of victory over anything that stood in her path. If you could put lipstick on a steamroller, that was what it would be like, that smile bearing down.

After I slammed the cab door on Delbert's monologue, I climbed the steps. "You're up early," I said, flopping down in the chair beside her.

That kind of threw her. "What?"

I yawned as if she'd never been away.

She was wearing a bunch of silver bangles, and she ran them up and down her arm. "It was just temporary."

"What was?" Her life, I hoped.

She was really frustrated. "My . . . fugue state."

Whatever "fugue" meant, it wasn't Ree-Jane's state.

She leaned her head back and smiled up at the porch light or at the collection of moths at its bottom, dead or in a fugue state. "Rafe is wonderful, isn't he?"

"No," I said.

"What? What do you mean, 'No'?"

"No, he isn't wonderful."

Now she leaned, as if in confidence sharing, over the arm of her chair, close to me. "We wouldn't be just a teensy bit jealous, would we?" Back on track.

"Why would I be jealous of Ralph?"

"Rafe, not Ralph."

"Why would I be jealous of Ray?"

"*Rafe,* for God's sake. *Rafe.*"

"Why would I?"

Her flushed face was what Emily Dickinson might have found "hectic." "I don't mean of him. I mean jealous of *us*!"

I feigned puzzlement. "Why would I be jealous of us?" I could have kept this up all afternoon if I hadn't been due in the kitchen ten minutes before.

Now she brought a fist down on the chair arm. "Not you and me! Me and Ralph."

"Rafe."

She flew up, sending her chair back on its rockers. "Oh, you think you're so smart!"

Back on track.

As she slammed the screen door, I set my hand on her vacated chair, rocking crazily—me, the great calmer.

I was, of course, avidly interested in what had happened and made a beeline for the kitchen, where my mother used her most guilt-inducing tone.

"I'd think you'd manage to get here on time to serve Mr. Muggs."

Mr. Muggs was the Poor Soul whom I had glimpsed through the dining room window above the wooden walk that ran from the side door to the kitchen.

"He's been waiting for nearly a quarter of an hour and so have Miss Bertha and Mrs. Fulbright."

I leaned stiff-armed on the counter. "I was stopped on the porch. Ree-Jane's back."

My mother tapped her wooden spoon against a double boiler containing what smelled divinely of her creamed chicken. "I know. A nurse at Tri-State called her mother this morning. Ralph went to get her."

I waited but there was no further comment. Of course not, as there was food to be served. She had split buttermilk biscuits and arranged them on plates, and now was pouring the creamed chicken over one, adorning it with a little pimiento strip and parsley sprig. To the plate she added her vivid green peas and a broiled tomato. Carefully, she wiped a tiny overflow of gravy from the rim of the plate. It looked, as always, artful. Sometimes she sifted a mixture of ground peanuts, paprika, and a mystery spice over the top of this dish, but not today.

I swept up the tray, barged into the dining room right past Miss Bertha as she barked at me. Or snarled. It came out less "Emma" than "Rummma."

But I just sailed past and set the tray on a serving table next to Mr. Muggs's table for two.

"My, that looks delicious, Emma." He tucked his napkin into his collar and rubbed his hands. I filled his water glass and asked him if he'd like coffee now or later. He said later, and I peeled away.

"Ruuummmmmma!"

I turned and fluted, "Yes, Miss Bertha, I'll have your lunches up directly." I held my empty tray up on my fingers and swanned back into the kitchen, ignoring whatever question she was about to ask.

Their lunches were ready and I set them on the tray. Then, seeing my mother busy over at the pastry table, I replaced the pimiento on Miss Bertha's plate with a little strip of habanero pepper (which my pepper research had told me was the hottest member of the family). I picked up the tray and asked, "What's for dessert?" I was backing into the dining room.

"Floating island."

"Oh!" I nearly swooned with delight before I carried the tray to their table and set plates before them. Miss Bertha poked her food around and Mrs. Fulbright murmured her approval of the meal.

I went to Mr. Muggs, who had nearly finished his chicken. "Floating island for dessert," I whispered.

His "Oh!" sounded much the same as mine had.

"Be back in a jiff!" I said.

The jiff was interrupted by a yelp from Miss Bertha, followed by her bouncing from her chair with cries for "Water, water!"

Gunga Din couldn't have called for it better.

I sighed. You'd think by this time she'd be familiar with every known pepper on the planet, and know that water was the very worst thing for its heat.

I filled her glass and handed it to her.

Mr. Muggs and Mrs. Fulbright received their floating islands— a dessert as magical as its name. Miss Bertha couldn't eat anything else because she was fanning out her mouth and would be making noises for the next fifteen minutes at least.

After they'd all left, I cleared their plates away. Mr. Muggs's plate was always cleaned of every morsel, almost as if he'd been eating shadows.

And after *my* two helpings of floating island, I took off for Britten's.

"Na Ow," said Ubub.

"Ake Or," Ulub corrected him.

I had asked them where Morris Slade had gone the night before; had they continued following him? I made out "Lake Noir," but was stumped by the next detail coming from Ulub: "Nilva Air." I did not want to spend the rest of the afternoon interpreting the Woods' dialect. "Where's Mr. Root?"

"Niside," said Ulub. He cocked his head toward the store.

I climbed the wooden steps and said hi to the two old-timers chewing tobacco and sitting on crates. I wondered since when did Mr. Britten offer the comfort of crates to his customers.

From him I got my usual lowered-eyebrow reception. Mr. Root was happier to see me. He was buying some Mail Pouch and a package of Twinkies. When I asked him about Morris Slade and what Ulub meant by "Nilva Air" he said, "Yeah, last night, he went out t' the Silver Pear."

"He went by himself?"

"Yeah, by himself."

"What time?"

"Oh, mebbe around seven, seven thirty. Got to the restaurant about eight."

"Didn't he meet anyone there?"

Mr. Root pondered. "Well, he could've, I guess. I mean, somebody might've been in there waiting, or come after."

This was very vague. "Then where'd he go after the Silver Pear?"

Mr. Root was getting a little defensive. "I don't know. We couldn't hardly wait all night. He was in there an hour, hour and a half by the time we left. How long does it take to eat?"

I felt like saying any good private eye would have waited all night. Of course, any good private eye would be getting paid too. "Well, never mind that, Mr. Root. You all are doing a great job."

"Well. You want a Twinkie?" He'd opened the package and held it out.

"Thank you, but I just ate a big lunch." That had never kept me away from a Twinkie before.

I whisked myself out of the store, waved to Ulub and Ubub, and hurried back to the hotel to call Axel's Taxis.

51

M r. Root or the Wood brothers would have given me a ride, but I wanted to think. Delbert, of course, wanted to talk, but I could ignore him in a way I couldn't ignore the others.

"Silver Pear? My God, girl, you can afford to eat there?"

The priciness of the restaurant interested him more than that a twelve-year-old was going there by herself.

"I sold my bike," I said as we drove through La Porte and out the other side to open land.

Delbert said, one, that he'd never seen me on a bike; and, two, that he was surprised I'd sell it. Then he started talking about what was best to do with a person's money and I tuned him out and watched horses in an otherwise empty field. As if words were water, Delbert's ran on and on. He might as well have dived into a lake of words, for the talk went down down down.

This might be a trip worth taking or it might not. But I was depending on the curiosity of the people at the Silver Pear. After all, Morris Slade turning up in that fancy sports car would trigger curiosity in a person much less nosy than the owners of the restaurant. They would have wondered, questioned, watched him.

I looked out at two black-and-white cows that had propped their heads on a split-rail fence, chewing and musing. I mused along too until I saw Lake Noir in the middle distance, through a million pine trees.

We turned off onto White's Bridge Road (called "the Lake Road" by the snobby owners of the luxury houses on Lake Noir). The Silver Pear didn't sit right on Lake Noir, but it was near enough that you could see it, like a silver plate through the dark trees.

Delbert had stopped talking and I hadn't registered this until we were bumping along a rough section of road. He was as silent as if he'd drowned in the lake, and I hoped that wasn't a drowned man driving.

Gaby and Ron were the owners of the big Victorian house that they'd turned into this expensive restaurant. The first time I was here, I tried to give the impression an adult just might show up and we'd have lunch. I had studied the menu with a kind of horror, seeing dishes like Lobster Thermidor and Filet Mignon à la carte for four times what the hotel charged for an entire meal.

I'd been here a couple of times since, and I hoped they wouldn't remember me and grow suspicious as to why a twelve-year-old was here again, empty-handed, no money in sight.

But I'd forgotten that I wasn't empty-handed! I had fame to spend. I kept forgetting I was by way of being a celebrity now, gaining more with each new installment I wrote.

"Really," said Gaby or Ron, hard to tell apart, both of them posted by the dining room door, hugging menus. His voice was high and breathy as he said it again. "Really, that was *so* brave of you!"

He was referring to my walk at gunpoint and being forced into a rowboat. "Not really," I replied. I asked them what was brave about going where a gun told me to go. (Of course I thought it was brave, but I "eschewed"—another favorite word—bravery in favor of a kind of jaunty, jaded attitude toward danger.) I said if I'd grabbed the gun, or yanked Miss Devereau into Spirit Lake after me, instead of just doing what she wanted, that would have been brave.

They naturally thought I was being modest and that was okay with me. I said, "If you read the *Conservative*—"

They nodded, yes, yes . . .

"—then maybe you read my account—"

Yes, yes . . .

I thought they might go into a tap dance in their polished shoes and seersucker suits. "Now, do you happen to recall a man driving up in a red sports car last night?"

"I certainly do. An Alfa Romeo two-seater. Just gorgeous!"

Alfa Romeo. Here might be another word my mind could taste that would go with "poinciana," "bougainvillea," and "Tamiami." I shook my head a little to get the words out of it. "He had dinner here?"

"Of course," said Ron or Gaby. "The Lobster Thermidor."

Wouldn't you know?

The other one said, or whispered, "We heard he'd been involved in a great scandal years ago over near Spirit Lake? At that big hotel that burned down?"

I nodded. I wasn't about to go into detail about the scandal. "Did he meet anyone here?"

"No."

"No."

"He didn't say anything about visiting friends at Lake Noir or anything like that?"

"No," said Gaby. I knew it was Gaby, for he added, "Ron?"

Ron shook his head.

Of course, why would Morris Slade talk to them about his plans? But then, why was Morris Slade here on his own?

I thought for a moment, but could come up with nothing else. "So he just left and went back to the highway." This seemed obvious, so what Gaby said next surprised me.

"No. As a matter of fact, he drove off toward White's Bridge." He pointed not toward the highway, but away from it. The bridge was just a short distance from the restaurant.

My eyes opened wider. That really made me wonder.

Them too. "We couldn't figure out where he'd be going. No one lives around here except for an old man, down the road from Mirror Pond. That's where the road just turns to dirt. We've never been on it."

Past Brokedown House and several miles beyond, dwindling and widening and dwindling to hardly more than a path, all the way to the back of Spirit Lake.

Ron said, "Of course, you know about the shooting there." He nodded toward a point just beyond the bridge. "That was something." He shivered, it seemed, with delight.

Gaby whispered, "Business was better than usual. I expect people are a bit ghoulish." He flapped his hand. "Don't quote me."

They were speaking of Fern Queen's murder. I said, "I won't. But he would have to have come back by the restaurant here. Did he?"

"Not unless it was after we turned in, and that wasn't till around one, one thirty."

Ron bit his lip. "Well, there *is* that old man. . . . Could he be a friend or relation of some kind?" He switched the menus to his other arm. "I never thought about that until now, that the car didn't come back."

"Maybe you just didn't see it, I mean, with all of your guests."

"Not last night; there weren't more than six or eight people. . . ." He mused. "We ran out of pheasant, I recall."

My mother would probably remember in this way, running out of something. I said, "I'd better be going."

"How did you get here?"

"Taxi."

Gaby turned. "I'll call you one."

"Not right now, please. I'm going to walk over to Mr. Butternut's."

They raised quizzical brows. They looked enough alike to be twins.

"The old man," I said. "That's his name." They'd been here for years and didn't know that? That was the restaurant business.

They shook their heads. Ron said, "My, but you are intrepid!"

I smiled at whatever that meant and left the Lobster Thermidor and pheasant-scented room.

I crossed the short expanse of White's Bridge, barely a dozen yards, curved around Mirror Pond, where the shooting of Fern Queen had occurred, and walked the dirt road as far as Mr. Butternut's small house, a cabin really, one great big room and a kitchen and a bedroom.

The place was lit up like a wildfire, even though it was broad day outside. A big bulbous porch light hung directly over the doorway, moth-shrouded like the ones at the hotel. He did not come directly to my knocking, so I called out, "Mr. Butternut! It's me, Emma Graham!" I heard him reply, but distantly, and there was a shuffling about before he pulled open the door.

"Well, what in tarnation?" He sounded pleased.

I was sure for anyone to visit him was an occasion. I don't think he had any family left at all, and being stuck out here with no one around must have been hard on him.

"Hi, Mr. Butternut. May I come in?"

"Yeah, sure. You want some cocoa?"

We'd had it when I was here before, right after Fern Queen's murder. "Okay. I see you've got a good fire going in your stove."

It was an ancient cast-iron one and the fire was so hot the air felt blistered.

"Come on, come on, set yourself down."

There were two armchairs drawn up before the stove and I perched on one, then sat back as far as I could to get away from the heat. I think old people tend to be colder. "Listen, did you happen to notice a red sports car around here last night?"

"Sure did." He was rattling pans around.

I straightened, surprised I'd hit pay dirt again. I waited for him to go on, but he didn't; he just plunked down a small pan and now was getting milk out of his little icebox.

"Well . . . where? I mean, did it go by here?"

"You bet. My Lord, why any fool would want to drive a fancy roadster like that down this good-for-nothing road's beyond me. I ain't got no marshmallows." He was looking into an almost-empty plastic Jet-Puffed bag that I could see held a couple of marshmallows stuck in a corner. He just didn't want to share them, was all.

He poured milk into the pan and added cocoa and sugar and stirred this into a paste before adding more milk. He made pretty good cocoa.

"Then what happened?"

"Nothin'. Things ain't always goin' on around here like in town."

He said this with his back turned, and I could tell from the crinkle sound and his arm moving that he was sticking the marshmallows into his cup on the sly.

"I mean, where do you suppose it was going?"

"No place to go except Brokedown House and nobody don't live there except ghosts." He laughed silently, shaking like a custard. "Just Calhoun spooks. Now it used to be a lot of Randalls lived down this road, Bud Randall was one, and then there was . . ."

He went on with the same history about past families he'd done before. It must be that old people had to check up on the past to see if it really had been there.

"But you'd have heard the car coming back."

"Yeah."

I waited. "Did you?"

"It never come back."

"Well, didn't you wonder about it?"

He was pouring out the cocoa, evening it up between the two cups. "Yeah." He carried the cups to the chairs, placing his on a little table kind of hidden by the arm of his chair so I wouldn't see the white swirl of marshmallow; they were melting.

I sighed. "Well—?"

"Well, nothin'. Wonderin' never caught no raccoons."

"Then the car must've gone to Brokedown House and maybe is

still there." The idea of someone like Morris Slade spending any time at all in that house, much less a whole night in it, was laughable, except it didn't make me want to laugh.

"Mebbe." I could tell he was sucking the marshmallow off the surface of his cocoa.

"Come on." I wanted him to think I was simply assuming he'd go with me. I wasn't going to Spook Hall all by myself.

"I ain't drunk my cocoa!"

He sat firm until the last drop. I felt like taking him by the ear.

He said, "Anyways, I can't see why you want to hotfoot it down there. Last time you got lost, if my memory serves."

"It doesn't. *You* got lost."

We argued for a couple of minutes while he put down his empty cup and got up and creaked over to a table and picked up his briar stick.

"Don't forget the flashlights," I said.

"Why? It's broad daylight."

I wouldn't be going to Brokedown House if it weren't. "You know how thick those woods are. It's pitch-black around there." I wouldn't be going if it were. "Come on."

As we banged out through his screen door he was asking why some people couldn't leave a body in peace.

52

We stopped, both together coming to a standstill. I think both of us knew that car's being there was not good. I don't want to think of Brokedown House as a dead end, although it appeared to have been for some people, liks Iris Devereau and her fiancé, Jamie Makepiece.

My memory was searching for a road, any road, that led out on the other side, and I remembered the old one that led from here to Spirit Lake, the lake itself. "Mr. Butternut, isn't there an old road that goes between here and Spirit Lake?"

"The one we're standin' on. But half a mile past here it's mostly growed over."

I don't know why I wanted there to be one; the red sports car hadn't taken it.

"Well, we best go look."

For once it was him and not me taking the initiative. Me, I didn't want to look. I was afraid to. But after all my jawing and cajoling, I knew I had to go in.

Mr. Butternut was already by the car when I caught up. There was nothing in it but water pooled beneath the dashboard, I guessed from an early-morning shower we'd had, and crisp brown leaves fanned out over the tan leather seat. The top was down, so the car was open to whatever chose to inhabit it; it gave me a chill.

I didn't think he'd meant to be here long.

Some tartness had returned to me and stiffened my spine and I turned toward the house. It was more a cottage than a house, and I'd been in it several times. Its roof was partly gone; everything—car, cottage, landscape—looked as if overcome by the elements or by gravity and sinking slowly into the sod. *"Under the sod."* I thought of the Robert Frost poem, and Ulub saying it.

I meant to go inside, but I still didn't. Instead I walked around the house, or, rather, beat my way around, for the ground cover was so thick, simply walking was impossible. There were trees so old and heavily branched they seemed to want to twine together.

Something scampered, things fell—acorns, small branches, twigs of clustered leaves, as if dropping down from the sky. Elsewhere, it was summer, but not here. Here it was always autumn.

You would think, knowing me, I'd be excited by all this happening. But I was sick of this. I was really sick of it. I heard a noise, a shout. It was Mr. Butternut yelling. I had to turn and go to the house then. I didn't want to: I knew there'd be something wrong. And I was afraid I knew what.

I crunched through the undergrowth, the shavings of bark and the saw grass and grape hyacinths, and considered how they had survived all of this bad news.

Mr. Butternut was at the back door, propping himself up, arm outstretched against the doorjamb.

As I got closer he called, "They's somebody inside—" He hitched his thumb back over his shoulder.

I stopped. "And he's dead."

"'N a doornail." He put a hand on his chest. "My heart's a-weakenin' as I stand here."

I moved through the door, Mr. Butternut's heart buoying me up. He came behind.

At first I thought my eyes must surely be deceiving me; certainly my eyes had done a lot of that.

He was in the parlor, lying on his back with his arms splayed out as if he'd been making snow angels. Which was a stupid thing to think because there was no whiteness around him, only blood, the blood he was lying in, the blood that was part of the mess that had been his chest.

It was stupid, but then I thought of snow angels because that's what I wished he'd been doing, doing something like a little kid. For I wondered if he'd ever really had the chance to be one.

Mr. Butternut, breath raspy, said, "That's him, ain't it? That Slade fella?" He was gasping for air as if what was left of the living, he and I, didn't have enough to go around.

I shook my head. "No. His name's Ralph Diggs."

53

"Anyplace there's trouble," said Donny, thumbs hooked in his belt as he swaggered around Brokedown House, "you sure manage to be there." His look said he was 100 percent right.

"Get out there and check on that car," said the Sheriff, who was hunkered down beside Dr. McComb.

Donny hitched up his pants as he passed me, looking at me as if this were all my fault. He walked out mumbling something about a "granny gun."

I didn't care anymore about what Donny said. I didn't even bother to look at him. I cared only about Ralph Diggs and Morris Slade. I meant to pick up my feet and move but they were welded to the floor.

Mr. Butternut had discovered he had feet and he'd walked them as fast as he could back to his house to call the Sheriff. I had stayed.

Amazingly, I hadn't been afraid to stay, for I thought someone ought to keep Ralph company, ridiculous as it sounded. I think fear had been knocked right out of me by the shock that a person could lose so much blood, that there could *be* so much blood in anybody. It was as I was looking at the blood that I decided to be scared and hightailed it out of there, fast.

I met up with Mr. Butternut just coming out of his house, hurrying back.

State police had come next, three cars of them nosed up behind the red sports car, eight or nine policemen inside and outside the house. I don't know how they'd gotten here so fast.

The Sheriff seemed to have forgotten I was standing there, me, Emma Graham, looking at this dead body of Ralph Diggs, lying in a pool of blood that had trickled into the cracks of the old floorboards.

He looked over his shoulder. "Emma?"

I just shook my head.

Dr. McComb, who had arrived ten minutes after the Sheriff, levered himself off the floor with some difficulty. "That's all for now. Autopsy will tell us more. But not much, probably. Hell of a blast. It wasn't done with that twenty-two, that's for sure." He nodded toward one of the troopers, who was on the floor beside the body, retrieving a small gun that Butternut and I hadn't seen.

I turned then and went out the front door and sat down on a bench beside Mr. Butternut, who just stared straight ahead. I saw Donny looking the car over, making notes in a little spiral book.

The Sheriff walked out, looked over at Donny, then at us. "What happened about Ralph Diggs?"

Mr. Butternut looked up. "We done told you."

I liked his waspish tone. I think I'd been misjudging Mr. Butternut. He had a lot more grit than most.

"Yes. Sorry. I guess I'm asking what you think." He was looking at me. "Ralph Diggs worked at the hotel. What do you know about him?"

I didn't feel like this. "He called himself Rafe; I think that's short for Raphael."

"I know. You told me that."

"You didn't seem to hear it. *Raphael.* 'Fey' for short." I looked up into the Sheriff's glacier blue eyes. "The kidnapped baby. It was a boy, not a girl."

The Sheriff rose and looked as if I'd just handed him part of the darkening sky, as if he'd run out of daylight. "What do you mean? How do you know that?'

"Raphael. After Mr. Woodruff, old Mr. Woodruff, the grandfather."

"Did he—Ralph or Rafe—tell you this?"

"Of course not. I'm just putting it together. Remember? Raphael was that baby's grandfather's name. So they called him Fey. The Diggses must have been the people in Pennsylvania that bellboy took him to. I guess they shortened Raphael to Ralph." I glared, as if for some reason this was the Sheriff's fault. "You've seen his face. How much he looks like Morris Slade." I frowned, not at the Sheriff this time, but at myself. I'd said something like this before. What was I missing? I was missing something pitifully obvious, and I knew it.

The Sheriff shook his head, musing. "Why in hell did Slade leave his car? Where did he go? Did they come here together?"

I knew he wasn't really asking us, me and Mr. Butternut, but I answered, "No. You can ask Gaby and Ron at the Silver Pear." I thought about it for a moment. "Morris Slade could have walked back to the highway, back across White's Bridge there." I tilted my head.

The Sheriff shook his head. "It doesn't make much sense he'd leave his car for the police to find."

"No, it don't," said Mr. Butternut, who'd been silent through this questioning. Now he slapped his knees and got up. "I'm goin' home if you don't need me anymore."

The Sheriff nodded. "I appreciate your help. It was a pretty bad experience for you, sir. You thought quickly. Thanks."

Mr. Butternut just nodded and walked off the small porch, back to the road.

Dr. McComb had come out and was standing beside the Sheriff, his black bag shut. "Nothing more I can do here, Sam. I been talking to the trooper in there. There's no sign of the shotgun. Shooter would've taken it with him."

The Sheriff nodded. "If you're leaving, take Emma home, won't you?"

I did not protest. My old self would have. My old self would have made up some good reason why I should stay. But my new self felt distant; maybe I was in shock. "If you're in shock, don't you act strange?" I asked Dr. McComb.

He nodded. "All kinds of strange. Affects people in different ways."

I stood up, ready to leave. "Well, maybe Morris Slade's in shock. Maybe he left and he's in the woods. Lost. You never went deep enough." I said this to the Sheriff.

Dr. McComb held the door for me to get into his old jalopy. When he tried to get it going, it choked up a lot. But finally we were bumping back over the road.

We passed Mr. Butternut, who raised his hand to me in a kind of salute, and I saluted back. I had to say about Mr. Butternut that he operated pretty well under pressure.

Dr. McComb slowed as he went around Mirror Pond, then over White's Bridge. "Well," he said, shifting gears about twenty times. "Sam'll sort it out."

I looked dully at the Silver Pear as we rumbled by. "Sure. He'll go after the wrong man."

54

could have been a celebrity again, I thought, but somehow celebrity wasn't as appealing as it was a week ago.

I thought this as I walked heavily up the back stairs to my room. I'd asked Dr. McComb to please go around to the back driveway and let me off so I could go inside without having to talk to people. But I realized, stopping on the landing between floors, that tonight there really weren't any people to talk to.

There had been no guests for dinner, not even Miss Bertha and Mrs. Fulbright, for some friend or relation of Mrs. Fulbright's had come to take them both out. And my mother and Mrs. Davidow had gone to a party at the Custis house across the highway.

By the next morning the Hotel Paradise had gotten the news. Mrs. Davidow, Ree-Jane, and my mother were gathered in the kitchen waiting for me to come foggily down to breakfast. If Ree-Jane was up before eight a.m., ever, the possibility for drama was increased by a hundred.

Ree-Jane was "prostrate" at the news about "Rafe, poor Rafe." I told her she'd better lie down then, as she couldn't be prostrate and still walk around with her arm flung over her eyes.

Mrs. Davidow wanted to know every detail and was about to

offer me a Bloody Mary until she remembered I was twelve. "Who shot him? Did Morris Slade shoot him?"

"Oh, my God! My God!" wailed Ree-Jane.

My mother was tying on her kitchen apron and said that if I didn't feel like waiting tables, Walter could help. "Maybe it was suicide," she said in a puzzled way.

"It definitely wasn't," I said. She shrugged and told Mrs. Davidow she'd run out of spice for her pumpkin chiffon pie.

Here I had just found a dead body, and one belonging to someone they knew, and it might as well have been a dead beetle for all the effect it had: they were just exaggerated versions of their same selves.

My mother turned to the stove; Mrs. Davidow smoked and talked six to the dozen, probably rehearsing for the reporters sure to come; Ree-Jane walked and wailed.

I asked Mrs. Davidow if she'd make one of her Bloody Marys for Great-Aunt Aurora, and she said she'd be happy to. She was always happy to make a drink, no matter whose.

Here we were at eleven a.m. on the front porch with two reporters. Or rather here *I* was, but Mrs. Davidow and Ree-Jane and my mother couldn't yet get the hang of it, me being famous.

When Ree-Jane had heard reporters were coming from Cloverly and even Pittsburgh, she right away changed out of her walking shorts into a Heather Gay Struther dress, this one a cheery Good Morning Yellow, which might not have been good for a death in the family, but was certainly good for photographers.

I pointed out to her that any pictures, if taken and if used, would be black-and-white. She was undeterred in the arranging of a peachy-orange-colored scarf and said that, given everything that had happened around here, this story would wind up in *Vogue*.

She arranged herself on the porch rail, the skirt spread out, a hankie at her eyes, and asked when the photographer would come. She had known "Rafe"—and pointed out the English pronunciation to the two reporters—better than anyone.

But the two reporters knew me better than anyone, for they were the same ones who had been here after I had been shoved into a row-boat without oars and shot at. There was also the attraction of Lola's Bloody Marys and my mother's coffee and pastry. It was as close to a party as they'd get, in the circumstances.

They found out what the crime scene had looked like.

I found out the police had arrested Morris Slade.

"They arrested Morris Slade," I told Aurora as I handed her a Bloody Mary at noon.

"That don't surprise me. He was found with a dead body, after all."

"No, he wasn't. He wasn't there."

She paid no attention; she was too busy with her own theories. Smacking her lips over the drink, she recited a verse:

> By the pricking of my thumbs
> Something wicked this way comes.

She set down her drink for a moment to hold up her thumbs.

"What? If you're talking about Ralph Diggs, he wasn't wicked, I don't think." I don't know why I felt the need to defend him now. Yes, I did. Because he'd been murdered.

"That boy"—her voice squeaked upward—"was a sneaky one. And he was too much in love with hisself, for one thing. I don't think I ever did see anyone so self-satisfied."

I was puzzled. "How do you know? You never met him."

"Of course I did, miss. That day you was so busy messin' around in what was none of your business, he brought me lunch and dinner. Well, don't think I didn't hide my bearer bonds and my jewels right after lunch. No, ma'am—!"

"Bearer bonds? Jewels? You don't have any of that."

"That's as much as you know. I can tell a good-for-nothin' sly boots of a thief when I see one. The way his eyes hit on every object in this room, just looking for something to rob me of, or maybe somebody to murder. Remember *Night Must Fall*?" She shivered and drank the tail end of her Bloody Mary.

Since I was the main rememberer of that movie, I didn't comment except to remind her I was only twelve.

"So how do you know," she slyly said, "that movie's older than twelve years?"

She should work for Perry Mason. What bothered me was how it clicked: she had recognized, just as I had, the similarity between Ralph Diggs and the sinister bellhop. As a matter of fact, she could be the old lady who had almost become his victim.

"It certainly looks as if Morris Slade shot him." I didn't want to believe this.

Aurora rattled ice that had melted to slivers, holding the glass toward me. "They trace that gun back to its owner, they'll know. Just like in the movies."

I sighed and took her glass.

But halfway down the stairs, I reimagined the scene at Brokedown House: the Sheriff down on one knee; Dr. McComb hanging over the body; Donny Mooma walking about like king of the hill, saying something about shooting a granny gun.

I ran down the rest of the stairs and into the back office, where the phone was. I plunked down Aurora's glass and grabbed up the metal phone pad, pushed the pointer to "M," and clicked it open. There was Dr. McComb's number.

"Be there, be there," I said to myself, and danced around like I had to pee.

"Dr. McComb, this is Emma."

He was surprised. "Emma, you should be—"

"What did Deputy Mooma mean about a 'granny gun'?" I hadn't time for my roundabout ways.

" 'Granny'?"

I pinched my eyes shut. "He was talking about the gun, I think, that was lying on the floor."

"Oh yeah, I recall. It's a small one. Now, listen, Emma—"

"What about it? What. A. Bout. It?" I said this through gritted teeth so he would know I wasn't fooling around and that I meant business.

He knew. He told me.

I ran all the way back up the stairs. Aurora had her cards out and was playing her version of solitaire.

"About time! Well, where's my drink?"

"Where's your gun?"

"Your crazy brother wanted it for some theatrical extravaganza."

"You let Will have a *gun*?"

"Oh, don't be so dramatic, miss!" She slapped a jack of clubs down on a queen of spades. "All you Grahams are. You all act like you was auditioning for every play on Broadway. Now, we Paradises, we come from solid, no-nonsense stock. You wouldn't catch us running down some fool story about murder or going crazy out in the garage, putting on some fool play—" *Slap* went the jack of hearts on the queen of diamonds. She even cheated at solitaire.

"So you let Will have your gun. Well, that's a real example of Paradise no-nonsense stock. That really is."

She raised a bony hand like one of *Macbeth*'s witches (which I was familiar with only because Will and Mill talked about putting it on). "Now you mind how you speak to your elders, miss! I said the gun wasn't loaded. I ain't going to loan some kid a loaded gun."

"You shouldn't be giving him any gun—" Aurora not being the soul of generosity, I added: "Wait a minute—why did you?"

She sniffed. "We made a trade."

"Trade?"

She put down the cards and wheeled over to her steamer trunk, which always stood open. She fussed around in the bottom, underneath the hems of dresses, and pulled out a bottle of Myers's rum.

I could scarcely believe my eyes.

"I can't say where he got it." She sniffed self-righteously.

"Will? He's got a still out back."

My feet took wing. I was up at the Big Garage inside of two minutes. I felt like kicking in the door, but if the gun was still in Will's possession he'd probably shoot me.

I knocked.

"Yeah?"

"Open this door right now, Will!"

There was, of course, no rush to open the door. I just stood there, furious. After another half minute, I yelled: "I'm not going away!"

The door opened fractionally. "What?"

He had on one of those vaselike hats with a tassel that they wore in Morocco. "What are you wearing?"

"A fez."

Despite everything that had happened, I was still fascinated by Will's craziness. "Why? Does the plane refuel in Morocco or Cairo?"

"Is that why you're here? To ask about my fez?"

"No. Let me in."

Will threw back the door and I walked into a strange land of lights and shadows. Pale shades of green, blue, and pink washed back and forth across the floor, accented by a couple of spotlights. The garage roof had been converted into a night sky, a pattern of stars cut from something shiny tossed across it, a small sliver of neon bright moon. Back in the dark corner was Chuck, the one who did all this, the lighting genius.

I had to admit it was great.

"So what do you want? We're busy."

"The gun. Aurora's gun that she traded you for a bottle of rum."

"Oh, that. Yeah, we were just looking for it. We think maybe Paul took it."

"Hello, missus!"

Paul was up in the rafters.

"Paul? Then why isn't he down here—"

"He was. He never took it." Will had his fez off, looking into it as if the gun might be in there. "Anyway, it was out of ammunition; it wasn't loaded."

"No? It is *now*. Ralph Diggs was in here yesterday, wasn't he?"

Will and Mill exchanged a look. "Yeah. Why?"

Of course they hadn't heard the news. Stuck here in the Big Garage, beneath the fake stars and shaved-off moon, how could they have? "Because the gun the police found by his body could be that one."

"Body?" Will said.

"Body?" Mill said.

They stared at me and then at each other.

For once they actually went slightly green. Or maybe that was just Chuck's light playing over their surprised-for-once faces.

55

called the Sheriff's office and got Maureen. The Sheriff was at the crime scene and Donny was at the Rainbow getting doughnuts. She would get hold of the Sheriff by the car radio immediately. Of course, he'd want the gun identified. "Ab-si-tive-ly!"

Twenty minutes later, a police car came roaring up the drive, spitting gravel when it braked. Given it was Donny, I was surprised he didn't have the siren blaring and his own gun drawn.

He got out, slammed the door as hard as he could, and pounded up the porch steps and into the lobby. He was carrying a small black satchel and wearing a menacing look, a look that he probably practiced in front of a mirror.

"Where's this Paradise woman? We need an ID on this old revolver." He held up the black bag. "Murder bag."

I wasn't the only one watching *Perry Mason*.

I directed him up the stairs, pointing the way to the fourth floor, but stayed on the third floor myself. I wanted to hear the yelling, not necessarily the words. I was pretty sure I knew the words. I was not disappointed in the yelling.

Donny Mooma was no match for Aurora Paradise.

I ran back down to the lobby when I heard him leave her room.

He hurried down the stairs, stopping only at the head of the last flight to make it appear a casual descent.

In the meantime, Mrs. Davidow and my mother had come to the lobby, seen the police car, watched him come down.

"What is it? What's wrong?"

Donny touched his cap in a respectful way, pretty good for him. "Police business, ma'am. You'll be hearing about it, I imagine."

I followed him out onto the porch. "It never happened the way you all thought, did it? It was Ralph Diggs that tried to kill Morris Slade, wasn't it? And there was some kind of—"

To me, he didn't have to be respectful. "Now why don't you just go mind your own beeswax, girl?" He got into his car and slammed the door.

I smiled. It *was* my beeswax. I went back into the office and phoned Axel's Taxis.

"Well, I couldn't hardly believe you was the one found that guy shot!" Delbert said this over his shoulder.

"I couldn't hardly believe it either." I said this to the hill outside of Britten's as we drove past. "And I didn't. Mr. Butternut found him."

At the top of the rise Ulub stood with his book, waving his arm, and Mr. Root sat, listening. I took out my change purse to make sure the bit of poetry I'd written down was still there. Why wouldn't it be? Because things are always disappearing. I also checked to see if I had enough money for both an ice-cream soda and to tip Delbert.

"Well, that fella worked at the *ho*-tel. He got shot over there near the Silver Pear . . . Well, hell, girl! That's where I took *you*!"

As if I didn't know. I thought maybe Delbert would twist the steering wheel off its stem and we'd go crashing into Walter's house (which we were now passing) if I didn't say more. "Well, it's too bad."

"Bad? *Bad*?" Delbert was really enjoying handing me this news, something he knew for a change that he thought I didn't. "Killed *dead's* how bad!"

I guess one or the other wasn't enough for Delbert. "Poor Ralph Diggs."

"Well, goodness' sake, girl, I'd think you'd feel worse'n that. You knew him!"

I slid in my seat. "Not much. He'd only worked for us for a couple of weeks."

"Yeah, well . . ." He bumped his hand against the wheel, trying to think up some other reason I should feel bad.

We were nearly at the courthouse before he remembered the other 50 percent of the story. So he didn't have time to make much of Morris Slade, especially since I slammed the door halfway into his description. I was that mad listening to Delbert telling me how I should feel.

"The fact that he brought it does not mean he used it."

The Sheriff was talking about Ralph Diggs. I couldn't believe my ears. "It was Aurora Paradise's gun," I said. "He stole it from the garage. It was meant to be used in Will's new play."

"You don't know what you're talking about, Emma," said the Sheriff, sitting hard in his swivel chair, as if circumstances were pushing him down.

"Thing is," Donny said, "if he'd come to kill Morris Slade, how come he didn't have his own gun? Yeah." Donny chortled.

It might have been the first bright idea he'd ever had.

"And he's the one that's dead, or have you forgot? And it's him that was kidnapped, don't forget either. It ain't the rich Morris Slades of this world that wind up bleedin' out, oh, no—"

"Donny. Shut it."

"Yeah, well, I was just sayin'—"

"You said it." The Sheriff gave him an icy look.

I stared from one to the other. I saw what it was: it was going to be another "hearsay" evidence thing. Not that, precisely, but another example of the Sheriff's mind being made up. If he didn't see clearly right now, he was never going to see it, because it was one of those things of such blinding clarity that if you blinked you'd miss it.

Ralph Diggs had taken a gun to Brokedown House to kill Morris Slade because he hated him. He hated him because Morris and his mother had abandoned him—no, worse than that. Ralph thought his father had had him "kidnapped," taken to an untraceable place. Or perhaps the luckless bellhop from the Belle Ruin was supposed himself to abandon the baby, like Moses being left in the bulrushes.

Ralph Diggs had probably had plenty of time to make up scenes, acts, a whole play to explain his hatred of Morris Slade. For some reason, the mother, Imogen Slade, didn't figure into it. I didn't understand why.

I said, "Ralph's having the gun doesn't *prove* it, but if he brought it, it sure wasn't for rabbit hunting."

Donny opened his mouth, then shut it when the Sheriff gave him another look as sharp as a knife. Then the Sheriff said to me, "Emma, I think you're in over your head on this one."

I could feel again the cold waters of Spirit Lake. "No. My head's right here." I made a ledge of my hand and rested my chin on it. "Your head, that's down here." My hand went atop my head. "You're the one under the water. Excuse me." I turned and walked out.

Hands on hips, sitting on that stool of hers, Shirl gave me an iron look.

"Well, I guess I'll have a chocolate frosted with sprinkles." I gave Shirl a smile, took my doughnut on a napkin Wanda supplied, and walked back to the last booth, where I sat and went on being mad. I sat and looked at my doughnut and wondered if I wanted to eat it.

Maud appeared with a glass of Coke and set it before me, then sat down herself. "You look as if you're sucking a lemon."

Frostily, I said, "The Sheriff doesn't believe me."

"About what?" She lit a cigarette.

"About Morris Slade."

I was facing the front of the Rainbow. Because the back of my booth was so tall that I couldn't see anyone coming in, I didn't see the Sheriff until he was there. He removed his dark glasses and stuck one of the stems into his shirt pocket. He leaned against the end of the booth and smiled. "Hello. Hello."

I was silent for a few heartbeats. "Have you got him in jail? I mean, I guess you arrested him, even if he didn't do it."

"Correct. I like to arrest the innocent."

"How are you so sure about this?" said Maud.

"Could I get a cup of coffee? Or don't you serve the local law anymore?" he said to Maud.

"Oh. Is that what you are?" She smiled sweetly. "It sounds to me as if you're ignoring some evidence, like why would a man like Morris Slade have a shotgun? He just doesn't strike me as a shotgun sort of guy."

The Sheriff put his dark glasses back on the way someone else might settle a hat to show they were leaving. He said, "You don't know one goddamned thing about it, Maud. Not one damned thing."

Then he turned and walked out, not returning good-byes from the counter sitters or Wanda. I knew because I leaned sideways and watched him go.

There was a heaviness in the air.

"I guess I shouldn't talk so much," I said.

She looked over. "You weren't the one doing the smart talking: I was. I don't know why I can't shut up sometimes."

"Don't the state police do anything? They were there."

"Sure, but—"

"Maud!"

Shirl was yelling. Maybe it was just as well. It let Maud go.

I wished something would let me go too.

56

I was so lost in thoughts of another person that it covered over the anger of Morris Slade getting arrested. For I knew there was another person.

Wondering who this other person could be made me nearly miss Souder's Pharmacy. Yet, some part of my mind registered the long gloves and perfume and powder window display, so I backed up a few feet and went in.

Souder's in the summer was the coolest place in La Porte, with the blackest shadows, the coldest marble, the airiest ceiling fans, the best ice-cream sodas. But for once I hadn't come for that.

I went to the rear of the store to see where Mrs. Souder was, and as I was about to ding the little bell, she came out, the beaded curtain swirling around her tall, thin shape, the beads sending out their tiny clattering sound.

It surprised me greatly that she seemed almost glad to see me.

"Oh, Emma. Well, how are you? I suppose you want a soda? Come on."

Apparently, all of this new friendliness had to do with my articles in the *Conservative*, for she complimented me as she put the chocolate syrup in one of the tall ribbed glasses, her head twitching as if it were on the strings of a puppeteer. Mrs. Souder had "an affliction"; I had no idea what it was.

She called my piece a "truly interesting overview." After adding two scoops of ice cream, she blasted it all with fizzy water. I thought she enjoyed that part of it; it must have allowed her to let off steam. A spiral of whipped cream topped off the soda. Then she said what was really on her mind:

"Well, I can tell you we were completely shocked about what happened! And you—you must have been just frightened to death!"

"Oh, I was. But it wasn't me, really, that found him; it was Mr. Butternut that lives out there on the same road." I don't know why I was being so precise about my secondary role here. Maybe it was because I didn't want to be the one who first saw Ralph Diggs dead. Maybe it would make me feel less responsible, or something.

She talked about the Slades and the Souders and the Devereaus for a while as she smoked a cigarette, leaning back against the big mirror that ran the length of the counter. I was surprised to see her smoking.

"You know Rose was one of us Souders?" she said.

I nodded. "My great-aunt Aurora told me so."

Her thinly penciled eyebrows went up. "Aurora Paradise? Is she still around?"

"She was this morning." I licked my long spoon. "They looked a lot alike, Rose Queen and Morris Slade."

Mrs. Souder stubbed out her cigarette and started in wiping down the soda fixture, already polished to a high gloss. "Looked alike, they certainly did. Of course, he was lots younger."

"How old would he be now? In his forties, maybe?"

She nodded. "He's around the same age as our eldest, and she's forty-three."

I didn't even know the Souders had an "eldest." I'd never seen any of their children. I worked it out. Twenty years ago, when Rose was murdered, he'd have been around twenty-two or three, if Mrs.

Souder was right. I wondered. "He must've been sixteen or seventeen years younger than Rose."

"Round that, yes. Rose wasn't a Devereau, except by her mother marrying the father. She was a Souder. Her mother was Alice Souder and she was married three times: to a Souder, then a Slade. He got custody of Morris, which certainly was a surprise, him being such a drinker and all. Then she married old Mr. Devereau. Rose's daddy was Albert Souder, a cousin of my husband's."

I frowned at all of these complications.

She went on. "I think Rose looked on Morris as sort of a kid brother. He seemed to idolize her."

It was strange, but as she reminisced, her twitching stopped completely, as if going back to the time when she was young had a calming effect.

"Yes," she went on, calling up this memory, "Morris kind of doted on her." She shook her head, but it was a real shake, not a twitch. "Well, that was long ago. A lot has happened since. Most of it bad."

The thin, filmy voice of Mr. Souder called her back to the other side of the bead curtain, and she left and was soon soaked up by shadows. It was bright light outside and yet in here it might as well have been night.

She had forgotten to collect the money for my soda, so I opened my purse and rooted out a quarter and a dime. As I did the scrap of paper with the poem on it fell out. I unfolded it:

This saying good-by on the edge of the dark . . .

Quickly I jammed the bit of paper into my coin purse as if the words left to lie on the marble counter too long would catch their death of cold.

By the time I was climbing the steps to the newspaper office, the anger that had retreated behind the chocolate soda was back.

I told Mr. Gumbrel about Morris Slade being arrested, but he already knew.

He shook his head. "Thing is, you've got to admit the circumstances seem pretty cut-and-dried, Emma."

He had listened and given thought to what I'd told him, his fingers massaging his temples as if it were all too rich a story for his town paper.

"What if the story never gets heard? What if *your* reading public never finds out that Morris Slade only shot in self-defense or that it was an accident?"

He sighed heavily—"We got enough surprises what with finding out that F-a-y really was F-e-y, and a boy, not a girl. That's enough right there of a surprise. And there's still your next installment. You finished that yet? I want to get it in next week's paper."

"I'm just polishing it." To curtail any further talk about my next piece, I got up and left to go and do my polishing.

By the time I'd left the newspaper office it was after four o'clock and I wanted to talk to Dwayne, even though he'd probably get smart about things. He was still what you'd call a good sounding board, even when he was under a car.

Delbert was sitting in his empty taxi, idling by the curb outside of Axel's Taxis.

"Are you waiting for a fare?" I asked him through the window.

"Huh? No, ma'am. I'm just setting here, thinking."

I got in and told him to take me to Slaw's Garage out on 219.

"Well, don't you think I don't know where Slaw's is? Ain't I dropped you off there before? I don't see why you want to hang out at that garage, anyway—"

I slid down and watched the world go by.

"You're *so* much help," I said to Dwayne, sarcastically, after I'd told him what had happened and he just kept *wham wham whamming* away with his wrench.

"As if you needed it." His voice was distorted by the bottom of the pickup truck he was under. "You and your riotous imagination."

"My what?" No answer. "Well, what do *you* think happened?"

Clang clang clingclingclingcling c-l-a-n-g. It sounded like a mess of tambourines. It was as if the truck were answering the question. It probably would have done just as well.

He said, "Two men, two guns. They draw. One dies."

"Where's the other gun then?"

"The shooter took it with him."

"Okay, then you're saying that person is Morris Slade."

"Sounds like it." *Clang.* Pause. "One thing's interesting. Why didn't this guy Ralph Diggs go after his mom? Did he think that crazy kidnapping scheme was all his dad's idea? That—what's her name?"

"Imogen."

"That she had nothing to do with it?"

There was something ghostly about Dwayne's disembodied voice, as if Dwayne had gone, leaving only enough words behind to keep me thinking he was still there, long enough for him to make his get-away. This talking to him while he was looking at a vehicle's underneath was tiring. I jumped down from the tire stack and took the board You-Boy had been using and rolled it to the side of the truck and lay down.

Dwayne turned his head. There was a lantern hooked onto some part of the pickup's works that cast long shadows across his face. "What are you doing?"

"I'm tired of talking to a truck. I'm just going to lie here."

He muttered and rolled out and stood. So did I. From his hip pocket he took out the old oily rag and started wiping his hands.

"What's wrong with my theory?" I asked him.

Carefully, he wiped each finger. "What's wrong is you're dragging a third person into this showdown. That just makes for complications, nor does it explain anything better." He stuffed the rag into his pocket and pulled out a pack of Juicy Fruit.

I shook my head when he held out the gum, offering a piece. I was running out of reasons. "Well, what would Morris Slade's motive be? Why would a father murder his own *son*?" I said this self-righteously.

"You of *Medea*-fame are asking that? Although I will admit the motive seems a lot more convincing if it's the son shooting the father." He folded a stick of the gum into his mouth and leaned back against the truck.

At least he was allowing that. I said, "Remember, Ralph came armed."

He shrugged. "So did his dad . . . if he is the dad."

I ignored the "if" part. "What Morris Slade's doing is he's protecting the person who must have saved his life. The person who shot Ralph Diggs when he was about to fire."

Dwayne crossed his arms, chewed his gum, looked at me. "You really think people would go to that length to save someone else?"

"I certainly do. Like Ben Queen taking the blame for Fern. Sure, they go to that length. *You* would."

Dwayne laughed. "You mean, like, for you, maybe?"

"Of course I don't mean me."

Of course I did.

I walked out.

It was a tossed salad I was supposed to be making, so I tossed it, chucking lettuce leaves onto salad plates, plunking cherry tomatoes atop the leaves, boomeranging onion slices.

"What are you doing?" There was Vera, risen like Venus on a clamshell, or whatever that picture was, announcing her displeasure I was still alive.

"Nothing," I said, in my surly way.

"Be sure you make a cross with the Roquefort cheese dressing."

So many replies to that rushed into my mind that she was gone before I could choose my favorite. I made crosses with the Roquefort dressing, except on Miss Bertha's. She despised Roquefort, so I slid a teaspoonful into the middle of her salad, hid it with the lettuce on top, and drenched it with French dressing.

While I was busy, Ree-Jane slipped in; that is, she didn't seem to come all at once, but like a vapor trail, which I believe was her "model's walk." A hilarious smile twitched on her face; apparently the short run to the mental hospital hadn't done much to wipe it off, nor had the shooting of Ralph Diggs had any sustained effect. You'd think she'd never heard of him.

"Guess where I'm going tonight?"

"Hell-and-gone? That dress looks like you're on fire."

She actually drifted around in a circle to give me the full effect of yet another Heather Gay Struther outfit. "It's new. Red."

No kidding? Since I hadn't guessed, she said it again: "Guess where I'm going?"

I was silent. Hell hadn't worked.

Now she was whispery: "Pat and I are going to the Double Down. Perry's place."

"The bar."

That irritated her. "It's not a *bar*. It's a club!"

I plunked pepper rings on a couple of salads and watched them slide off. "You have to be twenty-one to get in."

As if she had the perfect answer to that, she said, with a sticky smile, "Not if you're a special friend of Perry's."

"That's right. Then you have to be *forty*-one."

"Don't be stupid." Then, thinking over that dumb insult, she added, in a manner she regarded as smooth, "I've always liked older men." She simpered.

I turned, full face; I was really angry. "No kidding? Is that why you were so moony over Rafe? And 'prostrate with grief' this morning?" Her face was reddening up. "You know—Rafe Diggs, the dead guy. The murdered guy. Rafe."

Her mouth worked, but she could think of nothing to say. The color was leaving her face as if the color at least had grace enough to flee.

And so did she, finally.

57

The following morning I was back in La Porte, having walked the two miles myself. I thought about the Sheriff and felt maybe I should go and see him and, if not exactly apologize, as I didn't think either Maud or I had done anything wrong the day before except be sarcastic . . . well, maybe there was something to apologize for in that.

When he'd told Maud she didn't know "one goddamned thing about it," maybe he'd been right. We acted too much a lot of the time as if we knew more about the law than he did.

"Yeah, I guess I know one kid that's gettin' her comeuppance," Donny said, swaggering around, hitching his belt up and looking at me with a sharklike grin as if I were a school of minnows swimming by.

"Meaning?" I had no idea at all what he was talking about. But I figured I wouldn't like it, not if it made Donny happy.

The Sheriff had gone out somewhere.

"Well, ain't you got this great story about—?"

Maureen broke in as she yanked a paper from her typewriter. "Donny, you shut up, now. Sam wouldn't want you talking about this."

He turned slowly to Maureen. "Begging your pardon, ma'am?

Hell, Maureen, I didn't know you was deputy." Maureen had only spurred him on rather than settling him down. He turned back to me. "Yes, sir, you're the one that's been defendin' the great Ben Queen, ain't you?"

My stomach went so far down it could have hit the floor. I heard Aurora's voice: *"By the pricking of my thumbs . . ."* I felt it, felt my fingers tingle.

Then Donny said, smiling until the corners of his mouth nearly met his earlobes, "The great Ben Queen. Big hero. Saved your life."

"I know you're sorry about that." My thumbs still tingled.

"Maybe he ain't such a hero after all, him and his sainted wife—"

"Donny!" Maureen was picking up the phone. "I'm calling Sam."

"Oh, for God's sake, woman. He'll be in Cold Flat Junction by now. I'm just doin' a little kiddin' around."

But I heard whom she asked the operator to put her through to: the Queen residence.

What did he mean?

That Donny knew what had happened and even sounded like he knew why—that it was Donny who had this in the palm of his hand—made me feel like all my hard work didn't amount to much. The Sheriff knew it, but that was different; he deserved to know it.

I walked like I had no feet, just blocks of lead, to the taxi office. I looked over at Souder's; the pharmacy was right across from Axel's. *Sainted wife.* I thought Mrs. Souder might know about Rose Queen—that is, something about her that had or could have spoiled her reputation. . . . I had a sudden sense of dread that it might have to do with Mary-Evelyn Devereau, that maybe Rose had done something—

No no no. That mystery was solved. I refused to unsolve it. Rose wasn't even there at the Devereaus when Mary-Evelyn drowned.

His sainted wife.

Big hero.

So I had been right: there *was* another person. Ben Queen. But why would he have shot Ralph Diggs?

Dinner was as straightforward as my mother's menus could get: roast beef au jus, oven-browned potatoes, green beans almondine. No involved combinations or fancy sauces. In other words, there was nothing in it to argue about.

Miss Bertha managed to argue: roast beef too rare, potatoes too hard, beans . . . beans . . .

"Too almondine?"

Curtly, she nodded.

"Too bad." I turned with my tray and left. I did not have time for this.

Vera's table was a party of four people I didn't know, except for the fifth one, Mrs. Davidow, who was loudly making it a party of five. But the only one who minded, really, was Vera, for now she could not pretend to be in charge; Mrs. Davidow was in charge, and sending her out for more rolls, for more au jus, for more wine. I could see the steam coming off Vera like off the steam table in the kitchen.

I for one was delighted Mrs. Davidow was in the dining room because that meant she wasn't in the office. My mother was not in the kitchen, though, and that was a surprise. Walter said she'd gone upstairs to change. I told Walter to take in Miss Bertha's bread pudding when they were done.

Then I filled a glass with ice and made for the front of the hotel and the back of the office. I poured an inch of Myers's, another inch of Jack Daniel's, and just a little Gordon's gin over the ice. I added some Orange Crush from Will's stash. Then I poked a little paper umbrella into a maraschino cherry and put that in. I decided to add some of the juice from the little bottle of cherries, which turned the drink a pleasant pinkish brown color, and called it "South Sea Sunset." I guess I was just good with names.

* * *

"What's this?" said Aurora, reaching for it no matter what it was.

"A South Sea Sunset."

"Well, ain't that pretty!" She drank a good third of it in one go.

"Morris Slade turned out to be Ralph's father."

Aurora, for once, was stunned. "Now, girl, that about knocks my socks off!" But not the drink out of her hand. "You're telling me that young fellow working here was the kidnapped child? Good God! Sounds like one of your crazy brother's plays."

"If you mean *Medea,* Will didn't write it. The thing is, there were two guns at the scene—one of them yours, if you recall. And one was a shotgun that I don't think belonged to Morris Slade. And I don't think he shot Ralph. There's suspicion someone else was there."

She stopped jiggling the ice in her glass. "Who?"

I told her what Donny had said. And the way he'd said it. Dripping sarcasm.

"Ben Queen?"

I nodded.

She looked truly puzzled.

"What did Donny mean?" I must have sounded a little too desperate, for it put her on her guard.

She flapped her hand at me. "You're too young to know all that."

"If I'm too young to know it, it's got to be sex."

" 'It's gotta be sex.' " She tossed her palms up and mocked me.

I chewed my lip.

She smiled, showing her uneven teeth: "How about putting on Patience and Prudence before you go."

I went to the phonograph and rooted "Tonight You Belong to Me" from the stack of records.

She said slyly, holding out her glass, "Get me another and maybe we can talk about s-e-x."

I took the glass. "I'll get you a drink and maybe you can s-h-u-t u-p."

But she was already singing along with Patience and Prudence:

I knooow with the daw-aw-aw-aw-awn
That you-hoo-hoo-hoo-hoo
Will be gah-ah-ah-ah-one
But to-night you be-loong to meee.

I made my way downstairs, wondering, in my own story, who belonged to whom.

58

I was lying down on my bed, trying to make sense out of things and knowing I probably never would. I could not understand why all of this was happening. Not just about Morris Slade and Ben Queen and Ralph Diggs, but about everything.

Look at the Big Garage. There's Paul in the rafters and a gun on the pilot's seat of a sawed-in-half airplane, and yet nobody falls to his death or gets shot.

They have all of these colored lights, spotlights, all hooked up on extension cords that stretch nearly to Lake Noir and put so much load on the electricity you'd think the place would explode. But nothing bursts into flame and burns.

They've got knives, saws, hammers, drills that they don't know how to use right, yet no one ever gets an eye poked out or a limb sliced off.

If there's anyplace imagination ever ran riot, ever shot around like the wildfire that leaves them unmolested, then it's up in the Big Garage.

But no harm comes.

And yet out here, in the wide, wide world, spread out all over the place, a few people, without wanting to, come together almost by accident and *boom!* It's all over.

It sounds like the ones who drown and shoot and die, that the Hand of Fate is in that. For these people are drawn like magnets together, drawn into trouble.

But in the Big Garage, they must live a charmed life. No matter how many times they put themselves in the path of a speeding train, the train always switches tracks.

I seem to be saying it's all a game; it's all like a night at the Double Down. Yet surely, it's not luck. I could not say to Ben Queen, Oh, bad luck! Your wife is a victim of a bloody murder? Bad luck. You're the one convicted and hauled into prison? Bad luck. It's your daughter who did it? Bad luck. And then she's murdered? Bad luck, bad luck.

And now there looks to be another piece of bad luck coming your way, another thing forced on you—

(Big hero.

Sainted wife.)

—forced on you by your sainted wife, Rose Devereau? What did she do?

I almost set my feet on the floor to go up and talk to Aurora again. Only Aurora wouldn't know; she'd just be guessing.

But there was one person who would know: Ben Queen himself. And Ben Queen might still be holed up at the Devereau place.

It was worth the walk. But I would have to think about it. I didn't much like the idea of the Devereau house.

I thought about the poem I was carrying around and that I'd read so many times I could say it off by heart:

> *As slowly (and nobody comes with a light)*
> *Its heart sinks lowest under the sod.*
> *But something has to be left to God.*

No. It was something more meant than luck, but not as much meant as God.

59

After a double helping of pasta gruyère (my mother's upmarket version of macaroni and cheese), I went out to sit on the far end of the front porch. There I rocked and thought and made a cat's cradle of a piece of dirty string and wondered if I had the nerve to walk to Spirit Lake and pass the dock and the water where I'd almost drowned.

I watched the light filtering through the big oaks and determined there should be another couple of hours of it and decided, yes, I had enough nerve without rounding up Mr. Root and the Woods (and anyone else with a gun, like the Sheriff or Dwayne).

I went down the steps and around to the road that ran beside the Pink Elephant and, farther down, along the big vegetable garden. There were times I truly marveled at the size of the Hotel Paradise grounds, as if this were a little world all of its own, and I guess in many ways it was. I wondered if I would still marvel when I was old, like thirty or thirty-five, or if the marveling was just a kid's thing.

Walking the half mile or so to the lake, I couldn't help but look over my shoulder a few times to see if anyone or anything happened to be following. I don't know what or who I thought it would be.

I reached the near end of the lake, and skirted it as far as the wooden boardwalk that stretched out to the dock. I would not walk out to the dock itself. This I couldn't do. I continued on between clumps of vegetation growing so thickly on each side of the road, it nearly met in the center. I was walking toward the spring.

Here was the alcove where the tin cup was kept for drinking spring water. I was of two minds about the cup: On the one hand, it was kind of romantic to think of all of us, strangers to one another, drinking from the same cup. I know Father Freeman would say it was highly spiritual.

But what my other mind wanted to concentrate on was more the disease element, for who knew what state the people had been in who drank from this cup. So if I wanted water, I just put my hands under the pipe the water flowed from. I wasn't too enthusiastic about the pipe, either, as it looked pretty rusty.

I sat down and watched the woods lose light as the lake seemed to drink more in. Its surface was glassy with it. I could see a corner of the Devereau house in the distance and thought about how I'd last seen Ben Queen.

I got up from the low wall and made my way into the woods.

Ben Queen came around the corner of the house in his long light coat, the kind I'd seen in Westerns at the Orion movie house, his big-brimmed hat pulled down. He was carrying a rifle or a shotgun—I didn't know, except it looked like the gun he'd used to shoot Isabel Devereau when she was forcing me to stay in the rowboat and drown.

"Hello, Emma."

He broke the shotgun he was carrying over his forearm, as if he'd just decided not to shoot me.

"The Sheriff was looking for you." For small talk, that would have to do.

"He always is, ain't he? Does he know I'm here?"

I shook my head. "I'm surprised you still are."

"Good a place as any." He was holding open the screen door at the side of the house. "Care to come in for a bit?"

I went in and looked around this living room as the screen door stuttered shut behind me. The same record was on the turntable, the same music on the piano bench. I would have sworn these were the same motes of dust hanging in the vanishing light.

I sank into an armchair too big for me. I looked younger and smaller, dwarfed, when I wanted to appear older and bigger. "They arrested Morris Slade."

He had set the gun in a corner and was looking at the photographs on the wall. "Yeah, that figures." He put his finger to one of the Devereau sisters, as if he meant to straighten out or silence them. He was not saying anything about Morris Slade.

"The gun they found was only a little handgun; it wasn't the one that killed Ralph Diggs. That one was a shotgun or a rifle." I turned to look at the one standing in the corner. "Like yours."

Ben Queen turned from the photograph and gave an abrupt laugh. "Not 'like' mine. It was mine."

I didn't bother pretending to be shocked. "Why?"

"Because the damned kid was going to shoot Morris Slade. Morris didn't have no gun."

I waited. My questions came slowly because I wasn't sure I wanted the answers. When I found out the answers, would I have to write *The End*? "But why were you there?"

"Because I thought there'd be trouble. Morris came to see me over in the Junction. He told me they were meeting. I told him maybe it'd be better not to."

"Morris Slade was his father, wasn't he?"

He was standing at a window now, looking over the lake. I wondered if it looked like winter to him too. "Yeah."

"Ralph Diggs must have found out who his parents were and what had happened."

Ben Queen turned, angry, not at me but at everything. "What old man Woodruff and that damnable daughter of his did was terrible, and the guilt of it got put off on Morris Slade, though he had nothing to do with it. Leaving a baby out somewhere in the woods to expire . . . That's what that bellboy that worked at the Belle Ruin was supposed to do. Leave it or drown it or whatever." He shook his head and turned back to the window. "Can you imagine?"

I didn't have to. Moses in the bulrushes, Mary-Evelyn Devereau. And me. Almost me. I didn't have to imagine it. "He was a scapegoat." I had meant Morris Slade, but it could as easily have been Ralph Diggs. It was certainly Ben Queen, who'd been blamed for two murders he didn't do.

Ben Queen smiled slightly. "You remember that story."

I nodded, then said, with some accusation in my voice: They were all scapegoats. "Why did you leave Brokedown House?"

"We both left. In my truck."

"You should have—" Something. I didn't know what.

"Should have what? Morris wanted me out of the picture. He said he owed me."

"For saving his life?"

"Not just that."

None of this was my business to ask, but I had to. Always. I came as close to it as I could, saying in a scrappy tone, as if I were on the school yard with my friends, tittle-tattling, "Imogen Woodruff wasn't his mother, I bet."

"No, she wasn't." He wouldn't go any closer.

"Are you going to do anything?"

"About Morris? I already have." He stood up as if he meant to do it that minute.

Of course, I wondered what he meant, but if he wasn't inclined to say, I wouldn't ask.

"Are you okay for walking home before it gets dark? I could give you a lift, but the thing is, we can't drive except to go up that old road back there." He tilted his head toward the back of the house. "It'd make it a long way, a really roundabout way to get to the hotel."

I couldn't help but smile at that, thinking of my roundabout ways. "I'm okay." I wasn't. But I got up and walked with him to the door.

He put his fingers to his hat, said, "Well, good-bye, Emma. Nice talking to you. It always is. I'm going back to my truck." He collected his gun.

We both walked out and stood for a minute as if we didn't know what to do.

He hoisted the shotgun, still broken, said, "I'll see you, then, Emma." He walked back around the corner until the woods swallowed him up the way the lake had swallowed the light.

"Good-bye," I called, and thought I heard my good-bye echo, or maybe it was him, saying good-bye on the edge of the dark.

60

As soon as I could get away from the dining room that morning, I'd borne Delbert's chatter on the way into La Porte and was out of the taxi almost before it stopped. I didn't tip him.

If it hadn't been for Donny, I would have gone to the courthouse. But I didn't want to try and talk to the Sheriff with Donny around. I only hoped that Maureen had told the Sheriff about Donny telling me "police business." If she hadn't, I would.

Maud came back and, though it was only ten a.m., offered me some chili. I was eating a vanilla iced doughnut as a kind of breakfast dessert and thanked her, but said no, holding up my doughnut by way of explanation.

As she slid into the booth she said, "Did you hear what happened?"

"I never hear anything."

"Ben Queen went in to see Sam this morning. He gave himself up, I guess you'd say."

I guessed I knew that was going to happen from what he'd told me the night before. But he'd said he'd "already" done something about it. What? That must have been why Donny already knew something, or maybe Donny was just guessing.

I set my doughnut down. It was all so unfair. Ben Queen, Morris

Slade, and even Ralph Diggs were being punished for what others had done.

"You don't seem surprised."

I was so sad, I'd forgotten to be surprised. I tried to patch over my lack of it. "Donny as much as told me Ben Queen did the shooting."

She frowned. "Donny did? He shouldn't be talking about police business."

"Just what Maureen said. She was trying to call the Sheriff and tell him. Anyway, yes, I was surprised. Do you know what went on that night?"

Lighting up a cigarette, she shook her head. "Sam didn't tell me."

"There were two guns—I know that. The one they found belonged to—guess who?"

Maud just frowned. She hated "guess who's" and "guess what's."

"Aurora Paradise."

Her mouth fell open; the cigarette stopped halfway to it. "You're kidding. What in God's name—?"

"It was just a small gun, a revolver, I think, she's had from when she was really alive."

Maud laughed. "That's more frightening than ever Ben Queen would be. But how—?"

"She crazily loaned it to Will for their murder-mystery play. Well, it wasn't loaded, of course. Until Ralph Diggs found it."

"Dear God." Then she turned to lean across the seat and look at the door. "Sam said he'd be here around now." She looked at her wristwatch, in a worried way, then leaned over the seat again to look toward the door. "Here he is."

He was wearing his cap, which he removed to hang on one of the metal hooks at the top of the booth. He was carrying a coffee mug that advertised Sinclair oil.

I didn't waste any time. "So you're going to send him to prison."

"Who? Ben Queen?" He looked from me to Maud and back. "I'm going to? I wrote the laws?"

"Is he down for murder?" asked Maud.

"Not first-degree, I don't think. Manslaughter, probably. But I don't know. The thing is, he went to that house with a shotgun, which I'm sure would be construed as premeditation by any prosecutor."

I said, "He always carries it around. I would too if I was him."

The Sheriff sipped his coffee. "Always? Just how many times have you seen Ben Queen?'"

"You mean besides the time he saved my life?" I tried to make my tone acid, but I wasn't sure what that sounded like. "No times," I lied. "His brother George told me. Anyway, he was only trying to protect Morris Slade."

The coffee mug made a serious thud on the table. "You always seem to have more information than I do. Just what do you know about this?"

I should have said, "Only what Donny told me," but I wasn't stooping to pettiness, at least not yet. "It's obvious, isn't it? The other gun was brought there by Ralph Diggs. He went to use it. I mean, he would have, except Ben Queen stopped him. And it's ridiculous to say Ben Queen went there to kill Morris Slade, if that's what you're thinking. He could have done that in Cold Flat—" I stopped. Only Ben Queen could have told me he'd actually talked to Morris Slade in Cold Flat Junction.

The Sheriff leaned toward me. "Cold Flat Junction? What's that about? What've you—?"

Maud groaned with irritation. "Sam, stop it! Ben Queen turned himself in. He did the shooting; that's it."

I said, or more whined, "But why would he shoot Ralph Diggs except to save Morris Slade? He didn't have any reason to."

The Sheriff went sort of quiet. "He had a reason."

I have heard people saying they blanched, their face whitened. I blanched inside.

Maud raised her eyebrows. "Well, what?"

The Sheriff was holding his mug, swirling the coffee. When he said her name, he sounded meditative. "Rose."

"Rose? Rose Queen?"

Quickly I said, and knew it was to stop him from saying more, "This is all unfair. Where's the justice in it?"

He looked at me. "I've only got the law to go by, Emma." He set the mug down hard on the table, as if he were mad at the coffee, or the Rainbow, or us. Or not us, but everything. "I guess justice has to be left to God." He rose and took his cap from the hook. "Sorry. I'm not in the best mood. I've got to talk to the Diggses."

I sat up straight. "The Diggses? You mean the adopted parents?"

The Sheriff smiled a little. "In any case, the couple who brought Ralph Diggs up."

Maud asked, "Do they have to, you know, identify his body? The poor souls."

The Sheriff nodded. "Afraid so. They're coming in from Doylestown." He looked at his watch. "Pennsylvania."

He shook his wrist as if that might make time stand still. "They're probably already here. Maureen can take care of them until I get there. I've got to see the Mayor before I see them."

Already here? I was fairly itching to go with him, not to see Mayor Sims, but to the courthouse.

He read my mind. He could do that. "Forget it, Emma. You can't talk to them."

I changed my expression from whatever it was. "Who said I wanted to?" I pressed up the crumbs of my doughnut and licked my finger and gave the Sheriff a look of what I hoped was indifference.

"They're in mourning, Emma. They don't need a pile of questions thrown at them."

"As if I would. Anyway, you're going to ask them a ton of questions."

"What's necessary, that's all." He checked his watch again. "I'll see you."

As soon as he was out of the door, I jumped up. "Excuse me," I said to Maud, and nearly ran to the front. Her question, "Where are you—?" followed me to the baked goods cases, but didn't get answered. I told Wanda I wanted a half dozen doughnuts with sprinkles—vanilla, chocolate, rainbow. I bought four cups of black coffee, cream and sugar on the side, which she crated up. I carried the whole caboodle across the street and into the courthouse. I couldn't go very fast because of the coffee.

I stopped outside of the Sheriff's office door and listened. Donny's voice was the loudest, of course, but I heard a woman's voice too, which was not Maureen's. I pulled myself up and balanced the doughnut bag on the tray of coffees and opened the door.

Donny swung around. "What're you doin' here?"

He had on his "in-charge" manner, walking around to no purpose, thumbs hooked in his belt. It had been a couple of big days for him and he was enjoying them. He was telling the Diggses a trooper had just found Ralph's car, half buried in the woods across from the Silver Pear.

I said, "You mean he left it and walked the rest of the way."

"Now I don't see this is any of your concern."

I tried to look embarrassed and awkward. "Only, the Sheriff said that Mr. and Mrs. Diggs had come all the way from"—I forgot the name of the town—"from Pennsylvania, and I just thought they'd like some coffee. . . ." I looked at the middle-aged couple sitting beside Donny's desk. They were both heavyset, with brown hair and pale skin.

Mrs. Diggs spoke up. "Now, that's real sweet of you, dear." She had a handkerchief balled up in her hand. Mr. Diggs said thanks. He sounded choked up and sat with his head down.

"Brought some for you too," I said to Donny, "and Maureen."

From her desk in the back, Maureen smiled and waved thanks.

"Well, yeah, okay." Donny helped himself to a cup and took two sugars. "Them doughnuts you got there?"

I handed him the bag. He did not offer it to the Diggses after taking out a chocolate iced one and inspecting it. He grunted a thanks and gave back the bag.

I offered the tray of coffee to the Diggses. They both took a cup and he took a creamer. She just drank hers black and said no thank you to the bag of doughnuts. I guess if your son's just been murdered, not even a doughnut looks appealing.

"I'm so sorry," I said, remembering what I'd heard the Sheriff say, "for your loss."

They both nodded. She pressed the handkerchief to her nose.

The Sheriff would walk in at any minute, and I searched my mind for maybe the one question I wanted answered. But there were too many. How stupid of me not to work this out beforehand. But I hadn't even known Ralph's parents were here until fifteen minutes ago.

"Ralph was really nice. Everybody at the hotel liked him a lot. You know he worked at my mother's hotel for a short while."

Mrs. Diggs shook her head. "No, we didn't know anything. Didn't even know he was going—"

"Now, Mame. No need to talk about that," said Mr. Diggs. He sounded resentful more than sad.

The door opened and the Sheriff walked in. When he saw me, he stood there and shook his head, but then he went to the Diggses and introduced himself. "I'm Sheriff DeGheyn, Mrs. Diggs, Mr. Diggs. I'm terribly sorry."

For your loss, I added in my head, in a prompting way.

And he, of course, reading my mind, turned. "Emma?"

I hung my head, but only a bit, as the Sheriff knew I wasn't the head-hanging type. "Sorry. I just thought—"

Mrs. Diggs came to my rescue. "This here's one nice little girl, Sheriff. She brought us coffee and doughnuts. It was real sweet."

I kind of scuffed my shoe on the floor, but stopped, as he also knew I wasn't a shoe scuffer. I scratched my ear. I didn't look at him. "Well, it's just they had this long drive. . . ."

Donny was standing there now. "Thought you told her to bring the stuff over, Sam. That's what she said."

"I did not say any such thing!" I paused and turned to the Diggses. "Oh, I'm so sorry to be fussing at such a bad time for you."

I cast Donny what I think is called a "baleful look."

The Sheriff said, "That's very nice of you, Emma, to be so concerned. But we have a very sad undertaking here, so maybe we'll see you later."

He actually smiled. I could not read the smile. But I kept looking at it as I passed through the door.

61

"**TRAGEDY TOWN.**" Sitting at one of the tables in the Abigail Butte County Library, I set down that title with as heavy a hand as I could, pressing hard with my pencil, thickening up the letters until I nearly tore the paper.

I spent some moments doing this, as I didn't know what was to follow. Why not? Hadn't I just shown the last thing I'd written to Mr. Gumbrel a few days ago? What was it with writing? Did there have to be this feeling you were just born ten minutes ago and didn't even know that pages had writing on them? That you weren't supposed to write on air with your fingertip the way real babies did?

I put my head in my hands. It wasn't that I didn't know what I wanted to write about; there was plenty of it in my head. I just didn't seem able to begin, despite that.

I heard a car stop suddenly out on the road, its tires screeching as if to avoid running into something. I hoped Ree-Jane was crossing the street.

I slid down in my chair and stared up at the slow-moving ceiling fan on which a couple of flies were riding as if it were a fly merry-go-round. Then I forced myself to sit up and look at my page.

TRAGEDY TOWN: There was music. There was moonlight. There was dancing.

I wished I hadn't already written that so I could write it now.

There was music. There was moonlight.

Maybe I could continue with that line about families that I'd thought I read or heard somewhere. I wrote down: "All families are unhappy." No. That was too obvious for anyone to bother writing down. "All families are happy or unhappy." No. "All families are unhappy, but differently." That was okay, but somebody had already written it. But if another writer had written this, I couldn't use it, not because it would be dishonest, but because somebody would probably recognize it and write a letter to the editor.

So I decided to ask Miss Babbit and took the page up to the desk where she was stamping cards.

"Hello, Emma."

"Hello." I told her my problem and read her the line.

Miss Babbit looked a little perplexed, then told me to follow her, and we walked into the fiction shelves. She knew, I think, every book in the library, for it took her exactly one minute back there to find the book she wanted. I considered becoming a librarian. You really knew what you were doing if you were one.

The book she was holding was pretty thick; I read the title on the back: *Anna K*— Her finger was over part of the name. She read: " 'All happy families are alike; each unhappy family is unhappy in its own way.' It's by Tolstoy."

I'd heard of him. I think he was one of the Russians. They were all crazy. "I guess that line is pretty famous, isn't it?"

She nodded. "Of course, you could use it, Emma. Just put quotes around it."

I wasn't about to give him space in my story. "Thank you, Miss Babbit."

She returned to the front and I returned to my fate. I plunked down as if the chair were to blame.

And then I recalled what Maud had said about a writer who had a clock on his desk and forced himself to write a certain number of words every fifteen minutes. He just wrote the first thing that came to mind about his story.

Then I would do that. I looked at the big regulator clock on the wall—and picked up my pencil. There was music. There was moonlight. There was dancing. There was a ladder... Should I keep the ladder? Or did it kind of spoil the romantic sound of it? I shrugged and went on with the new episode. I thought about Bing Crosby singing "Moonlight Becomes You" to Dorothy Lamour. I gritted my teeth and thought of Morris Slade. I wrote: "He's charming. He's rich. He's in jail— Morris Slade."

Wow! That wasn't a bad opening! I went on:

Morris Slade was arrested after the body of a young man was found in Brokedown House, out near White's Bridge Road.

Mr. Butternut, longtime resident, discovered the body, and had this to say:

I could get a quote from Mr. Butternut. He'd love appearing in the paper, and he was probably on his way to being a celebrity. I started in again:

I call this story "Tragedy Town" because so many of them have happened around here. Some of this tale has appeared in earlier editions, such as the drowning of Mary-Evelyn Devereau, the murder of Rose Queen over in Cold Flat Junction, the recent murder of her daughter Fern, again near White's Bridge ...

Once again, I forgot about me, and sighed, and went back:

and the near murder of yours truly, Emma Graham, over at Spirit Lake.

I went on:

What you haven't heard are the details about the disappearance of the Morris Slades' baby from the Belle Ruin Hotel, an alleged kidnapping.
But now we know what happened. . . .

I looked up at the clock: eighteen minutes! I tossed my pencil up in the air, and as it came down I saw the Sheriff up at the front desk, talking to Miss Babbit.

What was he doing here? I didn't recall ever seeing the Sheriff in the Abigail Butte County Library.

Now he had seen me and was walking over to my table. He pulled out the chair opposite. "Mind?"

"Oh, do you read?" I said.

He smiled, you could say, thinly, a knife smiling. "Come down off your righteousness cloud and listen—"

My what? "I hardly ever think I'm right." I think I was still on my righteousness cloud, though, because I almost always thought I was right. I recalled what Maud had said: being right can be harder on a person than being wrong. I was still trying to figure out what she meant, exactly.

"How did you know I'd be here?"

"I didn't. I came to speak to Miss Babbit."

"Okay, I'm listening." I said this kind of managing a yawn at the same time. I patted my mouth with my hand.

"Morris Slade wants to talk to you."

That certainly stopped me in mid-yawn. "What?"

"He won't talk to anyone but you. Of course, you don't have to."

Don't *have* to? Was he kidding? I sat there looking serious as if I were really considering. Then, after a few moments of fiddling with my notebook and pencil, I said, solemnly, "Well, all right. If you think it would help."

62

When Donny brought Morris Slade into the room, I stood up. I don't know why I did this, for it seemed to be some mark of respect.

The Sheriff yanked me down.

Morris Slade smiled at this little display of temper (mine nice, the Sheriff's not) and sat down. He looked rumpled and in need of sleep, but otherwise the same.

The Sheriff, who was sitting beside me in this small room he'd told me was for "interviews," began to ask Morris a question.

Morris Slade kept the smile on his face, but shook his head. "Uh-uh, Sheriff DeGheyn. I told you I'd talk only with Emma."

"I'm not leaving you alone with her."

"Wait a minute!" I said, popping up again. "That's for me to say—"

Again, he yanked me down. "You're twelve, Emma. You don't get to say."

Morris Slade cocked an eyebrow. "Do you think she's in danger? Do you think I'm going to reach across the table and strangle her?"

The Sheriff shook his head briefly. "Not at all. I'm thinking more of a hostage situation."

Hostage! Me? This would be my second brush with death. I saw it in my mind, a scene where Morris was marching me out of the courthouse, gun at my back, then into his red car. . . . Or was the car still at Brokedown House? Then I noticed both of them were looking at me.

"Don't look so eager, Emma," said the Sheriff. "It's not going to happen."

"Why did you and Ralph Diggs meet at Brokedown House? That's way out. Nobody goes there now." Nobody but me, I should say, and Mr. Butternut.

He looked at me. "That's why."

"You mean so nobody would know you were meeting? Or that you knew each other?"

He nodded. "Or so that I'd never be found. Fey said, 'You can lie here until you rot.'"

I sat back hard. I really felt the effort of that, his own son saying that. "That's terrible."

The Sheriff put his hand on my arm, but not for comfort. I guess to keep me from talking.

"We'd abandoned him. He'd disappeared. He thought it would be fitting if the same thing happened to me."

The Sheriff said, "Ben Queen. What about Ben Queen?"

At first he didn't answer. Then he leaned toward the Sheriff, his arms on the table. "What do you know about Tragedy Town?" His smile was crooked.

I was surprised he remembered and puzzled he was bringing it up.

The Sheriff was puzzled too. "I don't know what you're talking about."

"I know you don't." Morris sat back. "I've already told you what happened at that house. I tried to get the gun away from Fey. It went off. Now he's dead." Morris wiped his hand across the table, as if he were sweeping crumbs. "I didn't mean to kill him."

To me, he looked incredibly sad. Almost to the point of heartbreak.

"You don't believe me," he said, looking up at the Sheriff.

The Sheriff said nothing and I couldn't read anything in his expression. I guess he was a really good policeman.

Morris Slade asked if he could smoke.

The Sheriff nodded and shoved the pack of cigarettes toward him, then lit the cigarette with an old Zippo. Maybe he didn't want Morris reaching into a pocket, or maybe he was just being nice. "Why did he want to kill you, Mr. Slade? Will you tell me that much?"

Morris Slade sat smoking for a few moments, I guess turning that over. The why was a big part of the story. He looked at me, then said, "Because he was angry he'd been abandoned. He was more than angry, he was raging. I certainly can't blame him for that."

"You're—you were his father. Is that right?"

He nodded.

"It was really more than abandonment, though. You—or someone—had him kidnapped."

Again he nodded, then said, "I didn't know about it. That's the truth. And that's all of the story I'll tell you." He looked at me again. "I'll tell Emma the story. I mean, beyond, or before, the shooting. What she can do, if she wants, it's up to her, is write it up and print it as part of her piece in the paper."

"If it's going to be made public, Mr. Slade, why not tell me now?"

"Because you don't deserve it, Sheriff."

I was glad to know I was humble enough to be staggered by Morris Slade—or anyone except maybe Maud—talking like this to the Sheriff. But more than that, I thought it was one of the strangest things I'd heard. *". . . don't deserve it"?*

There was a long silence while the two of them regarded each other.

When the Sheriff finally pushed back his chair and said to me, "Emma," I slowed down leaving by asking the first question that sprang to mind: "Why'd you call him Fey instead of Ralph?"

He smiled. "Because my father's name was Ralph, and I hated him."

"Emma," the Sheriff said again, drawing me forward.

All I could think of was all of the information, the answers, I'd never get. *Why did you come here now? Why did Ralph not go after his mother, Imogen? Why did they have him kidnapped? Why did you go to Cold Flat Junction looking for Ben Queen?—And what did it have to do with Rose?* That last question, I don't think I wanted to ask.

When I glanced back over my shoulder at Morris Slade, he looked at that moment as if he were a true inhabitant of Tragedy Town. He seemed to think this was enough; he wanted Ben Queen kept out of it and must not have known that Ben had given himself up.

They were saving each other.

63

The heavy church door closed behind me with a deep sucking sound. I passed down the nave and wondered where I thought I was going. I didn't know, so I sat down in a pew and looked around. The stained-glass windows were pretty, bright broken pictures, pieces of brilliant blues and reds.

St. Michael's Church was right behind the courthouse and across the street. I wondered where Father Freeman was and pulled one of the hymnals from the rack and leafed through it, stopping to read now and then. Nothing there could compare with Robert Frost.

I thought I knew why. The hymns were all about hope and victory. Even if the words didn't appear to be, when the end came around, it was clear the end was about hope and victory, with a big helping of glory thrown in.

Father Freeman came out of a door up there on the side and walked across to the long table where the things for the Catholic service were kept (you could say) under wraps. He appeared to be rearranging things, candles and chalice and so forth, as if for a dinner party. He made his various bows and scrapes and signs of the cross and I wondered how much of it he believed.

He turned to look out over the absent congregation, probably sensing a presence there, having a priestly turn of mind. He saw me and waved, then disappeared through the doorway again. In another few moments he reappeared, minus the white smock.

"Hi, Emma," he said, and sat down in the pew before mine and turned to face me. "Did you come to see me?"

"No, to see God, but he's not around, so you'll do."

"Thanks." He was silent, giving me, I suppose, a chance to speak, but I didn't.

He said, "I heard about Ralph Diggs. That was terrible. How do you feel about it? I know he worked at the hotel, but was he a friend?"

I shook my head. "Not especially. I felt bad about who they arrested and who's going to prison for it."

"You mean Morris Slade?"

"I mean Ben Queen."

"Oh." He frowned. "That I hadn't heard. The Sheriff arrested Ben Queen?"

"He did the shooting, but it was only to keep Morris Slade from getting shot." I didn't bother to add my thoughts about the guilty ones going free. I was riffling the pages of the hymnal like Aurora shuffling her pack of cards. I unfolded the piece of paper with the poem on it.

"What are you reading?"

"Poetry and hymns. They don't have much in common." I slid the hymnal back behind its strip of wood and folded the paper with the poem into even smaller squares.

"What poetry is it?"

"Robert Frost's."

Father Freeman held out his hand as if he had every right to see it. I didn't give it to him. *You don't deserve it.* I think I knew what Morris Slade had meant.

"Well, will you read it, then?"

The way he settled his arms along the back of the pew and settled his eyes on me meant the answer had to be yes.

"No."

"Emma, what are you so angry about?" He rested his chin on the tips of his fingers, prayerfully.

I was amazed that he wondered. "I just told you."

He frowned. "Ben Queen?"

"He has to keep being blamed and punished and coming back again. Nobody helps; nobody helps either one of them. Morris Slade didn't do anything either."

His chin, which had lifted for a moment, came back down on his fingertips, putting him in praying territory again. "You think you should be able to do something about it?"

I stared at him. Of course I should be able to do something about it. But so should he, so should a lot of people. I unfolded the paper and read:

> *I wish I could promise to lie in the night*
> *And think of an orchard's ar-bor—*

Just as Ulub had, I stumbled—

> *-bor-e-al plight,*

I raised my eyes and drilled them into his, and came down hard on the line:

> *When slowly (and nobody comes with a light)*
> *Its heart sinks lower under the sod.*
> *But something has to be left to God.*

I drilled another hole into him with my eyes.

"You believe that, Emma? That something has to be left to God?"

I got up from the pew. "Something. But not much."

I walked out.

64

Why I then took refuge in the back room of the *Conservative* offices among the old newspapers and dusty magazines, I don't know, but I felt somehow comforted, looking at ancient ads for BB Bats and Campbell's soups; for Jell-O in fancy molds; and for Morton's salt with its picture of a girl holding an umbrella, unaware of the salt leaking out behind her. There was Tangee lipstick in little tubes just waiting for Miss Isabel Barnett to shoplift them. And I knew that for some reason, that was what gave comfort to Miss Isabel: shoplifting.

Some of these papers went way back to the 1910s and '20s. And all of these things were still around, and would still be around in another forty years. I marveled at that: these things would last longer than we would, and I found that very strange. Here was a 1930s stove that only my mother would love. We had one in the small back kitchen that burned wood and had black iron plates you lifted with a handlelike device. It sounded more like something Aurora's mother (if time went back that far) would use.

I lined up all the magazine covers I could find that pictured the Fadeaway Girls: *Good Housekeeping, Life,* the *Saturday Evening Post.* I studied each one, thinking the pictures might tell me something about how to write the story that I was having trouble with; that is, the pictures might reveal something of the understory. For there was more to the story than the facts of the Devereau sisters' drowning of Mary-Evelyn; more than the facts of the murder of Rose Queen; of Fern's murder; of Morris Slade and Ralph Fey Diggs. And of me.

The *Life* cover reminded me of Vera, except for the girl's being young and pretty: the maid in a black uniform kneeling and looking through a keyhole. I had to admit I didn't think Vera would do that. Her black uniform faded into the black wall behind her.

Here was the Christmas issue that I liked so much, the red-coated girl in front of a wrought-iron fence, slipping a Christmas card into a mailbox. The background was red and part of her coat faded into it.

Here was the amber-haired girl, in the amber woods, walking with an amber and white collie. If you wanted to see the whole of her, you had to imagine her out of the background.

Maybe a person never knew the whole of a thing because it kept coming and going, never wanting to meet the eye dead-on. A shoe here, an arm there. But, no, not even an arm, for the sleeve that covered it faded into the background.

Is that what I was trying to do? To imagine people into their background so deeply they'd disappear?

Maybe that was the understory.

65

The big papers would take the first part of "Tragedy Town" away from me, as the shooting at Brokedown House and the arrests of Morris Slade and Ben Queen were too big to be confined just to the *Conservative*. That news would make it to much bigger papers and maybe even to the New York ones, given that Morris Slade and Imogen Woodruff were part of it.

That Imogen Woodruff was the cause of it all—that would not be reported. Imogen and her awful father, Lucien Woodruff. The only ones who knew all of the story were Morris Slade and Ben Queen. The Sheriff might have known all of it, but I kind of doubt it. From the way Morris Slade was talking in our interview, I wouldn't think so. Ben Queen might have been more willing to talk to the Sheriff, but I doubt he'd tell all of it either.

I knew some of it, but I hadn't worked out the rest.

"Fern never had no kids."

Jude Stemple had said this, some weeks ago, when he'd been one of the first people I'd talked to.

"Fern never had no kids."

In my mind I sat down again in the Windy Run Diner watching that look move around the counter sitters, Billy and the rest.

"Fern went off with her mother for several months."

"His sainted wife." Donny's voice.

A woman with a newborn wants to put it up for adoption: that had been one of my theories.

"He said he owed me." For saving his life? *"Not just that."*

Jude Stemple had described Rose in perfect detail that first time I talked to him. He had described the Girl. And that's why I thought she was Fern's daughter.

And that was also how I came to realize what had been so painfully obvious all along. How much Ralph Diggs looked like Morris, forgetting that he looked exactly like Rose.

"Rose." The Sheriff had said the name, but nothing more.

"His sainted wife," Donny had said, with his usual leer.

If I were Imogen Slade and discovered that the baby I thought was adopted was actually my husband's by another woman, what would I do? If, mind you, my own mind worked in the mean way of Imogen's and her father's.

I'd have him kidnapped.

What greater punishment for Morris Slade could there be than what was done?

Morris Slade was freed, of course.

I don't know what will happen to Ben Queen, but the Sheriff said "mitigating circumstances," which I think means being in such a bad spot that you didn't have any choice but to do what you did.

I was going over all of this on the train to Cold Flat Junction.

As the train pulled into the station, I thought about maybe asking Morris Slade if this story I'd come up with was true.

When I stepped down from the train, I did not go right away to the Windy Run Diner or any of the other places I seemed to make myself welcome at: the Queens' house, or Louise Landis's, or Jude Stemple's, or Gloria Spiker Calhoun's. I was surprised I could call up half a dozen others, but I could.

Instead, I sat down on one of the old benches placed on the platform for passengers to use. Here is where I'd first seen the Girl; I thought I might see her again. But why? For it was just as likely I'd see her in Spirit Lake or on the grounds of the Devereau house or at the Belle Ruin.

The train began to move, and between the cars I caught glimpses of that flat and empty landscape across the track. When the last car had passed, I could see that line of dark trees, standing in a regimental way, solid as soldiers. Then they seemed to sway a little as I looked, the way things appear to move if you stare at them long enough.

I wondered if the trees stood there at the edge of the dark, guarding a great mystery.

Or was all of this just my riotous imagination?

Martha Grimes is the author of twenty-two Richard Jury novels—most recently, *The Black Cat*—as well as the acclaimed fiction *Dust*, *Foul Matter*, and *Belle Ruin*. She lives in Washington, D.C. Visit her Web site at www.marthagrimes.com.